Ah, my love,
my only love,
consume me,
fill me
with rapture,
enough to last
until the
moments
of our
next rendezvous.

Books by Cassie Edwards

Published by Zebra Books

Rapture's Rendezvous

CASSIE EDWARDS

ZEBRA BOOKS
KENSINGTON PUBLISHING CORP.
http://www.kensingtonbooks.com

ZEBRA BOOKS are published by

Kensington Publishing Corp.
119 West 40th Street
New York, NY 10018

All Kensington titles, imprints and distributed lines are available at special quantity discounts for bulk purchases for sales promotion, premiums, fund-raising, educational or institutional use.

Special book excerpts or customized printings can also be created to fit specific needs. For details, write or phone the office of the Kensington Special Sales Manager: Attn. Special Sales Department. Kensington Publishing Corp., 119 West 40th Street, New York, NY, 10018. Phone: 1-800-221-2647.

Zebra and the Z logo Reg. U.S. Pat. & TM Off.

ISBN-13: 978-1-4201-1957-2
ISBN-10: 1-4201-1957-5

First Printing: September 1982

10

Printed in the United States of America

To my son Brian,
who understands what I am all about

Oh! She has passions which outstrip the wind,
And tear her virtue up, as tempests root the sea.

—William Congreve

Rapture's
Rendezvous

The first sign of dawn was making its presence known as pale orange streaks began to dance along the horizon, casting shadowed images on two lonely figures walking at the edge of the country road leading to Pordenone. They were dressed in dark, tattered trousers and matching black waist-length coats, and their wide-billed hats were pulled down low to hide their hair.

They both stood tall and walked in the same brisk manner as any other sixteen-year-old boys might do . . . except that one . . . was . . . a . . . girl.

Maria Lazzaro squinted her eyes, watching the September morning sunrise as it was filtering through the foggy haze that hung low over the ground. She knew that once the fog began to slowly lift, it would be like smoke from a fire, revealing tall houses in the distance.

She turned her gaze toward her twin brother Alberto, who had been unusually quiet since having left their Gran-mama's house. Maria knew that Alberto was also growing weary of their daily chores, but just hadn't spoken his mind about it, obviously not wanting to worry Maria.

Maria suddenly broke the silence. "How long has

9

Papa been gone now, Alberto?" she asked, wiping a black smudge from the tip of her nose. Oh, how she hated the endless duty of cleaning chimneys each day. The soot had seemed to change her olive coloring to a dull, ashen gray. And the filth beneath her fingernails. It took away from the dignity of having been born a female.

Alberto rested a long-handled brush against his shoulder . . . the brush itself even more black than the clothes that hung loosely from him and his sister. He shut his eyes and began moving his lips, a mere whisper of numbers barely audible to Maria.

Maria prodded impatiently. "Well, Alberto?" she asked, blinking her long lashes nervously. She was glad that she and Alberto had been given special schooling by her Papa before his departure to America. Numbers had been Alberto's favorite study, while mastering the English language had been her own. She had decided that being able to speak fluently after they arrived in America themselves was of much more importance than being able to add numbers in the head. "Well?" she further demanded, thinking him to be so slow.

"I'm counting. I'm counting," Alberto finally answered. "Let's see. I marked it on Gran-mama's wall. Yes. Now I remember. Papa left on the fifth of September and it is now the twenty-eighth of September. One year and twenty-three days. That's how long."

"It seems an eternity, doesn't it, Alberto?"

"Papa said that it would take a while," Alberto answered, eyeing Maria sympathetically. "The boat trip to America probably took weeks. Maybe months. Who knows? And then Papa had to find work."

"What if Papa forgets all about us, Alberto?" Maria

10

asked, watching her brother, seeing once again how handsome he was. His dark brown eyes were large like her own, and his skin, when it was clean, was smooth and olive in color, and his determination showed by the solid set line of the jaw. His lips were thick, and his nose had the "Italian curve" in it, and he looked much older than his years as he held his wide shoulders back, proud to display his six-foot height.

Slinging an arm around Maria's waist, Alberto hugged her to him. "You've got to learn to be more patient about things in life, Maria," he said thickly. "Papa said he'd send for us. So rest assured that he will. Papa has never lied to us."

"But I so hate to clean chimneys."

"You should be proud to be able to say that you're earning money," Alberto argued, dropping his arm away from her, to thrust his free hand deeply inside his trousers pocket.

"I'd much rather be making money while playing my violin," Maria pouted, kicking at a stone in the road.

"You know how Mama felt about you playing your violin on the street corners of Pordenone," Alberto grumbled. "She said you were no better than a beggar."

"Mama is no longer with us, to even worry about it," Maria said stubbornly.

"Maria!" Alberto stormed. "Shame be upon you. You make it sound as though you're glad that Mama is dead and buried."

Maria hung her head sadly. "I didn't mean it that way," she murmured. "I only meant to say that I am free to do as I please now that Papa is in America . . . and poor Mama. . . ."

"You are *not* free to do as you please," Alberto inter-

11

rupted. "I am the one who has been left in Italy to see after you, and I won't have my sister standing on a street corner like a waif. Even if it *is* while playing the violin. We have respectable jobs while being chimney sweeps. You should be proud."

"Well, I hope Papa finds us a nice place to live in America where there are no chimneys," Maria said, pouting more openly.

Alberto laughed heartily. "Maria, *all* houses have chimneys. Even in America."

"Well, maybe Papa won't make *us* clean them," Maria said, placing a hand before her eyes. "I've not seen clean fingers on my hands since we've become chimney sweeps."

Alberto took her hand in his and clutched tightly onto it. Her fingers were slender and lean, like a true violinist's for sure, and he did understand her love for the instrument. But he would *not* let her play for money to be tossed at her feet. He just wouldn't. She was destined for better . . . greater things . . . a future of wealth in America . . . the land where only the rich live. . . .

He gazed at her beauty. Beneath her billed hat lay a mass of dark, wavy hair that hung to her waist when set free. And the gentle curve to her jaw, accentuated by the full sensuousness of her lips took one's attention from the one flaw of her classic Italian features . . . a birthmark of a strawberry color, the size of a small mole, on the slight dimple of her right cheek. When she laughed, it would be as though erased, as it would tighten and blend in with her dark olive skin tones.

Alberto laughed to himself. His own matching birth-

12

mark was well hidden . . . but in a more embarrassing place. . . .

His gaze lowered, feeling a racing of the pulsebeat in the hollow of his throat. Maria was not yet aware of how her curves could affect a man . . . even a brother. Evenings, while sauntering around the house after bathing, and in more skimpy attire, Maria hadn't yet learned to be modest of herself. Her large, ripe breasts seemed always to be loosely bouncing when she walked, and when she stretched out on the makeshift bed of leaves that they shared, she didn't know to not cuddle up so close to Alberto . . . having done so since childhood.

Suddenly seeing that Maria was studying him, Alberto felt a blush rising upward from his neck and turned his head quickly away.

"What were you thinking, Alberto?" she asked, leaning in front of him, to look up into his face. She loved his tallness . . . even though she could almost boast of being the same. A slight bit of stretching was all that was required to be standing nose to nose with him.

She and Alberto had never ceased to surprise the Lazzaro family—first to be born only seconds apart, and then to grow to such a height. All their other blood relations were short and squatty, and none too pleasant to look at.

Maria smiled smugly to herself. She had liked being different, but was glad that her brother was the same. And their love for one another kept them even more apart from the rest of the family. No harm would come to either of them . . . ever . . . as long as they had one

13

another. She just knew it.

Alberto cleared his throat nervously. "Nothing much," he stammered.

"Want to know what I'm thinking, Alberto?"

"Sure. What?"

"I'm hungry. I'm starved," she answered quickly. "My stomach is growling and my lips are parched. It's always such a long walk from Gran-mama's house."

Peering into the distance, Alberto was glad to finally be able to see that the houses were growing more visible. Some people of the village paid by milk and hot bread. Sometimes that was even more welcome than money. But Maria was hungry now and Alberto usually tried to please her whenever she showed signs of needing something. He was dedicated to her. Fully.

His gaze traveled to the large fields of grapevines that now stretched out on both sides of them. The grapes that had been ignored by the pickers were so ripe, most had burst open, with their juices dripping down their thin, browned stems. And the air! It was filled with the sweet aroma.

"I'm hungry, Alberto," Maria whined further, hardly able to contain herself any longer.

Alberto looked around, then from side to side. "No one will miss a few of those grapes, Maria," he said. "It seems those that have been left will even soon be gone because it's almost time for the grower to prune the vines for the winter. Come on. Let's have our fill before heading on into the village. It's going to be a long day for us."

Following her brother's movements, Maria thrust first one grape then another into her mouth, savoring the sweetness as it seeped between her teeth and swirled

14

around her tongue. And after she stuffed her pockets full with more of the delicacies, she fell into step beside Alberto, hurrying on toward Pordenone.

"You know, Alberto, the one thing I'll miss most about this old country will be the grapes," Maria said, licking her lips of the still clinging sweet juices.

"I'm sure there are grapes in America," Alberto said, laughing.

Maria's eyes widened. "Really? Do you think so?"

Alberto stood more erect, suddenly feeling more knowledgeable than his sister. "Sure," he said. "America has everything. Just wait. You'll see."

As they finally entered the village, their pace became slower as their gazes traveled from house to house. Only the rich people lived in such big stone houses. The houses all appeared to have been built alike with their red-tiled roofs and fancy balconies leading from the upper-story rooms. And the yards. It almost took Maria's breath away, seeing the freshly trimmed green grass and the many varieties of flowers in the yards, as well as in window boxes . . . nothing like her Granmama's house, which was surrounded by dried, cracked earth, with cows, goats and sheep running free.

Maria's eyes shifted upward, the chimneys reaching into the sky drawing her full attention. "Which house do we go to first, Alberto?" she asked, stopping.

"Does it really matter?" Alberto mumbled, walking on ahead of her toward a house, eyeing the chimney with distaste. Maybe today the tickets for passage will arrive from America, he thought sadly to himself. Yes. Maybe today.

It had grown dusk, but the fireplace was burning

brightly, lighting the room around Maria, keeping her awake. The bed of leaves she was lying on felt good to her. But she rubbed her elbows gently. They throbbed from her having used them to climb up the steep insides of the many chimneys that she and Alberto had cleaned this long, hard day. She looked toward Alberto, eyeing his elbows. But even though his elbows looked raw and red, there was a lazy smile on his face.

Then Maria's gaze settled on the tickets being held tightly in Alberto's hands. Maria also had to smile. It was such a gratifying sensation to know that her Papa had remembered and had finally sent tickets for her and Alberto to join him in America.

Yes. What a pleasant surprise it had been when Maria and Alberto had discovered the tickets for the boat trip waiting in the mail when they had returned to their Gran-mama's house earlier in the evening.

"When can we go?" Maria asked, suddenly rising up to lean on an elbow, to face Alberto. She spoke softly, not wanting to wake her Gran-mama, who was asleep only a few feet away, on her own bed of leaves.

Alberto reached up and touched a lock of Maria's long, dark hair. "In the next few days, Maria. We'll have to help Gran-mama get things settled around here first."

Maria sighed heavily, her eyes seeking the sleeping figure of her Gran-mama. "I wish Gran-mama could go with us."

"Papa wanted her to go. But she refused. She doesn't want to leave Mama's and Gran-papa's graves. It would make her too sad."

"But won't she be terribly lonely?"

"Maria, we are not the only members left of the

16

Lazzaro family. You must remember Aunt Helena and many, many more. No. Gran-mama won't be lonesome. She'll miss us. But she won't be lonesome."

Maria turned over and stretched out on her stomach. It still felt warm and good from the huge bowl of *polenta* that she had eaten for supper. And the chestnut soup and fresh goat's milk had completed the feast.

"Alberto?"

"Yes, Maria?"

"I wonder what type of house Papa lives in?"

"I don't know. But you needn't worry about that. I'm sure it will be nice."

"Alberto?"

"Yes, Maria," Alberto said impatiently, suddenly feeling the need of sleep. He had many days of responsibility for Maria's safety stretched out before him.

"I wonder if the house will have a place where we can take a bath and real beds to sleep on," Maria said quietly.

"I'm sure all houses in America have bathing facilities and beds," Alberto answered. "Now, will you please get to sleep?"

There was a short pause. The only sound that could be heard was from the scratching of the dog that lay stretched out in front of the hearth.

Maria squirmed uneasily, her gown having worked up above her knees. "I wonder what type of work Papa found?" she whispered again.

"Hmm. It's funny. He never wrote of that," Alberto said.

"And, isn't it just awful, Alberto?" she said even more softly.

"Isn't what awful?"

"Oh, you know. Father warned us of the cruelties of a man named Nathan Hawkins and how terribly mean he is to the Italians who have settled in the same town Papa has."

"Aren't you even a bit afraid, Maria?"

A burning anger made her dark eyes flash, trying to envision such a man. The Italians had planned to find a better life in America. *Not* a life of slavery. "No. I'm not afraid," she hissed. "I am anxious to meet this evil man."

"What?" he gasped loudly.

"Yes. I want to meet this man who is treating Papa and our people so poorly."

"Why the hell would you want to meet him? He'll try to be just as cruel to us."

Maria had never been given cause yet in her life to hate . . . and was now feeling the difference it made inside herself as this hate continued to build, causing her to even suddenly feel like an entirely different person. She frowned deeply. "Why? Because there must be a way to make him pay for treating people so badly."

"Maria," Alberto sighed heavily. "Sometimes your sense of adventure gets in the way of logic."

"But there does have to be a way, Alberto," she said, sighing deeply. "There just has to be a way."

"Get to sleep, Maria," Alberto grumbled. "We've much to do in the next day or so."

"Okay, Alberto. Good night."

Maria felt a warmth next to her body, and welcomed her brother's arm thrown across her back. . . .

18

One week at sea, and Maria and Alberto feared the worst . . . that possibly they wouldn't even have the opportunity to see the great expanse of rich land called America.

Huddled together in a corner, beneath a water-soaked blanket, they trembled in unison.

"I'm so afraid, Alberto," Maria whispered, feeling a fresh, wild spray of seawater washing over the flooring of the ship, settling around her. "If only we could have afforded a cabin. What if we're even washed over-board?"

The ship continued to heave and pitch, and the wailing of the wind matched that of the many others who were also seeking a new way of life in America. Alberto lifted a corner of the blanket, to search his eyes around him, seeing once again the jammed upper deck of the crude ship called the *Dolphin*. As far as the eyes could see through the blur of the rain and the seawater's haze, bunks were lined up, filling the empty spaces of the upper deck, and on these bunks were members of families, huddled, sharing what had suddenly become a nightmare for all.

Feeling a sick ache at the pit of his stomach, Alberto pulled the blanket back down, a barrier being used to separate him and his sister from what mounting fear that he could . . . a fear that seemed to increase with each added lurch of the ship. He placed his arm around Maria and pulled her closer to him.

"It'll be all right, Maria," he said thickly. "You'll see. It'll be all right."

Maria reached for her violin case and placed it on her lap. "My poor violin," she cried. "It will be warped for sure. Then how can I pull beautiful notes from it? How, Alberto?"

"If anything happens to your violin, we shall purchase you another one when we reach America. I promise you that."

"But I only want this one."

"We shall take care of it as best as we can," Alberto said, helping to hold the case, pulling it to rest partially on his lap.

"And the animals on this ship stink so," Maria blurted, wrinkling her nose. "I thought the rains would at least wash the decks free of that stench. But it only seems to have worsened."

"I sure hadn't expected to share our boat trip with horses, mules and sheep," Alberto grumbled. "But we do have to, and the smell is one thing you'll have to learn to tolerate, Maria."

The ship rose, fell and rolled some more, making the timbers creak in an almost weary-sounding fashion.

"When ever shall it end?" Maria sobbed. Her stomach ached both from the tossing of the ship and the lack of food, and her feet and fingers had grown numb from the continuing wet, cold dampness.

"Please quit fretting so, Maria," Alberto said. "That won't make things any better."

20

Maria chewed her lower lip. "Alberto?" she said softly.

"Yes?"

"When the storm is over, can I please take these wet clothes off and put on a dress?"

He answered immediately and gruffly. "No. You cannot wear a dress," he argued. "You know the dangers of that."

"I still don't understand."

"To wear a dress would be to show this ship's crew that you are a woman. You *do* know the dangers of that."

"No, I do not," she said angrily.

"I've told you. Over and over again."

"I think you are wrong, Alberto," she persisted. "I am not beautiful. No man would . . . did you call it . . . seduce me. You are funny, Alberto."

Tensing, Alberto glared at Maria. "Maria, if you flaunt your . . . shall I say . . . your curves to these women-hungry seamen, you are asking for trouble. And, yes, my sister, you are quite beautiful. Even a brother knows the beauty of a sister."

"But to wear this ugly chimney sweep outfit for even another day almost breaks my heart," she moaned. "I thought that once we left Italy behind, it would also mean to leave dingy ways of dressing behind. I so long to wear long, pretty dresses. The one Aunt Helena gave me is so lovely with its lace and bows. Please let me wear it?"

"No, Maria," Alberto stormed. "I am to see to your safety and, damn it, you shall wear what I say. And please be sure to keep your hair hidden beneath that hat. That alone would give away the fact that you are

21

not my brother."

"Oh, all right," Maria grumbled, then grew silent, listening. "Has the storm stopped?" she whispered. "The sea seems to be a bit calmer and I hear no more close thunder. Only occasional slight rumblings."

Alberto quickly raised the blanket and searched the sky. There were still many gray, low-rolling clouds racing along overhead, but a rainbow filled another part of the sky in misty multicolors.

"Look, Maria," Alberto exclaimed, tossing the blanket aside. "Isn't it so beautiful?"

Maria's eyes sparkled as she stood and straightened her back, looking upward. "They say that a pot of gold can be found at the rainbow's end," she whispered. "Do you even think the one end of this rainbow stops where America lies waiting for us?"

"Maybe so," Alberto said, looking slowly around him, stomping his feet alternately, sending small showers of water from his clothes. Since the storm's abatement, the activity on the ship had taken on a different note. The rain-soaked people began to move from their bunks, coughing, sneezing, wringing the water from their clothes and hair, and checking the welfare of their belongings.

The ship's crew scurried around, clearing the outer deck of fallen debris and shouting crude obscenities as they pushed their way through the throngs of people milling about.

Alberto leaned into Maria's face. "Now you remember what I said," he whispered. "You keep that hat pulled down to hide your eyes and walk a bit stooped so no sailor will see your . . . uh . . . the size of your breasts."

Feeling a blush rising, Maria cast her eyes downward. "All right," she said. "I will." She clung to her violin case as she watched Alberto reposition their trunks further up the deck, then scoot their bunks closer together.

"There. That's better," he said. "If the sun ever shines again, at least we'll be where it can reach and warm us."

Maria placed her violin case on one of the bunks. "Will it be as cold for the whole trip, Alberto?" she asked, shivering. She wrapped her arms around her chest, hugging herself.

"It is the month of October," he said, walking to the ship's rail, to look far into the horizon, seeing gray meeting blue. Would he ever see land again? Had his Papa had such doubts when he had traveled from Italy to America? Setting his jaw firmly, he swung around on a heel to clasp onto Maria's shoulders. "Yes, it is the month of October," he blurted. "And cold as it is, you must remember that in November even, we shall be sitting comfortably in front of a cozy fire in Papa's house. By God we will. Just you wait and see."

Having suddenly pulled courage from Alberto, Maria lunged into his arms and hugged him to her, resting her cheek on his shoulder. "You always make me feel so confident of things in life," she murmured. "Alberto, whatever would I do without you?"

Alberto hugged her tightly. "I will always be here for you, Maria." But his gaze had traveled further up the deck, seeing a cluster of men taking their usual positions next to the ship's round, soot-covered smokestack. The storm had sent them fleeing for whatever protective covering they could find, but now they had returned, squatting, playing their same card games and

23

smoking long, thick cigars.

Maria had heard a different tone in Alberto's voice and she had sensed his body grow tense. She pulled from him, searching his face, then turned to follow his gaze. Yes, it was the same men. Alberto had been almost mesmerized by the silly card games they were playing since the ship's moving out into the open sea. "Alberto?" she whispered, tugging on his sleeve. "Alberto!" she persisted, when he ignored her. She looked toward the men again, then downward at the money being shoved back and forth between them. She understood that this thing they were doing held a fascination for Alberto mainly due to the stacks of green bills being exchanged from one hand to another.

Maria reached up to touch Alberto's cheek, suddenly afraid, seeing a strangeness in his eyes . . . a look of need . . . a look almost the same as lust as he licked his lips feverishly. "Alberto, come and sit with me," she pleaded.

"I've got to see how they play that game," Alberto said, jerking away from her, then gazed at her with his wide, dark eyes. "Now you sit down on your bunk and I'll only be a minute."

Maria clutched at his arm. "You don't want to even get near those men," she whispered harshly. Her own dark eyes widened, pleading. "Can't you see they are evil men?" She shuddered visibly, seeing the thick black whiskers of most of them, and the filthiness of their shabby clothes. "And they're so dirty. Even dirtier than the clothes we have had to wear."

"They might be all those things," Alberto said. "But don't you see the money in their possession? God. They must be rich."

24

Maria scoffed. "Rich? How could they be and dress in such a way? Bank robbers would probably be a more appropriate way to describe them. Please, Alberto, stay away from them."

"It looks too exciting, Maria. You know how boring life has been up to now for both of us."

"But I'm afraid to be left alone."

"I will only be footsteps away. Didn't I promise to always be here to look after you?"

"And I'm hungry, Alberto," she whined, gathering the bottom of her shirt in her fingers to twist it.

"The women folk will soon be cooking. You'll see."

"If I could show that I'm a woman, I could help with the cooking," she further pouted. "I've noticed that the ones who do the cooking sneak extra food beneath their skirts. I could even do that for us, Alberto."

Alberto frowned, busying himself, removing from his inner pockets most of his money and already purchased train tickets for the long trip from New York to Illinois, then quickly thrust this into Maria's hands. "Here. Hide this," he said. "Maybe the men are wicked as you say. No need in taking a chance of getting our money and tickets taken from me."

Maria looked downward, mentally calculating how much he had given her. She wasn't skilled with numbers, but she did know enough to realize Alberto hadn't given her all the money they possessed. She circled her fingers around what she did hold and eyed him questioningly. "Where is the rest, Alberto?" she whispered.

His face flushed crimson as he looked quickly away from her. "A man apparently doesn't go sit to watch that card game without money of his own," he mumbled, awkwardly thrusting his hands in his rear trousers pockets.

"Alberto!" Maria scolded. "You cannot do this thing. I know harm will come from it."

Alberto's eyes grew wider when he watched one of the men thrust a huge wad of bills inside a wallet, laughing, then moving away from the men, to go and wrap his arms around a young, beautiful woman. He further watched as they disappeared below deck. He had heard whisperings about these women with the painted faces and low-cut dresses, and what the men paid them to do. His heart pounded against his chest . . . wondering how it would feel to reach up inside the skirts of a woman. He had seen enough of his sister Maria to stir his insides to an almost burning inferno. . . .

"Alberto?" Maria whispered.

He leaned down into her face. "Hide the money and tickets," he said quietly.

"But where?"

"Inside the violin case. No one will ever have a chance to take it from you. I know how you watch it like a hawk."

"Then you still insist on going to sit with those men?"

He held her face in his hands. "For a little while, Maria," he said thickly. "Please understand. I'm a man. A man needs more than to sit idly by watching everyone else have fun."

Maria batted her lashes nervously. "All right, Alberto," she said. "But please. Not for long. I do want to be able to stand in line with you when the meal is completed and ready for serving."

"I'm just as hungry as you, Maria," he said, laughing

softly. "My stomach is aching just as badly. Don't you know that?"

"Then please hurry back."

"I shall."

Maria stood trembling as she watched Alberto move slowly toward the men, and then tensed as all eyes turned to study him before inviting him to join them. Fear and dread surged through Maria, wondering if Alberto truly understood the dangers of doing so. But he was a man . . . and men had to know how to protect themselves. Surely Alberto could also.

Hunkering down beside the bunk, watching to see that no one was looking, Maria pulled her violin case back onto her lap. Then reaching upward, she pulled a tarnished chain from around her neck to remove a small, square key from it.

Again watching around her, she hurriedly unlocked her violin case with this key, then looked downward onto her highly varnished instrument that lay in silence on its soft bed of crimson velvet. She so wanted to pluck the strings that were stretched tautly across their bridge, but was afraid that to do so would be to draw more attention to her and what she so desperately had to get hidden.

With the swiftness of her long, lean fingers, she placed the money and tickets in a small pouch at the inside far end of the case, hiding these snugly beneath packages of extra violin strings and a square cake of rosin.

"There. That should do it," she sighed quietly to herself, then drew in a quick breath when a dark shadow fell over her and her violin.

Hurriedly covering the pouch with her hands, she

looked upward into a man's face that was framed by hair that was more golden than rays from an afternoon sun. Their gazes then met, making Maria's body become as a thousand heartbeats. The color of this man's eyes was blue . . . as blue as the deepest waters of the ocean. He was so unlike anyone she had yet to meet, accustomed as she was to the Italians' dark eyes and hair. He had to be American. Wasn't he dressed as an American, in his ruffled, white shirt, dark waistcoat and tight-fitted breeches?

"I caught sight of your violin when you raised the lid of your case," he said, stooping, openly admiring the instrument. With a quick flick of the wrist, he had plucked each of the strings. "Hmm. A beautiful tone. Do you play?"

Pulling the brim of her hat to hide her eyes, Maria sat as though in a spell, afraid to speak, knowing that this man would most definitely be able to tell by the pitch of her voice that she was indeed female. She quickly shook her head back and forth, hoping that to be answer enough.

A deep laugh surfaced from the man, causing Maria's eyes to move upward again. She could see amusement in the half smile playing on his lips and wondered if he had already guessed what was behind her silence. His clean-shaven face and the gentleness to the curve of his jaw made her want to trust him. And didn't she have a need for excitement . . . the same as Alberto? Even now, she felt strange stirrings inside herself, a strangeness she hadn't ever experienced before. Was it because this man of blue eyes kept watching her with a smile so gentle? Why . . . was he even flirting with her? Had he truly guessed that she was a female?

"So you don't speak English?" he said, squatting down more closely beside her, so close even, she could sniff the aromas of a man's expensive cologne and richness of cigars. And his clothes were clean . . . and *dry* . . . which had to mean that he had possession of a cabin for this long voyage to America.

Shutting the lid to her violin case, she shook her head in affirmation, then locked the case with her key.

Another deep rumble surfaced from inside this man's chest. "Who are you trying to fool?" he laughed, pulling a half-smoked cigar from an inside pocket. He lit it and inhaled deeply. "If you couldn't speak English, how could you even know to answer my questions with the nod of your head?"

Maria's face reddened as she jumped to her feet. She searched for Alberto and found him deeply engrossed in his new card game. What was she to do? This stranger was going to discover her true identity. She just knew it. She tried to pull the chain that held her key over her hat and gasped openly when the hat went tumbling to the deck. She bent to grab it, but knew that she was too late. Her hair was tumbling loosely now around both her face and shoulders.

"Well, I'll be damned," the man said thickly, rising, catching her in his arms as she stumbled sideways. "I was right. You are a female. Why in hell are you dressed in such a way?" he blurted, tossing his cigar aside, to hold her at arm's length. His eyes traveled over her, seeing the darkness of her eyes, sheltered by thick, long lashes. Her lips were sensuously full, trembling now, from noticeable fear, and he saw this slight birthmark of a strawberry color on the slight dimple of her right cheek. That damn hat had hidden much from

29

his eyes.

His gaze lowered, seeing now the swell of her bosom, as it heaved in and out with each breath taken. Now that she was standing with a straightened back, there was no disguising what God had so blessed her with. And then there were the trousers. "Why, I've never seen a woman wear trousers before," he quickly added, thinking her to be so stately tall and shatteringly pretty. He felt the heat rising in his loins, knowing that he had to have a taste of what lay hidden beneath the dark, soiled clothes. Beneath those clothes, there was a woman, a woman pulsating with womanly desires. He could almost smell the animal needs of them both . . . intermingling with the sharp sea air, whining around them. But wasn't she one of the unfortunate immigrants headed for the disillusionment of the coal mines of America? Nathan Hawkins's coal mines? Should he risk mingling with her? What if she found out who *he* was? Would it interfere with his mission . . . ?

"Please let me go," she said, begging with her eyes, then searching around her again for Alberto, but feeling a slow death rising inside her when she realized that Alberto was now in another world, a world of gambling. . . . Hadn't she only moments ago, before her encounter with this stranger, heard some women whispering of this card game they called gambling . . . and how it *was* the devil himself . . . luring decent men into a wickedness they could no longer say no to?

"Again I ask you," the man persisted. "Why *are* you dressed in such a way? Do you not own anything more fashionable? Like even a dress?"

"Sir, I shall dress in any which way I see fit," she hissed, knowing that she now had to take command of

30

the situation. Alberto had betrayed her. He had chosen a game of cards . . . over her. . . .

"You're beautiful, even in such garments as these," the man said, freeing her, now realizing that no matter what, he had to have her. "But aren't you cold? I see how wet you are since the storm. Might you want to follow me to my cabin? I have a small stove with a soft fire burning inside it. Might you want to join me?"

With wavering eyes, Maria studied him more carefully, feeling an increased pulsebeat in her throat. He was even taller than Alberto, but not any more gifted with shoulders than her brother. And wasn't this man so very persuasive in his smooth way of speaking? And yes, she *was* cold. She *was* hungry. If he had his own cabin, surely he also had some nourishment to share with her.

She gazed toward Alberto once again, seeing his lack of interest in her, then set her jaw firmly. "And what might your name be, sir?" she asked, with her chin tilted upward.

"Michael Hopper," he answered, feeling hope rising inside himself. He didn't want to have *any* part of those riverfront whores who traveled these ships . . . making their fortune from the gambling fools. No. He wanted a female who appeared not to lie with each man who asked her. He was afraid of diseases. He eyed Maria once again. True, her clothes were dirty . . . but her skin was shining clean, and he guessed that the clothes were a planned decoy . . . to keep men from taking advantage of her.

And the violin? Was she a trained musician, searching for a place to show her skills, knowing that America was a land of opportunity?

"Michael Hopper," he added again, offering her an arm. "Michael Hopper at your service, ma'am."

She took her violin case by the handle with her free hand and draped her other arm through Michael's. "Maria Lazzaro, to you, sir," she stated flatly, feeling secure now with what she was doing. She could fend for herself. She was no longer a child, whimpering by a brother's side. She was a woman desired by a well-dressed American. No. She was no longer afraid. The warning of being seduced was quickly brushed from her thoughts. . . .

Letting her hair blow loosely in the wind, she followed alongside Michael, feeling eyes on her watching her every move. She laughed to herself, knowing what a pair she and Michael made . . . she with her soiled chimney sweep costume, and he with his impeccable, freshly pressed outfit.

Whisperings followed along behind them as women moved together in clusters around one small stove in the center of the deck. The aromas of grease heating and raw salmon waiting to be fried clung to Maria as she moved on away, hoping that maybe this one evening she would be offered more than fish and potatoes for supper.

"Maria is a lovely name," Michael said, as he guided her toward a door that led downward, below deck. "It fits you, you know."

"You really think so?"

"Yes, I do," he answered, then eyed the violin case. "And do you carry that with you everywhere you go?"

Maria clutched more tightly to the handle. "Almost," she said softly.

"And will you play for me?"

"I think not."

"Who do you usually entertain with your music?"

Maria felt a blush rising, knowing that she could not reveal to this fine class of a gentleman that she was mainly used to playing on the streets of Pordenone. She doubted very much if this was a custom of the Americans. "Myself," she quickly blurted.

Michael laughed deeply, opening the door, stepping aside, bowing slightly, gesturing for her to enter before him. "I'm sure that's no fun," he said, then offered an arm once again as he led her down a narrow, dark passageway.

"Playing my violin gives me much satisfaction," she said. "No matter if I am alone while playing it." She had hated it when her Mama had forbid her to play any longer in Pordenone. Oh, how she hungered for the opportunity of doing this again, but she now knew that was behind her. Forever.

She tensed when she heard many different noises surfacing from the rooms on each side of her as she passed by them. Above all else, women giggling and their taunting of men rose above it all, making Maria blush anew.

"My cabin is at the far end, away from all these others," Michael hurriedly added, having seen her uneasiness. "I'm sure you will find it to be quite pleasant."

Maria's eyes widened as a beautiful young girl swung a door widely open, revealing herself in her half-nude attire, with her breasts fully exposed above a torn chemise.

Michael hurried Maria along, almost yanking her from the spot. "Just a gambler having some fun with

33

one of the loose ladies who have chosen to board this ship."

"But, she looked . . . frightened. . . ." Maria whispered, swallowing hard. "Wasn't she trying to flee from that cabin?"

Michael laughed gruffly. "Caroline? Are you kidding?" he blurted. "She beds up with any gent who wears trousers." He eyed Maria stoically. "And you'd best watch out for her," he quickly added. "You also are wearing trousers. She might even try to get *you* to bed up with her."

Maria stiffened, feeling a sick feeling at the pit of her stomach. "Such a disgusting thought," she said, shuddering.

Michael doubled over with laughter and reached for a doorknob. "I *do* have me an innocent one at my side, don't I?"

"Innocent?"

"There are many ways of the world that I fear you may become acquainted with even before you reach American soil, unless you agree to let me protect you from them."

She set her jaw firmly. "I can take care of myself."

"And who might that fellow be who *has* been watching over you? I saw no wedding band on either of your fingers, so concluded he must be a blood relation. Am I correct in assuming that?"

Maria had almost forgotten about Alberto. Oh, how could she have? They had never been apart. Did this blonde American have a way of making her lose her wits? "Yes. He is my kin," she answered. "He is my twin brother."

"Damn it, you say."

"Yes. And may I ask you something, sir?"

"Michael. Please call me Michael."

She cleared her throat nervously. "Okay, Michael," she said, then added. "Can I ask where you are from?"

He opened the door widely, stepping into total darkness, except for what the small porthole emitted in wavy grays onto the low ceiling. "Good ol' Saint Louis, Missouri," he said. "In America, of course." He suddenly tensed, aware that he had just blurted out what should have been kept confidential. Damn. Damn. He knew that she would cause him to have a loose tongue. God. She was too beautiful.

Maria laughed. "How funny that name is."

"America?"

"No. Saint Louis."

"Yeah. I guess it is at that," he mumbled, searching for the wick of a whale oil lantern, then struck a match and lit it.

Maria stood straight-backed, watching the soft glow of the lantern, with her eyes growing wide, seeing the way in which this cabin was furnished. It was as though she had stepped into a grand hotel suite, of which she had seen pictures in books. "It is quite fancy," she said, almost afraid to step onto the highly polished floor. Her gaze traveled more around her, seeing plushly upholstered furniture in a beige leather fabric.

But the one piece of furniture that grabbed her attention most was a bed that filled the full depth of the far end of the room. Not a hard, uncomfortable bunk or bed of leaves . . . but a true . . . bed.

An aroma of mustiness filtered upward to be fast dispelled when Michael lit a fresh cigar and settled down onto a chair, crossing his legs before him. He couldn't help but feel a bit guilty, seeing the look of disbelief in her eyes as Maria continued to look around her. His cabin *was* quite elaborate, in comparison to the way the immigrants were traveling.

But having had to travel on such a long journey as this, he hadn't been able to say no to what the ship's captain had offered in the way of luxury. But the captain of the *Dolphin* had no idea of Michael's true identity. If he *had* . . . Michael would have been treated even more poorly than a rat that is discovered on ship. . . .

"And would you like to put on something less wet?" he asked, eyeing her between squinted eyes.

"What?" she gasped.

He laughed softly. "Don't be alarmed," he said. "I only want to give you loan of my robe, until we can get your clothes dry."

Maria looked further around her, seeing the small stove glowing orange in a corner, and a desk and built-in dressing table next to a basin that had been attached to the wall. Beneath the basin was a commode, making Maria turn her eyes quickly away.

She shivered again, realizing just how cold and uncomfortable she was. She eyed the stove once again and inched her way toward it.

"Well? What do you say, Maria?"

She turned to face him with wavering eyes. "I am a bit cold," she whispered.

He pushed himself up out of the chair and went to a closet, pulling from it a maroon-colored satin night robe. He tossed it to her, then sat back down, watching her.

She placed her violin case on the floor and clutched

the soft fabric to her. "Could you please close your eyes?" she asked quietly. She had learned to not be ashamed of her body while living in such close quarters at both her Papa's and Gran-mama's houses, but she had yet to let *any* man . . . not even . . . Alberto . . . see her fully unclothed. She had become aware of the size of her breasts and sensed that that was what most men liked about a woman's hidden proportions.

"Sure," he laughed, standing, to move to his desk, to busy his fingers while turning pages of his journal, in which he had yet to record on this damn blustery day. His brows furrowed, remembering the storm. He had been quite aware of the creaking of the ship's timbers. Was this to be the last voyage of this ship *Dolphin?* Had it seen its last days of bringing immigrants to America's soil? Damn it. He hoped so. He had yet to see any immigrants treated fairly. They would be better off if not given passage to a land that didn't truly welcome them with open arms. . . .

Kicking her shoes off and stepping from her trousers, and then having pulled her jacket over her head, Maria worked quickly to cover herself with this sleek, shining fabric that had been so generously loaned to her. She liked the feel of it next to her skin, almost a caress, it seemed, as she tied its belt securely around her tiny waist.

"I'm now fully covered, Michael," she said, curling her toes leisurely onto the warmth of the flooring beneath her feet. She flipped her dark hair away from her face and over her shoulders, smiling shyly as he turned to face her. The strange look in his eyes made a weakness settle in her knees and an ache begin between her thighs. She touched her forehead lightly and quickly turned to put her back to him, stooping to pick her clothes up, to arrange them on a chair next to the stove.

The pounding of her heart was a true warning of what was happening inside her. It had to be because she was suddenly being awakened to the desire for a man.

"You are quite a beautiful woman," Michael said, clearing his throat nervously. He had known that the loose clothes had hidden many things . . . but he hadn't expected to find such exquisite proportions as his eyes had feasted on until she had turned from him. Such large, firm breasts compared to such a tiny waist? Yes, he had made quite a discovery here.

"And I do love the robe," she said, running her fingers over its smoothness. "I've never had such softness against my skin."

He went to stand beside her, but didn't dare attempt to touch her. He was afraid to move, lest haste only result in waste. "But it is only my night garment," he said, puffing on his cigar.

"My night garments have only been of cotton," she whispered. "As well as all my day garments."

He ached to touch her. "You were made for satin, Maria," he said, then turned with a start when a knock on the door interrupted their awkwardness. "Damn," he uttered beneath his breath, crushing his cigar in an ashtray. "Who the hell?" he mumbled further, going to the door to open it with a jerk, then smiled, remembering having ordered this before taking his stroll on top deck. This was perfect. Maybe he could tempt Maria with food and receive a reward for all his generosities . . . ?

Maria's eyes widened when she saw a ship's steward

offering Michael a huge tray of silver-ornamented covered dishes. The aromas soon met her nose, making her lick her lips hungrily. She *had* been right. To be in Michael Hopper's presence *had* meant dry clothes . . . food. . . .

"Thank you, Shawn," Michael said, accepting the tray. He placed it on a table that sat between two chairs and closed and latched the door, turning to smile again, but this time toward Maria.

"A feast is what I now offer you," he said, gesturing with a hand for her to sit down opposite him.

She put her hands to her throat. "For me?" she whispered, watching hungrily as Michael lifted first one lid and then another from the dishes. Steam spiraled upward, curling around her, enticing her even more, as she saw a deep-browned baked duck, sliced carrots swimming in a cream sauce, and slices of cheese and apples piled high on another platter.

"Come. Sit," Michael encouraged, popping a cork from a wine bottle, to pour the crimson liquid into two tall, thin-stemmed wine glasses. "There's enough food and wine for two. Please enjoy it with me."

Maria sank down onto the chair and accepted a glass of wine, then a dish piled high with food. She hesitated before eating, feeling a sudden guilt, remembering poor Alberto and what he would be fed on top deck. But she set her jaw firmly, thinking it to be his own fault for having left her side for a silly card game. Had he not, he would most surely be sitting beside her in the warmth of this cabin, also being served such delicious-smelling food.

She took a quick sip of wine, then set the glass down, to be able to eagerly pick at the meat with a fork. Smiling at Michael, she savored the mixtures of tastes and the pleasant, calm feeling they were creating inside her stomach. "It is so very good," she said, then sipped on the wine again, this causing a rosiness to creep up into her cheeks.

Michael cleaned his plate and emptied his glass, then leaned back against the chair as he lit another cigar. "Now tell me a little about yourself," he said, placing his folded hands on his lap, twiddling his thumbs.

Maria licked her lips and relaxed against the back of her own chair after having placed her empty plate and glass on the table before her. "What would you like to know?" she asked, feeling deliciously contented.

"Where are you and your brother headed?"

"To America."

He laughed. "I know, my sweet," he said. "But where in America?"

"I forget," she said, blushing. She scooted to the edge of the chair, causing the robe she wore to fall clumsily open. Her blush deepened as she pulled the edges closer together. "I have the name of the town in my violin case," she said quickly. "I can look, then tell you."

His brows furrowed as he turned his cigar between his lips. "The name is unimportant," he murmured, looking toward the floor. He cleared his throat nervously, now eyeing her closely. "And what type of employment will your brother be seeking?"

Maria leaned against the back of the chair again, pulling her legs comfortably beneath her. "Whatever Papa has found for himself and Alberto," she answered. "But I cannot tell you what. Papa failed to mention it in his last letter to us."

"Oh, I see," Michael grumbled. "And it is your Papa

who sent tickets for your passage to America?"

"Yes. After waiting so long, he finally did so."

He felt a bit confused, having thought all along that most aboard this ship were headed for the coal mines owned by Nathan Hawkins. But . . . yes . . . there had to be a few who weren't. . . .

"And how about yourself, Michael?" Maria said eagerly, shaking her head to free her eyes of some loose strands of hair.

"Eh?" he said, not having expected her to blurt out that sort of question so suddenly.

"What is the purpose for you being on this ship?" she asked further, gazing around her once again, at the plushness of her surroundings. Then her gaze met his. "Are you even the owner of this ship, Michael?"

Michael began laughing, choking on his cigar smoke. "Me?" he said. "Not quite."

"Then what *do* you do, Michael? How do you make a living for yourself?"

His face became all shadows as he leaned over to pour two more glasses of wine. "I'm with a winery," he finally answered. "I've been to Italy . . . to . . . uh . . . check the quality of the grapes, to choose which of these we want to plant in our fields back in America."

He watched her eyes, relieved to see that she believed him, as had also the ship's captain.

"Then America does have grapes?" she asked eagerly.

"Yes. Many," he answered. "More wine?" he added, smoothly, holding a filled glass before her.

"I don't know why not," she giggled, having liked the way it had warmed her insides. Another glass might even make her so warm, it could linger with her on into the night, when she would be lying, shivering, on top deck.

She took a sip, then another, realizing that the usual tingling was working up her spine, as always happened when drinking any wine . . . even her own Papa's homemade brew that had been so sorely missed after his departure to America.

"And did you find our country's grapes to your liking?" she asked, then bolted upright when a sudden commotion erupted outside the closed door. "What was that?" she whispered.

Michael rose and went to her, but still refrained from touching her. "As you should know, there are many strange noises on a ship," he said. "It's nothing to worry about."

A louder thud and men cursing loudly prompted Maria to lunge for Michael, then suck in her breath when she found his arms enfolding her.

"Maria?" he said softly, eyeing her questioningly with his blue eyes, then moved his lips to cover hers, causing Maria's heart to thump wildly against her chest. He kissed her softly . . . testing . . . then pulled her closer to him in such a quick way, her breath was almost taken from her.

She opened her eyes, searching this face so close to hers, seeing how he had his eyes tightly closed, as though in a swoon, while continuing to kiss her.

It was a first for her. No man had ever kissed her before and she found that Michael's lips were creating many more pleasurable feelings inside her than she had ever thought possible. She closed her own eyes, squirming, to shape her body to his, not caring when the gown she wore flew open, making her feel even more clearly the hardness of his manhood pressing against her.

She knew that she should be feeling wicked, but the warmth coarsing through her veins and her heart pounding so rapidly convinced her that in no way could such a sensation of excitement be wrong.

She moaned throatily as one of Michael's hands moved to secure a breast, causing her nipple to draw tightly, aching as his fingers teased and pulled at it.

She threw her head back as his lips left her mouth and exchanged places with his fingers, now licking and sucking on the hard points of each breast, until Maria felt she might melt onto the floor into one throbbing mass of flesh.

"Maria, you are so damn beautiful," Michael said thickly, then scooped her up into his arms and carried her to the bed.

"And you, Michael?" she whispered. "You've set me on fire inside." She reached her arms out to him, begging him to come to her, wanting more, but had to remain patient as he began to undress in front of her.

"Remove the robe, Maria," he said, tossing his shirt aside, revealing to her a broad expanse of chest, covered by thick, golden curls. "I want to feast my eyes on the whole of you before we share the ultimate of feelings shared between a man and woman."

Maria smiled sheepishly as she sat up, to let the robe fall freely from around her. She straightened her back, proud of her breasts, hungering once again for his lips to devour them. "These feelings, Michael," she said. "I've never experienced them before. Have you? With many different women already?"

Michael's eyes widened and his fingers stopped unbuttoning his breeches. "You've never been with a man before?" he blurted, wondering about how experienced

43

she had appeared only moments ago. And she was ready to give herself to him willingly. Most women were too bashful that first time to be able to relax and enjoy it . . . much less to encourage it.

"Not in a sexual way," she said, running her fingers over the softness of the bed, relishing this moment of firsts . . . her first bed . . . her first love . . . "I've only been with my brother Alberto," she quickly added.

Michael took a step backwards, teetering. His face had turned ashen. "Your brother?" he gasped.

Maria bounced from the bed and went to Michael, laughing softly. She ran her fingers through the hairs of his chest, then fingered each nipple, thinking them to be so rubbery, not tight and stiff like her own now were. "Not as a husband with a wife," she giggled. "I said I hadn't been with *any* man in that way. My brother and I? We're as close as being one person. You see, that's because we are twins."

Michael reached for her, laughing awkwardly. "I see," he said. "And you're now ready to be taken sexually? By me?"

"Yes, Michael," she purred, fitting her body into his again, wrapping a leg around him, teasing him.

He held her to him, caressing the smoothness of her back, then lower, to the curves of her buttocks. "Why me, Maria?" he asked thickly.

She looked up into his eyes, smiling sweetly. "You're so different, Michael," she said. "You're even beautiful. Now please kiss me, will you?"

"Will I? God. Yes," he answered and consumed her fully with his lips, again lifting her, to stretch her atop the bed. He positioned himself above her, also on the bed, as his fingers quickly released his manhood from its tight confines and searched eagerly . . . hungrily . . .

for that soft place between her legs, glad to find her open, ready.

"I'll be gentle, Maria," he said. "You'll see how gentle a man can be."

Slowly he pushed his manhood to the part of her that had been readied for a man's entrance and began to probe. . . .

Maria felt feverish with desire, touching him everywhere, wanting to remember this moment. He hadn't let her see the part of him that was now like a hot rod exploring deeply between her legs. But she hadn't had to see it. All that was important was how it was making her feel.

She arched her back upward, sighing from the strange, pleasurable sensations inside herself, now waiting for his complete entrance inside the deepest part of herself. "Please, Michael," she whispered. "Now. Please do it now, Michael."

Michael's body stiffened as he thrust inward, groaning as the warmth of her vaginal walls closed around his throbbing manhood. Only a slight trickle of blood covered his entrance and now he was free to pull from Maria all the warmth and sweetness she was giving to him. He moved his body inward and outward, closing his eyes to the building of pressures ready to explode from inside himself, then crushed her mouth beneath his as the spasms of release became so close. . . .

"Oh," Maria whimpered as he had made the entrance, but the pain quickly turned once again to pleasure. She wrapped her legs around him and began to work with him, panting, meeting his every thrust, enjoying to the fullest this sensation of wild, sensuous pleasure invading every fiber of her being, then felt the urgency building . . . a frantic passion that made her cling to him . . . nibble at his shoulders . . . dig her fingers into his buttocks . . . until together, they began to tremble . . . to moan and groan in unison . . . until they soon lay spent . . . wet with perspiration . . . panting.

Michael stretched out on his back beside Maria and threw an arm over his eyes, still feeling the thumping of his heart. "God!" he blurted. "God."

Maria curled up next to him and began to trace his body with a finger. "Was I so bad?" she pouted, thinking him to be angry.

Michael turned to face her, laughing throatily. He squeezed a breast softly and kissed the tip of her nose. "Surely you don't think I'm disappointed," he said.

"Then you're not?"

"You're very skillful at lovemaking, Maria," he murmured. "And did I hurt you?"

"Only for a moment," she whispered. "Then I experienced the most heavenly of sensations."

"And I also, my love," he said, kissing her again.

She continued to trace his body with her fingers, and with wide eyes stared at the part of him that had just given her so much pleasure. "Why, it is so small and soft," she said aloud, then blushed when she realized what she had said.

Michael laughed, positioning himself so she could see it more easily. "Touch it again," he said.

Maria's fingers pulled away from him. "You want me to . . . touch . . . it . . . again?" she whispered.

He laughed again and took her hand in his, guiding it downward. "Touch it. Even hold it," he encouraged, feeling the heat begin to swell inside it as her fingers gently enfolded it.

"But it *is* so small," she repeated. "It felt much larger . . . when . . . inside me."

"Caress it, Maria," he said thickly, stiffening his legs.

"How?"

"Just move your fingers on it. You will soon understand."

She did as he suggested, thinking this thing to feel so warm. Her eyes widened as it suddenly began to thicken and grow in her hand. "Why . . . it's . . . alive . . ." she gasped.

"Very alive," he laughed, then turned to lift her to lie atop him, inserting his manhood inside her again. "And now, let's show you just *how* alive," he groaned, thrusting wildly inside her.

She wrapped her arms around his neck and closed her eyes, feeling her breasts bouncing against his chest, stirring her to sexual bliss again, surprised that it could happen again so soon. She wanted to scream . . . yell . . . she felt so wonderful . . . but soon it was all over again, leaving her to lie completely exhausted and even ready for sleep.

She moved from atop Michael and lay panting, wondering if her heart would ever beat normally again. . . .

"Can you stay with me, Maria?" Michael asked, brushing hair back from her eyes, tracing her strawberry-colored birthmark with his forefinger, but not mentioning it, for fear of embarrassing her. He could not be sure of her feelings for this one flaw about her features. "The voyage is to be a long, boring one," he quickly added.

Her eyes opened wildly, suddenly remembering Alberto and how frightened he might be and how frantically he must be searching for her. She climbed

47

from the bed and began to dress in her clothes that had succeeded at drying beside the stove. "My brother," she said breathlessly. "I simply forgot all about him."

Michael rose from the bed, buttoning his breeches. "He's old enough to fend for himself, Maria."

"But we've never been apart. Never."

"This would be a good time to start," Michael argued. He went to her and pulled her to him, exploring with his hands beneath her jacket. "It's not normal for brother and sister to be so close. You have to break that bond. And soon."

Maria jerked from his hold, with anger flashing in her eyes. "We shall never break our bonds," she hissed. "Ours is an alliance of love."

Michael stormed away from her and grabbed his shirt to pull it on. "Can his love warm you at night?" he shouted. "Can his hands caress and excite you as mine can?"

Maria's fists doubled at her side. "You are filthy-mouthed, Michael," she screamed. "How could I have let you touch me?"

He laughed sardonically. "Because for a while there, you realized there was more to life than being a sister."

Maria flung her hair around her shoulders angrily, now realizing that she had left her hat on the top deck, lying beside the bunk. Now everyone aboard this ship knew that she was a female. A fear gripped her insides, remembering Alberto's warnings. She had *wanted* to be seduced by Michael . . . but not anyone else. . . . But at this moment, that was the least of her worries.

"I'm getting out of here," she said, buttoning the last button of her breeches. She hurried toward the door, but stopped to eye the apple and cheese slices, worrying about Alberto and what he had probably had to eat

48

for his evening meal. "Can . . . I . . . ?" she whispered, begging with her eyes.

"Hell, yes," Michael pouted. "Take it all."

"Oh, thank you, Michael," she murmured, scooping as much food into her pockets as was possible. Then she eyed Michael with a long, lingering look, again feeling the warm, pulsating between her thighs, knowing that no amount of anger she felt for him could ever make her hate him. She was in love with him . . . and would be . . . forever and ever.

He moved toward her and secured the cork in the wine bottle. "Here," he said, handing it toward her. "Take this also. It gets quite cold topside. But you already are aware of this, aren't you?"

Tears sprang up at the corner of Maria's eyes. "Oh, Michael," she whispered. "Thank you." She tucked the bottle beneath an arm, picked up her violin case and stood aside as Michael unlocked and opened the door for her.

"Good night, Maria," he said, leaning to brush a kiss against her lips.

"Good night, Michael," she replied, then turned and began to flee down the long, dark passageway, being guided by only slight flickerings of whale oil lanterns positioned on each side wall.

Moving onward, keeping her eyes forward, anxious to reach the steps that led upward to top deck, she suddenly stumbled against something sprawled at her feet. She leaned against the wall, feeling desperation rising inside herself when she looked downward to see what could be blocking her passage. Then a loud scream surfaced from the depths of her throat when she discovered it to be the body of Alberto . . . lying lifeless . . . in a fetal position . . . with blood gushing from

49

his nose and mouth.

Slumping to the deck, Maria let the wine bottle crash to the floor. She placed her violin case next to Alberto, then lifted his head to rest on her lap. "Alberto," she moaned, rocking back and forth, with tears streaming down her face. "My sweet, sweet Alberto."

A sudden rush of feet brought Michael to her side. "Oh, my God," he groaned, stooping to see how Alberto was. He checked his pulse. "He's just knocked out, Maria," he said. "He'll be all right."

"Why would anyone do this to Alberto?" she cried, feeling a part of her dying inside. She could almost feel his pain. She cradled him closer to her.

"Many evil things can happen on a ship," Michael said. "Come. Let's take your brother to my cabin."

"No," she snapped angrily, remembering the cruelty of Michael's words of only moments earlier about her love for her brother.

"Why not?" he snapped back at her.

"My brother and I have our own bunks. Up on top deck," she said stubbornly.

"Then you refuse my help?" he argued, rising, glowering.

"I would appreciate it if you'd help Alberto to his bunk," she said softly, with wavering eyes.

"You sure you want me to help to even do that?" Michael boomed, placing his hands on his hips.

"Please, Michael?" she pleaded, sobbing openly.

"Oh, God, Maria," Michael answered, stooping to lift Alberto's arm over his shoulders. "Don't cry, Maria. Please don't cry."

She wiped her eyes with the back of one hand and lifted her violin case up with the other and walked beside Michael as he semi-dragged Alberto until he had him stretched out atop his bunk.

"There," Michael said, panting, then staring around him at the immigrants watching, seeing fear etched on each of their faces. It made Michael feel so damn helpless. But maybe once he reached America, they could all have a chance to thank him. Yes, once his mission was accomplished. . . .

"Alberto," Maria said, resting on bended knees beside his bunk. "Please wake up." She accepted a handkerchief from Michael and began gently wiping the blood from Alberto's face. Then she remembered the commotion she had heard outside Michael's door . . . shortly before she and Michael had fallen into bed, wrestling, pleasuring one another. She closed her eyes as they burned with tears, knowing that this noise had been her own brother being beaten while she. . . . He had probably been searching for her. . . .

"Is there anything else I can do, Maria?" Michael asked, touching her hand.

She jerked free of him and glared upward. "Yes," she said darkly. "You can leave me and Alberto alone. I will not leave my brother's side for the rest of this journey. It is he who now needs me to watch over him, and I shall do this, no matter what."

Michael clamped his lips together tightly and swung around and stormed away, leaving Maria with an aching, throbbing heart. "But I *do* love you, Michael," she whispered after him.

Then her eyes traveled around her, searching the faces, anger swelling inside her, hoping to find out who was responsible for her brother's injuries. . . .

Chapter Three

The ocean had changed its mood. It now lay quiet . . . a canvas of blue stretched out as far as the eye could see. The only ripples in the water were from the ship's movements, and it didn't even appear to be making any headway.

Maria peered across the endless body of water, thinking to never see land again and all the comforts it had to offer. Oh, if only she hadn't taken for granted such things as fresh drinking water . . . the softness of grass beneath one's feet . . . the song of the birds in the brush. She licked her lips thirstily, feeling the dried cracks of flesh peeling from them. No. Never again would she even be able to run with her brother through fields of tall grass, or be able to share a bed, where late in the night they could exchange their secret thoughts.

Maria leaned down over Alberto, trying to shade him with her body. Now the rains would be welcome, for the sun was even worse punishment as it continued to beat down onto Maria's head, making her scalp tingle in a strange way. It had been this way for days. Nothing but sun and sea. The colors of blues and yellows meeting were now a constant blur to Maria. And she had to wonder if it was the same for Alberto, as his eyes looked into the distance in a bulgy, silent stare.

"Alberto?" Maria whispered, dipping a cloth into a pail of water, then touching it softly to Alberto's lips. "Please suck on this cloth. Please, Alberto. You need the moisture in your body, or you might even dehydrate and die a slow, lingering death." She squeezed the cloth, watching the droplets settle onto his closed lips, only to run, as drool might do, down his chin and onto his sweat-soaked shirt.

Alberto blinked his eyes and moved his head slightly, but still lay mute, as he had now since Sam's fierce blow upon the head. Maria gently turned his head and checked the head wound. It had finally quit seeping a colorless liquid. Guilt flooded her senses, as she remembered not having found the wound for two full days after his accident. Even the ship's doctor hadn't seen it. Doctor Rawson had fleetingly checked Alberto over, saying he would be all right in time, to not fret. But when Maria had continued to worry as each day had passed, seeing no change whatsoever in Alberto she had insisted that Doctor Rawson take a closer look at Alberto. That was when the head wound had been discovered.

"It don't look good, missie," Doctor Rawson had drawled in a cockney sort of dialect. "It appears to me that your brother might or might not make it now that I see his head. Sure willpower will be the only thing to pull him through now. We will just have to wait and see."

"You *will* be all right, Alberto," Maria said, smoothing his shirt with her hand, so wanting him to awaken and pull her into his arms, to reassure her that indeed he would arrive on America's soil with her. Even to think of seeing his body heaved from the ship, into the ocean that had become a grave for many since having left Italy, made Maria's stomach turn into massive quivers.

Looking down into her pail of water, fear gripped her heart even more. What had been rationed her and all on board just wasn't enough to keep her and Alberto's tongues wet, let alone to use it for anything else. Her eyes searched all around her, seeing all the others who were suffering from different maladies. The ugly moods of the weather continued to take their toll. Coughs and sneezes wracked all, it seemed. The children were the ones who had managed to stay the healthiest. But the elderly? So many . . . oh, so many hadn't made it.

Maria clutched at her chest, coughing herself. Her eyes continued to travel through the throngs of people lining the rails of the ship, now looking for the familiar stance of Michael. He had let her be . . . since that night she had attacked him verbally for his having spoken so wickedly of her and Alberto's relationship.

Now? She wished that her stubborn side hadn't been dominant that night. Now? She wished she had said yes to Michael's invitation for her and the wounded Alberto to share his cabin. Ah, to be in the comfort of his cabin . . . attired in comfortable clothes . . . being given all she desired to eat and drink. Yes, even Alberto would most surely agree that that would have been best for them. Maria now feared that Alberto might possibly have a sunstroke, instead of the usually fatal disease called pneumonia. She hadn't decided yet which was the worst. These past several days she had seen so much of both.

Feeling suddenly exhausted, and oh, so sad, Maria

stretched her legs out beside the bunk, pulling her breeches legs up beyond her ankles, and placed her head on Alberto's chest, sighing. She again hadn't seen Michael, but she knew that he was smart to stay below deck, where he was able to forget the stench of top deck and all those who were suffering so.

With tears burning at the corner of her eyes, Maria took one of Alberto's hands in hers and let herself be lost to all that was around her . . . dreaming sweeter dreams than those of the present . . . reliving her one time with Michael . . . wishing it could be again. She didn't see Alberto's lips begin to move, or feel his heart-beats hasten against her cheek. . . .

Alberto was aware of Maria's closeness. He wanted to reach out to her. Comfort her. Explain how he had happened to ignore her that day. Explain how he had happened to be below deck . . . where Sam had assaulted him. . . .

Alberto had loved the feel of the cards between his fingers and the power that each card represented when he would spread them out, face side up, on the ship's flooring before him. He had found that the Aces were the best to be dealt, and that he had been dealt many of those. It was all so vivid in his mind now . . . so easy to recall. . . .

"Damn lucky, ain't ya, lad?" one man sneered, dealing cards once again, as Alberto scraped in his winnings.

"Yeah. Guess I am," Alberto boasted. He liked the coins even as much as the green bills. He knew that if he had several of those, there were many things that could be bought for himself. His eyes traveled behind him, smelling the sweetness of the beautiful lady who was leaning over him, running her fingers through his hair. When their eyes met, she winked enticingly toward him, licking her lips, making her painted lips shine like fresh raindrops just fallen onto the petals of a rose. Velvet. Pure velvet. That was what her lips were, he thought hungrily to himself. When he looked lower, he could feel his face reddening. What lay before him were two mountains of breasts, heaving, trying to fall free from the dress that revealed the deepest of cleavage and the smallest of waists.

Turning, Alberto placed his cards in his hands, smiling widely, spreading the cards, seeing three Aces and two Kings. Yes. A full house was what the men had called this. Surely he was going to win again. Damn. How had he ever existed without playing this exciting game? He felt more alive now than ever before.

"What's yore bet, lad?" a man with a heavy beard and cigar hanging from between his lips asked.

"The highest I can go," he said daringly.

"What's that you say?" another shouted, frowning.

"What's the highest I can bet?"

Laughter bounced from man to man. "All of it, sonny boy," one encouraged. "All the damn money in yore pocket if ya be brave enough to do it."

Alberto ran his fingers across his brow, contemplating his fate. His eyes jerked from one man to another, seeing apprehension, possibly even fear etched across their faces. "All I have?" he said softly.

The man next to Alberto spat chewing tobacco into the wind, and with an elbow, nudged Alberto in the side. "Shore, son," he boomed. "Why not? What do ya have to lose?" Then he tore into a fit of laughter, taking his billed hat from his head, tapping it against his leg, watching Alberto's reaction.

Setting his jaw firmly, Alberto searched inside his pockets. He felt that he was being made fun of. He felt that they didn't think he was smart enough to know what he was doing. Well, he would show them. He had won so much, what would it matter if he lost this time? And, anyway, he had given Maria the largest amount of their money to keep safe.

His heart stopped short. His head swung around, seeing the absence of Maria beside their bunks. *Oh, God,* he thought to himself. Where was she? Then his eyes captured her hat . . . lying on deck. . . .

He pushed himself up with one quick motion, ready to dash back to where he had left Maria, when soft hands covered his own.

"Where're you goin', darlin'?" the honey-dipped voice said from behind him.

Alberto felt something tighten in his groin as he turned and found this beautiful creature moving closer to him, placing her body so close he could feel the largeness of her breasts crushing against him. His eyes glanced downward, seeing the deep cleavage once again and what lay on each side. His manhood began to swell inside his breeches, suddenly feeling a need he had for so long been forced to keep quelled. And now? Was this lady . . . willing . . . to let . . . him . . . ? His eyes widened when he felt a hand brush lower, against the tightness of his breeches.

Loud laughter brought him to his senses. The men were all watching, enjoying his embarrassment of the moment. He looked down into the eyes of this woman . . . the eyes of a cat . . . so green and flash-

57

ing . . . then pulled her lips to his and damn well showed the men that he indeed knew what to do under such circumstances. He even grew bold enough to let a hand wander upward and touch the softness of the flesh of a breast. His heartbeats consumed him as his fingers continued to explore, circling this part of a woman he up to now had only been able to admire from afar. He had so often wanted to even touch Maria . . . but had been afraid to ask. . . .

"Hey!" a man boomed from the ship's deck. "Are ye a goin' to play cards or pussy?"

Hating to set this woman free, Alberto clung for a moment longer, then whispered into her ear, "You're so beautiful."

"Win this hand and ya can touch more than my tits, darlin'," she whispered back, blowing into his ear, making goose bumps ride his spine.

"Then win it I shall," he said, giving her breast just one more squeeze. "And your name? What might it be?"

"Just call me Grace," she said, giggling.

Alberto had to join in the quiet laughter. Grace didn't seem the appropriate name for a woman who gave of her body so freely. But it didn't matter. Nothing mattered now, except that knowing how to win at cards would be to also win at something even more important. He would soon know the secrets that lay hidden beneath a woman's skirt.

"Let me win this hand," he said. "Then we can get on with the most pleasurable side of life." He released his hold on her, smiling crookedly. Scooping the cards back up into his hands, he squatted and checked them once again. Yes. He had a winning hand. Yes. He would bet all he had in his pockets. With one thrust, he threw all his coins and green bills onto the pile of money that had already been bet by the other men.

With a pounding heart, he watched as each man spread his cards out on the floor in front of them, revealing a various assortment of what could be winning hands . . . except that Alberto's had the most Aces, with two Kings to confirm his win.

"Damn it all to hell," one man grumbled, puffing angrily on his cigar. "A damn full house. You did it again, lad. Don' know how, since you never did play before. But, you sure as hell took my money from me."

"I'm quitting for a while, gents," Alberto said, grinning from ear to ear. "I've better things to do, if you know what I mean." He began to pull the money toward him, but was stopped when a boot lowered, to rest on his hand. He looked up into beady, dark eyes, surrounded by thick, scraggly whiskers.

"Not so fast, sonny boy," the man said, increasing his weight on Alberto's hand, making Alberto wince.

"I won fair and square," Alberto said, feeling the bones in his fingers straining to be set free.

The man glowered, spitting chewing tobacco next to Alberto's knee. "In this game o' chance, you don' just play to keep the money," he said darkly. "You give the men a chance to win it all back. Don' you see? Tha's part o' this game, sonny boy."

Grace moved lithely toward this man attired in garments that reeked of sweat and tobacco juices. "Now, Sam," she purred, wrapping her fingers around his hand, squeezing it. "You know it doesn't really matter. Now does it?"

The low-cut dress gaped open even more at the top,

catching Sam's eyes. Grace swung her hips around so the back of her arched against the front of Sam, then back around so her breasts barely brushed against his arm. "Do you understand? Huh?" she added, winking.

Sam's face became all smiles as his foot released Alberto's hand. "Sure. Don' know whut I was a thinkin' on," Sam laughed. He reached down and began to help Alberto with the money, even thrusting it into Alberto's breeches pockets. "Go on, lad," he added. "Take yore leave. Damn sorry if I bothered you. Don' know what gets in my head at times."

Alberto's thoughts were swirling, not understanding at all what could have changed this man's mind so fast. But one look upward at Grace made him understand how and why any man could be swayed by such a smile as hers. And her fingers. She did have a way of touching a man. How could any man say no to her?

A slight tinge of jealousy raced through Alberto, though. He knew that Sam would more than likely be reaching up inside Grace's skirt also, probably even right after Alberto had finished. It was apparent that this was Grace's way of life. He knew that it should disgust him, but it only excited him more.

Leaning down, Grace whispered into Alberto's ear. "Ready?" she said. "I have a cozy cabin below deck. I'll show you things there you never dreamed imaginable."

Feeling the pulsebeat quickening in his throat, Alberto pushed the last of the money inside his pockets and straightened his back. "Show the way," he said, putting his arm around Grace's waist, following along beside her. He felt proud that he was one of the many who had first chance with Grace this day. Maybe if he played this newest deck of cards right, he could spend even the full day with her.

With a fleeting glance around him, pangs of conscience pierced his heart, like arrows being shot into it. He knew that he should be searching for Maria, but knew also that this chance to be with a woman might be too fleeting to pass by. And wasn't Maria capable of taking care of herself? Surely she was just wandering around on top deck, exploring, as she was prone to do. He had teased her about this adventurous side to her nature many times. So often while on the outskirts of Pordenone, she would tarry behind and get lost in some field, straying, hunting for some beautiful butterfly, or dog that had gone yapping into the underbrush. Surely she was only noseying about now. The rains had washed the decks clean. Before, she hadn't wanted to wander off because of the filth. Now? She had reason to.

"And might you have a friend on deck?" Grace said, seeing Alberto's steady gaze around him. "Do you have a wife who might, uh, miss you for a while?"

Alberto cleared his throat nervously. "No," he said thickly. "I don't have a wife." Did he look old enough to have a wife? Maria had often told him that he looked older than his age of sixteen. Had she been correct in saying this? Damn. It made him quite proud of his six-foot height and broad shoulders. He felt like an older man, with feelings fast encompassing him that he knew older men must have every day of their lives. But older men usually had wives to share these feelings, with whom they could release their sexual tensions.

This day he would take from this wench all she was capable of giving him. He hastened his footsteps as they reached the doorway that led downward.

"So you are alone on this voyage?" Grace asked, finding it hard to keep up with his long stride. God. Did she have an eager one on her hands. But, he would soon find that he shouldn't have been so easy.

"No. Not quite," he answered.

Shadows fell across Grace's face. "Then . . . who . . . might you be with?"

Alberto now bent his shoulders and leaned down, for to stand upright would mean for his head to scrape against the low ceiling of this long, low hallway that he was being guided down. He stepped high, to miss a stray, empty wine bottle that was suddenly at his feet. He squinted his eyes, seeing only the dim lighting from the whale oil lights that lined this wall. "My sister Maria," he finally answered, brushing his hands along the wall, to steady himself as Grace stepped in front of him, to place a key into a lock.

Grace turned to Alberto, reaching up to touch his face before pushing the door open. "Then you have no father or mother aboard this ship?" she asked coyly. "Just you and your sister?"

"And why does it even matter?"

"I only wish to show interest in anyone I take to my personal bunk," she answered. "That's all."

"Then now you know all you have to know to take this man to your bunk," Alberto said, taking the liberty to swing the door aside, revealing a semi-dark room, occupied only by a long, thin bunk. Discarded, uneaten food lay scattered across the floor, along with more strewn, empty wine bottles. One lone whale oil lamp flickered in pale goldens on the cabin's outside wall. Alberto screwed his nose up, wiping it with the back of a hand. The aroma of this cabin was one similar to dried urine and feces, making his stomach almost turn. His eyes tilted in wonder. "And this is your cabin? It isn't as clean as I imagined . . . or as fully furnished."

Grace swung her hips smoothly as she walked on past him, making her fully gathered blue silk dress rustle enticingly. Her hair shone in rustic coppers as it bounced atop her shoulders and her lips moved seductively as she talked. "A bunk is all that is required for my services," she said. She pulled at his hand, urging him onward. "Now isn't that right, darlin'? And a maid I'm not. Who worries about a bit of filth when there are more interestin' things to set a mind to wanderin'?"

When she had succeeded at getting Alberto inside the cabin, she shut the door and turned to him, slowly tantalizing him with her lips and fingers as she began to unbutton his shirt.

"Yeah. I'm sure," he mumbled, then couldn't help himself when he yanked her into his arms, smothering her with kisses on the fullness of her lips, then downward, to brush his tongue across her breasts. She was right. There were more things of interest in this cabin to make one forget any ugliness about it. She was here. His heart thundered inside him . . . anxious. . . .

She giggled noisily, pulling away from him, teasing him with her eyes. "Whoa. Slow down," she purred, reaching back to unfasten her dress. She stepped out of it, slow but sure, all the while watching him and how he was openly panting after her. "Well?" she added. "You gonna do it with your breeches on?" She stopped long enough to touch him where his swollen member throbbed against the tight confines of his breeches.

"No," he said, laughing awkwardly. "Guess not." His fingers busied with unbuttoning his breeches, then stepped from them as she continued to shed her clothes, until she stood nude before him, appearing eager, ready. . . .

He wanted to hurry with his attack, yet she looked so lovely with the whale oil lights reflecting onto her skin of ivory. It was as though a sunset was in this room . . . casting warm glows of gold rippling down the front of her. "You are so breathtakingly beautiful," he whispered, reaching to touch her. His breath began to come in short gasps as she leaned into him, fitting her lower bush of hair against his erect manhood.

"You can have me now if you want," she whispered, tilting her chin upward, so his mouth could hit the target she was offering.

Alberto lunged toward her, not knowing which part of her he wanted to touch first. She was all woman . . . so fully blown. . . .

"Let's lie down," she encouraged, taking him by the hand, leading him across the room.

He followed after her, breathing hard. He didn't hear the door open behind him, but soon felt hands other than Grace's grasp him by the wrist. "What the hell . . . ?" he shouted, then felt a point of a knife scraping against his backside.

"Just shut yore mouth, sonny boy," the unseen man drawled.

Alberto tensed, quickly recognizing the voice. It was Sam. The man who had stepped on Alberto's hand just only moments ago when Alberto had been trying to fill his pockets with his winnings from the card game. A prickly sensation flooded his senses, throwing caution into his thoughts. "What are you doing here?" he snarled, but uttered a low moan when the blade of the knife left a thin trail of blood down his back.

"Just do as you are tol', and we'll see to it tha' you don' get hurt none," Sam growled.

Alberto swallowed hard, gritting his teeth. He didn't want to show a cowardly side to his nature. But he didn't want to get hurt, either. He had not only himself to protect, but also Maria. "What do you want?" he said quietly, knowing the answer to that before he even spoke. Sam had come for the money. Alberto had been set up. He looked toward Grace and saw the look of mockery flashing in her green eyes, making them look even more like those of a cat. His eyes raked over her nakedness, so sure it wasn't he who would be sleeping with her now. He had lost . . . and more than money . . . it seemed.

Sam shoved Alberto onto the bunk. "Get 'im ready, Grace," he growled. "You know wha' I mean."

Alberto was now able to see all around him. His heart throbbed wildly when he saw Sam standing there with a knife in one hand, and the other resting on a holstered gun. Hopes of coming out of this alive quickly dwindled.

"Come on, darlin'. Relax," Grace purred, stretching her body out next to Alberto's.

"What the . . . ?" Alberto gasped, suddenly realizing that Grace was continuing with her efforts of seducing him. Her fingers traced a path downward, stopping on his manhood, fondling it until it sprang up again, even though there was an audience. He closed his eyes, not wanting to be a part of this ugly scene, but he couldn't control the lusty urges building up inside him. When Grace's tongue replaced her fingers, he stiffened, breathing wildly, feeling the warmth seizing his insides, ready to erupt into a million spasms of delight. Then Sam stepped forward and took Grace by the hand. . . .

"Enough, little woman," he snarled.

Alberto opened his eyes, startled. He watched as Grace went to stand across the room to watch while Sam approached Alberto with his breeches removed. "What do you think you're going to do with me?" Alberto shouted, trying to climb from the bunk, but stopped when a gun-toting Grace walked across the room, pointing it at Alberto.

"Now, just you shut up, darlin'," she purred, smiling wickedly. "You're soon to find out just how we get our pleasures aboard this movin' vessel. There's more to life than playin' poker. . . ."

"You . . . can't. . . ." Alberto whined, then felt Sam's fingers twist around his hair to yank him from the bunk.

"We . . . can . . . and we will, sonny boy," Sam growled, moving around to Alberto's behind.

"Stop. . . ." Alberto moaned when he felt the stiffness of Sam's sex press against his buttocks. When the lunge was made inside him, he gritted his teeth together, to keep from screaming. He closed his eyes. It was all too humiliating. He tensed when the pain began to wrack his body. He was being raped . . . but . . . by a . . . man. He had never felt more degraded in his life. He would be nothing but grime when these two finished with him.

He began to tremble as cold sweat began to pop out along the full length of his body. He opened his eyes momentarily, to see a look of hungry desire in Grace's eyes as she continued to stand and watch. When Sam's body became all tremors, Alberto felt as though his body was going to be torn in half. He couldn't help but let out a loud sob as he was pushed to the floor in a heap. He rolled up into a fetal position, waiting for the final insult . . . death. But he would welcome it now. . . .

"Git up and get yore clothes on, sonny boy," Sam growled, already dressing himself.

Alberto's eyes opened widely. He looked around the room, searching for his clothes. He felt anger rising inside himself when he saw Grace emptying his pockets of everything. They had taken his male virginity from him . . . and now they were also taking his winnings. He had lost. Everything. Everything . . . but . . . Maria. "Oh, Maria," he thought desperately to himself. "How can I ever tell you?" He knew that they always shared everything. But this was one thing . . . he could never share with her.

"Did ya hear?" Sam growled, kicking Alberto in the ribs with the sharp point of a boot. "Get yoreself up and get dressed. Do ya think we wan' to be stuck with the likes of you all evenin'? We have other crops to pick."

Groaning, Alberto pushed himself from the floor, feeling an unusual heaviness in his body. Each movement was as though he was a tied rope . . . ready to snap. He wasn't sure which part of him ached the most, but he managed to get to his clothes. Piece by piece he struggled, until he was finally fully clothed. Then he eyed Sam and Grace, wondering what to expect next.

Sam slithered toward him, waving the opened knife in his face once again, chewing on a fresh wad of tobacco, now fully clothed. "Now, sonny boy, if'n ya tell who it was who done this to ya, I guess I don' have to tell ya whut to 'spect from me," he drawled.

Alberto's eyes widened. "I won't tell," he mumbled. "Honest."

"Too bad you didn't get to get into Grace's pants," Sam laughed boisterously. "She has a way of showin' fun, like no other whore has."

Alberto felt a brief brave tremor surge through his veins. He set his jaw firmly and said, "Then why did you do . . . that . . . to me? Why didn't you just . . . go . . . to bed . . . with Grace?"

Sam spat tobacco juice onto the floor, laughing raucously. With one brow raised higher than the other, he slapped Alberto softly on the cheek. "Sonny boy, don' you know you're just as purty as a woman?" he snickered. "Not too often one comes along like you. When they does? I has me my fun."

Alberto's face flamed. He had never been compared to a woman before. His fury was kindled even more. "You can't be from my country," Alberto snapped. "None of my people could be as filthy-minded as you."

"You guessed it right and proper, sonny boy," Sam said, winking. "I make it my pleasure to ride these ships from New York to Italy. Gets me more rich each trip. Tha's why I couldn't let you step away from that poker game with all my money."

"I'd gladly have given you all you asked for," Alberto said glumly. "But why did you have to degrade me so? Why?"

"Like I said. You're an extra purty one, you are."

"I'd like to kill you," Alberto snarled. "And I must tell you, if I get the chance, I will."

The knife blade moved closer to his throat. "Now, I don' like hearin' talk like that," Sam growled. "I thought you had agreed to forget wha' happen here."

68

"I agreed to not tell anyone. But I didn't agree to forget. I can never forget. This nightmare will live with me for the rest of my life."

"Oh, you poor child," Sam teased, then walked away, whispering to Grace as she hurriedly dressed.

Alberto saw a possible chance for escape. With two steps of his long legs, he was at the door and out into the hall. But after taking only two more steps, he felt a rushing blow against the back of his skull and was suddenly drifting into a black, swirling mist of nothingness. . . .

Not able to remember anything else, Alberto's mind switched back to the present. The flesh of his face felt on fire. He tried to lick his lips, to moisten them, but nothing. He still couldn't awaken fully enough to arouse Maria, to tell her of his needs. If he didn't get food and water inside him soon . . . he knew the surety of his fate. His insides were begging for . . . food . . . and water. . . .

Blinking his eyes, trying to keep the rays of the sun from scorching his eyeballs even more, he felt a sense of relief when tears managed to trickle from the corner of an eye. When Maria began to stir and looked upward onto his face, he waited for her to discover . . . the tears. . . .

Maria's breath came in quick, short gasps when she saw the first signs of Alberto's possibly coming out of the darkness of near death. His eyes were open as they had been at times, but now there were tears, which had to mean that he was aware of things . . . people . . . around him.

Leaning down into his face, Maria whispered,

69

"Alberto? Sweet Alberto. Do you hear me? Are you going to be all right?" Sobs shook her body as her fingertips ran across his dry, cracked lips. "Please tell me that you are going to be all right. If you die, so must I. We are one . . . you and I."

Alberto opened his mouth and managed to force three words from between his lips. "Maria . . ." he mumbled. "I'm . . . hot. . . ."

Maria's heart leaped with glee. He *was* awakening from his long bout of deep sleep. He *was* going to be all right. "Alberto, Alberto," she sobbed, wrapping her arms around him.

Alberto strained with all his might and managed to speak some more, saying, "The . . . heat . . . Maria. . . ."

Hurriedly reaching to pick up the dampened cloth, Maria began to bathe his face. "I know," she purred. "I know." A fit of hacking coughs suddenly seized her, along with chills that encompassed her body from her head to her toes. Fear grabbed at her heart. She had seen so many die after many such seizures of coughs. Was . . . it . . . meant that she was now to have the dreaded pneumonia herself . . . and die . . . ?

Her eyes searched desperately around her. The heat was the tyrant. She had to remove herself and Alberto from this top deck, or most surely Papa would not have two children to wait for in America. They would be a part of the sea . . . never to rest in a final grave beneath a protective covering of earth. . . .

Alberto's hand reached upward and brushed a few strands away from Maria's face, relishing in the touch of her soft skin. But there was something else this day. There was a clamminess about her. God. She was ill. He wanted to reach for her . . . protect her . . . when

70

she began coughing violently again.

"Maria . . . ?" he whispered. "You must get . . . help."

Maria clutched at her chest, feeling pain stabbing the insides of her lungs. The damp, cold night air and the extreme change to hot, dry days had done its damage. "Yes. I know," she replied. Her gaze settled on the door that led downward, where Michael ate and slept in comfort, but where also . . . she had found Alberto . . . injured . . . and left to die in a most cruel way.

But Alberto was alive. He was going to be all right. But he would have a much better chance for a complete, healthy survival if she went to Michael and asked for assistance. Reaching up to smooth her hair back from her face, securing it with a comb on each side of her head, she knew what she had to do. "Alberto," she whispered, licking her lips, trying to wet them. "I know I promised to not leave your side. But I must. For a moment. Then I will return. Do you understand? I am going to seek help. I know . . . of . . . someone who will willingly help. Then you and I . . . we . . . can be more comfortable . . . and even eat and drink as one should."

Alberto tried to raise himself upward, but groaned noisily when the pain struck him at the back of his head. "Who . . . ?" he whispered.

"An American," she answered. "That's all I can tell you now. Just trust me."

"Can . . . *he* . . . be . . . ?"

Maria touched Alberto softly on a cheek, smiling. "Yes. He can be trusted, Alberto," she said, then turned her head to cough once again. The pain was worsening in her chest with each fresh bout of coughs. She knew

71

that she must hurry. If she got too ill to care for Alberto . . . then she had to be sure there would be someone else who would be willing to. Surely Michael would do this for her. Hadn't he shown such a gentle side to his nature? Hadn't he truly cared for her . . . not just for what she had shared with him? She had seen more than lust in the depth of his blue eyes. She had seen love . . . compassion. . . .

Pushing the legs of her breeches back to cover her ankles, she kissed Alberto softly, then rose and began to make her way through the throngs of milling people. Her hair blew in dark streamers behind her and her birthmark seemed larger with the steady rays of the sun seeming to mark her face in even more strawberry reds.

A tightness moved around her chest as she pushed her way onward, then a fresh bout of chills sent bone-aching tremors up and down her legs, chest, and arms. She covered her mouth when she began to cough again, seeing the door that led downward to Michael through a haze as her eyes misted in gray blurs.

Stumbling, she opened the door and almost fell down the stairs. Her knees were growing weak, as was the alertness in her head. She cringed when she began to walk down the narrow, dark passageway, fearing someone might even grab her into one of the rooms, possibly even rape her. When she had been in this passageway before . . . she had been with Michael. But she had to shudder . . . remembering when she had been alone . . . and had found Alberto. . . .

Chapter Four

Maria turned to lie on her side, sighing leisurely. The splash of the water beneath her had a lulling effect, and the steady movement of the ship made her feel as though she was in a cradle, rocking. Then her eyes moved quickly open, darting around her. Where was she? She didn't recall having been brought here. A long, crimson velveteen curtain hung from the ceiling next to the bed, hiding all else from her eyes.

"A bed," she thought to herself. "I'm lying on a bed. How?" A slow smile curled her full, sensuous lips upward, now running her fingers across the softness of the sheets beneath her. She had only known one bed. Michael's. And it was his bed that she had somehow become acquainted with once again. Then her fingers began to feel down the full length of her body, relishing in the luxuriousness of Michael's night robe that had again been so generously loaned her.

A slow flush rose upward from her neck, wondering if it had been Michael who had shed her outer *and* undergarments. If so, had he taken liberties with her body . . . when she had been unaware of it . . . ?

Maria closed her eyes and thought hard, trying to remember how and why she had come to be in Michael's cabin this second time on this voyage. She had been . . . worried . . . about Alberto. . . .

Her eyes flew open again, a slow desperation causing her to push herself upward. Where was Alberto? Was he all right? Feeling a cool sweep of air settle on her breasts that were now fully exposed from Michael's night robe having fallen agape in front, Maria clutched at it, holding it together. Then she slowly pulled one end of the curtain aside, breathing much more easily when she discovered Alberto stretched out in an apparent deep, peaceful sleep on a bunk at the far end of the room, covered with a blanket up to just beneath his chin.

From what Maria could tell, Alberto was all right. But he did need a fresh shave. A thick patch of dark whiskers framed his lips.

Her thoughts moved swiftly to Michael: "Michael, oh, Michael. You really do care. Or why else would you have taken both me *and* my brother in?" she whispered, feeling a delirious warmth of desire surging through her blood. She leaned closer to the curtain and pulled it further aside, craning her neck, searching the cabin around her. She moved to her knees, feeling the thunderous pounding of her heart when her gaze settled on him.

Michael was slumped over his desk, writing in his journal. His shirt front was unbuttoned halfway to the waist, and the dazzling white of the shirt was accentuated even more by an abundance of ruffles spilling over his thick, golden chest hairs.

He placed the tip of his pen to his lips, lifting a thick brow as he gazed toward Alberto. He knew that Alberto's strength had to have returned. Each evening, Michael had learned that to be sure that Alberto

74

would eat, all he had to do was take leave of the room for only thirty minutes or so after having placed the tray of food on the floor beside Alberto's bunk. Always when Michael returned, the food would be gone and Alberto would once again be playing his game of pretense, lying so still, appearing to be asleep.

"Damn it. Why?" Michael fumed to himself. He turned a bit sideways in the chair, now thinking about Maria. He dropped his pen to the desk top and bolted upright, discovering Maria peering back at him from the lifted corner of the curtain. He whispered her name and hurried to her side, not caring when the velveteen curtain jerked loose from the ceiling and crumpled to a heap on the floor. He sat down on the bed beside Maria, taking one of her hands in his, lifting it to his lips, kissing it with soft, feathery touches.

"Are you really all right, Maria?" he said thickly. His gaze raked over her, leaving no spot untouched by the caress of his eyes.

Maria settled back onto the bed, in an almost swoon. She wasn't sure if this was caused by Michael's presence, or a sudden lightheadedness from a piercing hunger gnawing away at her insides. "How long have Alberto and I been in your cabin, Michael?" she asked, placing her fingers to her brow, breathless. She now knew the intensity of her weakness and suddenly recalled how ill she had been the day she had decided to seek Michael's assistance.

"Several days, my sweet," he replied. With the back of his hand, he reached upward and touched her cheeks, then her brow. "But I believe your fever has broken and you're on the road to recovery."

Maria fluffed a pillow and placed it behind her back,

leaning into it. "And was I so ill?" she asked. "So ill that I cannot even remember these past several days?" She felt her face coloring, looking at the bed and the empty space beside her. "And did you . . . did we even . . . ?"

Michael laughed throatily. "No. I, nor we, didn't," he said, leaning closer to her. "And my, aren't our thoughts a bit on the wicked side? It's a sure sign that you are well." He leaned even closer and whispered into her ear. "You're a wench. A she-devil. Did you know that?"

"Michael. Please," Maria said, glancing toward Alberto. He was lying much too quietly. Not appearing to even be breathing. Could he be feigning sleep? Was he indeed hearing all? Her face flushed even redder, imagining what could be going through her brother's mind if he had heard. Alberto hadn't known of her one time with Michael. If he did, or would ever find out, Maria even suspected that Alberto might become guilty of violence.

Michael reached for a cloth and wet it, wringing it out to be almost dry. Then he began to smooth it across Maria's face in slow, even strokes. "I'm sorry," he murmured. "I didn't mean to embarrass you."

Maria leaned her face into his caresses. "That feels so good," she sighed.

"I'm sure my doing this daily helped to pull the hated fevers from inside you," he said, moving down to her neck, lifting her hair.

"You've done this? And I wasn't even aware of it?"

"You've been quite ill, darling."

Maria's eyes darted to Alberto once again. "Michael, please do not call me sweet names. Not in Alberto's presence."

76

"He is asleep, Maria."

"I'm not so sure. . . ."

Michael turned and studied Alberto. "Yes. I know what you mean. He has a way of fooling a body."

"And is Alberto going to be as well as I?"

"I'm sure he is already," Michael grumbled, resuming his strokes with the cloth.

Maria's eyes widened. "What do you mean, Michael?"

"It's been the damnest thing," he grumbled further. "At times, I'm sure I feel his eyes on me when I least expect it. But when I turn to look at him, his eyes are closed again."

"But why would Alberto not talk to you, if he is well? Surely you're imagining things."

Michael glared toward Alberto, tensing inside when the same feelings of apprehension raced through him. Even now, he could tell that Alberto was indeed feigning sleep. This made his trust for Alberto wane even more. It didn't seem Alberto and Maria were from the same mother's womb, much less twins. Their personalities were too much of a contrast. He turned his gaze back to Maria. "Damned if I know," he finally said.

"And you're so sure Alberto is well?"

"After I got him in out of that sweltering heat, he began to improve quite readily," he said. "I don't know why you and your brother chose to stay out in that damned weather when I had so eagerly offered the comforts of my cabin," he added, furrowing his brow.

Maria didn't want to explain the whys. Doing so would be to reveal how angry Michael's words had made her when he had accused her of having more than sisterly feelings for her brother. Even now it angered

77

her. But she did feel a deep sense of gratitude for Michael now, and renewed strange feelings swirling around inside her because of his nearness and the gentleness of his strokes as he continued to caress her face and neck with the dampened cloth. "I do appreciate what you've done for Alberto and myself," she murmured, fluttering her eyelashes nervously as his gaze met hers and held. His blue eyes were like pools, luring her into them, making her insides begin a slow melting.

"And will you stay on here with me in my cabin even now that you are well?"

Maria's heartbeats faltered, glancing toward Alberto once again. "No. I think not," she said. "As soon as Alberto is able, we must return topside. It is the only decent thing to do. One can take only so much advantage of another."

"But you might have a relapse," Michael said, placing the cloth back on the table, leaning down closer to Maria. He felt the heat in his loins as his eyes lowered, seeing the heaving of her bosom, so large, tempting his hands to reach upward to touch. But, no. He had to remember. She had just recovered from an illness so close to having become pneumonia, and also, her damn brother who was too close, ready to pounce if Michael made the wrong move. The curtain had been hung for privacy. He would have to tack it to the ceiling once again.

Maria stretched her long, lean legs out in front of her, crossing them. "And how far away are we from America?" she asked softly. "I am so anxious to see this new world. And also my Papa. It's been so long. I only hope he is well."

78

"I'd say about another week of travel should get us there," Michael answered, moving to sit beside Maria, crossing his own legs. He couldn't keep his eyes from venturing along the smoothness of her olive-colored legs, and then on upward. Surely he could hold her again . . . have her all to himself . . . before the ship reached its destination. For once they had reached New York, the confusion of the docks could very well separate them forever.

"Can you tell me about it, Michael?" she asked, eyes wide.

"What do you want to know?"

"What I will first see when the ship draws near to the New World."

Michael crossed his arms and began speaking softly, intending his words only for Maria's ears. To hell with Alberto and his nonsensical ways. "When the ship moves into the harbor, you shall first see a huge statue."

"A statue?" Maria exclaimed. "What kind of a statue?"

Michael laughed hoarsely, loving her innocence. "It's called the Statue of Liberty. It stands for 'Liberty Enlightening the World.' It was a gift from the French to the American people, commemorating a century of American independence."

Maria pulled her legs up and hugged them to her. "It sounds fascinating," she sighed.

"It is the landmark most looked for by immigrants like yourself and your brother," Michael continued. "It's a symbol of welcome to every shipload of immigrants entering the harbor. One of the first things to be seen of this New World, as you choose to call it, as the ship moves up the bay."

"Then what else will I see, Michael?"

"Then you will see the largest suspension bridge on earth. The Brooklyn Bridge. And after that, you will get your first look at the lower Manhattan skyline. A sight to behold. But I won't tell you anymore. It will spoil it all for you."

"Please tell me one more thing, Michael," she said. "After Alberto and I leave the ship, will we go immediately to the train and start our trip to my Papa's home?"

"Not exactly," Michael said even more softly.

"Why not?"

"There's a place called Ellis Island. All immigrants have to go there. I guess you could say you have to go through a process of Americanization."

"Like what? What do you mean?"

Michael laughed. "Honey, you don't have anything to worry about. The ones who do have are convicts, insane persons and persons likely to become public charges. You are none of these things. Right?"

Maria giggled, snuggling down more onto the bed. She pulled the blanket up over her, having felt a sudden chill. Then her stomach played an overture of grumbles, reminding her of her hunger. She glanced upward at Michael, smiling coyly. "I'm very hungry, Michael," she said.

He jumped from the bed, smiling broadly. "Those words are like music to my ears," he said. "It's further proof of your regained health. You have to know you haven't had much nourishment these past two days."

"And have I had any? If I have been asleep, how could I have eaten?"

"My dear, you were fed by me. Don't you remember?"

Maria blushed. "You did this for me also?"

"Some of the best clam chowder prepared aboard this ship. Spoonful by spoonful."

"Oh, Michael," Maria sighed. "You are so good to me." Then her gaze moved to Alberto. "And Alberto? He has eaten also?"

Michael's eyes became cold. "He has indeed," he grumbled. "For a man who was supposedly near to dying."

Maria was confused by Michael's tone. It was as though he hated Alberto. Even his eyes showed his dislike. "What do you mean, Michael?" she said softly, looking from Michael to Alberto, then back to Michael once again.

"What do I mean?" Michael asked, crossing his arms. "He has managed to put away quite a stomachful of duck and all the trimmings each time I have left food for him."

"How do you mean . . . left food for him? Didn't he eat while you did?"

"Never. He would always wait until I would leave the cabin, then he would eat it all. Every bite of it. Damn strange behavior if you ask me."

Coldness seeped through Maria's veins. Had the blow to Alberto's head caused him to lose his senses? Or maybe the heat of the sun had done its damage to his brain before she had asked assistance of Michael. She began to chew her lower lip, watching Alberto, crying inside for him . . . her brother . . . her other self. "I'm sure he is all right," she mumbled. "If he's eaten, then

81

he's all right. No matter how he has chosen to eat . . . or act. . . ."

"Yeah. I'm sure of it," Michaël said, buttoning his shirt. He went to his chair and lifted his black waistcoat from it and slipped it on. It fit him so perfectly, Maria saw how much it emphasized the broadness of his shoulders. Then her gaze lowered, seeing the tightness of his matching breeches and how they exposed to the eye the gift of his manhood that bulged out in front beneath the layer of cloth. Her face flushed red, realizing just how breathless he could make her by the removal of those breeches.

"As you might notice, it's quite late," Michaël said, motioning toward the ceiling, at the darkness beyond from the skylight. Whale oil lamps flickered in soft goldens on each wall, making the room almost one of intimacy. "I might have a bit of trouble securing much food," he quickly added. "But I'm sure we can come up with something." He combed his fingers through his hair, then headed toward the door. He turned and took one last look at Maria as he opened the door. "I won't be long. You will be all right, won't you?"

Maria smiled warmly. "Yes. I'll be all right," she said. "And you be careful," she said further, shadows crossing her face. "I remember the darkness of that passageway. I don't want anything to happen to you like it did with Alberto."

Michael reached down and patted the inside of his lower leg. "I don't believe anybody would take that chance," he boasted. "Not with the knife I can so rapidly wield."

Maria's fingers went to her throat. "You wear such a weapon?"

82

"Beneath my breeches leg. I have worn it since having found your brother in such a condition," he said flatly. "Just let some son-of-a-bitch come after me. There won't be an inch of his body left untouched."

Maria smiled weakly as he moved on from the cabin, shutting the door after him. Then her gaze moved to Alberto. Quickly, she brushed the blanket aside and moved across the floor, stopping to stoop next to her brother. "Alberto," she whispered. "Alberto. It's me. Please say something." She shook him gently, then gasped when his eyes flew widely open.

"Maria," he said thickly, eyeing her with dark, brooding eyes. "I'm so thankful that you are all right. I would have wanted to die myself if you hadn't pulled through that terrible illness. Each cough from inside you was the same as myself experiencing it." He reached his hands upward and touched the softness of her cheeks. Damn. They were much too flushed . . . and . . . he knew . . . not from fever. There was more to her and Michael Hopper's relationship than there could be had they just become acquainted. If he ever caught Michael placing his hands where he shouldn't, it would be Michael who would feel the touch of his own knife on his flesh.

Maria reached up and took his hand, leaning her face into it. "That is because we are twins, Alberto," she said. Then she dropped his hand, setting her jaw firmly. "And you? What kind of games are you playing, Alberto?" she spat. "Why are you acting so crazily? You know as well as I that you are capable of getting up from that bunk and acting civilized. You know that you are no longer ill. Why, look at you. You've even gained a few pounds, it seems."

Alberto laughed, pushing himself up on an elbow. His hand reached upward and caressed his beard. "Oh, you must mean my beard," he said. "That's reason enough for my face to look fuller."

Maria doubled up a fist and pounded it on his arm. "Oh, Alberto," she cried. "You know what I mean. Why are you doing this thing to Michael? He's been so nice. You and I both would have probably died if we had stayed out in the weather. You know that, don't you?"

"I do appreciate his generosity," he grumbled, lowering his eyes. "But people are only generous if they expect something in return." His eyes shot upward. They had become as two dark coals. "And you do know what kind of reward he will expect from you now that you are well, don't you?"

Maria pushed herself up and crossed her arms, glaring downward at Alberto. "Alberto, that is quite enough of your filthy mouth," she said coldly. "Where has your trust gone? Is it because of what happened to you? Michael is not like the ones who did that horrible thing to you. Michael is good. He would never do anything to hurt either one of us. Please quit acting as though your brain has shriveled up to a nothingness."

"If he ever does touch you. . . ." Alberto hissed, moving from the bunk. "This is why I lay so quietly. To listen. I'm sure in time he will approach you. And the best way to watch out for you is to not get too close to this man myself."

Maria grew quiet, remembering so vividly when Michael *had* touched her. Her blood surged in a wild thrill even now when she thought about it. Then she paled when she saw the look in Alberto's eyes. She knew that he meant business. She knew that he would indeed possibly harm Michael if Michael would even so much as try to kiss her. "But, Michael won't," she murmured. "Please don't fret so."

Alberto moved around the cabin in bare feet, stretching. "I have to admit, it does feel damn good being off that bunk for a while," he said.

"Then you will stay up? Join Michael and me when he returns with some food?"

"No. I will not," Alberto said flatly.

Maria moaned softly. "Then you will continue to play your games? You will lie back down and close your eyes like some ninny?"

"I don't wish to mingle, Maria," he said solemnly. "Not at least until we get to Papa's home. Then I can talk with people of our own kind." He turned and went to Michael's desk and began to flip the pages of Michael's journal. "Michael is not of our own kind. I do not wish to have anything to do with him."

"So. You will take his cabin, and eat the food he gives you, but still refuse to act civilized around him? Is that what you're saying?" Maria stormed, stomping a foot in rage.

Alberto moved on around the cabin, touching the softness of the bed, and the fineness of the paneling that covered the walls. "Exactly," he said. "Exactly."

"You are a brother I do not understand anymore, Alberto," Maria said, going to the bed, sinking down onto it, sulking. She pulled the blanket up around her, feeling a chill once again.

"Maybe I have changed," he said, going to his bunk, stretching out on it.

"One unfortunate incident in your life changes you

so much, Alberto?"

Alberto glowered, remembering. "It was more than that, Maria," he murmured. "It was much more than that." His fingers reached up and touched his fresh growth of beard once again, feeling its stubbiness. One day soon, it would be fully grown. Then he wouldn't be recognized. Then he would get his revenge. He would play that same card game and take all of Sam's winnings, then when Sam and Grace tried to lure him into Grace's cabin, Alberto would be the one who would win also at that game. He laughed to himself. Suddenly his life had become one big game. He liked that. Yes. He liked that. And no one could ever say he looked like a woman again. Not with a full face of whiskers. Damn that Sam. Damn him all to hell.

The door opening made Alberto turn with a start. Putting his back to Maria, he listened as Michael made his way into the room once again. The aromas of stewed chicken and scalloped potatoes filtered across the room and upward into his nose, making him hungry all over again, even though he had had a complete feast of the same only about an hour earlier. He licked his lips and lay even more quietly, at least glad that Maria was to be the recipient of these tasty morsels. She needed to gain her strength if they were to move from this man's private room. Alberto had had enough of this pretense. He was ready to return topside and set his plans in motion. Plans that would cause him much pleasure. He hadn't yet had the opportunity to experience the fulfillments of a woman. And this he would do before arriving on America's shores.

Michael kicked the door shut with the toe of his boot then hurried toward Maria. "We were in luck," he said, smiling broadly. "The captain was having himself a late supper and had plenty enough to share with you." He sat the tray of food on the bed next to Maria, lifting the lids, revealing steaming, hot food, so tempting Maria lunged for a fork and began to eat in near desperation.

Michael poured two glasses of port, handing one to Maria. "God. I've never seen anyone so hungry," he said, sitting down beside her, sipping on the wine, amusement lighting his eyes as he continued to watch her.

Maria wiped her mouth with the back of a hand, blushing. "I didn't mean to eat so greedily," she mumbled, swallowing hard.

A deep laugh rumbled from deep within Michael as he stretched a leg out beside Maria. "Eat on," he said. "I'm enjoying watching. I don't like women who pick at their food. It's not healthy."

Maria cleaned the plate of food then leaned back against the bed, sipping on wine, feeling deliciously content. "I do feel much better now," she said. She glanced toward Alberto, tensing inside, knowing that he was listening, waiting for a wrong move to be made by Michael. She hated this. For she wanted Michael to complete this contentment bursting from inside her by kissing . . . caressing her . . . to send her mind into another world. But not as long as Alberto was near. She would have to devise a way to be away from Alberto before the ship reached America. She had to be with Michael intimately once again. At least one more time before saying their final farewells.

"And now that you have filled your stomach with nourishment, I think it's time to get you down for the night," he said, removing the tray from the bed. "Rest will make you even stronger at this stage of your recovery."

Maria scooted down onto the bed, watching Michael as he moved around the cabin, turning the wicks of the whale oil lamps down, turning the room into a cave of dancing shadows. When he moved toward the bed, she tensed, looking quickly toward Alberto. Was Michael actually going to climb in bed with her? Surely . . . not. . . .

She watched even further as he removed his waistcoat, and then his shirt, revealing the tightness of his shoulder and chest muscles. "Michael, are you . . . ?" she said, watching him pulling his boots off.

"I need my rest also, Maria," he said, moving toward the bed.

"But, Michael," she murmured, glancing toward Alberto once again.

"Never fear," he said, climbing onto the bed, with his breeches still on. "Rest is all I am after."

Maria tensed as he stretched out next to her. How could she be so close and not touch him? It was too much of a temptation for her. Inching her fingers across the sheet, she felt a passionate thrill shoot through her when she touched the hairy back of his hand. Then she gasped lightly when his fingers moved around and captured hers in his. When his body turned and his gaze met hers, she moved her body toward him as though he was a magnet, pulling her.

All thoughts of Alberto were forgotten as Michael moved closer to her and embraced her. His fingers went to her hair and smoothed it back from her face, then his lips sought hers and kissed her ever so gently as his hands moved on downward, capturing a breast.

A loud cry of outrage filled the room as Alberto lunged onto the bed. He pulled Michael from Maria and threw him from the bed, all the while cursing vile profanities at him.

Maria jumped from the bed, crying, clutching at Michael's night robe that she still wore. "Alberto, please stop. Please," she sobbed. "You're acting like a madman."

"Go and find your clothes and put them on, Maria," he shouted, standing with doubled fists at his side, daring Michael to take another step closer.

Michael pushed himself up from the floor, then stood in a daze, watching.

"But, Alberto," Maria whined.

"Did you hear me?" Alberto shouted, taking a step closer to Michael. "If you don't, I'm going to lay into this lover of yours."

"But where shall we go?" Maria asked, searching around her, finding her clothes lying in a neat pile next to the stove. She began to put them on hurriedly.

"Where do you think?" Alberto growled. "Where we were supposed to be in the first place."

"It's too soon for Maria to be exposed to the sea air," Michael said in a tone of voice that was a bit too monotonal. But he was waiting. He would defend Maria against her own brother if the need arose.

"I shall be the one to determine that," Alberto said, turning his head, seeing if Maria was indeed dressing.

Michael took a step toward Alberto, but Maria rushed to Michael's side and took him by the arm. "Please, Michael," she said. "Please don't get into a fight with my brother. I am well enough to return topside. I feel very strong now. It's best that Alberto and I return to be with the rest of the immigrants."

Michael framed Maria's face with his hands and leaned down into it. "Are you sure, darling?" he asked quietly, studying her facial features, as though it would be the last time he would be near her.

"Yes. I'm sure," she said, reaching up to touch his hand, then flinched when Alberto came and jerked her away from Michael.

"Come on, Maria," Alberto shouted.

"I must first get my violin," she said, searching around her once again.

"Hurry up then. We must find a place to rest when we get topside. It's already dark, you know."

Michael ran his fingers through his hair, frowning. "If you insist on moving topside, let's go about it in a civilized manner," he said thickly. "Let me get assistance to help get your belongings moved. You will need your bunk and all the heavy blankets you can get. I'll see to it that you have the best."

"We don't need any more of your help," Alberto stormed. "You already tried to take payment by touching my sister and kissing her."

"I don't need payment for anything," Michael said flatly. He moved toward the door, ignoring Alberto's further accusations. "I'll go topside and make all the arrangements. We have to do what's best for Maria, Alberto. Whether or not you believe I'm doing it for her."

When Michael disappeared out into the passageway, Maria went to Alberto and glared upward into his face. "Oh, Alberto," she cried. "How could you? Michael didn't mean us any harm."

"I watched as he started to kiss you," he said, glowering.

"It is I who made the first advance," she said, tilting her chin up into the air, then walked on out into the passageway in her soiled chimney sweep costume, carrying her violin case with her.

Alberto's face drained of color. "Surely I heard wrong," he murmured to himself. "Maria wouldn't say such a thing. My Maria? My sweet, innocent Maria . . . ?"

He moved on out into the passageway himself, tensing when he passed the spot where he had been left to die. He hurried along, still wondering about his sister. . . .

Chapter Five

Two more days at sea and America's shores would be reached. Maria lay crouched beneath a heavy layer of blankets watching Alberto. He appeared to be asleep, but she didn't want to take a chance that he might see her sneak to Michael's cabin. She would have to wait a bit longer. But she did have to see Michael this night. If not, she might never be able to feel his arms around her again. America was a vast land. She had no idea where this Saint Louis was, where Michael had said he was going. She tensed, seeing a movement on Alberto's bunk. Though it was dark, she just knew that she had seen him reach down and pull a boot on! Where did he think he was going? He had stayed close to her since having left Michael's cabin. But he had been acting strangely, all the while keeping his face hidden from the card players as he continued to watch them. Surely he wouldn't. . . .

Alberto looked slowly around him, making sure no one was witnessing his preparations for his departure from his bunk. So far, no one had paid any attention to him. And now that his beard was fully grown, he was ready to make his move. Just thinking about holding the cards in his hands again made his heart pound. And then what he had planned to do later made his blood surge wildly with delight. He would show them. Sam and Grace would wish they had never even met him.

Eyeing Maria closely, Alberto smiled to himself. She was most assuredly asleep. She would never miss him. He pulled the last of their money from his breeches pocket and stacked it neatly in the palm of his right hand. He would make this back double, he mused to himself. Maria would never know. . . .

Tears burned at the corners of Maria's eyes, watching Alberto move from the bunk and head toward the dim lighting of a whale oil lamp, beneath which huddled the usual group of men playing poker. Through her mist of tears, she watched as Alberto settled onto the deck, now one of the men who played the devil's game. Cigar smoke circled upward and all eyes turned to Alberto, silently studying him for a second, then fell back to playing, mouthing crude obscenities as each card turned up in each of their hands.

Maria had wanted to reach out and stop Alberto, remembering what had happened to him before, but her inner tormented feelings of need for Michael had urged her to remain silent, pretending to be asleep. She knew that if Alberto was busy playing cards, he wouldn't see her leave for Michael's cabin. Yes, it was a perfect cover. And, for some unknown reason, Maria felt that Alberto just had to know what he was doing. For it was he who had taken the beating, and he would surely have devised a way to keep this from happening again.

She sighed to herself. She hated to admit it, but she even felt relieved to be away from Alberto's side for a while. Since his personality change, he had been most unpleasant to have as a companion. She had to hope that once they reached their Papa's home, Alberto would return to his old self and be just as lovable as before.

Pushing her blanket aside, Maria crept from the bunk, still attired in her hated chimney sweep costume and drab, dark shoes, and began to walk cautiously across the deck flooring. She barely breathed as she moved toward the door that led below deck, all the while watching Alberto. But he was already absorbed in the card game. He wouldn't see, or miss her, for hours.

Fear made shivers ride her spine as Maria moved down the steps, seeing the semidarkness of the long passageway that led to Michael's cabin. She knew that she was foolish, not having warned Michael of her plans to be with him. He could have met her. Protected her. But she hadn't known the true time that she could have left the bunk. She would just have to keep quiet so no one in any of the other cabins would hear her approach.

Noises from all sides of her made her cringe. They were as before. Gigglings from loose women who were paid to share their bodies with any man who asked, and the drunken, rowdy laughter from sailors who had finished with their duties for the night.

Hugging her arms tightly around her, Maria hurried to Michael's door and tapped lightly. In only a matter of moments, she would be with him. He would again teach her the mysteries of life and in the most sensuous of ways.

She tensed when he did not answer. A terrible thought seized her. What if Michael had paid for the services of one of these . . . wenches . . . ? She tapped more noisily, looking around her, trembling. If he didn't open the door soon, someone else on either side of her might, and then what?

The door jerked open quickly, revealing a half-drunken Michael to Maria. "Michael?" she whispered, seeing his hair all tousled in layers of gold. And even though there was only a dim lighting, she could see swollen mounds beneath his eyes and the red streaks that surrounded the blue of his eyes.

"Maria?" he said in a thick speech, almost teetering.

She eyed him once again. He wore the night robe that was so familiar to her and it gaped open in front, revealing that he wore nothing beneath it. Her face reddened when she caught sight of his manhood. It wasn't in a state of arousal and even looked funny as it hung so loosely from his light-colored patch of pubic hair. She would always be amazed at how something so tiny could grow to such proportions to give her such pleasure. Tremors of passionate lust raced through her, making her move on inside the cabin.

When she heard the cabin door shut and the bolt lock slide in position, she turned and waited to see what Michael would do next. She had never been around an intoxicated man before. And she hated seeing Michael in this state. Especially when she had expected so much more from him this night. She tensed when she saw him reach for the wine bottle and pour himself another drink.

Taking a large swallow, Michael began to walk around Maria, eyeing her questioningly. "And how did you manage to get away from that damn brother of yours?" he asked darkly.

"I did manage. That's all that's important," she said softly. "You are glad to see me, aren't you?" she quickly added, wanting to reach up and touch him, even cling to him.

"But what if he realizes you are gone?" Michael continued, taking another large swallow, burping noisily as he placed the empty glass down on a table.

"He won't," she said flatly.

"And how can you be so sure?"

"He's playing that card game again," she answered, lowering her eyes.

A raucous laugh filled the dark corners of the cabin as Michael moved toward the bed, falling down onto it. "He is a damn idiot, that one. I also love the lure of the cards, but not among the scum that travels these ships," he said, still laughing. He stretched out on the bed, watching Maria once again. "And why did you come?" he said further, in a quiet drawl.

Maria stood still, even though her heart was pounding wildly inside her, seeing him on the bed, so tempting. She felt full of the devil this night, so very, very wicked. But she knew that only Michael could cause her to act in such a way. Only Michael. "Don't you know, Michael?" she asked, casting her eyes downward.

"I'm not sure," he said, a smile lifting his lips playfully. "Come. Show me."

"But aren't you too . . . uh . . . drunk . . . ?"

Another laugh from Michael jolted Maria's nerves. "Too drunk to do what, honey?" he added, reaching over on a night stand to pick up a half-smoked cigar. He placed it between his lips and lit it, suddenly enjoying this little game with Maria. The heat in his loins urged him to hurry on along with it, but he would let her make the first move. It would be more exciting that way.

He puffed eagerly on the cigar, watching her move toward him. Damn. Even in that ugly garb, she was the most beautiful woman alive. He loved the color of her skin . . . the dark olive tone that he remembered being so soft to the touch. And didn't she appear to be a tigress now, as she moved her stately tall body toward him? Her dark, wavy hair hung to her waist, and her eyes were hidden beneath thick, heavy lashes, which were now fluttering like butterfly wings as she bent down over him.

"Michael, you know what I mean," she said, lowering her full, sensuous lips to cover his.

"God," Michael groaned, reaching for the ashtray, dropping the cigar into it. He then pulled Maria atop him and kissed her hard and long, letting his fingers begin to unbutton the shirt that hid her large, full breasts from his hungry mouth and eyes.

Maria pulled away from him, devouring him with her eyes. "Michael, please make love to me," she murmured, touching his face, tracing it with a fingertip. "Just like you did before. Please?"

Her skin quivered when he touched her ever so gently beneath her shirt, still searching out her breast. When he made contact, she moaned with ecstasy. She squirmed, making her breast more accessible. And when his fingers circled the breast and squeezed a nipple to tautness, she felt her head begin to reel.

"Undress, Maria," Michael said thickly. "Stand beside the bed and do it in front of me. Slowly. I want to watch."

As though hypnotized, Maria pushed herself off the bed, then stood with a straight back, watching him as his eyes caressed her. Swaying gently, she first removed her jacket, then, teasingly, finished unbuttoning her shirt, slipping her arms from each sleeve, smiling wickedly as her breasts came into full view.

Feeling indeed wanton, she reached up and began caressing her breasts, seeing the desire for her increase in Michael's eyes as they widened and became as two coals, burning with passion. She looked further down and saw that he was ready for her as he lay with his night robe spread apart, revealing his most intimate part of himself to her in its full glory.

Letting her fingers move slowly from her breasts, down across the flatness of her stomach, she unbuttoned her breeches and stepped out of them, and then her shoes, and then, like a snake, slithered down onto the bed beside him. "Love me, Michael," she whispered, reaching up to touch his lips. "I am yours. Tonight, I am yours."

Michael laughed hoarsely, reaching for her. "And you thought I was too drunk, huh, Maria?" he said. "Darling, I was drinking because I didn't have you. My thoughts have been in tortured torment ever since our first time together. Now? Yes, I shall make love to you. Over and over again. Until you are completely satiated."

His mouth covered hers, setting her afire inside, feeling the familiar warmth sweeping through her that only he alone had ever aroused in her. His lips were hard, demanding, and when his tongue made entrance between her lips, searching, probing, she wrapped her tongue around his, further enjoying the reckless passion being awakened inside her. She ached for his lips to search out every inch of her body. She arched her body upward, inviting this from him. And when his hands began to fondle and caress, she moaned with pleasure, hating it when his lips left hers, but glad when they began to wet the nipple of a breast, making it stiffen, turn to a peak of raw passion. He sucked and chewed, letting his fingers travel downward until they had found the secret place between her legs. Without any abandonment, she spread her legs apart, shutting her eyes, feeling her heart beating with a rapid pounding as his fingers searched up inside her, then withdrew and began to caress her love mound with slow, but sure strokes.

She trembled as she became further alive beneath his caresses. The feelings inside her were building to such an intensity, she gasped when his mouth traveled further down and sought out the soft spot between her legs, replacing his fingers with his tongue.

"Oh, Michael," she whispered, writhing, running her fingers through his hair. It was as though she was soaring, mindless even, as he continued the assault with his tongue and lips. Panting wildly, she cried, "Now, Michael. Please take me now." She reached down and urged him upward.

He lunged inside her, stiffening his body and gritting his teeth when he felt the warm wetness of her vaginal walls close around his manhood. He moved his body slowly in and out, relishing the pleasure he was taking from his Maria, now knowing that no other woman could ever compare. He could feel the heat building . . . climbing . . . and began to thrust harder . . . reaching up to entwine his fingers into her hair. Then his mouth crushed against hers in a hungry devouring kiss of passion.

Maria lifted her legs around his body and locked her ankles together, moving her hips, letting the waves of pleasure splash through her, feeling them grow higher and higher, as though she might drown in this ocean of ecstasy.

With a fierceness, he gripped her more tightly in his embrace and together their bodies exploded in earth-shattering spasms, making them both cry out in unison, until they lay clinging, trembling, and slippery from nervous perspiration glistening along their bodies.

"Ah. Now I am truly drunk," Michael sighed, kissing Maria softly on the temple.

Maria giggled a bit. "And I am also," she purred, still feeling a throbbing between her thighs . . . a throbbing that told her she was ready for more of the same.

Michael's left hand drifted lazily over her body, touching each crevice knowingly. "Maria, I don't think I can say goodbye," he said.

Maria's heartbeat raced. "I feel the same," she murmured.

Moving from atop her, Michael reached for his cigar, relighting it. He sat with his back braced against the outside wall, furrowing a brow. "Then why do we even have to, Maria?"

"What are you saying . . . Michael?"

"We could wed. Make this a proper union."

Maria bolted upright, eyes wide. She knelt on the bed at Michael's feet, looking up into the blueness of his eyes. "You mean . . . you . . . are . . . asking my hand in . . . marriage?"

"And why not?"

Excitement sent small electrical impulses through her. Then she remembered Alberto and how he felt about Michael . . . and then remembered also her father who was waiting for her in America. Loyalty to family had always made the bond strong in the Lazzaro family, as it did in all Italian families. It was in their blood. An alliance that no outsider could understand . . . *nor* interfere with.

No. Her family had to come first. Her face became all shadows as she cast her eyes downward. "It's impossible to do so," she murmured.

Michael flinched as though he had been hit. "Why not, Maria?" he said, tilting her chin up with a forefinger, so their gazes could meet. "You do profess to love me, do you not?"

Tears burned at the corner of her eyes. She fluttered her lashes nervously, then said, "I'll never love anyone else."

Michael rose from the bed, pacing the floor. "You say you love me but you won't marry me," he blurted, kneading a brow, with the cigar hanging limply from the corner of his mouth. He came to an abrupt halt and glared toward Maria. "Tell me the reason why you refuse, Maria," he demanded hotly.

Maria pulled the night robe Michael had shed from his body around herself, suddenly conscious of her nudity. She hugged herself, feeling a slow trembling rising inside. "You wouldn't understand," she finally answered.

"Try me," he said flatly.

"It's because of my family," she uttered, flipping her hair to hang in a long, thick mass down her back.

"Damn it, Maria. Why would your family object? I'm respectable enough. Or is it because I am an American? Do Italians have to marry Italians, or what?"

"No. Nothing like that."

"Then damn it. Why?"

Her eyes flew upward and she set her jaw firmly. "I cannot desert Alberto and my Papa," she said. "My Papa is all alone in America. He's waiting for me and Alberto. And also, Alberto. He's not behaving rationally. I must stay with him until he's acting normally once again."

Michael hit his forehead with the palm of his hand, groaning. "Alberto, Alberto," he shouted. "Always Alberto." He went to Maria and pulled her up from the bed, clutching onto her shoulders. "Can Alberto do this?" he said thickly, then kissed her fully on the lips as his hand worked at disrobing her again until their bodies fused and began moving together, creating the wondrous desirous feelings inside Maria once again.

"Oh, Michael," Maria gasped as she felt the hardness of his manhood probing between her legs.

"Can he, Maria?" Michael murmured, showering her breasts with kisses, then lower.

"No. He cannot," she sobbed. "But it makes no difference, Michael. My mind cannot be changed."

Michael lifted her to the bed and stretched out beside her. "Then, my darling, we must not waste any of our moments we have left together. We must make love. Over and over again this night. We must, for I feel I can never get enough of you."

"Yes, my love," she whispered, feeling passion weaving its way through her heart. "Oh, yes, yes. . . ."

*   *   *

Alberto pulled his hat lower in an attempt to hide his eyes, knowing that his eyes could be the reason that he could be recognized. And even though his clothes were the same as he had worn before, he knew they were like those of most other men aboard this ship, filthy and tattered, so he didn't believe that Sam would remember him from just that one confrontation with him.

Letting his eyes wander about, Alberto's hate grew within him as he found Grace leaning over Sam, teasing him with her fingers. They were a pair, they were. Sam with his beady, dark eyes, and thick, scraggly whiskers that had threads of chewing tobacco stuck throughout, and Grace with her low-cut gowns, revealing a tempting pair of breasts for all men to drool over, but looking so wicked with a constant glint in her cat-green eyes. Her copper hair fell around her face, framing it, looking as though she had already wrestled many men this night.

"And how about you, stranger?" a voice spoke from beside Alberto, making him jolt to attention.

"Huh . . . ?" he said, straightening the cards in his hand.

Then Sam grumbled. "Place your bet, damn it," he said. "We ain't got all night, ya know. If'n ya plays cards with us, ya stays alert. Now bet or move on with ya."

Pinpricks of hate raced along Alberto's nerves, eyeing Sam darkly. "You're going to get yours, you damn bastard," he thought to himself. "But now I'll play along with you." He gazed down at his cards, smiling amusedly. Damn. He was lucky. Another winning hand for sure. "My bet?" he drawled, trying to disguise his voice. "One American dollar. That's what my bet is."

He checked his cards once again to be sure. Yes. There was a ten, Jack, Queen, King, and Ace. All of different suits, but that didn't matter. What he had was called a Royal Flush. He did remember that name, for sure. It was the best he could get. He furrowed his brow, kneading it with his free hand. Should he have bet more? It could even speed up the game a bit. But, no. He would have a next time.

The men on all sides of Alberto placed their own bets, then the time came to reveal the hands. Straightening his shoulders back proudly, Alberto placed his cards on the deck, slowly, one at a time, feeling his heart pounding, knowing that all eyes had seen that he had indeed won with the best cards among them all.

"Damn it. A Royal Flush," one muttered. "Ain't seen one of them in a long time. Damn lucky."

Sam glared at Alberto in silence as Alberto scraped in his winnings. He took another mouthful of chewing tobacco, licking his fingers before dealing another hand of cards. Then he began dealing, occasionally glancing Alberto's way.

Alberto cringed, seeing that maybe he was getting too much attention too soon. He knew that Sam could possibly remember that one other time, and how lucky Alberto had been at playing this game. Could Sam see him and his true features through his thick crop of whiskers? But, surely not. It was dark, even foggy, with shreds of wet mist hanging in the air.

As the new hand of cards fell on the deck before him, Alberto scraped them in one at a time and positioned them in his hand, not believing how his luck continued to be with him. Even so, should he bluff and pretend he had nothing this time? He didn't want to work too fast. He had to be cautious, or he would fail once again at having a woman's flesh against his own. So he frowned and drawled a slow, "Damnation. Ain't got nothin' this time." He smiled to himself when muffled chuckles rose from the throats around him. When he discarded, he threw away three Aces and drew another Ace and two Kings, making him frown, knowing that even now, he had a full house, after having kept an Ace and a King in his hand before having discarded. His face flushed crimson, looking around him, knowing what to expect when he placed these cards on the ship's deck before him, letting all see what was probably once again a winning hand.

"Got ya all beat this time," Sam laughed. "What's yore bet this time, stranger?" he added, looking Alberto's way.

Alberto couldn't resist the temptation of getting the better of his enemy. "Five big ones," he drawled, counting the money out, slapping it onto the ship's deck.

"Damn it you say," Sam growled, spitting a wad of chewing tobacco into the wind behind him. "Well, ah'll raise ya five," he quickly added, laughing throatily.

"I'll call you," Alberto said, throwing out five more dollars, feeling guilty and reckless now, remembering how Maria had worked so hard beside him when cleaning chimneys, taking so long to even earn one Italian lira. But he would win it back. Double. Plus in doing so, he would be able to touch the secret parts of that wench Grace. His eyes moved to her, just as she began to creep around to snuggle down behind him. He swallowed hard, remembering so vividly how it had happened before. She was making her first move. Well, he would play along. She would soon find out how her plans would be changed this night. How he would be the one in authority.

"Okay, stranger," Sam grumbled. "Show us yore cards."

Alberto smiled amusedly as he placed his three Kings and two Aces on the ship's deck for all to see. His gaze traveled across to Sam and he could see the hatred forming in his beady eyes. "And yours? What are you showin' this hand, stranger?" Alberto asked, placing a distinct emphasis on that word "stranger."

"Yore whippin' my ass tonight," Sam growled, slapping his three Queens of Spades and four and five of Hearts on the ship's deck.

"So I am," Alberto said, smiling widely. He looked at all other cards in front of the other men and saw that he had indeed beat them all. As he scraped his winnings in, he glanced quickly toward Sam and knew that the time was drawing near. He knew that if he waited too long, Sam would probably understand just what was happening.

"And where've ya been on this here trip before tah-night, stranger?" Sam suddenly blurted, counting out more money to place on the ship's deck before him.

The color drained from Alberto's face. "Uh . . . I . . . well . . . you see, I've been ailin'," he quickly said. "Yeah. Had that damn dysentery. Guess it's been the drinkin' water on this death trap called a ship. Didn't think anyone would like gettin' round me." He felt beads of perspiration on his brow, seeing Sam studying him even more closely.

"Tha' right?" Sam growled.

"Yeah," Alberto said, then he felt the softness of a

106

hand reach around and cover his own.

"And you're feelin' better now?" Grace purred, blinking her green eyes at him as she leaned her face down into his.

Alberto's color returned to his face. "Yeah. Much. Sure am," he mumbled, feeling that same damn stirring in his loins that he remembered from before as her fingers worked a button loose on his shirt and inched her way beneath it, curling in the thickness of his chest hair.

"I'm glad," Grace said further, pulling her hand away, settling down next to him. "You see, I'd like to get to know you better."

Alberto swallowed hard. "You would?" he stammered. He had wanted to act confident, fully in control of himself, but this beautiful woman was causing him to react much differently than planned.

Grace leaned over and whispered into Alberto's ear. "I've got a private cabin all to myself," she said. "Want to see it?"

Alberto glanced quickly around him, seeing all eyes on him. Then his gaze met Sam's and held. A further intense feeling of hatred lured him to his feet. He knew that no more hands of cards were necessary. He had come to the point of no return now. He placed his money in his pocket, then turned and locked his arm around Grace's waist. "Sure. It'd be my pleasure to see your cabin," he drawled, glancing once again at Sam and seeing that look of triumph in Sam's eyes, knowing that Sam would be thinking that soon he would have himself some fun with this newest stranger. But Alberto would show both Sam . . . and Grace. . . .

"And might ya be alone on this journey?" Grace

purred, clinging, making sure a breast mashed against Alberto's left side. He felt a delirious sense of need rising inside him, making his face flush even more.

"Sure am," he lied, knowing this was only a part of her plan, as before. He knew that if she thought he was a lone traveler, she and Sam would have more freedom to abuse . . . his . . . body. He swallowed hard once again, leaning down as Grace led him through the door that took him below deck, where her filthy cabin waited. He had to wonder how many innocent men had been taken there and used. A weakness at the pit of his stomach made him feel like wretching, remembering exactly what Sam had done to him earlier. But not this time. No. Not this time.

"No wife?" Grace asked further.

"No. None. Ain't needed a wife yet," he drawled, laughing awkwardly, looking around at the dismal passageway, cringing when he again remembered the last time he had been there. He managed to pull his arm more tightly around Grace's waist, even making her squeal out with pain.

She jerked away from him. "Hey. Watch it," she stormed. "What do ya think I am? Don' you know I'm a fragile female? Just ya remember that."

Alberto had to laugh, remembering the way she had held a gun on him. She most certainly hadn't looked fragile to him then. "Beg your pardon," he said, trying to force his lips to quit trembling with the need to want to laugh at her further.

She walked on ahead of him and pushed a door open with one quick stroke. She stepped aside, holding her head tilted a bit. "This here's my cabin, mister," she snapped. "You can enter if'n you treat me like a lady."

Alberto moved on past her, quickly darting his eyes

around him, seeing that nothing had changed. She still had a cabin full of filth. His gaze moved to the bunk, knowing that soon he would have her on it and be taking from her just what he demanded. She would even beg for mercy, if he had anything to do with it. "So this is where you pass your evenings when you're not watchin' that card game, huh?" he asked, moving on around the room, touching everything gingerly. He tensed a bit when he heard the door shut behind him.

"My castle," she purred sarcastically. She went to Alberto and leaned up into his face, reaching down to touch the bulge in his pants. "Don' you think it's as purty as anyone else's castle? Huh?"

Alberto became breathless as her fingers began to work on him, then expertly unbuttoned his breeches with skilled fingers, reaching in, touching him more freely. "Yes. A castle," he stammered, closing his eyes, gritting his teeth, knowing that this was where his self-control had to be used. He moved away from her.

"Hey. What is this?" she shouted, standing with hands on hips. "You knew what we was comin' down here for. So whut's yore game, mister?"

Alberto eyed her smugly as he rebuttoned his breeches. "Did you say . . . game . . . ?" he growled.

"I don' play any games, mister," she said, beginning to unbutton her dress that hung in green silken folds from around a dipped-in waist. Her breasts rose and fell, two mounds inviting Alberto to almost forget what he did have in mind. He so wanted to bury his nose between the depth of those two pieces of swollen flesh. He so wanted to place his lips on the nipples, suck hungrily from them. But first things first.

He went to Grace and grabbed her by the wrists and tightened his hold. "You know that is a lie, fair lady," he grumbled. "You know that's the only reason you are on this ship. Just to play games."

Grace's head snapped backward as she stared upward, studying Alberto more closely. "Wha' do you mean?" she said softly, her green eyes flashing.

"Don't you recognize me, Grace? Huh? Don't you remember playing that little game with me once before? Then leaving me for dead out in the passageway?" he growled, furrowing his brows into a deep vee.

"You . . ." she gasped, now recognizing him. "It's the whiskers. They hide your true identity. If Sam. . . ."

"If Sam what?" Alberto said, shaking her.

"He'll surely kill you this time," Grace said, laughing shrilly.

"You mean if I don't kill him first," Alberto said, laughing darkly.

"Then you mean . . . to . . . ?"

"I'm not sure yet," Alberto said, laughing once again. Then his one hand went to her hair. He grabbed his fingers full and jerked her head back, glad to hear her groan with pain. "And before Sam has time to get here, I have to make my move," he said. "Where's your gun, Gracie girl?"

"My . . . gun . . . ?" she said, panting hard, trying to pull free, but only moaning more when her hair began to pull harder.

"Damn it," Alberto hissed. "I'm through with your little games. Where's that damned gun?"

"Over there. On the table. Beneath . . . beneath that scarf."

"Just come along with me then," he said, moving an inch at a time, forcing her to walk with him. "I'll be the one making use of that gun this time."

Grace began to kick and scream, but stopped when

110

Alberto hit her across the face with the back of his free hand.

"We'll have none of that stuff," he said darkly. "We don't want to warn Sam, now do we? We know that Sam will be here shortly to have his sick fun. Right?"

"He'll be here all right," Grace said, wiping her red, swollen cheek. "He'll kill you. And I'll stand and laugh while he's doing it."

"Yeah. I know you would. But you won't get a chance," Alberto said, releasing his hold on her when he had the gun secured in his right hand. He checked for bullets and found that it was fully loaded. He motioned with it toward Grace. "Get over there. By that door. And damn it, if you make one sound when Sam starts to open that door, I won't only kill him, but you also."

"You . . . wouldn't. . . ."

"Just try me, slut," Alberto said. "All I have to do is remember what Sam did to me while I was in this cabin the last time, to spur me to murdering both you and him."

Grace stumbled sideways as Alberto gave her a shove. "Now just stand there and be quiet," he added once again, waiting. He stood, tense, listening, and when he saw the door begin to open, he reached upward with the gun, and as soon as Sam's head came into full view, Alberto came down with a full force, hitting Sam over the back of the head with the butt of the gun.

Grace gasped in disbelief beside Alberto, as Alberto kicked Sam away from the door so he could shut it. Then he leaned down and checked Sam's pulse, relieved that the bastard was still alive. He didn't want a murder rap hanging over his head before he even had the chance to get to America. He had many plans. No fool like this Sam character was going to take those plans away from him. He turned and glared toward Grace. "Now. Tear some of your garments away and use them to gag and tie Sam," he ordered.

"I won't," she said, setting her jaw stubbornly.

Alberto hated having to strike a woman once again, but felt he had no other choice. He went to her and struck her across the lips, flinching even himself when he saw a thin stream of blood begin to run from a corner. "Do as you're told," he said, motioning with the gun once again.

He stood in silence as she hurriedly tied both Sam's legs and arms and then gagged him. Alberto's pulse-beat was racing, knowing what he was going to demand of her next. There was no way he was going to leave this cabin without first getting what he had that first time come down here for. He began to tremble when she stood, challenging him with her eyes. "Now what?" she hissed, hands on hips.

"Undress," Alberto ordered, eyes wavering.

"Undress . . . ?" she said in disbelief.

"You heard me. . . ."

She laughed tauntingly. "Sure, mister," she said, slipping her dress down from her shoulders, revealing that she wore no undergarments beneath it. As she stepped out of it, her shapely body was revealed to him in its entirety. He raked his eyes over her, taking inventory of all her body's dips and crevices. He licked his lips hungrily. "Now. As I hold the gun, you undress me," he ordered, placing his feet apart and his arms part way up into the air.

"Jesus," she muttered, sauntering toward him.

When her fingers began to touch his bare flesh, he

112

could feel goose pimples rising, rippling. An anxious greed for this woman's body made him reach downward with his free hand and caress a breast, causing soft moans to begin to surface from deep within him. He had never felt anything so soft. He squeezed harder, making her eyes move upward and tease him seductively with them.

"You want my body?" she purred, standing, stretching, touching herself now knowingly.

"I'm taking your body," he said flatly. "Move to that bunk."

She inched her way toward it, watching his gun. Then she stretched out across the bunk, smiling wickedly toward him. He reached down and picked up his belt and moved toward her. He saw a fear enter her eyes, making shadows crease her face. "What are you going to do with . . . that . . . belt . . . ?" she gasped, working her way to the other side of the bunk.

"Lie on your stomach," he ordered, standing over her.

"Why . . . ?"

"I'm going to tie your hands," he said. "Do you think for one minute I could trust you while I was getting my pleasures from your body?"

"Don't tie me up," she begged, her eyes pleading. "I promise I'll be good. I cain't stand to be in bondage. I've been treated that way before. Some guys get their kicks by tyin' me up. But I cain't stand it."

"I'd be a dumbass if I listened to you."

She jumped up from the bunk and went to him and placed her lips to his. "I promise. I'll show you a good time. Anybody who has the guts to do what you've done to Sam deserves a good time. Please believe me. I'll be good to you."

Alberto's pulse raced and he could feel the heat building in his loins. "All right," he murmured. "But you know that I can get the gun faster than anything you can do. Just remember that."

"I will," she said, then wrapped a leg around him, drawing him to her, making his head begin to reel. He slung the gun down on the one end of the bunk and let her lead him downward, until he was stretched out on the bunk and she was kneeling over him, teaching him the tricks she knew with her mouth and tongue. He wanted to close his eyes, to enjoy to the fullest what he had so long been waiting to experience. But he didn't trust her. He placed his right hand closer to the gun, then with his left, reached down and grabbed a handful of flesh, squeezing the breast as he felt her lips begin to nibble along his body. His legs stiffened and his stomach muscles grew taut, afraid he would explode any minute, releasing all the pent-up emotions that had been building in him since that very first time he had realized that Maria had been more than a sister . . . that she had blown fully into a woman . . . more beautiful than any other Italian woman he had ever seen.

He had known it was wicked, but he had so desired to explore her body . . . see . . . feel . . . the secret parts of her body that he had known were so different from his own. But he had never approached her, had only let his mind enjoy the pleasure of dreaming.

"Come here, wench," he said, tired of waiting. He laughed to himself. He could tell by her eyes and the flush of her face that she was enjoying this just as much as he was. He positioned her beneath him, holding on to her wrists, then stretched his body over hers, sighing, enjoying the feel of her breasts against his chest and the

114

softness of her skin against the full length of his.

"Now, wench, I'm going to explore your body," he said thickly. "But that doesn't mean I can't beat you to that gun if you try anything. Do you understand?"

Grace lifted her hips and ground herself into him. "Honey, all I want from you is your body," she purred. "To hell with the gun." She turned her gaze to Sam, who still lay unconscious. "And to hell with Sam. Compared to the likes of you, he's just a weasel."

"Then show me the best that you know, Gracie baby," Alberto said, surprised at his own boldness. He was acting as though he was experienced, when in truth, this was the first woman he had ever seduced.

Grace reached up and pulled his head down, crushing his lips to hers. When her tongue probed inside his mouth, he felt the throbbing of his heart and a melting sensation flowing through him, to end inside his manhood. Her fingers pressed into his back, then lowering, positioning him, ready for him to begin his thrusts inside her. "Now," she groaned. "What the hell are ya waitin' for?"

"Huh . . . ?" Alberto stammered, suddenly feeling a bit awkward.

"Put it in me. Now. Don' you know nothin'?"

She opened herself to him, still waiting. He fumbled with himself, but suddenly felt a coldness surging through him. He was deflated. Nothing was there. The throbbing was gone and the sensations of floating had been replaced by a trembling fear. He pulled away from her, crimson-faced. He looked down at himself, unbelieving. Only moments ago, he had been ready. He had been so sure. But now? Nothing.

Grace crept from the bed, frowning. "Well, I'll be damned," she purred. "I've run into a few like you.

Poor bastard. What a life you've got ahead of you. No woman will want the likes of you. First you're as virile as they come, even better, then the next thing I knows, you're a nothin'."

She flew into a fit of laughter, filling Alberto with dread. He pulled his breeches and shirt on, then his shoes, grabbed Grace's gun, and fled from the room, panting.

He was ashamed, humiliated all over again. And again in front of the same lady. He stopped in the passageway and hung his head in his hands, sobbing. "I'm not even a man," he cried. "What the hell's wrong with me? What can I do?"

He stumbled onward, grabbing at the wall, then went out onto top deck, eyeing the men who still played their card game, then at Maria. Had she been innocently asleep all the while he was . . . ?

"Oh, Maria," he thought to himself. "Oh, sweet Maria. So innocent. So very much my own. Your brother isn't even a man."

He stumbled further until he fell on his own bunk, wanting to die. His dreams of having the fulfillment of a man had just been shattered. Disillusionment swept over him. Would it always be this way for him? Tears wet his cheeks as he pulled his knees up to his chest, shivering in the chill of the night.

He placed the gun he had taken from Grace next to his cheek, feeling its utter coldness. Maybe . . . maybe he should just go and shoot himself just like he was a horse that was no longer of any use to anyone. Maybe in time . . . that's just what . . . he would have to do . . . to himself. . . .

Chapter Six

Those of the immigrants who were healthy and strong enough crowded against the ship's railing, watching . . . waiting. They had been told that in only a matter of minutes they would get their first view of "America's golden door." All were quiet. Even the children were no longer crying. The air held a spirit of cautious hope. The water now splashed in only mild sprays of bubbly effervescence against the ship's bow, as the ship's boilers ceased to be fed coal by the work-weary crewmen, who had mainly seen only the dark dungeon of the mechanical works of the ship since leaving the Italian shore.

Maria snuggled more closely to Alberto. "I'm so excited," she whispered, reaching up, checking to see if her hair was completely hidden beneath her billed hat. She once again would be playing the role of a boy until she reached her Papa's home. Alberto had warned her of the many strange men that they might have to encounter, and knowing only one American, this Michael whom Maria had taken a quick fancy to, and the way he had so reacted to Maria's beauty, Alberto had thought to expect the same from *all* American men. Alberto wanted *no* man to take advantage of his sister's sweet innocence. *No* man.

Alberto leaned down into Maria's face. "The gun, Maria," he whispered, glancing quickly around him, making sure no one saw or heard. "Is it well hidden?"

Sighing, Maria fluttered her thick lashes nervously. "Yes. It is still well hidden," she whispered. "But I still don't understand why you want to keep it. Surely whoever lost it would have much more need of it than you or I. Why didn't you leave it just where you found it? Guns are ugly, dangerous things."

Alberto was glad that Maria had believed his story when she had discovered the gun hidden beneath the blankets of his bunk. At that moment, the only thing he could have said was that he had found it. He couldn't have revealed to her that in truth he had taken it from a ship's whore and had even used the butt of it to bust the skull of a rapist-thief partially open.

He looked all around him, studying the faces of the crowd. He hadn't seen Sam *or* Grace since that night, the night that Alberto had discovered that he was lacking in the knowledge of how to act as a true man . . . sexually. He didn't understand it. For even now he could feel his manhood come to life with just the remembrance of how soft Grace's body had been. But when the time would come actually to be with a woman, would Alberto's body fail him again? His heart ached, thinking of that possibility.

He flinched when Maria's elbow nudged into his side. His face reddened as he saw the questioning in her eyes.

"Alberto, did you hear me?" she whined, still worrying about his state of mind. He was still behaving strangely. Even more so after his night of playing that card game once again. She at first had worried that he

118

might have lost all their money. But when he had shown her that he had even won a few lire, she had been a bit proud of him. So she knew that it hadn't been the money that had caused his loss of spirit. Would she ever find out? Were she and Alberto truly drifting apart? She had never thought that possible. They had always seemed as one. Ever since birth.

"Oh, the gun," he stammered, thrusting his hands inside his front breeches pockets. "I felt that it became mine the minute I found it. I felt that we might need it once we arrive in America."

"But America is a land of opportunity. Not a land to fear," she argued.

"Remember what Papa has said about that Nathan Hawkins," Alberto grumbled. "He's an American, and it sounds as though he's one to not trust."

"Yes, I guess you're right," Maria murmured. "But, Alberto, why must I carry the gun? It's so cold and hard against my belly. And that rope you have tied the gun to my belly with is itching my skin so."

Alberto hung his head. "In case we have to be checked to enter America and they discover you are a woman, they won't go so far as to have you remove your breeches and shirt," he mumbled. "With a man, they may have no qualms about it. Please understand."

Maria twisted her body, trying to stand so that the gun wouldn't irritate her so severely. "Oh, all right," she said, then stood on her tiptoes and let out a loud gasp. "Alberto. Look. See," she said, suddenly panting.

Through a low-hanging haze, the New York harbor slowly began to take shape. Alberto removed his hat from his head and squeezed it between his hands, eyes wide, first noticing the 152-foot-high Statue of Liberty.

"My God," he shouted, now aware of all the other cries and shouts of glee surfacing from all the rest of the immigrants who crowded around him and Maria.

Maria's heart seemed to lunge, now remembering how Michael had so carefully described it to her that second time during their last moments together, after they had made love to one another, over and over again. "And did you know that a person can stand in the torch at the very end of the arm of the Lady of Liberty?" she blurted.

Alberto eyed her darkly. "And how do you know that, Maria?"

She cast her eyes downward, feeling a blush rising. "I read about it in a book, Alberto," she said quietly. "That's how I know."

Alberto seemed to have not heard. Something else had caught his quick attention. "Maria! Would you look at those mountains!" he exclaimed, pointing, as the ship moved on past the Statue of Liberty, closer to the piers.

Maria stood on tiptoe again, craning her neck. "What mountains?" she asked. "I see no mountains."

Alberto's voice grew impatient. "Those tall ones. Over there. Coming closer. Look at them. They're so strange. And why don't they have snow on them?"

The haze suddenly lifted, revealing the immenseness of New York's buildings. A smile erupted on Maria's face, which grew into a laugh of mirth. She had realized that her brother had been lax about reading and studying, even though their Papa had so eagerly urged them to do this, but she just hadn't realized Alberto was *this* slow in the ways of the mind. Her smile and laugh faded away. Perhaps this wasn't the result of a lack of book

120

learning, but from that blow to Alberto's head. She reached for his hand and held it in hers. "Alberto, those aren't mountains," she said. "Those are buildings."

He jerked his hand free, scowling. "Damn it, Maria," he argued. "Don't you think I can see that? It was the fog. It had hidden the truth from my eyes. I'm no damn idiot. Please don't treat me like one."

It was Maria's turn to scold. "And you, Alberto," she demanded. "Do not spoil this, my first arrival to America, by throwing filthy words into my face. You know how long you and I have waited for this day. Please be a bit more pleasant."

Alberto placed his arm around Maria's waist and pulled her to him. "I'm sorry," he said, replacing his hat on his head with his free hand.

"Oh, and look at the bridge," Maria squealed, quickly forgetting her anger. "It's named the Brooklyn Bridge." She glanced furtively toward Alberto, expecting him to question her further knowledge of these landmarks of America, but he stood, with mouth agape, also taking in all these wonders of the New World. So Maria turned her gaze to see the rest herself, continuing to rattle on. "And we are now in the harbor of Manhattan. Isn't it just too magnificent, Alberto?"

The ship inched its way to the dock. Maria drew in a deep sigh of relief, listening this final time to the noises of the ship . . . all its timbers creaking, the low drone of the rumble of the boiler that was becoming less and less noisy by the second, and that endless splashing of the water that had sometimes almost driven her to screaming.

The aromas of the ship's deck around her were what she was happiest to leave behind, the aromas of human waste, vomit, steaming fish and potatoes, and the ever present stench from the animals that had shared the far end of the top deck with the massive group of immigrants.

Feeling smug, so soon to become an American, to stand and walk atop American soil, Maria bent and reached for her violin case, ready to make her departure alongside her brother.

When she straightened her back, she let her gaze travel around the crowd, feeling an ache circling her heart. She was remembering the more pleasant side of her journey. That which had been shared with the man who she would always love. Michael. She so longed to get a glimpse of his golden locks of hair and the blue of his eyes. She so longed to search him out . . . run to him . . . fall into his arms . . . to confess her love for him . . . let him lift her into his arms and whisk her away.

But she knew this to be an impossibility. She had been the one to decline his proposal of marriage. She had been the one to walk away from possibly the only man who could turn her insides into a mass of rippling warmth. She had been the one to say no to what was to have possibly been a life shared with a man and the riches he possessed. Would he have showered her with jewels? Satin dresses? Furs?

Tears burned at the corners of her eyes when she found no trace of him on top deck. He most assuredly had stayed in the privacy of his cabin and would continue to do so until the ship had emptied of the poor and unfortunate, and the smells that seemed to cling to their skins and clothes.

Maria looked downward at her own attire and

cringed. Soon she would cast these filthy, ugly clothes aside. And once she was attired in a beautiful, lacy dress, breeches would never be slipped upon her legs again.

"Come. It's time to leave the ship," Alberto said, lifting their one trunk to rest on his right shoulder.

Maria moved along with the crowd, hearing the eagerness of all the Italian chatter around her. She smiled to herself, so glad her Papa had prepared her and Alberto so well by having taught them the American language. He had even sent American dollars to them, explaining that many Italians would get tricked out of their lire when exchanging them for American dollars upon their first arrival to America.

"Hey. What's going on here?" Alberto exclaimed as he and Maria stepped from the ship to the pier. They were being roughly shoved toward a small boat along with several other of the Italians. Many other small boats were lined up next to this one, also being boarded.

A man with dark hair, a large, thick moustache and pale gray eyes, attired in a dark uniform, grabbed Alberto by the arm. "Get aboard, lad," he ordered sharply.

"Why?" Alberto shouted. "We're in America now. We're Americans. You can't shove us around. We have the same rights as you."

The man laughed raucously. "You've got to be Americanized first, lad," he said. "Then *maybe* you'll be able to call yourself an American."

Alberto jerked away from the man, fists doubled, swinging them near the face of the man. "My father is here in America. So I will also stay. No one can tell me I can't stay." He continued to dare the man, though his heart was pounding so hard, he was fast becoming breathless.

Maria stepped to his side, shadowing her eyes with the back of her left hand. "Please, Alberto," she whispered. "You're creating a scene."

"I must. Don't you see?"

"This Americanization the man speaks of," she whispered further. "It is quite necessary. All immigrants have it to do."

Alberto's eyes wavered. "Really?" he murmured. Then his gaze lowered, his dark eyes burning a hole through Maria. "And how do you know?"

"I just know," she answered. "Now please do as the man says."

"Oh, all right," Alberto sulked, having become a bit frightened anyway when he had seen the man lift a long, dark club from a loop at the waist of his breeches.

Maria studied the name printed in bold red print on the side of the small boat as she stepped over the side, into it. *"The General Putnam,"* she whispered to herself, then stood in silence next to Alberto, clutching tightly onto the handle of her violin case, once again hearing the dreaded noises of water splashing, and the drone of a boiler's engine as the boat began to make its way from the pier.

"I didn't expect anything like this," Alberto grumbled.

"What did you expect?" Maria whispered, sidling closer to him.

"I expected our ship to be met by a cheering crowd of welcome. Maybe even gifts given to each one of us. But

124

not this. I feel like an animal. If this is what America is, we should've stayed in Italy."

"It will soon be better, Alberto," Maria encouraged. "You'll see. And when we reach Papa's home, just think of what must await us. Can't you just envision a house so beautiful that has several separate rooms among which to choose from to be in any time of the day, instead of one large drab room as we've just left behind at Gran-mama's house?" Her eyes grew wide in wonder. "And there will be beds, bathing facilities. . . ."

Alberto interrupted her. "Maria, will you just be quiet," he stormed. "Look ahead. Does that look like a place that welcomes Italians with open arms? Is that even the place we are actually being taken to? Damn. What have we gotten ourselves into? And did Papa have to go through all of this when he first arrived in America? Why didn't he warn us if he did?"

Maria's gaze followed Alberto's. Suddenly she was afraid. They seemed to have left the grandest section of America behind and were being taken to an ugly island. She eyed it closely, seeing that it was just a ragged rock jutting out of the harbor, covered with gray, drab buildings. Her attention was then drawn to the same dark-clothed man who had been so rough to Alberto. He now stood at the stern of the ship, beginning to speak to all who were standing as quietly as Maria and Alberto with fear etched on their faces and in their eyes. Maria clutched her violin case to her bosom, listening.

"I am an immigration officer," the man's voice boomed, seeming to echo all around him as the damp ocean breeze blew in icy shreds. "This boat is taking you people to Ellis Island. This is where you will have what you will get to know is called 'Americanization.'

125

It is nothing to fear, but is quite necessary before being set free on the streets of New York. It may take some time to get completed, so please try and be patient. And if it makes you feel any better to know this, all other immigrants before you had this to do also. It will go much faster for you if you will just cooperate." He spat into the wind, wiping his thick moustache with the back of his left hand, then quickly added, "And I'd like to take this opportunity to be the first to welcome you to our shores. We Americans welcome into our midst anyone who is not criminal or deranged. It is a land of opportunity. I hope you will be able to be as happy here among us as you were among your own people in Italy."

Trembling from the chill, Maria moved closer to Alberto. He was all she had now until she reached Papa's arms. And wasn't America such a large, vast land? Her fears seemed to triple just thinking about it. Her gaze moved to the ship *Dolphin*, feeling a sadness, wondering if Michael had yet left its ugly, smelly decks. Her thoughts wandered further. Was he missing her? Had he possibly even been watching her as she had left the ship and had as quickly been herded onto this smaller boat? Did he even understand what she was going through at this time? Had he known that so much was being asked of her and her brother now? He had warned her about some of it. But had he truly known to what extent she and Alberto would be treated so roughly?

Her eyes lowered. No. Michael wouldn't know. He was not an immigrant. He had never been an immigrant. All his knowledge of what went on at this point in her journey was only speculation, or from rumors that he most surely had heard. The thrill of what had so long been a dream of hers, to become an immigrant, was slowly turning into a nightmare.

Eyeing the island as it grew closer, Maria grew even more tense. It appeared to be a prison. Not a place she wanted to be taken to, even if it did mean that in the end she would indeed be an American. There was something about the buildings on this colorless island that gave her a sense of dread. Was it because she saw no one around it? Were the immigrants herded into these buildings like animals, just as they had been while being ordered onto this smaller boat?

Then her gaze moved upward. Against the gray horizon, many seagulls were circling overhead, crying eerily as their large, white wings spread, soaring, dipping, moving closer to the boat. Maria loved birds, but these with their dark, imploring eyes made her even more afraid. It was as though they were studying her. She had to wonder how many immigrants these birds had seen pass through these waters? Oh, if only they could talk. What a tale they could probably weave.

"Alberto, I only wish this was over. I wish we were on the train, on our way to Papa's," she whispered.

"I know. Me also," Alberto said, shifting the heavy trunk atop his shoulder, feeling a slow aching beginning in his body. His eyes darted around him, seeing sadness on the faces of all who surrounded him. He knew that most were weary from the trip. He knew that most were losing hope for the future now. The cheers from the ship *Dolphin* had faded away to a silent, gloomy nothingness. It hadn't been at all as any of them had expected.

"Maybe it will go quickly," Maria sighed, seeing the

127

boat now being secured at the pier. Once again she found herself being shoved along with the rest of the immigrants, now onto the wetness of gray rocks, so slippery she almost plunged into the water.

"Here. Take my hand and hold on to it. Don't let go," Alberto ordered, reaching for her.

"All right, Alberto," Maria murmured, moving onward, watching all around her, seeing how quickly they all had been ordered into one of these buildings that she had been studying from afar. Once inside, she looked quickly around her. She was now standing in a huge room that held many stalls, and in these stalls there were lines and lines of other immigrants, most looking bone-weary, waiting and watching around them.

The same dark-clothed, moustached man shoved Alberto, then Maria into one of these stalls, along with the others. "You just stand there and wait your turns," he said, pushing and probing even more into the small space that smelled of perspiration and dried urine.

Maria eyed Alberto questioningly, seeing the confusion in the dark of his eyes. She knew what he had to be feeling. That they were like cattle . . . being herded. How many more times would this happen to them before coming face to face with becoming an American?

Then Maria's eyes moved on around her. A huge American flag graced the far end of the room, making goose bumps rise on her flesh. She had always dreamed of the day that she would see this symbol of freedom. She had read that the Stars and Stripes had been always the most popular name for the red, white, and blue national flag of the United States, standing for the land, the people, the government and the ideals of the

United States, no matter when or where it was displayed. Surely in this place, its presence meant that freedom was only footsteps away, Maria thought to herself.

Looking further around her, she saw many uniformed policemen standing with arms crossed, watching. This further increased her feelings of having just stepped inside a prison. She glanced quickly in another direction, frowning. The room was filled with total confusion and noise, even scenes of near chaos. Maria shuddered when she listened to the mothers shrieking at their children; then at the many tormented cries from the children; and at the coughs and ramblings that rose from the cubicles. Maria soon discovered that Italians weren't the only ones who were a part of this horrid transformation into Americans. There were many nationalities. She could tell by the many languages being spoken.

From what she could tell, most immigrants' possessions were few. What she did see were mainly battered wicker trunks and bedding rolled into tight balls, being held tightly in the arms of many, as though to lose these was to lose one's soul.

Maria ached inside. But she had only to think of the future. Once this ordeal was over, she and Alberto would be on their way. And wouldn't they be seeing Papa in only a matter of days now? Oh, how anxious she was. She closed her eyes and let her thoughts dwell on this, on their reunion, on how she would make her Papa's house a showpiece. She would plant flowers in flower boxes, she would place beautiful lace doilies on all his furniture. . . . Her eyes were jolted open when a loud voice boomed from beside her. It spoke fluently in the Italian tongue.

"It will be a while now. Please just be patient," this man said. "Your turns will arrive." He moved closer to the group, looking from person to person. "I am the immigration officer officially working with you Italians," he added. "I would like to ask that when it comes your turn, please answer the questions asked of you as quickly and accurately as possible."

"Turn? What does he mean?" Alberto said. "What the hell are we going to have to do now to be able to move on to Papa's home?"

"Patience. That's what you have to have now, Alberto," Maria whispered. She was just beginning to feel tired, even sleepy. It had been a long, exciting day. She looked for a place to sit, but there wasn't even enough room to do this. All were squeezed together, even mingling breaths. She closed her eyes and leaned against Alberto, feeling a wetness surfacing around her eyes. If only they would hurry, she thought to herself. "Please, God, let them hurry."

But hours upon hours passed. It seemed that no one was going to be admitted into the land of America. And then suddenly, the immigration officer began taking them one by one to a table and chair, inviting them to sit. Maria listened carefully, hoping to hear the questions, but couldn't, so she just waited her turn. When she was guided to the chair, she was all ears and eyes, knowing that it was coming to an end. Hopefully coming to an end. Surely she and Alberto would be allowed to move on as soon as they had completed this questioning.

She settled down onto the chair, relishing its comfort, even though it was only hard wood pushing against her sore, aching bones. She placed her violin case on her lap and leaned her elbows against it, resting her head in her hands.

"And what is your name?" the immigration officer asked, eyeing her closely with steel-gray eyes and pointed nose.

Maria gulped back fear. His eyes told her that he possibly knew the truth of her gender. She glanced quickly at Alberto, then back at the immigration officer. She had still wanted to remain as a boy until she was safely at her Papa's house. She flinched when the immigration officer reached upward and jerked the hat from her head.

He laughed hoarsely, flinging the hat onto the table. "Well? Lad?" he mocked. "Thought I had me a beauty here. No male could have such a beautiful face. Now tell me. What's your name so we can get along with this thing."

Maria's gaze lowered. She swallowed hard, then spoke. "Maria. Maria Lazzaro," she said in perfect Italian, since that had been the way in which she had been addressed.

"Birthplace?"

"Outside of Pordenone. In my Gran-mama's house."

The officer laughed hoarsely. "Yeah. I bet," he chuckled further, tapping the eraser of his pencil on his chin, studying her lower than her face, tilting a brow when he could see the largeness of her bosom, though covered by a dark, thick jacket. "And your destination?" he blurted.

Maria's gaze moved quickly to Alberto once again, having forgotten the name. "Alberto? What is the name of the town . . . ?" she asked, feeling desperation rising inside herself.

Alberto stepped to her side. "This is my sister Maria. I am Alberto Lazzaro," he said, squaring his shoulders. "We are on our way to Hawkinsville, Illinois. Our Papa awaits us there with lodging."

"Okay. Good enough," the man said, recording this information in a large journal. "And, Maria, how much is six times six?" he asked, smiling crookedly.

Her eyes widened. Such a question, she thought, remembering Alberto and how good he was with numbers. But herself? She didn't know how to answer so quickly. She began working with her fingers, counting them to herself, then bolted out an answer. "Thirty-six," she said, sighing, feeling her face flushing, knowing that this man had to think her quite dumb to have hesitated so long with the answer.

"Have you ever been in jail, Maria?" was the next question addressed to her by this man, who continued to study her closely, lowering his eyes usually to where she continued to breathe heavily from nervous tension.

Maria's jaw set firmly and her shoulders squared. "Do I look like a person who would have been in jail, sir?" she snapped, her eyes flashing.

"I just ask the questions that are assigned, miss," he said, furrowing a brow. He then added, "And do you have any weapons on your person?" He again the same as raped her with his eyes.

She grabbed at her throat, remembering the gun. But she also remembered that no man would get near her to remove her clothes while Alberto was around. She knew that he would kill the person first. "No. No weapon," she said quietly. "Do I look the sort who would carry a weapon, sir?" she said, fluttering her

132

lashes nervously toward him.

The man's eyes wavered and a slow flush rose upward from his neck. "No. Guess not," he mumbled. He entered some more into his journal, then asked, "Is there anyone in your family who is insane? Mentally disturbed?"

"No. No one," Maria murmured, glancing quickly at Alberto, reminded to still be a bit worried about his state of mind.

"Anyone afflicted with contagious ailments?"

"No. No one."

The questions seemed to go on forever, then Maria was directed to another table, where a lady attired in white stood waiting. "Here, miss," the lady said, taking Maria by the arm. "You must remove your jacket and roll up your shirt sleeve of your left arm."

"Why . . . ?" Maria gasped, seeing the lady holding onto a long-needled instrument.

"You are in need of an inoculation. All whom enter into America must be inoculated."

"And . . . why . . . ?"

"It's to prevent one from acquiring the dreaded disease called smallpox. Now please, do as I say. Roll up your sleeve as soon as you get your jacket removed."

Maria searched in desperation around her for Alberto, but saw that he was now seated, answering the long line of questions, the same as she had just done.

"Please, miss," the lady insisted, moving even closer to Maria.

Maria sighed, hating it when she felt the trembling beginning in her fingers. She had wanted to be brave enough to get through this whole ordeal without showing her fears. She wanted to show that she had strength. That all Italians were strong and could with-stand anything. But she *was* afraid. Oh, so afraid of that needle that was waiting to be plunged into her flesh.

She placed her violin case on the floor before her and slowly pulled her jacket off, holding it in front of the gun's bulge beneath her shirt, then rolled up her shirt sleeve. She held her arm out, turning her face in another direction, closing her eyes. When the sharp point made its intrusion into her arm, and then over and over again, like several pinpricks being made over a small, circled area of her arm, she felt as though she might faint. She teetered for a moment, then ordered herself to stand upright. No Italian would faint just from pinpricks into the arm. No. She just couldn't.

"Okay. That's it, miss," the lady said. "Move on so the next person can step forward."

Maria's eyes widened. The whole area throbbed as though the lady was continuing her assault. She turned her eyes back around and looked at her arm, seeing a circle of redness where the needle had been inserted. "You are finished?" she whispered.

"Yes. Now please move along."

"Yes, ma'am," she said, pulling her jacket quickly on. Having been vaccinated in the left arm, she lifted her violin case with the right hand and inched her way through the crowd, all the while keeping an eye on Alberto. If she were to lose him, she would more than likely never see him again. She had never seen so many people at one time. They were swarming around her like bees.

She waited, anxious, until Alberto moved to her side, with the trunk lifted onto his right shoulder, mumbling some soft obscenities.

"Alberto?" Maria asked, going to him. "Are you all right?" His face had paled and the lids over his eyes had grown heavy.

"Such a crude way to welcome us into America," he continued to grumble, wincing when Maria touched him on the left arm, close to where his own vaccination now throbbed and ached.

"Are we now free to move onward? Is our Americanization over with?" she asked anxiously.

"I was told that a ferry awaited us. Out on the far end of the island. It will take us once again to the piers on lower Manhattan's shores."

"And from there? What then, Alberto?"

"I have already been directed to where we can catch the train called the 'National Limited' that will carry us to Papa's town," he said, beginning to move forward, anxious to be away from the drudgery of this large room, where children shrieked and women babbled so with one another.

Maria panted by his side, trying to keep up with the pace of his long legs. She knew that she was almost as tall, but her energies had almost been drained from inside her. As a man brushed against her left arm, she recoiled in pain. "My arm . . . it aches so, Alberto," she whined. "It feels so heavy. As though it might even drop off. Does yours feel the same?"

"Mine? It feels as though a knot has formed beneath the pit of my arm," he grumbled, inhaling deeply the freshness of the air as he finally reached the outdoors. "But that doesn't matter, Maria," he quickly added. "Let's get away from this place. Come. Hurry along now. We must reach the ferry before it leaves us

135

behind. I wouldn't want to spend a night on this wretched island. I imagine the rats swarm thicker than even the people once nightfall comes in its total blackness."

Maria stepped gingerly along the wetness of the rocks beneath her feet, remembering having almost fallen earlier. Then when they reached the ferry, she followed alongside Alberto as he stepped high and climbed aboard. As was the boat that had carried them to this island, this ferry was crowded with immigrants who were as newly Americanized as Alberto and Maria.

Maria smiled to all who squeezed in around her, glad finally to see hope flashing in their eyes once again. Their ordeal of Ellis Island was being left behind them, and only a bright future lay ahead of them.

Shivers of delight rippled along Maria's flesh, now being able to see and enjoy the tall buildings of New York without having to fear anything. Her neck craned, trying to see to the tops of the ones closest. She so longed to go inside one of these, but she was too anxious to get to her Papa. Maybe one day, later on in her life, she could return and fully explore the expanses of New York and its people's ways of living.

"Now stay close beside me, Maria," Alberto urged as the ferry moved next to a pier and was secured by a rope. "New York is almost another country in itself, it seems. It must be even as large as Italy. Now don't take your eyes off me for one second. Do you understand?"

Maria swallowed hard. "Yes. I understand," she said. She pushed and shoved her way along, next to Alberto, until they were finally walking along a cobblestone street that lined the waters of the harbor. Maria's heart swelled inside her, wanting to laugh and shout that she had made it. She was in America . . . and had just become an American. "Do you have my papers, Alberto?" she asked anxiously, not wanting to lose the only thing that proved that she had indeed gone through the complete steps of Americanization that were required to be able to stay in America.

"Yes. I have yours with mine. In my inside jacket pocket. Don't worry. I won't let anything happen to those. They could mean the difference between life or death for the both of us. I'm sure of it."

Maria sniffed, glad to be leaving behind the strong aroma of dead fish and horse manure. She stepped high onto a curbing and then saw that they had reached an area that was mostly horses and carriages and fine ladies and gentlemen entering and leaving the harbor area. She looked behind her. Not only had they left the unpleasant smells behind, but also the long line of ships and the hectic atmosphere of the waterfront, and had entered an area of business establishments. Small shops lined each side of the street, enticing her to stop and stare. But Alberto just kept trudging along, head held high, ignoring the better class of people that were milling along the streets.

Maria got a glimpse of herself in a large plate glass window of a store and soon felt her face reddening. She had never seen such a sight before as herself and her brother who walked beside her. Their outfits looked even more pitiful than when she had at first hated having to wear them. They now were wrinkled, filth-laden, and her hat had been crunched, leaving the bill of it to hang limply over her forehead.

Feeling so self-conscious of her appearance, she

hung her head, not wanting anyone to see her face. She was humiliated. What if even Michael suddenly appeared before her? But she had to remember. Michael had seen her this way. He had even taken her into his room and had made love to her after having seen her look so terrible. She just hadn't known at that time . . . just how terrible . . . she had looked. She hadn't had a mirror at her Gran-mama's house to gaze into, to see the qualities about her appearance that were good . . . or poor. Now she was even more eager to get to her Papa's house . . . throw these dreaded clothes into a fire . . . and even laugh as she watched them burn.

"There. Over there," Alberto said anxiously. "There is the marvelous train that Papa wrote us about, the one we shall ride to get to Papa's town. Hurry. We don't want it leaving us behind."

Maria's eyes widened. To her, the train looked like some sort of black monster. And the smoke billowing upward from the smokestack reminded her of a dragon, puffing. People were boarding, attired in all sorts of ways. Some were almost as pitiful in appearance as she and Alberto, and some were elegant, the women in fully gathered dresses of silk, and the gentlemen with black frock coats and matching hats and breeches. The thing that grabbed Maria's attention the most about the women she was admiring were the different styles of hats perched atop their heads. Some hats had large feathers blowing in the gentleness of the breeze, and others appeared to be gardens, filled with assortments of beautifully colored flowers.

She sighed to herself. One day she would own such a hat. One day she would look just as lovely.

"Our tickets. I must first get our tickets," Alberto said, stopping, setting their trunk down beside him. He searched frantically inside his pockets, then smiled broadly when he pulled the two tickets out. They had been somewhat damaged, due to the wet, damp temperatures aboard the ship, but they still represented further adventures for brother and sister. Alberto squared his shoulders, then kissed the tickets. "Let's go, Maria," he said. He lifted the trunk to his shoulder and moved on along and boarded the train after having let Maria enter first.

Almost breathless from excitement, Maria moved into a car of the train, looking slowly around her, seeing how crowded it was. She recognized the look in many of the eyes, and knew this to be a look of immigrants, such as herself. She noticed that on this particular section of the train, none of the more elegant people were present. They had apparently been directed to finer cars. This particular car was drab, colorless, almost the same as that dreaded Ellis Island that would haunt Maria's dreams for many months to come. This car even stank almost the same, only more so of stale cigar smoke and an occasional whiff of some alcoholic beverage.

"Where can we sit, Alberto?" she whispered, inching her way down the long, narrow aisle.

"Just keep moving until you see two vacant seats," Alberto said, furrowing a brow. He had expected more from such a fine train. He had expected possibly even velveteen seats and shades at the window. But only dark, ugly, uncomfortable-appearing seats, most of which were already filled with travelers, met his eye.

"I see two. Just up ahead," Maria said, moving more

quickly, afraid someone else might get there before her and Alberto. Breathing hard, she rushed ahead and settled down onto the seat. She placed her violin case on her lap, eyeing Alberto anxiously as he moved next to her, setting his trunk out in the aisle. Maria then watched all around her, wondering where everyone else aboard this moving giant was going. She held her head high. She was going to her Papa . . . Giacomo Lazzaro. How proud she was to be able to say his name . . . and know that he wasn't all that far away, now.

Michael was relieved to finally feel the vibrations in the floor beneath his feet, knowing that the train was moving away from the busy depot. He lit another Cuban cigar. He pulled a green velveteen curtain aside, then stood with hands clasped tightly behind his back, watching the New York skyline pass by him.

At one time, New York had been his playground. He knew all the nightspots. He had frequented them all with the most beautiful of female companions. But he had grown tired of this fast pace and had taken his fortune to the quieter, more conservative city of Saint Louis, Missouri. There, he had discovered the United Mine Workers of America and what the union represented to the poor, and hadn't been able to resist becoming involved, so vividly remembering his youth, and how his own father had slaved in a small shoe shop, barely scraping in pennies.

Michael had learned to hustle early in life. Lower Manhattan became his stomping grounds. His skills became that of a shoeshine boy, and he shined the shoes of the richest politicians and bankers. The tips he would receive were quickly turned into higher earnings when he learned the art of gambling. Dark rooms in back alleys at the age of thirteen had been the beginnings of Michael's wealth. And now? At age thirty-five, he could buy and sell most of those people who had been the recipients of his skills as a shoeshine boy.

A rustle of a skirt behind him made Michael turn with a start. A slow smile curved his lips upward, seeing Alice Moberly standing at his side, waiting patiently for his acknowledgment of her presence in this magnificent private car of the famous National Limited Train.

Michael's eyes wavered as he pulled the cigar from between his lips, realizing that he had ignored Alice. He studied her now and how shatteringly pretty she was, attired in a pale green serge traveling suit that accentuated the smallness of her waist and the soft curve of her breasts, and her blazing red hair circled in a fancy pompadour atop her head. Her facial features were petite and her coloring much too pale, but highlighted with a touch of pink rouge on the shallow slope of her cheeks.

She flashed her green eyes upward, smiling seductively as her tongue wetted her lips. In the past, this would have set Michael's blood to racing, but not this time. Maria, and what they had shared, were too fresh in his mind. An emptiness had been left inside him when she had walked away from him and his offer of marriage.

"Michael, you haven't said two words to me," Alice purred, lifting her fingers to smooth a lapel of his navy blue, pin-striped woolen suit. She formed her lips into a soft pucker, as though ready to kiss him, then turned and walked away from him, sulking. "Not even a kiss,

141

Michael?" she said, turning on a heel, facing him once again, her eyes now narrow, anger reflected in deeper colors of green.

Michael placed his cigar in an ashtray and went to her, taking only a hand in his. "I'm sorry," he said. "I've much on my mind."

"It's been a long time between kisses, Michael," she said, tracing his lips with a forefinger. "I know of your restlessness. Your needs. Why is it you haven't pulled my clothes from me and thrown me across the bed? Has this trip changed you somehow?" She jerked her hand free, with lips suddenly straight and sealed, studying this man's blue eyes, the gentleness to the curve of his jaw and the hair that had now grown to curl in gold at the top of his shirt collar.

She had always marveled at his stubbornness when she had suggested that he wear the popular pomade that was used to slick a man's hair. Instead, Michael had preferred letting his hair lie in loose waves, curling at the ends, having liked being different, even though the sleekness of hair was more fashionable for men. He even parted it on the side, instead of in the middle, and these things made him appear more handsome than most men of his same age.

"Or is there another woman, Michael?" she whispered between clenched teeth. "Is that it? Did you meet another woman? Among the foreigners did you find someone who could please your sexual fantasies even better than I?"

Michael turned his back to her, knowing that the answer lay in the depths of his eyes. He knew that all she would have to do would be to take one look now, while his thoughts *were* so full of Maria, to reveal the truth to this woman who had been his steady female companion for two full years now.

Marriage had never been spoken of between Alice and himself. The sensual side to their relationship had begun shortly after Alice had become his private secretary, assisting him in his business, the mammoth Hopper Shoe Company that had grown to be known all over the country.

Alice, being closer to Michael's age than Maria, had already left a trail of tumultuous love affairs behind her, and this alone was reason enough for Michael to have chosen not to ask for her hand in marriage. He had been watching and waiting for the right woman . . . a virgin . . . an innocent . . . to take as a wife.

Maria. Oh, how he now ached for Maria. She was all that he had wanted in a wife, and even more so, being so gifted in beauty and bodily proportions. "Oh, God," he worried further to himself. She had trustingly given up her own virginity while in his arms. And now he had let her slip through his fingers. She was now gone from his life, to never be again. . . .

"Michael," Alice stormed, moving to his side. "You haven't heard a word I've said. Please tell me. What is it that's bothering you?"

Michael went to a desk and opened his journal, reading a few entries. "When will you begin typing the report, Alice?"

"Is that all you have to say, Michael? Are my skills as a typist suddenly more important than my skills as a lover?"

Michael scowled, slamming the palm of his hand on the desk top. "You must remember that you do get paid for clerical services," he said darkly.

"Michael . . . please. . . ."

"The journey was a long one, Alice," Michael grumbled. "I am tired. Please excuse the sharpness of my tongue."

An abundance of white lace was revealed when Alice slipped her jacket off. She smoothed her skirt with her fingers then went and sat down on a cushioned chair behind the smaller secretarial desk that sat facing Michael's. She rolled a sheet of paper into the Remington typewriter that Michael had purchased for her own private use shortly after she had been hired as his secretary. In only a matter of weeks she had mastered this new "contraption," as Michael still continued to call it.

"Hand me the journal, Michael," Alice said, straightening her back. "If work is what you want, work is what you shall get."

Michael closed the journal and carried it to her. "I would like to have the report ready for the union meeting upon my arrival in Saint Louis," he said. "You see, I also have duties to perform. I was asked to make this trip with a specific purpose in mind, so it is only proper that I be ready for any questions from those union members who put their trust in me."

"But, you are so somber," Alice said, reaching into a top drawer, pulling out a cigarette.

Michael struck a match and lighted it for her, then relighted his cigar. He went and sat down behind the larger desk, positioning his feet to rest on the top, crossing his legs. He inserted his hands into his breeches pockets, fitting his thumbs to hang over the outside. "The immigrants are a sad lot," he reflected. "Well, I should say most of them are," he quickly added. Maria's face flashed before his eyes, making the

144

pulsebeat throb in his temple. If he let himself, he could even feel the touch of her lips. . . .

"Most of them you say?" Alice asked coolly. "How can you tell one from another? All the ones that I have seen are dressed in drab clothes and slouch so as they walk, like scared peasants."

Michael pushed himself up from the chair, trying to keep from lashing back at her. He knew that to do so would be to reveal too many truths to her. Instead, he went to the liquor cabinet and poured himself a glass of port, then slouched down into a heavily upholstered chair, turning the glass in his hands, watching the overhead light reflect into it, like diamonds on display. "These . . . uh . . . peasants. . . ." he murmured, then jerked his head up to glower at Alice. "They are soon to discover what a mistake it was to come to this land of opportunity. The peasants? They will soon find out that only drudgery awaits them. Yes. They are afraid now, having left the only way of life behind them that they have known since the day they were born. But wait until they reach the town of Hawkinsville and meet up with Nathan Hawkins. Then they will really have just cause to be afraid and walk as though defeated. Because they will be. Only the union can give them hope. Only I can intervene and see that the wrongs are made right."

Once again his thoughts returned to Maria. He was glad that she wasn't a part of this train carrying these people to a life of impoverishment. At least Maria and her brother had been paid passage by their father, instead of by the likes of Nathan Hawkins.

"So you found out that what we all suspected was true?" Alice asked, flicking ashes from her cigarette into an ashtray. "Everyone aboard that ship did have their passage paid by Nathan Hawkins? They are all headed to work as slave labor for this man's coal mines?"

"It appears so, Alice," he grumbled. "It appears so."

"That's so horrible, Michael," Alice said, mashing her cigarette out, then opened the journal and began to study it.

Again Michael pondered over having discovered Maria and Alberto as part of this ship's passengers. He had thought the ship had been taken to Italy only at Nathan Hawkins's expense. It was Nathan Hawkins's ship.

Michael had only lucked out himself by having played the role so well of a buyer for a winery, saying that all other ships had been booked completely, and that he had a deadline to meet, convincing the ship's captain to let him travel along with him this one time. He smiled to himself, remembering even having been given the private cabin of the bastard Nathan Hawkins, since Hawkins hadn't taken this voyage himself.

Michael knew that if Hawkins ever found out the true identity of the man who had used his cabin in every way possible, the craggy face of Hawkins would grow even paler than Hawkins's eyes, which always appeared empty . . . unfeeling.

Damn. Michael so hated himself for not having found out the destination of Maria and Alberto. When he had asked Maria, she hadn't remembered, and when she had suggested she search in her violin case where she had the name written on train tickets, Michael had thought it hadn't been necessary, having thought they would have plenty of time to discuss this later. But as time went on, their moments together had been spent talking about other things besides where the journey would end for the both of them.

And then there was Alberto. Alberto had refused to even talk with Michael, let alone discuss such congenial and simple matters of life that Michael would have so liked to have shared with him. No. Alberto had been close-mouthed. He had mainly been there to protect Maria, whom he had hovered over as though he was the husband of the beautiful female at his side.

Damn. He had to quit thinking about Maria. She was no longer a part of his existence. His main concern now was for the welfare of this new group of immigrants and what the success of his findings could mean to the success of the unions in Southern Illinois.

"This private car of this train," he said, looking around him, seeing the plushness of the seats, the velveteen-covered bed at the far end, and the fringe-trimmed curtains at the windows.

"Did you say something, Michael?" Alice asked, eyes wide.

"I feel a sense of guilt, knowing I am traveling in such luxury, and the immigrants having to travel in such crowded, smelly quarters as the car they have been directed into. Is it even fair that I have the money to use to rent such a private car as this?"

"God, Michael. You carry the burden of the poor on your shoulders. Must you always?"

"I was just as poor once," he mumbled, pushing himself up from the chair. He walked to Alice's side, bending to turn the pages in the journal. He suddenly smelled the aroma of her perfume as it circled upward and into his nose. Why hadn't he noticed it before?

147

Wasn't it even the perfume he had brought back to her from France? He cleared his throat nervously, pointing to an entry.

"Do you see this?" he said. "This was entered on a day that two bodies were thrown over the ship's side. These two women died from consumption. They left behind two families in need of mother and wife. Their journey started on the mournful side, wouldn't you say? And I have many more of these same entries. This ship is a death ship. And even the ones who do make it to America too soon find that they wish they had been the ones tossed into the hungry claws of the sea when they find what is awaiting them."

"Did you speak with many of these people?"

"Those who were not too afraid to speak to a stranger."

"And each spoke of Nathan Hawkins?"

"They had only the deepest respect for the man who had paid their passage."

Alice rose from the chair, taking Michael's hand in hers, guiding him toward the bed. "Michael, you must relax. You must let me massage your neck and back muscles. I have never seen you so tied up in such bleak thoughts before. Let me help to ease this all from your mind."

Michael unsnapped the tie from his shirt, then slipped his suit jacket and shirt off, revealing his massive chest that was heavily covered with curly blonde chest hairs. He sighed deeply as he stretched out onto the softness of the bed. "Yes. I'm sure you're right," he said, turning to lie on his stomach.

He closed his eyes and let Alice's fingers begin to knead and rub his flesh, already feeling it loosening beneath her touch. When her lips exchanged places with her fingers, he tensed for a moment, then flipped onto his back and yanked her down atop him, crushing his lips against hers. She wasn't Maria but she was with him, ready, willing to help possibly erase Maria and all the mounting problems from his mind.

His fingers went to her blouse and reached beneath it. In no way did this woman's breasts compare with those of Maria. Maria's had been so large, so firm, so inviting to the touch from both his lips and hands. But as the need for a woman . . . any woman . . . built inside him . . . he grabbed Alice's breasts and began brutally to squeeze them.

"Oh, Michael," Alice moaned, reaching down to unbutton his breeches with trembling fingers. "It's been too long. I almost went wild without you. Darling, please . . . don't . . . leave again for a long time. These trips? They just mean loneliness for me. . . ."

Michael pushed her gently away from him. "Undress, Alice," he said thickly, kicking his shoes off, then slipping his breeches and undergarment down. He watched her hungrily as she removed the combs from her hair, letting her hair cascade in red waves around her shoulders.

Michael felt the familiar heat rising in his loins. The last time he had experienced these feelings, Maria had been the cause. Oh, Maria. My Maria, he thought sadly to himself, then reached his arms outward as Alice stepped from the last of her garments.

When Alice was beside him on the bed, he rolled over and climbed atop her, not wasting any time as he thrust his manhood inside her and began working anxiously in and out. He gritted his teeth and closed his eyes, moaning, and when the spasms began, he whispered the wrong name. . . .

Alice kicked and scratched, screaming. "Get off me you bastard," she shouted. "Do you hear? I hate you, Michael Hopper. I hate you."

Michael scooted to sit upright next to her, furrowing his heavy blonde brows. "Damn it," he growled. "What did I do?"

Alice began gathering her clothes, stomping angrily around the room. She glared toward him. "You don't know?" she whispered between clenched teeth, stopping to study him, not even knowing him any longer. He had changed. The voyage . . . someone on that voyage . . . had changed him. Someone named . . . Maria. . . .

"What the hell are you talking about?" Michael asked, stammering.

"Who is this . . . Maria . . . Michael . . . ?" Alice asked, stammering.

He turned, swallowing hard, paling. "What did you say . . . ?" he gasped.

"Who is this Maria whose name you just whispered when we were . . . making love . . . ?"

"God. Oh, God. Did I . . . do . . . that . . . ?" he blurted. He turned his back to her, hanging his head. He began to knead his brow, now knowing that he had to find Maria. He would look for her . . . even until his death, if need be. . . .

Chapter Seven

Placing her nose against the pane of glass next to her, Maria watched the land race by outside the train window. It seemed to her the further they traveled, the flatter the land became.

Illinois. She had just heard the whispers of those behind her that this land had been given the name of Illinois. The "Prairie State." And this land was where her Papa had settled. In only a matter of hours she would be able to rush into his arms, feel once again the security that those arms had always represented to her since the day of her birth.

As she continued to watch, she gazed upon a great sea of grass, an endless expanse that flashed and rippled in the wind in soft wine colors. It was a land where there seemed to be nothing but grass meeting sky, except where small towns would suddenly appear alongside the railroad tracks and in streamside groves.

"How much further now, Alberto?" she asked, turning her wide, dark eyes to her brother.

He was absorbed in a deck of cards that he had managed to steal from one of the card sharks aboard the ship. He was placing them on his lap, studying them, then stacking them back together once again to shuffle them.

Maria's brow furrowed, not liking this new pastime of her brother's. She could see a future of possible trouble for him if he persisted with such a thing. Hadn't it gotten him in enough trouble aboard the ship? Hadn't he yet learned that it was the devil's game?

"I'm sure it won't be long now," he murmured, pushing his hat back from his forehead, looking annoyed for having been disturbed.

Maria's eyes wavered. "Alberto, those cards. What you are doing is nonsense. Why don't you put them away? When we reach Papa's house, you will have more to do than play that silly card game."

"Don't start bossing me around, Maria," he scowled. "Sisters are to be seen, not heard. Didn't you know that? Especially a twin sister."

Anger seized Maria. She slapped at Alberto's hands, knocking the cards from them, making them scatter on the floor. "You've changed, Alberto," she said. "Since leaving Italy, you've changed."

"You pick up those cards," he growled.

"I will not," she said stubbornly. "And when we arrive at Papa's, please don't let him see them. I don't think he would approve. Especially since you always play that game with money. Alberto, what do you think Papa would think of that?"

Alberto laughed self-assuredly. "What would he think?" he boasted. "He'd probably be proud to see that I've learned another way of making lire, dollars as they call them here in America. And it's so simple. No hard manual labor. Maria, don't you know how long it took us to make just a few coins while we worked so hard cleaning chimneys in Pordenone each day? Why, this is easy *and* fun. One would be foolish to not do it, especially one who knows the tricks of the trade."

Maria crossed her arms. "And you do, Alberto?" she sulked.

"Very much so."

"And you forget the blow to your head that one time because you had let yourself get mixed up with such characters who play this game?"

Shadows crossed Alberto's face. He reached down and picked up the cards and thrust them inside his front right jacket pocket. "Must you always be reminding me of that?" he growled, knowing that she would most truly be shocked if she knew the truth of those nights with Sam and Grace. He closed his eyes, not even himself wanting to be reminded of it.

"As often as needed," she said, setting her jaw firmly.

Alberto reached over and took one of Maria's hands. He squeezed it fondly, watching her, pleading with the darkness of his eyes. "I really would rather you didn't speak to Papa of this card game I have grown so fond of," he said. "I guess he probably wouldn't like it that I have found such a way to play with money."

"Maybe Papa has found a pleasant job making good enough money so that we won't ever have to worry about such things again," Maria murmured. "Wouldn't that just be too grand, Alberto?"

"Don't count on it," he answered, looking around him at all the other immigrants who were now a part of America and its working force. And he had to remember all those who had come before them. How could the Americans have so many job opportunities and fulfill their own population's needs for jobs as well?

No. Something inside him told him that hardships could possibly be ahead. He sensed it. He had even read this between the lines that his Papa had written when he had sent the tickets and money for passage to America. If Papa had been well off . . . happy . . . secure . . . it would have shown in the words of his letter.

A conductor, thin and tall, dressed in all black, began to saunter down the aisle of the train, rambling, "Hawkinsville next stop. Please make sure you get all your belongings and step carefully from the train when it comes to a full halt. Nathan Hawkins will have a representative at the depot to direct you all to your assigned quarters."

Alberto and Maria glanced at one another quickly, eyes wide. "Did I hear right, Maria?" Alberto blurted, eyeing the conductor as he moved on away from him repeating the same speech over and over again. Alberto turned and eyed Maria once again. "Did he . . . really say . . . Nathan Hawkins?"

"Yes. I'm sure of it," she whispered, watching all around her as the crowded car became a hubbub of activity as people pulled baggage down from above them and children were made to calm down and sit on trunks that had been placed in the aisles next to the seats.

"Why would all these people . . . ?" Alberto said.

"Yes. Why would they all have association with this Nathan Hawkins who Papa wrote briefly about? What could be the connection with these Italians . . . and Nathan Hawkins? And the name of the town? It *is* the name . . . the same as. . . ."

"Yes. As Nathan Hawkins," Alberto grumbled. "Damned if I know what it's all about." He grew silent as the train's brakes began to screech loudly.

154

When the train depot came into view, Maria's heart began to pound. Was she truly only moments away from seeing her dear Papa? Would he have changed? She knew that she had. Would he be able to see the change in her? On this journey, she had become a woman. She felt no different, but she knew that it possibly showed in her eyes and the way in which she held herself. She had come of age . . . and she was proud of it. The only drawback was the fact that she had lost Michael in the process . . . when she had said her goodbyes to him. Oh, Michael, she thought to herself. Wherever you are, I shall always love you.

"I guess maybe this car is the only one to unload at this town," Alberto said, watching the people rushing toward the door when the conductor opened it, motioning with his hand for them to come ahead.

Maria remembered having seen the more fancily attired women and men at the New York train depot entering other cars all along the line. She was anxious to know where they were going. She lifted her violin case and listened to Alberto groan when he lifted the trunk to his shoulder, then moved on behind him toward the door. When she moved next to the conductor, she stopped and said, "Sir? Where might the people on the rest of the train be going?"

"To Saint Louis, Missouri," he said, then added, "But never you mind about them. You just move on out of this train and step aside so the train can get on its way. Like I said, Nathan Hawkins will have a representative to take care of your needs."

Maria lifted her chin into the air, fluttering her lashes nervously. "My Papa will be here to meet me and my brother," she said proudly. "We won't need the likes of a Mr. Nathan Hawkins." Then she stopped and put her hand to her throat when she suddenly realized what this conductor had said . . . about . . . Saint Louis. . . .

Saint Louis was Michael's destination. She now remembered his having said this. She reached out and touched the conductor on the arm. "Did you say . . . Saint Louis . . . ? That this train was going to Saint Louis . . . ?"

"Your ears work pretty good, young lady," he answered. "Saint Louis is indeed the destination."

Maria felt a desperation seize her. Had Michael been on this train? Had he been there the whole time she had, and she hadn't been aware of it? She wanted to rush back through this car and to the next and the next, looking for him, to get a glimpse of him just one more time. But a familiar voice made her heart leap. She looked ahead and standing outside the train with arms outstretched was her Papa. Tears filled her eyes as she raced down the steps of the train, almost tripping, and fell into her Papa's arms. She placed her violin on the cobblestone street and then hugged him strongly. "Oh, Papa," she murmured, over and over again, sobbing with delight.

Then as he pushed her away from him to hold her at arm's length, he said, "Maria. My Maria. Let me take a look at you." His eyes raked over her, then he said, "My, oh, my. You've grown into a lady for sure."

Through the blur of tears, Maria saw that he had changed. Giacomo Lazzaro had aged. He appeared much older now than his forty-nine years. He was no longer a strong-looking man. He even had a slight curve to his back. Maria wiped at her eyes, absorbing his presence even more, seeing that he looked more squatty and short than she remembered.

"Papa," she whispered. "Are you all right?"

His face was slightly distorted by the large dose of chewing tobacco he had tucked inside his cheek, and his hair had thinned to only thin wisps blowing in the gentle breeze.

Giacomo spat onto the street beside him and wiped his lips with the back of his hand. He appeared to be quiet with worry and it showed in the depth of his dark brown eyes. "I have us a place to stay and a job for Alberto and me," he said, forcing a smile. "What more could a body ask of the Americans?"

He turned to Alberto and reached his arms toward him. "And, son," he said proudly. "I see you got Maria and yourself safely across that large body of water. This makes you a man. I'm proud of you."

Alberto could contain himself no longer. He flung himself into his Papa's arms and hugged him tightly. "Papa. Oh, Papa, how glad I am to be with you."

"Such a show of affection for your old Papa?" Giacomo chuckled, patting Alberto fondly on the back. "Does this old heart good, it does. I'm glad to have you . . . home . . . with me . . . son." His gaze searched Alberto's face. "And whiskers? It makes you look even more to be a man."

The train whistle blew shrilly, making Maria turn with a start. She had forgotten about Michael . . . about Saint Louis . . . but now she was keenly aware of the train cars that were moving slowly on by her. Craning her neck, she peered searchingly into each of the windows, wondering if Michael might at any moment be at one of those windows and see her. If so, what would she do? Run after the train and demand

157

that it be stopped? Or stand and watch her heart being carried away from her once again?

But the faces that looked back at her were those of strangers . . . finely dressed ladies and gentlemen . . . but . . . strangers. Her heart ached when she saw the last car come into view. She looked even more closely into its windows, seeing that this car was quite different from any of the others. There were fewer windows and there were no people sitting beside them. These windows displayed the finest of green velveteen curtains, fringed on the edges, and behind these she could see only a slight movement of a person . . . a woman . . . with the reddest hair that Maria had ever seen . . . and attired . . . very . . . scantily. . . .

Maria's face reddened, and she looked suddenly away, knowing that car had to be a special car to have so few passengers. Remembering how she had traveled, in the heat and smelly surroundings of the crowded car, made her cast her eyes downward, feeling even a bit humble. She had to wonder how it might feel to have wealth . . . beautiful clothes. . . .

"Let's go home, children," Giacomo said, fingers snapping his suspenders, turning, waddling away in a walk that was only his own, his head bobbing nervously on his shoulders.

"Do you mind calling America and this house you are now living in home, Papa?" Alberto said, looking at the way his Papa was dressed in loose-fitted, dark breeches and matching shirt. They were so wrinkled, Alberto knew that no iron had been set to them. His earlier worries were now crowding in on him—that his Papa hadn't found an easy life here after all; in fact, it appeared that whatever work he did each day had

158

begun to make him into an old man much too soon.

"A home is what you make it, Alberto," Giacomo answered, spitting into the wind.

"How much further until we reach it, Papa?" Maria asked breathlessly.

"Just down the road a piece," Giacomo said. "Just a short piece and we'll be there."

Maria glanced backwards just as the caboose of the train made a turn on the tracks in the far distance and disappeared from sight. A longing shot through her, and she wished to be on that train, just knowing that Michael possibly was. Hadn't he left the ship at nearly the same time she and Alberto had? Wouldn't he have probably been as anxious to get to his American home as she had been to get to hers? Wouldn't he have boarded the nearest train that left the earliest? Just the same as she and Alberto had done.

She lowered her eyes, blinking back a tear. "All those people at the depot," she said, glancing backwards once again. "On the train, the conductor said something about them having to be met by a representative of Nathan Hawkins. You know. The man you made brief mention of in your letter to Alberto and me. What does it mean, Papa? Why would all these people who have come from Italy like Alberto and myself even be wanting to see this Nathan Hawkins?"

Giacomo's shoulders slumped even more and his brow furrowed. He chewed angrily for a moment, then answered in a deep, thick tone of voice. "This man . . . Nathan Hawkins . . . pretty much owns us all," he grumbled.

Alberto stepped in front of his Papa, glowering, reaching out to stop his father's pace. "What do you

159

mean, Papa?" he stormed. "How could anyone own anyone? I do not understand."

"Take a look at most of the people who stand waitin'," Giacomo said, turning, seeing the dark, drab clothes of those who waited still at the depot, and the desperation on their faces. "Most of these Italians—whom I know none of by name since they have come from all parts of our beloved country—have come to America to live in this town of Hawkinsville, which Nathan Hawkins settled and named after himself many years ago."

"What's that got to do with it?" Maria asked, looking into the distance, seeing what was probably the town that her papa was speaking of. It looked bleak . . . cold. . . .

"Nathan Hawkins bought and now owns all the houses in Hawkinsville," Giacomo continued. "He even owns all the stores, which are few, and the coal mine where I and all the rest of the Italians work."

The color drained from Alberto's face. "What's this you say . . . about . . . a coal . . . mine . . . Papa?" he blurted. "Did you . . . say . . . ?"

"Yes. I said I work in a coal mine. And that's where you will also be workin', Alberto."

Alberto placed his trunk on the ground and then his fingers before his eyes, still seeing the blackness beneath his nails and in the pores of his skin, from his years of working as a chimney sweep. Tears stung the corners of his eyes. He had thought his life in America would be one of cleanliness . . . with a job of honor . . . not degradation . . . as he knew the coal mines must make one feel, since one had to work in dark caverns many miles below the surface of the earth. "No, Papa,"

160

he mumbled. "You must be joking. Tell me . . . you . . . are . . . joking."

"It is a truth I hate to admit to," Giacomo said, wiping his mouth with the back of a hand. Alberto and Maria glanced quickly at their Papa's fingers . . . and then at his face, seeing the traces of coal dust that they hadn't noticed before. They had been too anxious to see their Papa to notice these things that had meant nothing to them . . . until now.

"Why, Papa?" Maria said, taking one of his hands in hers, feeling the veins, so taut, like the veining of a dried up leaf.

"I was among one of the immigrants bought and paid for by that Nathan Hawkins," he grumbled, reaching inside his shirt pocket, to get another plug of chewing tobacco to stick into the corner of his mouth.

"You . . . were . . . ?" Alberto gasped, paling even more.

"Yes. I never told anyone back home, but I had heard word of this man bein' so generous as to pay passage to America, guaranteeing a respectable job and house if a person would choose to take advantage of this rare opportunity. My dream was always of comin' to America. How could I refuse?"

"So you work for that man . . . and live . . . in *his* house?" Maria said in a near whisper, feeling something tearing at the corner of her heart.

"Yes," Giacomo said, faltering. "One of his houses. There are many."

Maria set her jaws firmly. "And us, Papa? Alberto and myself? Are we . . . also . . . owned . . . by this . . . man . . . ?" she suddenly blurted, trembling inside. She had thought she had come to a land of freedom, to a

161

house owned by her papa. It was all becoming a nightmare. Why? Her papa should have told them. Why?

"Yes," Giacomo answered, turning to walk on toward a horse and buckboard-style wagon that was at the side of the road, hitched to a tree limb. "When one lives in Hawkinsville, one is owned by Nathan Hawkins."

"God," Alberto moaned, kneading his brow. He lifted the trunk to his shoulder, but feeling more than its weight on his body. He felt the weight of a future of many years of labor . . . hard labor . . . pressing down upon him. And in the dark shafts of a mine? Where he would continue to get blacker and blacker? Would he ever be able to be a respectable citizen, dressed in fine clothes, and be able to flash clean, well-groomed fingernails? God. When he had played cards, how he'd hated letting anyone see the filth beneath his nails. Damn. He didn't want to work in a coal mine. Damn. Damn.

When Maria reached the wagon, she placed her violin in the back, then let her papa help her up onto the seat. "Our passage to America, Papa?" she said. "Did Nathan Hawkins . . . pay . . . for it?"

She scooted over so Alberto could position himself on one side of her and her papa on the other. Her papa lifted the reins, shouting loudly to the one lone black mare. "Yes, Maria, I had no other way," he finally answered.

"But, you never said . . . it wasn't . . . your money," Alberto said. "On board ship, no one mentioned it. We seemed to be apart from all the rest. Now I remember this. All the others seemed to stay to themselves."

"I persuaded Nathan Hawkins to let me do this in

this way in order to keep my dignity in the Lazzaro family," he answered. "I knew that you would have to be told once you arrived, but I didn't want your gran-mama nor Aunt Helena to know. Please understand."

"Oh, Papa," Maria said, wrapping her arm around his waist, hugging him. "It's all right. Truly it is. All that truly matters now is that we are together. Finally together. And nothing will ever part us again. We are a family . . . an alliance of love. We will fight for our freedom. Together."

"There ain't no way to fight," Giacomo mumbled. "There are no different jobs for us immigrants. Only these that Nathan Hawkins has given us. And if anyone threatens to leave Hawkinsville, to go to an-other city, he threatens right back, saying that he can find ways to send them back to Italy. We are caught up in somethin' ugly here, but at least we are alive . . . well, and alive. . . ."

Maria felt hatred simmering inside. She had thought "revenge" earlier when she had heard of this Nathan Hawkins and his evil ways. Now she felt even a stronger urge to get even with him for having tricked her people . . . her own papa. She would find a way. She didn't want her papa and Alberto to have to spend the rest of their lives working in the filth and dangers of a coal mine. America had meant hope . . . not despair.

As the wagon moved into the outskirts of the small town, Maria looked in silence all around her. Even the brightness of the sun of this October day couldn't help to improve the appearance of the surroundings. The streets were laid out like cowpaths, with only bits of sidewalk in front of the business establishments. Faded-out, false-fronted shacks were wedged in be-

163

tween undertaking parlors and saloons. Only a few men were standing, browsing at the doors of these establishments, but the noise surfacing from within made one quite aware of the boisterousness of those who were inside. The loud sound of pianos clinking and the high-pitched laughter of women made Maria cringe. It reminded her of the many books about the West that she had read. But this was Illinois. She had thought it to be filled with only gentle people . . . as gentle as the winds that blew across the straight stretches of the land.

"Are these people of our kind who frequent the saloons, Papa?" she whispered, looking sheepishly into the windows, trying to see who could be making so much of this type of noise. Surely they were drunk. But the women? What women would allow themselves to mingle with such men . . . unless . . . they were of the bawdy-house kind . . . ?

"Not too many," Giacomo said, glancing a bit sideways as someone was tossed from a door of one of these saloons. He slouched his shoulders a bit more then continued to speak. "They come from the next town. A town called Creal Springs. It seems they ain't allowed to raise such a fuss there. In fact, no saloons are even allowed there."

Maria looked into the distance. "Where is this town? Is it far away?"

"Only a few minutes' drive by horse and wagon," he said. "But I seldom go there. We Italians are encouraged to stay here in our smaller community . . . to buy from the country store that Nathan Hawkins owns. In fact, most Italians are eager to shop there because Nathan Hawkins doesn't make us pay for what we buy right away."

Alberto craned his neck to see around Maria. His eyes grew wide. "How can that be, Papa? If he's so evil, why would he let you buy things without paying for them at the time you're buying them?"

"Most miners need food way before they receive their paychecks," Giacomo said, slapping the horse with the reins. "So they are welcomed to Nathan Hawkins's where they are allowed to sign a slip of paper that states they will pay when their paychecks arrive."

Alberto began to knead his brow, settling against the back of the seat. "Doesn't sound quite right to me," he mumbled. "This Nathan Hawkins is up to something. I just know it." He scooted to the edge of the seat once again, eyeing his Papa. "Have you ever signed such a paper, Papa?" he asked thickly.

"Yes. Many times. . . ."

Maria's mouth went slack. "But, Papa, you don't even know how to count very well. Are you sure he isn't tricking you in some way? Are you sure when you pay, you are paying for only what you bought?"

Giacomo laughed hoarsely. "No one is goin' to trick me out of my money," he said. "And don't you know I knew enough of numbers to teach both you and Alberto? Maria, you don't have much faith in me."

Maria's eyes lowered. "I'm sorry, Papa. Truly I am."

Giacomo spat chewing tobacco. "I know it sounds fishy, but so far, no one has complained of any wrong-doings. Feedin' the kids is the first thing they think about. Anything else is of less importance. Always. Remember. Family . . . strong family feelings is the only way of us Italians."

165

Maria clasped her hands onto her lap, continuing to look around her, trying to not worry about all these discoveries. Then when her Papa guided the wagon down another street, what Maria saw made her insides begin to churn. On each side of her were row after row of tiny frame houses. None of them had been painted. They were bleak and were crowded together, with not even curtains at the windows. Behind the houses, Maria got her first glimpse of the coal mine and of its big sheet-iron tipple as it stood graceless into the sky. The houses had been crowded at the edge of the mine from which black, dusty chat seemed to have poured so heavily that it was apparent that neither trees nor gardens could grow. It was a barren wasteland all around the houses and the mine, and even the silence was led by silence.

Maria cringed more inside the further her Papa traveled down this street. She eyed each house as they passed, wondering which one would be the one she would have to be a part of. She ached inside, having dreamed of life so much different than what she was finding. Then her eyes shifted upward. Yes . . . these houses had chimneys. Why had she even thought they would not? But she did know that she wouldn't have to clean them. Alberto and her Papa had . . . a . . . job. She would not be required to work. She would devote her time to making her brother and father comfortable . . . as comfortable as possible . . . under the circumstances.

"This is it. Home," Giacomo said, nodding toward a house that was identical to the ones Maria had been gazing upon. Giacomo guided the wagon into a narrow drive and pulled the reins tightly, urging the horse to stop. He then jumped from the wagon and secured the reins around a low tree limb.

Maria climbed slowly from the wagon, then followed along behind her Papa and Alberto, clutching onto the handle of her violin case, looking all around her, feeling the complete loneliness of the surroundings grabbing at her. When she began to climb the steps that led upward onto a porch, she felt the steps give a bit beneath the weight of her feet. She grabbed for Alberto's arm and let him assist her the rest of the way. She gazed into his face, seeing the same torment in his eyes that she knew was in her own. What they had left behind, far away in Italy, had been better than what they had now come to.

But maybe once she was inside, she would see a difference, Maria thought to herself, hurrying her pace as her Papa opened a screen door, then the main door. He stepped aside and let both Maria and Alberto enter, then followed behind them.

Maria's hopes quickly faded. She sat her violin case down on the floor that was barren of any carpeting, a floor that had wide cracks between the oak strips of wood, showing earth beneath it only a few feet below her. She wrapped her arms around herself, feeling the draft even now. The aroma was that of damp earth and mustiness, making her nose twitch nervously.

Her eyes moved on around her, seeing one overstuffed chair that had its stuffing hanging from it in loose shreds of graying cotton; a lone kerosene lamp sitting on a table that had been made from strips of wood nailed awkwardly together; and a pot-bellied stove that glowed orange from the heat inside it.

The walls were the same as the floor . . . barren . . .

with tiny, gaping cracks, revealing the outside world if she looked closely enough, and the windows were stained a dirty yellow, void of curtains or shades.

Maria turned to her Papa, who had been watching her. "Papa, is this . . . really . . . your American home?" she murmured. She felt a deep pity . . . sorrow . . . for her father. She could see the remorsefulness in the depth of his brown eyes. He walked away from her and opened the stove, spitting into the flames.

"The best I can do, Maria," he finally answered, going to slouch down onto the one chair in the room.

"But this isn't even good enough for an animal," Alberto grumbled, placing the trunk on the floor. He felt insulted that this man Nathan Hawkins could get away with such a thing as this. He eyed the cracks in the wall and the flooring beneath his feet. He clenched his hands into two tight fists, determined to make things change. He would find a way. Maybe his Papa couldn't . . . maybe his Papa was compelled to let this stranger control his life . . . but Alberto just would not let this happen to himself. No. He had to find a way. He just had to. . . .

"And the rest of the rooms of this house, Papa?" Maria said, moving toward a door. "Are they the same?"

"The same," he answered, placing a fresh plug of chewing tobacco in the corner of his mouth.

Maria moved on into the kitchen, seeing first a makeshift table and three chairs in the middle of the room. They were unpainted and black from fingerprints where many people's hands had touched. Another stove glowed orange in this room, but it was not of the pot-bellied kind. It was broader, with space to place cooking utensils atop it. Maria had seen pictures of these in catalogues. At least this was one luxury that she hadn't had in Italy. She could remember her Gran-mama stooping before the fireplace many hours at a time, placing large kettles into the flames, even baking bread in the coals.

"There's no running water in the house, Maria," Alberto said, moving to her side.

She turned, eyes wide. "How do you know?"

"I just asked Papa."

"Where . . . do we get water for cooking . . . washing dishes and laundry . . . and for bathing? We at least had water at Gran-mama's house. We had to pump it up from the ground, but at least we had water."

"There's a faucet somewhere up the street that all the women use," Alberto said, going to the back door, looking out, seeing still no grass . . . nor trees. All he could see was the damn mine's tipple standing so tall and erect into the sky, as though it was a person, laughing at him, knowing that it would be pulling almost his soul from him when he went into the coal mine's bowels each day.

Maria had a look of weariness about her when she moved on into another room. She sighed with relief when she saw a bed . . . an actual bed . . . standing at the far end of the room. She went to it and touched the iron bedstead that had rusted from dampness, then the mattress. The mattress was thin, hard, but it was better than having to sleep on leaves as she had been forced to do while living at her Gran-mama's house.

"There is a bed for each of us," Giacomo said, suddenly entering the room. "I did see to it that we have that luxury in America. I spent my first several months'

169

wages on these beds. But it was well worth it. I get me a full night's sleep most nights . . . that is . . . when I'm not too cold. I can't seem to keep the fires burnin' all night."

Maria went to Giacomo and placed her arm around his neck. "It's the cracks in the walls *and* floors, Papa," she murmured. "No one could keep a house warm in such conditions."

"And we don't have stoves in the bedrooms. That's another reason," Giacomo said, moving back to the kitchen. "But I can't expect to have everything at once. What we have will just have to do for a while."

Maria followed behind him. "And there is just the one other bedroom?" she asked, going to a roll of shelves, picking up dishes and silverware, seeing how they were caked with dried food. Yes. This kitchen had been lacking a female's touch.

"Alberto and I will share the other bedroom," Giacomo said, placing a tea kettle on the stove. "We each have a bed, though."

Something grabbed at Maria's heart. "Papa, I had hoped . . . that . . . uh . . . your house would have . . . uh . . . a bathroom," she said, blushing.

Giacomo laughed hoarsely, pulling a chair up to the kitchen table, sitting down. "No. No bathroom. If you'll look out the window at the far left of the yard, you'll see a neat little privy for your important private needs."

"I had so hoped," Maria sighed, going to the door, seeing a small square of a building that had a door hanging loosely on hinges, gaping open.

"I'm sorry, honey," Giacomo said. "I know this ain't much. But maybe we can make it feel like home. Maybe with Alberto's wages and mine put together we can cheer this place up a bit with more furniture, and even some rugs on the floor to cover up the gaping flooring."

Maria hugged him tightly. "I'm sure of it, Papa," she whispered. "I'm sure of it."

When the tea kettle began to whistle, Maria went to it and carried it to the table where her Papa had placed three cups with tea leaves scattered in the bottom of each. "And do you have nice neighbors, Papa?" Maria asked, trying to force a cheerfulness into her words.

"Ah, yes," Giacomo said, smiling broadly. "There are the Valzanos, Collettis, Hurtados. They are the nicest of the lot. On Sundays, we usually sit around on our porches and have nice leisurely chats. You know. About Italy. About the vineyards we each left behind."

Alberto entered the room. "Speaking of vineyards," he said. "I can see off in the distance and I see a vague sign of a vineyard. Whose is it?" He sat down opposite his Papa, thumping his fingers on the table top.

Shadows creased Giacomo's facial features. He lowered his eyes, fidgeting with the cup. "That is just a small part of Nathan Hawkins's estate," he said.

"I didn't see it, Alberto. Where?" Maria rushed into the living room and opened the door and craned her neck, seeing only a glimpse of what Alberto was speaking of. She could see it in the distance . . . the ocean of dried grapevines against the horizon. And then when she looked even further . . . she saw the vague outline of a house. She now knew why she hadn't seen it earlier. She had been too absorbed by the house that her Papa was leading her to.

She continued to stare, eyes wide. "I've never seen such . . . a . . . house. . . ." she whispered to herself.

171

The mine whistle blew long and loud, making goose-bumps ride Alberto's spine. He glanced sideways at his Papa, wondering if he had truly gotten used to this way of life. He appeared to have accepted it, but Alberto had noticed that the old joviality was lacking in his eyes. It made Alberto's insides ache to see just how much his Papa had changed since having made this trip to America.

"Now, son, you stay pretty close to me these first few times beneath ground," Giacomo said, hooking his carbide light on the leather bill of his work hat. "Coal mining is one of the most dangerous works in America today. It kills many. There are always dangers of explosions and cave-ins. Just a small rock fall can be the end of a man."

Fear etched itself across Alberto's face. He knew that he lacked in bravery at times, and he was still amazed at himself for having gotten enough courage to put Sam and Grace in their places. His gaze lowered, feeling a sickness at the pit of his stomach, remembering how embarrassed he had been when he hadn't been able to succeed at seducing Grace. He would always remember her mocking laughter.

"Son? Did you hear a word I said?" Giacomo said,

leaning up into Alberto's face.

Alberto fidgeted with the carbide light he held. "Uh . . . yes . . . Papa," he murmured, knowing that his face was coloring. What a damn time to be thinking of women, he thought to himself. But he knew that when he wasn't thinking about cards, thoughts and fantasies of women filled almost every moment of his days . . . *and* . . . nights.

Maria. Ah, Maria. It was her fault. If she wasn't so beautiful and always so close . . . reminding Alberto of just what a woman did have to offer a man.

Guilt plagued him, remembering how he had just snuck to stand beside Maria's bedroom door to watch her undress. He had even hidden behind the privy and had watched her through a crack in the wall.

Something similar to a stabbing sensation made his stomach lurch, knowing that something evil was guiding him to do such unthinkable things. But he knew that it was because his needs to possess a woman had yet to be fulfilled.

"Then, son, it's time to get your hat readied with your carbide light," Giacomo grumbled. "There's nothin' darker than the insides of a coal mine with that carbide light blowed out."

"Okay, Papa," Alberto said, watching men scurrying around, stirring the coal dust beneath their feet, looking like black fog rising into the air. Ponies had been lined up and hitched to posts, ready to start hauling the coal once it was brought to the top. Alberto hadn't noticed before, but one stretch of railroad track lay in the depths of dried, overgrown weeds and ran along the ground to cross the tracks that had carried Alberto and Maria to Hawkinsville. The ponies would

173

carry the coal to the gondola cars of a train once a day, for the train to then carry and distribute this coal to different sections of the country.

Alberto pulled his soft-shelled hat more secure on his head, frowning, realizing that this hat with its top made of cloth offered no protection whatsoever against any rocks that might choose to fall on his head. But this was the only hat offered to the miners, so Alberto had no choice but to be the same as the others milling around him . . . to accept a fate that had been so unjustly handed his way.

He placed his carbide light onto the hook of the leather bill of his hat, then followed along beside his Papa, who was quiet with worry. His Papa had confessed that he already was ailing with a rupture from the constant handling of the heavy loads of coal. Alberto wondered what other sort of ailments could be an aftermath of working beneath the ground. Would one's lungs have to work harder to keep oxygen pumping through them? Would Alberto become like a bat, preferring the dark to the light?

"Here's how we get lowered to the city underground," Giacomo said, stepping up to a mesh-covered cage held upright by a pulley. "Come on, son. Step in beside me."

Alberto swallowed hard, looking quickly from one person to another. The faces were docile. The men stood, most with rounded shoulders, in dark, coal-stained clothes. The Italian exchange in morning gossip ceased as the cage began to be lowered, sliding gently into the darkness.

The shadows being cast against the wall of earth on each side of Alberto from the men's hat lights made him grow tense and his eyes strain. He scooted closer to his father, hearing the heaviness in the way he was breathing. "Papa, are you all right?" he whispered, focusing the dim light from his hat onto his Papa's face.

"The closeness of the air always seems to grab at my chest," Giacomo said, openly wheezing now. "I keep hopin' that my body will adjust. I'm sure in time it will."

Alberto began to experience such a tightness himself. He coughed, then reached up and loosened a button at his neck. He felt as though a dead weight was crushing in on him the lower the cage moved into the deepest recesses of the ground. "How much further, Papa?" Alberto said, feeling cold sweat beading his brow, though in truth the air had grown damp and cold.

A snapping noise above his head and an abrupt halt of the cage made Alberto aware that the pulley had stopped. A trembling rumbled through him, seeing how pitch black it was on all sides of him. He quickly remembered his Papa's warning . . . "There's nothin' darker than inside of a coal mine with lights blowed out."

God, Alberto worried to himself. Even with all the lights each man had on his head, it was still as dark as what hell must be like.

"Come along, Alberto," Giacomo said, guiding Alberto by an elbow out of the cage, as the rest of the men crowded out and around them. "Like I said. Stay close."

Alberto's eyes widened, now seeing so much more than before as he began to follow alongside his Papa on ground that crunched with scattered coal beneath his feet. The carbide lights were spread out more, on each side of him, reflecting onto beautiful different colors of

175

stalactites and stalagmites, almost taking Alberto's breath away. "I've never seen anything like this, Papa," he blurted. "Why, it's beautiful here."

"This is the underground wonder I failed to mention," Giacomo said, reaching into a pocket, pinching off a plug of chewing tobacco. He formed it into a ball and poked it into the right side of his mouth, wetting it with his saliva. "But what you'll soon step into ain't pretty at all."

"Why, Papa?"

"It's where we've picked and shoveled away at the earth. Where we've been workin' at gettin' the coal out."

"But you won't have to disturb this area to get coal," will you?"

"Sometime soon. There's lots of coal to be had here," Giacomo said, now chewing and sucking on his tobacco. He went to a wall and lifted two pickaxes, handing one to Alberto. "We must get to work. Ain't makin' no money standin' 'round beatin' our gums."

Once again, Alberto followed his father, hearing the steady drumming of pickaxes from the other miners who were busy burrowing their way through the earth. Alberto reached up and kneaded his brow. A slow ache had begun in his head and he had just begun his long day of duty. *God,* he thought. *Will I even be able to make it?*

He stopped to look around him once again. Some miners were spraying water from a long, twisted hose onto the face of the coal, to keep the dust down. Others were busy propping up the roof of the ground with timber.

"This is where one learns to curve his back, son,"

Giacomo said, moving into a narrow cavern that looked to be only thirty-six inches high. "You might even have to kneel because of your added height."

Alberto stepped into this part of the underground where fresh timber creaked above his head, but not high enough for him to stand erect. As his Papa was doing, he stooped, already feeling the muscles pulling at the base of his neck and spine.

Shivers rippled his flesh. In this part of the mine, it was even darker than the rest. It had to be the darkest dark there ever was or could be. It was darker than any night. The light on his hat gave him no consolation whatsoever. He now knew that he could never like working in a mine. His goal was to better himself . . . and as quickly as possible.

"Papa, what did you mean when you said that about making money? How do we get paid for a day's labor?" he asked sullenly.

Giacomo lifted the pickaxe and swung it heavily against the earthen wall, then another blow, and after another grunted exhaustedly with each jerk of his body. "We get paid by the buckets we fill with coal," he said, panting.

"Buckets?"

"See them? Over yonder? We keep track of them that we fill, then we get paid by Nathan Hawkins."

"Can't some lie and say they fill more than others?"

"Nathan Hawkins knows if there's one less or more bucket at the end of the day. After everyone speaks his number to Nathan Hawkins's representative, he has a way of knowin'. I think there's a spy among us, keepin' track for that devil. If someone tries cheatin', none of us gets our wages."

"God," Alberto groaned, beginning to work his own pickaxe into the earth once again. He stopped after only three blows, to wipe his brow. "How much per bucket, Papa?" he quickly added.

"Huh? What's that you say?"

"How much money do you make per bucket, Papa?"

"Ain't never the same," Giacomo grumbled.

Alberto's heart froze. "What . . . ?" he gasped.

"Ain't never the same from day to day," Giacomo repeated.

"Why the hell not?"

"Hawkins pays us also by the quality of the coal we've found on a certain day. . . ."

"That bastard," Alberto grumbled, now thrusting his pickaxe into the earth, blow by angry blow, imagining it to be Nathan Hawkins. He growled, hitting harder and harder until he felt a firm hand fall onto his shoulder. He stopped and looked down onto the puzzled face of his father.

"Alberto, you act like a crazy person," Giacomo said quietly. "Why are you attackin' the earth so? You have all day. You must save your energy so it'll last you till we're raised back up into fresh air."

"Sorry, Papa," Alberto said, leaning his pickaxe against his leg, wiping his brow with the back of a sleeve.

"Now work at a steady pace, son," Giacomo urged, spitting against the wall of black. "But don't kill yourself while doin' it. There's enough coal in this here earthen grave to fill many of our buckets."

Alberto looked away from his Papa, toward a man who was pushing a shovel over some sort of screen. "Papa, what's that man doing?" he asked, watching more closely.

Giacomo's gaze followed Alberto's. He flicked a suspender, making coal dust fly all around him, then said, "We have these little screens that you dump your coal that you dig on. You take a shovel and push it over the screen so's your real fine coal falls out on the ground. You can't sell that. We leave it lyin' here in the bowels of the earth. We only pass the big lumps of coal up to the ponies a waitin'."

"Oh, I see. . . ." Alberto said, then felt his heart leap when a loud, thundering blast echoed into his ears. A slow, moaning, rumbling of the ground and walls around him made Alberto close his eyes. He covered his head with his hands, flinching, looking sideways, waiting for the ceiling to come tumbling down upon him. He lowered his hands and turned wide-eyed toward his father, when he heard his father guffawing next to him.

"Son, you've got to get used to that," Giacomo said, wiping his eyes with the back of a hand.

"What the hell . . . ?"

"Just some blastin' goin' on up a further piece," Giacomo said, patting Alberto on the back.

"Isn't . . . that . . . a bit dangerous . . . ?"

"Not if it's done properly. It's an everyday occurrence. You'll get used to it."

Alberto laughed nervously, lifting his pickaxe once again. "I thought the whole damn thing was falling in . . . that the whole top was coming in on our heads," he said.

"I know, son. It took about a week fore I knowed whether to run or sit still. I know. Just be a bit patient. You'll learn in time."

Alberto began swinging the pickaxe again, letting his mind wander to more pleasant thoughts. If he couldn't afford to think of women, then he could think about his card game. He just had to find a place where he could play. It was like an illness . . . eating away at his insides.

Maria strained and pulled, then lifted the washtub of water and inched her way toward the back door. She closed her eyes and bit her lower lip, feeling muscles straining in every inch of her body. She wasn't used to this type of labor. No. None that she had found on this her first full day in Hawkinsville. She still couldn't believe that she had to walk several blocks to the only faucet allowed this small village of Italians to get her water for everything they needed in the house. And then to have to throw the filth of the water out the back door onto the ground for flies to buzz around so freely? "I hate it," she murmured. "I just hate it."

She kicked the screen door open, then leaned the washtub onto the top step, tipping it so the water could start running over the washtub's edge. She watched the white lathery suds wash along the top of the scales of black earth, then get swallowed up in gulps as they searched out the cracks that reached out like veins on the back of a hand.

Placing a hand on a hip, groaning, Maria let the washtub tumble downward, to rest awkwardly on its side at the foot of the steps. Breathless, she looked slowly upward, seeing the blueness of the sky and feeling the warmth of the sun. She knew that was something to be grateful for. Her father had told her that November in Illinois was usually a month for the first snowfall, and freezing temperatures enough to make one's bones ache.

"But this is only the first day of November," she said, rolling a sleeve up on her dingy cotton dress, feeling the heat of the sun caressing her arm. Her eyes traveled further around her, feeling the need to get away from the drabness of her surroundings. Surely she would only have to walk a short distance from this community to find something besides coal and coal dust. She was anxious to breathe some fresher air . . . see some grass . . . lean against a tree. Only then would she feel the freedom of the soul that she now so longed for.

"I will," she said determinedly, rushing back into the house. "I'll take a walk. Surely leaving my chores until later won't matter. I have to see what else this countryside has to offer."

Slipping her apron off, she looked down at the dress she now wore. She had chosen not to wear the new dress Aunt Helena had purchased for her. She knew that to do so while working in such filth would mean to ruin it in one day's time. No. She had chosen a simple cotton dress that didn't have any lace or bows to brighten it.

"Should I change into my newer cotton dress?" she pondered to herself, holding the thick gathers of her dress up into the air, letting it then cascade back around her. "No. I'd best not. It would take too much time. I want to leave now. And I must be ready to get right back to my work when I return."

She reached upward and touched her hair. She had already brushed it until it shone. Smiling, she pulled her combs from each side, letting her hair fall to hang loosely to her waist, wanting to relish the breeze of the day, to let it lift her hair from her shoulders, to give it a fresh smell.

She hurriedly chose a knitted shawl to wrap around her for warmth, pinched her cheeks for color, then rushed through the front door, not stopping to look back. She knew one thing. She wasn't going to go in the direction of the mine. Its tipple was a threatening sight for her. She knew that below it, somewhere beneath the ground, her Papa and Alberto were working with danger. She closed her eyes and shook her head, not wanting to let herself think such thoughts. She had to believe that her Papa knew how to protect himself, and knew that he would protect Alberto before he did even himself.

"They'll be all right," she mumbled, hurrying her pace, seeing a small bridge ahead, now knowing just where she was headed. It was the house that she had seen the day before that was luring her onward. She stopped for a moment, cupping a hand above her eyes, seeing the spaciousness of the house that still sat far in the distance. The heat rays from the sun were a wavy haze, distorting her full view, but she could tell that this house was like none other she had seen before. Not even in comparison to the homes owned by the richest of families in the city of Pordenone, Italy.

This house was of a red brick, two-storied, and had a wide, spreading porch on front, the roof of the porch supported by tall, white, round pillars. This house was Nathan Hawkins's. To go stand in front of it might even mean to get a glimpse of this evil man . . . a man who she was growing to hate with every fiber of her being. Some way, she would get revenge for herself and the small community of Italians. Some way. . . .

Drawing her shawl more securely around her arms, Maria moved onward, knowing that what lay between her and possibly Nathan Hawkins was a wide stretch of tall Indian grass that seemed magically to begin on the other side of the small creek that the iron bridge she had just stepped onto led her across. She could hardly wait to move through the blowing gentleness of the grass. Today, it could be compared to an ocean as it dipped and swayed in gentle greenish-yellows. It was such a relief to get away from the coal dust. Even the air around her had changed. She inhaled deeply as she left the bridge and made her first step onto a thick carpet of moss that laced the edge of the creek bed. Then she moved on into the thigh-high grass, now wondering about another house that had been hidden from her eyes by a thick grove of trees.

She stopped to stare in its direction, seeing that it was of much better quality than the one she now lived in, but yet not at all similar to the brick house that she had been heading for. She looked to the distance, studying the brick house, then glanced back at this white frame house, trying to decide which to seek out first. A sense of adventure made her choose the smaller house, full of wonder as to how anyone had succeeded at having such a nice house in this area that was supposed to be owned by Nathan Hawkins . . . a house painted a clean white, with a fence surrounding it on all four sides . . . a house much nicer than the ones that the coal miners and their families had to live in.

When Maria reached the trees and began to move beneath the towering oaks, their dried leaves rustled above her head, sounding as though they were heaving restless sighs while the prairie breezes continued to

183

blow its breath onto their faces of brown. A gray-tailed squirrel hopped from a lower limb, then picked an acorn up from the ground and began turning it in circles between its front paws as its teeth worked their way hungrily into the nutty center.

A sudden eruption of dogs' barks broke the serene setting that Maria had found herself surrounded by. She tensed and looked hurriedly around her, always having feared stray dogs. She knew that the tall grasses could hide the dogs from her eyes, but that it in no way kept them from smelling her presence.

She went to stand beside a tree, clutching at its trunk, watching for any sudden movements around her. But nothing. When the barking began again, she ceased breathing for a moment, listening closely, then knew that the dogs had grown no closer or further. She inched her way onward, pushing low branches of trees aside, feeling thorns from the brush that she had moved into nipping at her ankles, then found herself standing in the open, next to the fence that she had seen from afar.

Two huge brown dogs came racing toward her, yelping and snarling, showing their teeth, but unable to reach her because of the fence that stood so tall between them.

Maria flinched each time the dogs lunged toward the fence. But she began to move onward, now looking toward the house that sat in the middle of this fenced-in yard. It was two-storied, with drapes pulled shut at each window, and smoke spiraled slowly into the sky from a tall, brick chimney that reached upward from the ground, almost clinging, it seemed, to the side of the house.

A wide porch stretched across the front of the house with many white wicker chairs positioned on it. At the far end, a porch swing hung from the porch roof, swaying gently in the breeze, emitting a slow, creaking sound.

Now completely ignoring the dogs still following along beside her on the other side of the fence, Maria eyed the stately black carriage and two matching chestnut mares that were tied to a hitching post outside the fence, next to a gate that opened into the yard, where a path of white gravel led to the steps of the porch.

One of the horses whinnied as Maria moved closer. She reached a hand upward and touched the softness of its mane, but still looking around her, seeing the many leafless trees that surrounded the house, and how their limbs hung low over it, seeming to embrace it.

Her gaze moved lower, seeing the squared-off flower beds on each side of the walk. They showed signs of once having been filled with an assortment of flowers, but had turned into brown, wilting stalks, bent now, like an ageing man might do.

A stronger gust of wind sent Maria's dress hem whipping upward, causing a chill to creep up her legs and between her thighs. In haste, she pushed the skirt of her dress down and snuggled more into her shawl, stopping, gaping, when the front door of this house opened slowly, revealing a figure standing in the shadow of the alcove.

Maria swallowed hard and began to inch her way backwards, now realizing what an awkward circumstance she had found herself in.

A dark-skinned lady stepped out into full view and began to move down the steps toward Maria.

185

Maria stood wide-eyed, stunned. She hadn't been around any Negroes before. She had read of how they had been used as slaves, and how they still didn't have the same privileges as most white people. But this Negress didn't appear to have been affected in any way by such prejudices. As was Maria, this Negress was tall and stately and held her head high. She was attired in a long, flowing satin gown of a rose coloring that clung sensuously to her figure that was well-represented by its plunging neckline. Her pompadoured hair was of a reddish tint, but displayed roots of shining black. Her eyes were as dark as any dark Maria had ever seen and her thick lips had been painted red. Her wide nostrils flared as she reached the gate and began to talk. . . .

"What brings you here?" she asked in a deep throaty, slow drawl that matched the sultriness of her costume. Her long, lean fingers displayed many rings of ruby-colored settings that matched the small circles of red earrings on each earlobe.

"I was just taking a leisurely . . . walk . . ." Maria said, clearing her throat nervously. Somehow she felt inferior to this beautiful creature standing before her. The lady's dark skin was sleek and shining, and an aroma of expensive perfume traveled from her body upward into Maria's nose.

Maria eyed the lady's dress once again, feeling envy eating away at her insides. In Italy, this was what Maria had dreamed of wearing, when America flooded her thoughts both day and night. She had hoped that her Papa had purchased such a grand house and that she would be able to go and purchase closets of gorgeous clothes.

Her gaze moved upward, seeing the confidence in the

strong set of this lady's jaw. How had this person succeeded at getting so much in the world? How had a Negro . . . a female Negro . . . managed to have more than even the Italians? Maria had always thought the Italian race to be superior. Had she been wrong?

Maria's face colored when she felt this lady's eyes travel over her, feeling very self-conscious about the drab way in which she was dressed. She pulled her shawl even closer, clutching it in front of her.

"Are you of the Italian community?" the lady asked, patting one of the dog's head, as the dog moved to her side, panting.

"Yes . . . I . . . am," Maria stammered.

"You're the first female of that community to cross the iron bridge that leads away from their houses," the lady said, curving her lips in a soft smile.

"I . . . am . . . ?" Maria said, eyes wide.

"What's your name?" the lady asked, eyeing Maria's attire once again with a fleeting glance.

"Maria. Maria Lazzaro."

"Mine is Ruby. Just Ruby," Ruby purred. "Come on in out of the chill of the air." She lifted the latch on the gate and opened it.

Maria eyed the dogs cautiously. "But the dogs," she said. "They appear to be so . . . so . . . vicious. . . ."

Ruby's throaty laughter filled the air. "Only if I want them to be," she said, clapping her hands sharply, then shooing the dogs away from her.

Maria reached down and lifted the skirt of her dress, walking alongside Ruby, anxiety rippling through her. Had she found a friend? The color of Ruby's skin made no difference to her, for wasn't her own of a different coloring from all other Americans'? In a sense, Maria knew that this alone could make for a special bond between her and Ruby. But she was puzzled by something that Ruby had said.

"Why would I be the only female Italian to cross the iron bridge?" she asked, moving up the front steps. "Surely there had to have been others with the same need to get away from such terrible surroundings."

"Nathan Hawkins has etched a fear inside most of their heads, almost as though they've been branded by dangerous hot irons," Ruby said. "If not the females, their husbands, brothers, or fathers. Most females are warned against wandering too far . . . Most believe that Nathan would put them in bondage if he found them wandering on his private estate."

Maria paled, remembering her earlier plans of going to stand in front of Nathan Hawkins's house. "And is it true? Would he do such a thing?" she asked softly, stepping onto the porch.

Another laugh bounced through the air as Ruby reached for the screen door. "Hell, no, honey," she said. "He might have something else on his mind, but never anything like bondage. It's just a tale that got started by some fool of a husband who feared that his lovely Italian wife might wander off after becoming bored with washing a coal miner's filthy underthings and having only a house filled with children for company."

"This Nathan Hawkins. You do know him?"

"I've had many a run-in with the bastard," Ruby hissed, opening the main door, stepping aside so Maria could enter.

"He is an evil man, isn't he?" Maria said, stepping gingerly across the threshold, stopping, feeling her

188

heart hammering against her ribs when her gaze moved quickly around her. She took it all in, then stared questioningly at Ruby. "Why, it's so beautiful," she finally blurted. "How . . . ?"

Ruby closed the door then moved across the softness of a beige woolen carpet. "I see you are surprised to see how I live," she said, reaching for a long, thin cigar. When she placed it between her lips, Maria's fingers went to her throat, struck with amazement. She had already been stunned by the crudeness of some of the words Ruby had chosen to speak. And . . . now? To smoke cigars . . . as only a man was normally wont to do?

Once again Maria's eyes took in the room and its decor. It was a room of gentle colors, as though meant to make one relax . . . to forget any troubles that might be burdening one. It was a room of beiges and pale greens in both the brocade draperies hanging at the windows and the many upholstered chairs and matching sofa positioned for comfort in front, and on both sides of the six-foot-wide-and-high brick fireplace.

Wide-leafed palm plants sat in each corner of the room, and a grandfather's clock stood ticking away against the wall, where steps began that led upward to the second floor.

Maria knew that this house, and all that was in it, had taken much money to make it so beautiful. But . . . how . . . ?

"Come. Sit by the fire," Ruby said, flicking ashes from her cigar into the flaming logs on the grate. She settled down onto a chair, with her back held straight, drawing from her cigar once again.

Maria pulled her shawl from around her shoulders,

already feeling the warmth from the fire moving into her flesh, making her feel a bit languid. She went to sit opposite Ruby, clasping her hands tightly together on her lap.

Ruby removed the cigar from between her lips, then leaned forward a bit. "Do I make you uncomfortable?" she asked in her slow drawl.

Maria swallowed hard, reaching up to push her hair back from her shoulders. "No," she said. "And why should you?"

"I'm a Negro. Most white women turn their noses up into the air when a Negro approaches them, except if they are seeking one of my kind to do their dirty work for them. You know . . . cleaning . . . laundry . . . cooking. If this is needed, most white womenfolk can tolerate us. But that's the only reason they will confess to."

"If you will notice, my skin is not white," Maria said proudly, reaching up to run her fingers over the smoothness of a cheek.

"Yes. I noticed," Ruby said, smiling. "I also noticed how fluently you speak the American language. Have you been in Nathan Hawkins's Italian community long?"

The way in which Ruby had referred to "Nathan Hawkins's Italian community" sent renewed sparks of hatred racing through Maria. Her eyes blazed, showing her anger, though she didn't feel free to speak of it to this Ruby who was still only a stranger to her. "I've been in America only one day," she murmured. "My Papa taught me how to speak English while we were still in Italy." She paused, then smiled. "My brother Alberto and I arrived by train yesterday to be with our Papa, who was already here."

190

"Oh? A brother you say?"

"Yes. My twin," Maria boasted, flipping her hair, lifting her chin.

"A twin," Ruby drawled. "Hmm. Interesting. I've seen but only one set of twins during my lifetime." Her eyes raked over Maria, glimmering. "And does your brother Alberto look exactly like you?"

"Yes. We have the same color of eyes, hair, and even a birthmark of the same size and shape. Our heights are also the same." She paused, then added, "Yes, we are the same, except for personalities. Alberto has only recently changed."

"In which way?"

Maria looked away from Ruby, chewing her lower lip. "He has suddenly acquired the pleasures of a card game, one he was taught how to participate in while we were on board that wretched ship that brought us to America," she said sullenly. "It seems this game has captured his heart in almost the same way as a woman might one day succeed in doing."

"The card game you speak of I'm sure is what we Americans call Poker," Ruby said, laughing amusedly.

Maria's eyes flew upward. "So you do know about this . . . this evil game?"

Ruby rose from the chair and tossed her half-smoked cigar into the flames rising from the logs on the grate. She turned, standing with her back to the fire. "Yes. I'm very familiar with it," she said, laughing still.

Maria was puzzled by the amusement Ruby found in the mention of the card game. But Maria was puzzled by everything about Ruby. She rose and began moving around the room, touching the smooth finish of the redwood tables that sat beside chairs in the room. Then something caught her eyes. She leaned down over a lamp, seeing that behind its shade there was no sign of a wick with which to light the lamp. Instead, there was a tiny, pear-shaped bulb made of a delicate-appearing luminous material. She reached inside and touched it. "What is this?" she gasped, feeling its cold smoothness.

Ruby moved to her side. "You've never seen an electric lightbulb?" she asked.

"Is this . . . ?"

Ruby laughed, then reached over and switched the light on, reflecting a bright ray of artificial sun upward onto Maria's face.

"Yes. One of the first in the area," Ruby bragged, straightening her back. "Nathan Hawkins has the same in his house, and further down the road at Creal Springs it has become quite commonplace."

"Then you must be one of the rich Americans, Ruby," Maria said, reaching up inside the shade, marveling at the heat she could feel now radiating from the bulb.

Ruby threw her head back in another fit of laughter. "Not really," she said. "Just calculating and very smart."

Maria continued her exploration around the room. "I truly don't understand," she said. "If Nathan Hawkins owns all the land in this area, how is it your house is . . . uh . . . so much nicer than the one I'm living in?"

"That's simple enough to answer," Ruby drawled, moving to stand in front of the fire once again. "Nathan Hawkins didn't succeed in buying my father out those many years ago. This house was my father's, and before that my grandmother's. When my father passed away, he left the house to me. I made sure Nathan Hawkins had no chance to get his hands on it. And if he even tries to come near the place, I sic my dogs on him *or* his representatives."

"And your . . . mother . . . ?"

"She left when I was a baby. I've never even seen her. My father said she was a . . . uh . . . a tramp."

Maria gazed longingly around her once again, seeing the way she would truly like to live. Such luxury! "And I guess your father . . . uh . . . left you a lot of money? This house is so beautiful."

Ruby went to look up the staircase, furrowing a brow. "A nigger having a lot of money?" she said, laughing sarcastically. She swung her head around, eyes snapping. "That's what he was called. A nigger," she blurted. She went to the fireplace and stared down into the flames. "No. My money? I've made it. In the only way I know how."

Maria went to stand beside Ruby, eyes wide. "Maybe you could tell me how you did it," she said softly. "I'd like to have the same things you have." Her gaze moved over Ruby and the richness of her attire. "Your dress. I've never seen one so breathtakingly beautiful."

Ruby's eyes wavered as she turned to face Maria. "I doubt if you would want to live as I do," she said sullenly. "Yes, it appears that all is well here in this house. But you see, it is just that. A 'house.'" She gazed back into the flames. "A house . . . of . . . girls," she murmured. "I run a . . . house . . . of girls. . . ."

Maria gasped and stepped back away from Ruby as though she was the plague. "You . . . what . . . ?" she whispered, looking quickly around her. "This is a place . . . of . . . ?"

Ruby went to the door and opened it. "I knew your reaction would be one of shock," she said. "Now it's best that you be on your way. I don't need the likes of you to associate with anyway." Her eyes narrowed into two slits. "Just look at you," she hissed. "You're no better than a slave yourself. Get out of my house. I don't even know why I asked you in, in the first place. Soft in the head, I guess."

With a throbbing pulse, Maria inched her way toward the door, then stopped when she reached it. "I'm sorry if my attitude offended you, Ruby," she said, blushing. "It's just . . . that . . . I've never met face to . . . face with a. . . ."

Ruby placed her hands on her hips and tilted her chin up, proud. "A whore?" she hissed. "You've never been around a whore before?"

"Please, Ruby," Maria whispered, reaching to touch Ruby on the hand. "I truly don't care if you run this house. Please believe me."

Ruby stepped back away from Maria, making Maria's hand drop awkwardly in front of her. "Why would you even care anything about me?" she asked. "In most everyone else's eyes, I'm a cheap tramp, just like my mother."

"I think we could be friends, no matter your occupation," Maria said, lowering her eyes.

Ruby laughed sarcastically. "Your brother? What would he think of you associating with my kind? And your father? They would probably disown you for sure."

Maria glanced quickly around her once again. She knew that she would willingly accept any threats from her family, if only she could occasionally come to this house and sit beside the fire and chat freely with this woman of dark colors. Until she had found out Ruby's occupation, she had felt a closeness of sorts to her. She looked toward the staircase when another dark-skinned girl came sauntering down the steps. Maria eyed her closely. She wore only a thin chemise, which revealed the largeness of her breasts and a tiny waist. The girl moved stealthily across the room, toward the fire.

Ruby turned on a heel and raced across the room to stand with hands on hips next to the girl. "Isn't anyone stirring yet upstairs? What the hell do you girls think you're doing sleeping until noon? We have to get with it. We have to be ready for the rush this evening. The warmer weather brings the men out. You know that."

"Ah knows," the girl said, wiping her eyes with the back of the hand. "But we's been ovah worked lately. You knows that." Her eyes became as two dark coals when they turned to gaze upon Maria. "And whut is that white lady folk doin' in our house? Don't tell me you're goin' to put her to work side by side with us?"

"No. Not quite," Ruby said, turning with a small smile lifting her lips, nodding toward Maria. "No. She's just my friend. Nothing more . . . nothing less."

Maria smiled a bit awkwardly. She did indeed feel out of place standing in such a place as this . . . but . . . yet . . . Ruby did make her feel as though it *was* just another house, not one of prostitution. "Yes. We're friends," she said softly. "But for now, Ruby. I must go." She reached for her shawl that she had thrown over the back of a chair.

Ruby moved toward her, hand outstretched. "You

195

come by anytime," she said.

"I've much work to do at my Papa's house," María said. "But I'll sure try hard to break away." She took Ruby's hand in hers and shook it gently.

"You should try and make it soon," Ruby said, then opening the door for Maria. "It's best to even get your exploring done now. Real soon the snows begin to fall and it's hell getting around."

Maria's thick lashes fluttered, knowing that she would have to get used to this lady's way of loose speech, her smoking of cigars, and knowing that she was a madame of a . . . whore house. But she would. She didn't want to rot in that house of her Papa's alongside Alberto, who seemed content enough as long as he had a hand of cards to play with. "I'll remember your warning," she said, laughing softly, then moved on out the door.

Ruby moved out next to her, hugging herself with her arms as the wind whipped her dress up around her ankles. "I won't ever introduce my girls to you," she said quietly. "You see, most only have known the acquaintance of men besides the girls they work beside. They don't even know how to carry on a decent conversation. None have been educated except in the ways of their bodies. I hope you'll understand."

Maria swallowed hard, hugging herself, pulling the shawl more tightly around her arms. "Yes. I think I do," she said, wondering if Ruby had had an education, and if so, where . . . ?

The dogs began running toward Maria, making her stop, tense. She chewed on a lower lip, barely breathing as both dogs began sniffing at the hem of her dress.

"They won't bite. They sound vicious when a

196

stranger comes close beside my fence. But once I have let someone inside my fence, they sense that this person is my friend. Please go on your way without any fear whatsoever."

"All right," Maria gulped, inching her way toward the gate of the fence. "If you . . . think . . . so," she quickly added, hurrying through the gate, shutting it loudly behind her.

She turned and eyed Ruby quizzically when Ruby broke into another of her deep, throaty laughs. Maria smiled sheepishly, then moved on toward the thicket, then pushed her way through the thickness of the trees, wondering if all men were willing to fight their way through all this just to get to bed up with one of those colored girls? But she knew that the trees were a good cover . . . a good dividing point, along with the iron bridge, to separate Ruby's way of life from the simpler ways of life of the Italian community.

Maria sighed with relief when she stepped out into the clearing and began to make her way through the Indian grass, stopping to only glance toward Nathan Hawkins's house. She felt the hate brewing inside her, knowing that one day she and this Nathan Hawkins would meet. Maybe by then she would have a plan worked out . . . a way to accomplish the revenge that he most assuredly deserved.

Laughing lightly, she moved on, stepping onto the iron bridge, seeing rusty flakes of red hanging from its edge. She had to laugh, just knowing that someone had gotten the better of Nathan Hawkins already. Ruby had succeeded at this. In truth, this was the one main reason Maria had decided to truly become friends with Ruby. Ruby appeared to know the secrets of life and how to get what she wanted. Maybe she would be able to teach Maria just a few things. Maria didn't want to live the life of a whore like Ruby and her girls . . . but she did want to learn how to dress beautifully and how to carry herself . . . so that when she did meet Nathan Hawkins, he wouldn't even suspect that she was from the Italian community. She would trick him. Yes, that's what she would do. Trick him. Make him bow down to her. . . .

Chapter Nine

The steady drone of sewing machines echoed down the narrow hallway of the Hopper Shoe Company. Michael listened, proud. When he had first heard whispers that The Louisiana Purchase Exposition was going to be taking place in the city of Saint Louis, he had wondered how he could participate in the molding of it. He had known that many things would be needed in the preparations, since every state and territory of the United States was going to be represented with concessions and pavilions and official buildings, as were scores of foreign countries, as well.

When first mention of the need of flags for each of these buildings and pavilions had been made, Michael's mind had begun to work, knowing that was the one thing he could enjoy seeing taken care of. His building was large, with still many unused rooms waiting to be filled with whatever equipment he would desire. He had been admiring the skills of the seamstresses of the city and their abilities in using sewing machines, and he knew that the sewing machine was the tool of the future for the clothing industry. So he had decided to invest in several that could first be put to use making flags for the Saint Louis World's Fair, as The Louisiana Purchase Exposition was now being proudly called by the businessmen of the community.

Michael walked to the window and gazed outward, seeing the Wainwright Building, Saint Louis's first skyscraper. A pang of envy rippled through him. He had wanted to be the first to invest in such a building. He had wanted to have the recognition, especially since the Saint Louis World's Fair was going to draw people from all over the world.

Word had even reached Michael that President Roosevelt was going to attend. He was to be there for the opening events of the fair. How marvelous it would have been to have been able to show off such a magnificent building to such a man as Teddy Roosevelt. But now Michael would only be able to boast of having built the second tallest. He already had his plans in the works. His building was to overlook the muddy waters of the Mississippi River and to be built close to the Eads Bridge, where it would be accessible to all travelers to the "Gateway to the West," as Michael so fondly referred to this city of Saint Louis.

Reaching up, he ran a finger around the top of the detachable collar that he wore today along with his pure silk blue shirt. A diamond stud pin twinkled from the folds of his silk cravat, and his blue, pin-striped woolen suit and tight-fitted breeches made him appear to be of the rich class, which, in truth, he now was.

Michael moved toward the liquor cabinet of his office and removed a fancy crystal decanter from it and poured himself a glass of whiskey. He had felt the need of this strong beverage as of late. It seemed to be the only effective way of erasing the memory of Maria from his mind. He had tried to discover her whereabouts by checking back with the ship *Dolphin*'s

200

captain, but had found that neither the captain nor anyone else on board had remembered Maria or Alberto. They had just been two immigrants lost in the crowd.

"Four months," he grumbled, his blue eyes moody as restless waves on an ocean. "A damn full four months and I still don't know any more than I did. Where in the hell did she disappear to? Will I ever be able to see her . . . hold her. . . ."

"Michael, will you please sign these letters," Alice said abruptly from behind him, making him turn with a start, wondering if she had heard the words he had just spoken aloud. There had been a strain between the two of them since that day on the train. She had even shown this strain while they made love. Something was lacking in her touch . . . her kisses.

But Michael knew very well why. Alice wasn't Maria. No one could ever compare with Maria. His dreams were haunted by her full, sensuous lips . . . the softness of her flesh . . . the voluptuousness of her breasts. Even now he felt the heat in his loins, even though he knew that he could probably never possess her again. Before Maria, he had found what he had needed in other women's arms. But now all he ever thought about was her. There was so much about her . . . her haunting beauty . . . her innocence. . . .

Michael set his glass down inside the liquor cabinet, clearing his throat nervously. "Ah, I see you have the letters ready for mailing," he said, settling down onto a large, comfortable leather chair behind his magnificent desk of solid oak. He picked up his pen and dipped it into ink and began scribbling his name at the bottom of each page.

Alice, appearing the businesswoman she indeed tried to be during working hours, was attired in a black serge skirt with a scarf tied and cascading in colors of purples and greens down the front of her white shirtwaist blouse. The skirt rustled as she sat down on a cushioned chair next to the desk.

"And do you think we'll get the flags ready by May, as we've promised in these letters?" she asked, lifting a hand, repositioning a comb into the deep-piled head of red hair.

Michael lifted one letter after another, still signing. "No problem," he grumbled, not looking Alice's way. "Don't you hear the machines? Only two have broken down thus far. I'm damn proud of my investment. Making only shoes had become a bore."

"As I have also become to you, Michael?" Alice hissed, crossing her legs.

Tensing, Michael laid his pen down. The gentle slope to his jaw suddenly tightened as he combed his fingers through his thick mass of blonde hair. He set his lips firmly together, leaning back in the chair, looking with annoyance toward Alice. "Are we going to have to go into that again?" he said flatly.

His hands moved downward and held onto the arms of the chair, the knuckles whitening. He had known that it eventually would come to this. He had grown tired of her constant naggings, even though she was so damn beautiful with her green eyes snapping angrily right now, and her red hair flaming as though it was a million sunsets.

But her sour attitude had suddenly become just an annoyance. There were many secretaries in Saint Louis. Maybe he would just have to seek one of their services out and say goodbye to Alice.

Alice threw her shoulders back in anger. "What's the matter, Michael? Does the truth hurt? You know that you've been having trouble lately making love. Is it because you're not truly bored . . . but losing your skills as a lover?"

Michael pushed the chair back and rose angrily from it, tightening his hands into two tight fists at his side. "Alice, I think you've seen your last day here at Hopper Shoe Company," he fumed. "You know when you began giving me more than your secretarial services it wouldn't be forever. And if you must know . . . yes . . . I am bored. You are boring. Now how do you like having that thrown into your face? Can you be the one to face facts? Huh?"

He turned and walked to the window, placing his back to her. He clasped his hands tightly behind him, hating having lashed out at her in such a manner. And, damn it, they had been good for one another. Until Maria. . . . He felt a presence at his side and turned on a heel, finding Alice there looking almost humble as her lashes fluttered nervously. He withdrew when her hand reached out for his.

"I'm sorry, Michael," she said. "I don't want to lose my job. I know you won't have any trouble replacing me. Mrs. Smith's Secretarial School is just waiting for such openings. But they aren't as skilled as I. You know that."

Michael's eyes wavered. He went to the liquor cabinet and poured himself another glass of whiskey and swallowed it in one fast gulp, feeling it burning his throat, making him cough a bit. He went back to his desk chair and slouched down onto it, leaning back, placing his feet on the desk. He fitted his fingertips carefully together and watched Alice as she came to sit down, eyeing him questioningly.

"Alice, you do know it's over between us, don't you?" he said softly. "You do know that if you stay on here, it will be only for business purposes? You see, I do know that you are one damn good secretary . . . one I'd have a damn hard time replacing."

Alice paled. "If that's the way it has to be, I guess I don't have any choice," she said in a strained voice. She reached upward and wiped a trace of a tear from her eyes, surprising Michael, for up to this point in their relationship, she had put on the air of being hard . . . calculating . . . stubborn.

Damn, he thought to himself. Maybe she does care for me. Could she truly be in love? Naw. She only loves herself. This is only a big act. She's good at that also.

"So you do understand," he said, letting his feet drop to the floor, scooting his chair up to the desk. He reached into a gold-embossed container and pulled a Cuban cigar from inside it. He bit one end off, spitting it into an ashtray, swirled the cigar around his tongue to wet it, then lit the other end, inhaling deeply, the one thing that he was still able to enjoy . . . since . . . Maria.

"Yes, Michael, there will be no further harassment from me," Alice said, reaching for the stack of letters that were already signed. "And did you know that John Philip Sousa's famous band is going to be at the fair to play the opening song?"

Michael sighed heavily, seeing that she was smart to change the subject and return to the discussion of business matters, since he was determined to rid himself of her if she didn't. She had heard the determination in his voice. He was glad that this thing was finally settled. As for his sexual pleasures, he had ways of seeking out what release he could find beneath a woman's skirts. Alice wasn't the only woman available for such services in this large city of Saint Louis.

"Yes, I've heard," he finally said, beginning to dip the pen in and out of the inkwell once again, then proceeding with the placing of his signature at the bottom of the pages. "'The Hymn of the West.' That's what the official song of the fair is going to be called."

"And I hear that President Roosevelt isn't going to be able to make it after all," she said, stacking the letters neatly in front of her.

Michael's head jerked upward. "What . . . ?" he gasped. "Everyone was so anxious to meet him. God. The United Mine Workers of America were eager to see him come here. You know we had hoped he would come to a meeting . . . see what we are accomplishing. Damn. What bad luck."

"I know you were counting on it," she murmured. "But the way they have planned his participation is quite unique. He's to press some sort of telegraph key from his office in the White House that will turn on the electric lights at the House of Electricity that's almost completed here. It's supposed to be the greatest array of electric lights that has ever been seen. Anywhere."

"How is it that you know of these changes even before I?" Michael grumbled, flicking ashes from his cigar into an ashtray.

"Remember? I'm one top-notch secretary," she boasted. "I keep up with things. I heard this news on a local radio program today while getting ready for work."

"Wonders of the electrical age we are now beginning to be a part of," he sighed, then resumed with his name scribbling.

"Michael . . . ?"

"Huh . . . ?" he mumbled, not looking up.

"What have you and the members of the union come up with about the Italian community? Have you decided what you're going to do at Hawkinsville? Have you any plans in progress?"

Michael handed the rest of the letters to Alice, then leaned back in his chair. He removed the cigar from between his lips and mashed it out in the ashtray, sighing heavily. "No. We haven't been able to accomplish a damn thing," he grumbled. "Those people. They struggle so. They're a proud, hard-working people reaching up in what little ways they can for dignity and a measure of self-determination. But just as soon as it appears they may have accomplished something in that direction, Nathan Hawkins sends in his goons and scares the hell out of them."

"How? What could they do?"

"From the few times I've gone to the saloons in Hawkinsville, I've heard talk of some of the coal miners' having been grabbed in the dark of the night and beaten to a pulp. Such as that. It's a damn shame."

"I've worried about you going there," Alice said, placing the letters on her lap, crossing her hands over them. "You know Nathan Hawkins's men have to suspect something. That you're with the union. God, Michael. One of these nights, you're going to find a knife thrust between your ribs."

Michael laughed hoarsely. "Let 'em try," he said. "I've got my own knife. I can be just as fast as the next person."

"So you do plan to return?"

"Yeah. I have to continue to mingle," he said. "The damn thing about it, though, is the Italians have become close-mouthed. I can't pry any information from them. That community is Nathan Hawkins's. Bought and paid for. Why, most of the Italians owe their souls to the country store."

"What do you mean, Michael?"

"Ah, they don't know the first thing about figures," he grumbled. "They buy grocery and household supplies at Nathan Hawkins's general store and put it on account, then pay double without knowing it when it comes time to pay up."

"How horrible," Alice said, rising. She went to the window, holding the letters to her chest. "I do wish you didn't have to be so involved with the union," she quickly added.

"Alice . . ." Michael said, rising, going to stand next to her.

She smiled lightly. "I know," she said. "I'm getting too personal again. But Nathan Hawkins's goons? What if they *are* wise to you? You know Nathan Hawkins will not allow his coal mine to go union. He would kill anyone who interferes."

"Like I said. I mingle," Michael said, thrusting his hands inside his front breeches pockets. "I dress the part of something besides a rich businessperson or a coal miner. When I go to Hawkinsville, I dress the part of a drunken bum. Surely no one will guess that I have something besides whiskey on my mind. Unless. . . ." he quickly added, lifting his lips into a lewd grin.

"Unless what, Michael?" Alice prodded.

"Oh, nothing," he said, walking away from her, to pour himself another glass of whiskey. He couldn't have revealed his thoughts of that moment to Alice. To do so would be to cause her to go into another rage, even though she had promised to not pry anymore into the sexual side of his life. But he had been thinking about Ruby's house. He had discoverd it by the pure luck of listening to another poor drunken slob bragging about his conquests with the wayward women at the whorehouse that sat back by itself, almost in the shadows of Nathan Hawkins's house. It had surprised Michael to hear of such a house so close to Hawkins's estate, and he had been quickly prompted to seek it out himself. And hadn't he been needing some encouragement in the ways of women? Hadn't so much been lacking . . . since Maria . . . ?

The surprise had truly come, though, when he had found that the house had been one of only Negro women. This had been a first for him . . . to enter a house run by a Negro madame . . . a house of only Negroes . . . and very skilled in the ways of men.

His pulse raced even now, remembering the one night with Ruby and how skilled she had been with her tongue. She hadn't left one inch of his body untouched by the slick wetness. She had earned her title well . . . Madame Ruby. But she still didn't have what was needed to turn his soul to burning embers. She had just whetted his desires, making him long even more for Maria and the fulfillment she could give him.

A chuckle rumbled through him, remembering the ruby that he had discovered pasted inside Ruby's navel. "My trademark," she had purred, touching him on his fast-rising manhood. "No one will ever be confused in

208

the dark of the night when they have me on a bed. When hands and tongues explore my body, the ruby stone will alert them to the fact that it is Ruby they have the honor of being with that night."

"What are you thinking about, Michael?" Alice asked, pulling Michael's thoughts back to the present.

"What . . . ?" he gasped, moving quickly away from her, realizing that she had seen the bulge fattening beneath the buttons of his breeches.

"Something . . . or . . . someone got you aroused," she accused, stomping to stand beside him. "God. I can't do it, but thinking about someone else can?"

She stormed from the room, leaving Michael to stare after her. He kneaded his brow, not realizing what was happening inside himself. First he felt impotent, then the next thing he knew, he was as horny as hell. "Damn. Damn," he said, hitting the palm of his hand with a fist.

He tried to refocus his thoughts back on the struggles of the coal miners. He had only succeeded in speaking with a few to explain that the union made coal mining safer and more secure economically. But they had frozen up the last couple of times he had traveled to Hawkinsville.

Fear had them wrapped in its grasp. He needed an ally. A man who was a miner . . . one who could move among the others . . . to spread the truth. Michael had to find an ally . . . and . . . *soon*. It had become dangerous lately. He had feared that someone might even recognize him from the ship and tell Nathan Hawkins, in hopes of getting a reward.

But Michael had known all along that this was a dangerous game that he had chosen to play. And continue to play it he would! He wasn't going to be like most of the coal miners . . . docile . . . afraid. He would get that Nathan Hawkins to treat these people decently. Damn it! He had traveled clear to Italy in search of the truth. And now that he had it, he had to make things right. If not for the growth of the union . . . then for those beautiful, innocent people.

The town of Hawkinsville had become a prison. He knew that death threats hung over the ones who talked of leaving. Well, he would eventually see to it that even that changed.

He swallowed another gulp of whiskey and set his jaw firmly. He knew that he had himself to think of also. He had, this moment, to quiet the urges building up inside himself. He rushed to the door and moved quickly down the steepness of the steps until he reached the walk outside the building. The clanging of the Broadway Cable Car approaching made him step out onto the cobblestone of the street, waiting, feeling the brisk winds of March whip around him. Spring. A time for love. . . . He almost choked on those thoughts. Spring without Maria? Could he truly bear it? His eyes showed a quiet despair, knowing that he had no choice but to do so.

When he boarded the cable car, he took a seat with all the other dark-clothed, well-dressed men. Most sported hats and mustaches. But Michael still preferred a clean-shaven face, and he had utter contempt for hats.

He watched the city move on past him, seeing that this cable car was approaching the arch of gas lamps that gave the street he was now traveling on its night-time glamour. Portraits of all the presidents from Washington to Cleveland had been attached between the gas lamps and looked down on the noontime rush hour. Michael was proud of this added attraction to the city. He alone had suggested it. He had received nothing but favorable comments about this tourist attraction.

He settled down into the seat, crossing his arms, watching. Businessmen on their way to their private clubs scurried along the walks, and some women attired in their business costumes of black and white mingled with women attired in their fancy hats and long, flowing dresses of silks and satins.

Michael usually went to the Liederkranz for his noontime pleasures of sharing business talk and cigars with other businessmen. But this day, Michael had far more important things on his mind. He knew that in a room at the Planter's House Hotel there waited a woman who was paid top dollar by the classiest gents of the city. Maybe she would make him forget. At least for the moment.

The Broadway Cable Car clattered down the tracks, clanging its bells noisily when horse-drawn carriages got too close to the tracks. A loud whinnying from a horse made Michael glance sideways, tensing when he saw the ugly, almost distorted face of Nathan Hawkins behind the driver of the carriage that was also traveling down this busy thoroughfare.

"Damn. I can't even put him from my mind for one minute," Michael whispered to himself. "Now he's in Saint Louis to stir up trouble." He turned his eyes quickly away, for fear that Nathan might in the future recognize him as being one of the better-class gents of Saint Louis, not a drunken bum as Michael would continue to profess to being while in Hawkinsville.

But, Michael had also to remember, so far Nathan Hawkins hadn't made his presence known in the saloons of Hawkinsville. Normally, he would hire someone else to do all his dirty work. In fact, Michael knew that most of the Italian people hadn't ever met him. Only his representatives. No. Nathan Hawkins wouldn't want to dirty his expensive London-bought clothes by entering the town of Hawkinsville . . . even though it was his own name-given town.

The cable car drew to a halt, releasing many of its passengers out onto the walks of the city. Michael pushed himself up from the seat and joined the milling crowds along the walkway until he found himself standing in front of the several-storied-high Planter's House Hotel. He hurried inside, seeing all reds around him in the plushness of the carpet beneath his feet and the draperies hanging at the long windows.

He moved on past the desk clerk. He didn't have to ask the room number. He knew it by heart. He had heard many men talking of Sabrina. "Sabrina." What a beautiful name. He hoped she would be just as beautiful.

He began ascending the wide staircase, taking steps two at a time, and when he reached her door, he hesitated before knocking, fearing that another man might be inside. He hadn't called ahead. His needs had caused him to move in haste.

After taking a few deep breaths, he knocked, tensing. He smiled awkwardly when the door flew widely aside, revealing a lady of about fifty whose wrinkles had only begun to crease what was once a beautiful face.

"Yes? What can I do for you?" she asked in a low-pitched drone, leaning out a bit to glance up and down the length of the hallway.

"Uh . . . you . . . are you . . . Sabrina?" Michael asked, stammering. Was this aging person the woman the men gossiped so freely about? His gaze traveled over her, seeing the heaviness of her breasts and how the nipples thrust hard against the pale green chemise she had wrapped around her body. One look further downward revealed that nothing at all was worn beneath this thin material. It revealed a thickening waist and a blonde patch of pubic hair shaped in a sharp vee, to match the short-cropped blonde hair atop her head.

Michael stared upward at her hair, not having seen a woman with such a haircut as this. It was cropped short to hang just below her ears, and she had straight bangs hanging low to her eyebrows. Her lips formed into a wide, brightly painted oval as she motioned with her hand for him to enter her room.

"Sabrina is here to make you forget your troubles," she said, closing the door behind her. She went to Michael and smoothed her fingers over his brow. "You do have problems, yes? Your brow is much too furrowed for such a handsome man."

Michael felt a bit awkward in this lady's presence, having expected her to be much younger. He looked quickly around the room and spied the greatness of the mahogany bedstead covered by the sleek shine of flaming red satin sheets and pillow covers.

The rest of the room was like most other hotel rooms, with a wardrobe that sported a pier glass mirror set into its door, two upholstered chairs of brown horsehair, and a table beside the bed upon which sat a glass Bordeaux lamp. A china basin sat on a stand on the opposite side of the bed next to a long, narrow window where lacy, sheer curtains hung, pulled closed.

His gaze met Sabrina's and held, discovering her art of teasing with the pale grays of her eyes and the flickering of her tongue that seemed to be continuously wetting her lips. He reached for her, placing his arms around her waist, jerking her roughly to him. "Yes," he finally answered. "I am in need of someone to help me forget for the moment."

His head bowed, grazing her flesh with his lips, nudging the thin material of her chemise aside with his nose, until her breasts were fully exposed to him. Michael reached upward and squeezed one breast as his lips devoured the other, drawing a moan of ecstasy from deep within Sabrina.

"Aw, you are so hungry," she purred. "Come to my bed. Let me show you Sabrina's ways of making a man lose his senses."

Michael followed along beside her, hurriedly slipping his suit jacket off, then his collar, shirt and silk cravat. By the time he reached the bed, he had only his breeches and shoes to remove, but he found that he didn't have to use any more of his own efforts in doing so. The eagerness of Sabrina's fingers was already on him, quickly helping to expose his full nudity to eyes that were completely devouring him.

"Please lie back on the bed," she said sternly. "I wish to first wash you with my perfumed oils."

Michael's eyes widened. "You what?" he gasped, hesitating.

"It is my specialty," she said, removing her chemise, letting it cascade to the floor, to settle around her feet. She urged him downward, pressing her fingers against his chest.

Michael propped two pillows beneath his head, watching her as she moved toward the basin. When she reached inside and pulled a wet satin cloth from the glistening pool of liquid, his heart began to pound in anticipation. He could smell the perfumed oils. Was it some sort of aphrodisiac? The moment she placed the cloth against his abdomen and began to move it in slow, easy strokes, he felt a keen sense of sexual desire begin to build inside him. And as she continued to spread the perfumed oils, moving downward, across his thighs and then onto his manhood, he gritted his teeth and stiffened his body.

"So it does feel good, does it not?" Sabrina purred. She placed the cloth inside the basin, then climbed atop him, positioning herself so that one thrust was all that was required for him to plunge his manhood deeply inside her.

Sabrina's lips sought out his nipples, sucking, all the while working her breasts over the sleek wetness of his oiled body. He reached down and touched and probed between her thighs with his fingers, then guided himself inside her, knowing that it wouldn't be long before his peak would be reached.

"You're a skilled whore," he grunted, moving his hips hurriedly, holding her closer to him, as though she were in a vise. "Worth every damn dollar."

"Yes, yes," he quickly added, thrusting even harder, feeling his heartbeats becoming erratic from the building excitement. "Give it to me, baby," he groaned. "Show me just how much you *are* worth." He heard a low rumble of laughter surface from deep inside her as she reached back and dug her fingernails into his buttocks, making him groan even more loudly as this had

215

seemed to make his completion come in wild, angry spurts inside her.

His mind left him for those short, pleasurable moments of ecstasy, urging him to whisper, "Maria . . ."

His hand reached up around her neck and jerked her lips to his, kissing her fiercely, hungrily. "Maria," he whispered again. "I love you, Maria. Oh, my God, how I love you. . . ."

Another low, throaty laugh drew him to his senses. He set Sabrina free, watching her face twist in mockery as she continued to laugh. "You are not as all others I service," she said, climbing from the bed. "You still speak of another woman when you are with me."

Michael tensed. "I . . . did . . . ?" he whispered, remembering the other times.

"But I in time will change that," she purred, pulling her chemise on. She reached inside her wardrobe and pulled a towel from it, then tossed it to Michael. "Yes. In time I will teach you to forget. But for now, wipe the oils from your body and be on your way."

She went to the table and slid a drawer open and pulled a cigarette and match from inside it. She lit the cigarette, still watching Michael. "And what did you say your name was, handsome man?" she asked, slouching down into a chair, crossing her legs to swing one outward from her.

Michael climbed from the bed and began wiping his body with the towel. "I didn't say," he grumbled, still brooding over the fact that he had once again spoken Maria's name while in the arms of another. . . .

"You are not going to reveal it to me?"

Michael eyed her closely, remembering how she had been capable of making him soar to such heights of

216

gratification, even though he had once again been guilty of speaking Maria's name. Maybe this whore could make him soon forget. Then he would be free of all his haunting memories and dreams. "Michael," he said. "Only Michael." He hurriedly dressed, then pulled a roll of bills from his inside jacket pocket, handing her two fifties.

Sabrina went to her wardrobe and reached in, hiding the money. She turned to face him, licking her lips, then said, "And, handsome Michael, I can expect to see you again? Yes?"

Michael sucked in his abdomen, buttoning his jacket. "Often," he said, walking toward the door.

"You had better make a reservation before your next visit," she said, clinging to the door as he now stood with it open. "Safer that way. I have a good clientele, but yet, some might cause you some trouble if they see you taking up too much of my time."

Shadows creased Michael's face, feeling a bit dirty when she talked about so many men always using her body, the same as he had just done. "Yeah. Sure," he said thickly, then turned and rushed down the hall, stopping to stare down the staircase, checking to see that no one recognizable was in the lobby. He knew that even though he was a man with special needs, he still had to be discreet. His name was becoming more and more influential in Saint Louis. He wanted everyone to continue looking upon him as a citizen one could fully respect and admire.

"My God," he muttered beneath his breath when he caught sight of Nathan Hawkins approaching the stairs. No one could mistake that craggy face, with its briar-thicket eyebrows and bushy gray mustache. As

217

Nathan Hawkins stepped onto the bottom step, Michael stood as though frozen, seeing the lights from the ceiling reflecting on this man's bald head. When his narrow, gray eyes shot upward, Michael jumped aside, eyeing the area around him. He breathed a sigh of relief when he found a linen closet door behind him. He would have to hide there. In no way did he want to meet Nathan Hawkins face to face. The time for that was in the future . . . but only when Michael felt it necessary for the welfare of the union . . . and the coal miners.

With haste, he stepped inside the linen closet, leaving a crack from which to watch where Hawkins was going. When Nathan Hawkins knocked on Sabrina's door, Michael's face drained of color, thinking of himself having just left Sabrina's room. If he had been slower at getting dressed, he would more than likely have run head on with the bastard.

Then Michael couldn't help himself. He bent double, muffling a laugh, hardly able to envision the likes of Nathan Hawkins in bed nude with a woman.

"How could any woman . . . ?" he said, choking on the words. "Even . . . a . . . whore . . . ?"

Counting out the last few coins in the palm of her hand, Maria felt a weariness settling around her heart. She knew that Alberto's luck at playing cards hadn't been as good as it had been on the ship. Instead, he had drained the Lazzaro family of the last of their grocery money, meaning that Maria had to find a way to replace the money, or confess this obsession of Alberto's to her Papa.

"I don't like this responsibility of being in charge of the Lazzaro family's monies," she sulked, dropping the few coins into a fruit jar, screwing the lid on tightly. "Alberto is better at figures than I. But Papa said it was my duty since I am home all day with nothing besides household chores to do."

But she knew that Alberto had taken more charge than she had, taking it upon himself to remove money from the jar whenever he chose to do so, so he could go to Ruby's, which Alberto confessed to frequenting to Maria. "But not for the pleasures of a whore," he had said. Alberto had explained that there was an upper room at Ruby's house that was used only for gambling . . . that the finest-dressed gents from all over the area made it their habit to visit Ruby's house . . . both for card playing *and* whoring about.

Even though Maria had made a brief acquaintance with Ruby and had even decided to like her, the thought of Alberto's being a part of Ruby's house had disgusted her. It seemed to her that his personality continued to change. He had become a person with a warped mind. Hadn't she seen the way his eyes raked over her as of late? Hadn't she seen him lurking in the darkness when she made trips to the privy?

"Alberto, Alberto," she whispered, rushing to her bedroom. "I don't even know you anymore, Alberto." She lifted the corner of the mattress of her bed, hiding the jar of coins in the depths of the springs. "If it's not your gambling I'm worried about, it's something else," she added. "Why can't it be as it was when we were in Italy? Why have you had to change so?"

The rattling of the paned glass window beside her bed reminded Maria of the type of day it was. She went to the window and stood cross-armed, staring outward into a beautiful windy day of March. It now seemed

219

ages since the frozen water pipes of winter had sent her daily rituals of scrubbing, cleaning, and cooking into a tailspin.

The community water faucet had only dripped one continuing icicle, growing each day, it seemed, until the icicle had reached the ground and had formed what looked like mounds upon mounds of cut glass sparkling beneath the dull rays of the winter afternoon's sun.

Many trips with the horse and wagon had been made into the town of Creal Springs by Alberto, to buy small barrels of water, draining even more from the Lazzaro family account. They had used the water sparingly, as though it were an expensive champagne.

But, finally, the sun had begun to lean its velvet rays of gold closer to the small town of Hawkinsville and the warmer breezes had begun to blow, until the daily trips to the community water faucet had been made possible once again.

"But, now what shall I do?" Maria fretted aloud. "I have the water I so prayed for, but I do not have the money I need." She watched the freedom flights of the birds outside her window, envious of them. "I cannot confess to Papa that I haven't enough money to last until his next paycheck. To tell Papa this would be the same as tattling on Alberto," she whispered, turning to stare at the drabness of the house that continually encroached itself upon her. She hated this house. So far, she hated America. It had handed nothing her way except for the grief of the drudgeries of her everyday existence, and the heartache when she would let her thoughts wander to Michael, who had traveled on away from her to some strange name of a city called

220

Saint Louis.

Tears brimmed her eyes, as she remembered Michael's gentle smile . . . the blueness of his eyes . . . the blonde waves of his hair. At first glance she had fallen madly in love with him. She had loved his difference in appearance, so light-skinned, nothing at all like the Italian men she had grown so used to seeing on Pordenone's streets. She had never hungered for any of her countrymen's touches. Only Michael had stirred the embers inside her to a burning inferno.

"But, I shall never see you again, Michael," she said, flipping her hair to hang down in dark waves to her waist. "I must forget you. I must." She reached upward and pulled the tarnished chain free from beneath the bodice of her dress. She turned it in her fingers until she found the clasp, then unfastened it, letting the chain and the key that hung loosely from it ripple down onto the palm of her hand. When she would feel the loneliness eating away at her insides, she would remove her violin from its case and let her instrument speak to her in its soft, gentle voice as she pulled the bow across its strings.

She lifted the skirt of her dress up as she stooped to reach beneath her bed. She pulled the violin case outward and lifted it atop her bed, then unlocked it, remembering how it had pleasured her to play on the street corners of Pordenone—the only audience she had ever known.

Touching the strings, plucking them one by one, a thought seized her, making her pulsebeat increase. She had played her violin on the streets of Pordenone for . . . money. . . . Why couldn't she do it in the town of Creal Springs? Her Papa and Alberto would never need know. She would play only during the hours that they were in the bowels of the earth. And choosing to play on the streets of Creal Springs instead of this Italian community was much wiser, since the people of Creal Springs would most surely have coins to share with the less fortunate.

"Yes," she said aloud. "That's what I shall do. That could be the answer to many things." Tremors of excitement raced through her, as she thought that playing in front of an audience once again was so close at hand. Why hadn't she thought of it earlier? She wouldn't only be finally having some pleasure from life, but bringing home some coins at the same time.

"Now what shall I wear?" she said, looking down at her flimsy attire of a thinning, threadbare cotton dress. As she held the skirt out from her body, she could even see herself through it. No. That would not be appropriate to wear where people would be watching her.

She rushed to the wardrobe, pulling out the dress her aunt Helena had given her. Its sleekness of satin shone back at her in shimmering colors of greens and the velveteen bows and white trimmings of lace made her heart pound against her ribs. She wanted so to wear this, to look like one of the rich women who lived in the magnificent houses at Creal Springs.

But her brows furrowed. There were two reasons she could not wear such a dress. She did not want to reveal the curves of her body to men, knowing that to do so, especially while standing on a street corner on display, could possibly cause one to do her harm. She also knew that to wear such a fancy, expensive dress would be to defeat her purpose of wishing to look the part of a waif who did indeed need coins tossed at her feet.

"Then what shall I wear?" she murmured, placing the dress back inside the wardrobe. Her gaze settled on her chimney sweep outfit. It hung from a hanger, clean and crisp, yet it gave her such an empty feeling inside, thinking to have to wear it again. She hated its absolute drabness. She hated the breeches. But when she had taken it to the stove to burn it, as she had so longed to do while on the long journey from Italy, her Papa had stopped her, saying that it was a waste to destroy any clothes that still could have a possible use some day.

"Did he know that more would be needed besides coal mining to keep this family in money?" she wondered aloud. Had he thought she might even try her skills at chimney sweeping while here in America? A loathing made her face become all shadows. But she knew that today this outfit was the best thing that she could wear. It would make her look the role of a person in need, and it could be used to hide the fact that she was a female. She had mostly succeeded at doing this while on the ship and train. With her hair hidden beneath the confines of the hat, she knew that she could indeed play the role of a male once again. For her Papa? Anything! Hadn't she even refrained from returning to Ruby's because of her Papa . . . and what he might think of her for associating with her kind? Yes, for her Papa . . . anything. He came first. Now. Always.

With trembling fingers, she hurriedly changed from her dress to her black breeches and jacket. "Papa will never know," she said, sweeping her hair up atop her head, pinning it, then placing the cap snugly over it. "And the money I shall make will be spent for groceries. He'll just think I'm using the money he has earned. Only Alberto will know the difference, because it is he who is spending Papa's hard-earned money as well as his own. But Alberto can just go jump in the lake if he doesn't like what I'm doing. To tell Papa would be the same as telling on himself."

Maria stepped into her high-topped shoes and laced them, then placed her violin in its case and snapped the lid shut. Taking a deep breath, she hurried outside, glad to know that Alberto had decided to leave the horse and wagon at her disposal for use any time of the day for shopping or in case of an emergency. "Well, this is an emergency," she said softly, smiling, now anxious to carry this plan out.

She placed the violin in the back of the wagon, then pulled herself up onto the seat. The horse was stamping its feet restlessly, also anxious, it seemed, to get away from its drab surroundings. Maria lifted the reins and gave them a slap, looking quickly around her, seeing if anyone was watching her escape from her day of drudgery. Excitement was building inside her. She had grown so tired of her days of labor. She hadn't even been able to take her daily walks because of the cold, damp weather. She had wanted to return to Ruby's, but hadn't, knowing the disappointment it would cause her Papa.

She wondered now if Ruby would even remember her. Several months had passed since the day they had met, the day Maria had seen another way of life that she had only up to that time read about in novels. "A house of whores," she thought to herself, guiding the carriage out onto the narrow street, moving away from the row after row of shacks, on through the small town of Hawkinsville, and onto a country road of dried, muddy ruts. She stiffened, feeling her body being tossed about on the seat. But she was determined to move onward. She had only a few hours, then she would have to return before her Papa and Alberto would get home. She had to keep this from her Papa. At all costs.

When she reached the outskirts of Creal Springs, she stopped and pulled her billed hat lower on her forehead, hoping her eyes wouldn't be so noticeable. She knew that most males didn't have lashes to match her own. That alone could give her identity away. She had to be sure that no one discovered that she was a female. She would stand . . . mute . . . playing . . . then bowing a silent thanks if coins were tossed at her feet.

Slouching a bit, Maria urged her horse onward, now looking from side to side, seeing the nicely painted white-framed houses lining both sides of the town's streets. Each house was of a different design, and they had lawns of mowed green grass, and flower beds in shades of yellows, reds and purples.

Maria sighed, longing to live in such a way. Everything in this town seemed so fresh . . . so clean. And the houses appeared to have been built so that no cracks could possibly be found in the walls. She could envision a family living in luxury behind these walls . . . a family that probably hadn't ever had to want for food . . . for warmth. . . .

Determination made Maria slap the reins even more fiercely. She would get some coins tossed to her this day. She had to.

When she reached the outskirts of the business district, she eyed the buildings with awe. They were mainly of red brick and had huge windows of paned glass, in which could be seen displays of women's apparel, furniture, and many other items that made Maria's eyes widen, and her heart pound at a faster rate of speed. Pordenone wasn't anything like this. This town in America showed such a variety of wealth.

She guided her horse down a street that had even been made of laid red bricks. This street then led onto another street that formed a square around a magnificent building that displayed a huge, grand clock at the top. It showed its face and hands on four sides, so that no matter which street you were on, you could still look upward and see what time it was.

When chimes began to count out the hour of ten, Maria moved onward, looking for a corner that would be best for her to do her . . . entertaining . . . which she knew in truth would be called begging by the wealthier of the townspeople who might see her. But she didn't care. She was doing what she had to do, and she would enjoy it no matter what she might be called while doing it.

Maria studied the buildings carefully, and the people coming and going from them. Most of the men were dressed in neat suits and wore hats and exhibited fat, bushy mustaches. The women were dressed fancily in long, flowing dresses, and most displayed the fanciest of hats, each, it seemed, trying to outdo the next by the extremes of design.

Another longing rippled through Maria, hoping one day to be a part of this glamour. But she now knew that more than likely it would never happen. It was meant for her to remain just an immigrant. She was supposed to make life as easy for her father and brother as was humanly possible. The Lazzaro family had to stick together. But anger raged through her now, remembering Alberto, and his carelessness with the Lazzaro money. One day he would see the wrong of his new way of life. One day. . . .

A seven-story brick building drew Maria's keen attention. It reminded her of some of the buildings she had seen during her brief time in the large city of New York. This had to be the building meant for her to stand in front of. Surely the largest building of this town would be the one most frequently used by the townspeople. And upon closer observation, she read the name Creal Springs City Bank on a huge sign that reached across the front. She smiled. This indeed was the place to display her talents as a violinist. Surely people leaving a bank would be the ones to have the most coins to toss away. . . .

Hurrying to tie her reins to a hitching post, she then removed her violin and bow from their case and inched her way toward the street corner nearest the door of the bank building. She eyed the people sheepishly, seeing that just her presence alone was drawing much attention. She blushed a bit, knowing how terrible she had to look in her ghastly chimney sweep costume, but then she only ducked her head, fitted her violin beneath her chin, and began drawing the bow across the strings, letting her mind drift to the words being spoken to her from her instrument . . . so soft . . . so soothing. She played harder, until she could even feel the strings beginning to cut into her fingers. It was then that she heard the first tinkle of a coin against another coin landing on the brick walk at her feet.

Maria's pulsebeat increased, but she knew to not let herself make eye contact with the people being so

227

generous. She knew that to do so would be to reveal too much. Instead, she tucked her violin beneath her left arm and bowed deeply, keeping her head ducked.

She proceeded to play another song familiar to her, thrilling inside from the audience that she was drawing, and from the money that she was fast earning. She couldn't play fast enough, and the faster she did play, the more she heard the coins being tossed at her feet. Then the chiming of the town clock drew her quick attention to the time of day, and she knew that her fun would have to draw to a close. She had to shop for household supplies before going home. She was anxious to replenish their empty kitchen pantry. She would even get home in time to make a delicious stew. What a surprise for her papa and, yes, what a complete surprise for Alberto. He had known how few coins remained. He would know that she had worked for the food that would be placed on the table this night. She was anxious to see his face . . . to see the wonder in his eyes.

Not looking upward at the crowd that began to disperse as she began to collect the coins to slip into her pocket, she listened as they moved on away from her, hearing the comments of how fabulously "he" had played the violin. Pride swelled inside her. This alone was worth the disgrace of having to wear such an outfit once again. She would do it again. Yes. Tomorrow . . . she would do it again. . . .

Chapter Ten

A week of playing her violin on the street corners of Creal Springs had passed and Maria was still playing her heart out, hardly believing the response she was receiving. She had hidden a jar full of her earned coins away from Alberto's snoopings. He had guessed her pastime, but had kept his silence about it.

This day, Maria had found some competition. She drew her bow across the violin strings, glancing sideways at another Italian female, seeing her displaying her beautiful assortment of paper flowers that she had made for selling on the streets. The girl held the flowers in front of her for all to see as they passed by. Maria felt a twinge of jealousy when the girl was handed coins in exchange for the paper-shaped clusters of beautiful different colors.

The girl was of the same olive skin coloring as Maria, with dark, imploring eyes that could take the heart from anyone looking into their depths. Her dress was of a thin, fully gathered cotton that would wrap around her ankles as the winds whipped around the corners of the bank building she and Maria were standing before.

Except for the girl's nose that was tiny and tilted, her features were Italian. Maria knew that she was competing with more than artificial flowers for notice. This girl was shatteringly pretty. Maria knew that she had to let the pretty side of her own self be seen, no matter if doing so disclosed to all that she was a woman . . . not a man. Playing the violin for coins had suddenly become not enough. If she had to show the beauty of her long, flowing hair, and the brightness of her eyes that she had kept purposely hidden as best she could, then be that as it might. She would do just that. She needed the coins . . . surely more than the girl standing beside her!

Leaning momentarily to place her violin in its case, Maria watched out of the corner of her eye as the girl continued to sell her flowers. Haste was needed. Maria was losing out on coins this day.

She reached up and pulled her hat from her head, shaking her hair to come loose from its pins, to cascade lazily down her back in long, dark waves. She licked and sucked on the fullness of her lips, to cause them to darken in colors of reds, then loosened the buttons of her jacket down halfway to her waist, revealing the deepness of her cleavage. She felt a bit wicked but she knew that in such clothes, more than what she would usually reveal to the naked eye was needed. She was a woman. She would display this along with her talents at playing the violin. She had to remember . . . she needed the coins. She would try anything to get them.

Smiling, she looked toward the girl, seeing that she had been watching. "Now I shall be the one to get the coins," Maria said to her in Italian, picking up her violin.

The girl blushed, then unbuttoned her dress partially

down the front, deciding to play the game as well. "We'll see about that," she whispered, also in Italian, moving closer to Maria. "At least I look the part of a woman. I have never worn breeches. You look disgusting. Absolutely disgusting."

Maria's eyes snapped with anger. "Then you have never known the true meaning of being poor," she whispered back, ignoring the gathering crowd watching the feud developing. "I had to wear breeches in Italy. I was a chimney sweep. What did you do in Italy? Make flowers like a weakling? At least I proved my need for lira. By working hard. Ha! Now tell me you have worked so hard yourself."

"And what have we here?" a high-pitched male voice spoke suddenly from behind Maria, making her whirl around, eyes wide. "Two females on the verge of war?" he said further. "Shame be upon you. Maybe you need an intermediary. Shall I suffice?"

Maria clutched her violin to her bosom, words catching in her throat when she saw this craggy-appearing face staring so knowingly upward at her. She had never seen so ugly a man. His gray eyes seemed bottomless and his briar thicket of eyebrows and bushy, gray moustache bounced as he talked. His hat was held in his hand, revealing a head that shone back to Maria, almost like a mirror, as she looked downward. He was so short, she knew that she could very easily place her chin upon that head of glass. But she chose to not even stand so close to him. He had an air of aloofness about him. As though he truly didn't care about anything or anyone, except himself. Why he had chosen to intervene in this private argument was a question Maria didn't care to hear the answer to.

"No, sir. Your interference is not appreciated," she said flatly. "Now if you will please excuse me, I have a song I would like to play on my violin."

The man refused to move. He smiled crookedly as he pulled a fat roll of bills from his front breeches pocket. "Now if I gave you enough money for a full day's playing, would you think you might take time to speak to a lonely man?" he questioned, winking at Maria.

Maria stared open-mouthed at the money, then toward the young girl, whose face had paled. "But . . . sir . . . I don't know. . . ." Maria whispered, staring once again at the money. She had never seen so much at one time. Never. Oh, how much she could buy with it. Oh, how she ached to reach her hand out . . . accept it. . . . But she couldn't. She had pride. Coins were earned. This vast amount of money wasn't.

"This is only a small amount of all the money that I own, young lady," he said, holding the money out, motioning for Maria to take it. "If you wish, share this with the young lady at your side. Then you will no longer have reason to dispute. Money is the cause for your angry words being exchanged, is it not?"

Maria swallowed hard, inching away from him. This was too easy. Nobody gave away such amounts of money . . . unless . . . they wanted more than one was willing to give. "Sir, please be on your way," Maria whispered, looking from side to side, seeing that all the other bystanders had moved on their way, now that she had ceased playing her violin. Anger made her insides turn to boiling, realizing she had lost her chance at having many coins tossed her way because of this interfering old man whom no one could possibly enjoy being with. And no way was she so anxious to have extra money that she would have to accept it from the carefully manicured fingers of this gentleman.

She looked at his ruffled shirt and the sleekness of his black waistcoat and breeches. His boots shone back at her also in black, shining as much as his head, as though both had been waxed by carefully trained hands.

The man laughed out of the corner of his mouth. "Surely you are jesting," he said, placing the money back inside his breeches pocket. "No one refuses Nathan Hawkins anything. Especially an Italian. You are only in America because I was kind enough to pay your passage. Indeed this is true. And you have to know it."

Maria's face paled. She felt numb . . . absolutely numb . . . having heard this man's name spoken. "Did you say . . . Nathan . . . Hawkins . . . ?" she finally gasped, looking him up and down, now feeling like laughing after having visualized for so long that this Nathan Hawkins whom everyone despised and hated would be huge . . . virile . . . even possibly of a giant size for a man. But this man? He was so small . . . so grotesque in appearance. How could any man . . . or woman . . . fear him?

"So you do know of me," he said, smirking. He leaned closer to Maria, whispering. "And you do know that you owe me much, don't you?"

Maria bit her lower lip, wanting to say so much to him. Hadn't she practiced the words? Over and over again? Wanting so much finally to be able to meet him face to face? But now? They were on a street with too many ears to hear the words she had chosen to use on this man. Then she remembered the other Italian girl with whom she had been competing for space on this sidewalk. What was she thinking at this moment? Why hadn't she spoken her mind?

Maria turned to go to her, to maybe use her as an ally, instead of an enemy, to face up to this man whom Maria had hated for so long. But Maria found the girl gone. She had disappeared into the air, it seemed. Maria now remembered how the girl had shown fright upon first seeing Nathan Hawkins. Now Maria knew that it hadn't been the money that had sent the girl's face to losing its color. It had been the fact that Nathan Hawkins was there, speaking with them. It was apparent that this girl had indeed been warned against him.

Now what was Maria to do? Here he was, and what was he insinuating? That she owed him something? That she had been paid passage to America by him? She knew the latter, but she felt the only thing she owed him was hate . . . revenge.

She bent down and placed her violin in its case, feeling the need to flee. When he stooped, to be beside her, she tensed, not knowing what to expect next.

"I know who you are," he said, looking around, to see if he was being watched.

"No. I don't think you do, sir," she whispered, flushing. She clicked the locks securely on her case, then hurried to her wagon. She placed the violin in the back, then untied the reins, wishing there weren't so many miles between Creal Springs and Hawkinsville. There just wouldn't be any way to escape him if he chose to follow her.

He moved toward her, with his hat on his head now. He reached up and took the reins away from Maria. "I wish to see you, Maria," he said flatly. "You are to follow me home. My carriage is over there. You have no choice but to follow me. Do you understand?"

"Give me the reins, sir," she said, fuming. "I have no desire to go to your house. I have no desire to be near you. You have the devil in you. I don't wish to have anything to do with you."

Nathan Hawkins laughed as he handed the reins to her. "I like a girl with spirit," he said. "Yes. I like that. You are more beautiful even when you are angry. Now. You just follow me. Then I won't have to ship you and your brother and father back to Italy on my ship's next voyage. I think I make myself clear. Do I not?"

Maria's heart began to pound rapidly. "What did you say?" she said, clutching the reins, trying to hide the trembling in her fingers. She watched his eyes grow even lighter in gray. There seemed to be absolutely no bottom to them. And his craggy features worsened as he frowned.

"You heard me. Quite distinctly, I am sure," he said, walking away from her, toward a fancy carriage of black.

"I shall not," she yelled after him, slapping the reins, causing the horse to lurch forward. "Hahh!" she then shrieked to the horse, glad when she saw that the horse had finally decided to pick up speed. She had to return home in haste. She couldn't hide the fact that she was frightened. She couldn't believe that she could be, after seeing the smallness of this man. But his words terrified her. What had he meant about shipping them all back to Italy? Surely he couldn't have that much power over her Italian family? They were Americans now. They had been Americanized. Could Nathan Hawkins truly take this away from them?

She screamed at the horse once again, feeling the need to cry. She hoped that her Papa and Alberto would be home, but she knew that by the sun's angle in the sky that it was way too early. What if Nathan Hawkins did indeed follow her home? What was she to do?

She turned her head, looking behind her, searching the road, then breathed a sigh of relief when she found that he wasn't there. He wasn't anywhere in sight. Surely he had been only jesting. But she had to force the horse to speeds it wasn't accustomed to, to get her inside her house, where she could lock the door, just in case this crazy scheming man would decide to seek her out. And how . . . how had he . . . known . . . her name . . . ? Knowing that he did indeed know her gave her an eerie feeling. As though he may have been watching her long before now . . . just waiting to confront her. But why? Creal Springs was surely filled with beautiful, rich women. Why would Nathan Hawkins single her out?

The breeze continued to whip her hair around her face, sometimes even blinding her, but she continued to urge the horse onward until she guided it onto the street that led her past all the houses that were like her own, for once glad to be able to have this house to go to . . .

be a part of. Even though it was in no way a comfortable house in which to live, it was home. A hideaway. A part of the Lazzaro family now.

Maria pulled the wagon to a halt behind her house, then jumped from its seat to hurry to the horse, seeing how it was panting. Guilt plagued her for having worked the horse so hard. It had even worked up into a muddy lather. "Sorry, boy," she purred, wiping him down with a handkerchief she had pulled from her rear breeches pocket. "I won't do this to you again. Hopefully, I won't have a need to."

The approach of clattering hoofs sent Maria's heart into an erratic pace. She stooped behind the horse, watching the road, then sighed heavily when she saw that it was a neighbor, Mrs. Colletti, returning home from the grocery store with her daily supplies.

"I must get inside my house," she said, hurrying to remove her violin case from the back of the wagon. With quick steps, she rushed to the back door and almost fell into the house, then went to the front window, watching. She still felt that he would follow her. He had said that he knew who she was. He would also know where she lived. The only thing that she had going for her was the fact that she had never seen Nathan Hawkins, or the likes of his fine carriage anywhere near the street that she lived on. For him to come there would be to cause many eyebrows to tilt upward. Surely he wouldn't want the Italian community to know that he was after one of their own . . . for whatever reason he had. Would Nathan Hawkins even now send one of his representatives to ask for her presence in his house? Was that the way he did these things?

She continued to watch until her eyes ached. A chill on her chest reminded her of what she still wore and how it gaped open in front. She looked downward, suddenly remembering the time, and how she would have to search for words to explain this attire to her Papa should he come home and find her dressed in such a way. She wasn't ready for explanations. Too much had already happened this day. She had to change into her usual attire of cotton house dress before the mine whistle blew, a reminder that the men would be lifted to the surface and be set free from their ugly chores for one more night.

Lifting her violin case, she went to her bedroom, placing the case on her bed. Having the need to take one more look at her violin before slipping it beneath her bed, she unlocked the case, raised the lid, then gasped. She felt an ache circle her heart when she found that the rough trip back from Creal Springs on the floor of the wagon had been too much for her delicate instrument. A wide crack gaped open on the front of its body, just below its bridge, making the strings lie loose and limp from it. Tears formed in Maria's eyes, hating Nathan Hawkins even more. He was responsible for her haste. It was because of her haste that she had forgotten that her violin had to be treated as delicately as possible.

"Oh, how I hate you, Nathan Hawkins," she said, sobbing. She picked her violin up, hugging it to her. She had guarded it . . . protected it . . . coddled it as though it were a baby on that long voyage from Italy. And now? To have it broken because of Nathan

Hawkins? It added insult to injury. She had hated him for so long. Her wish to seek revenge was now building inside her once again. She would find a way. Yes . . . she would find a way.

A knocking on the front door made Maria tense, knowing that possibly her opportunity to do just that had arrived. If Nathan Hawkins was seeking her out, she would play a game with him. She was a woman. A woman had ways, much different than a man, to complete a plan of revenge.

The knocking persisted. Maria began to tremble, now suddenly feeling less brave. Had he truly come? Her knees had grown weak, imagining the likes of him knocking on her front door. "But I must go to the door," she whispered, placing her violin back in its case. "And I must do it quickly. Very quickly. For won't Papa and Alberto be home much too soon? What if . . . ?"

With a pounding heart, she inched her way to the door. She hesitated for a moment, then opened it slowly, swallowing hard when she saw that indeed it was Nathan Hawkins standing there, with hat in hand, circling it between his fingers. Their gazes met and held as Maria opened the door even more widely.

"What do you want?" she hissed, holding on to the door's edge until her knuckles whitened.

"I want you," Nathan said, smiling crookedly. "Let me come in. We must talk."

"No. You cannot," she said, leaning out a bit, to see if anyone was watching. Her Papa just couldn't hear about this. He just couldn't. It would worry him so. And didn't he have enough to worry about? His health

239

was failing. And it was all because of the cruelties of this man . . . Nathan Hawkins.

"You don't seem to understand," Nathan said, curling his lips in a lewd grin. "You don't have any say in the matter. This house you are living in is mine. I can enter whenever I wish. Now will you please step aside?"

"I will not," she said stubbornly, beginning to close the door, only to be stopped by his jerking it away from her. She gasped, putting her hands to her throat. She began to step back away from him as he stepped across the threshold and was indeed in the close confines of the room with her. "Please. . . ." she stammered, her courage suddenly having left her. She stood, trembling, as his eyes moved around him, seeing the shabbiness in which Maria and her family lived. Could she see a glimmer of laughter in his eyes? Did he enjoy making people live in such a squalid way?

"And how do you like the house I have given your family to live in?" he asked, moving around the room, touching the few pieces of furniture that were there.

"You know that no one could enjoy living in such a way," she said, lowering her hands to her side, circling them into two tight fists. Her hate for him was growing to such an intensity inside her that she found her courage slowly returning.

Nathan turned on a heel, reaching up to caress the thickness of his mustache. His eyes were narrow slits of gray this moment as they raked over Maria. "You don't have to live in such a manner," he said smoothly. He tossed his hat onto Maria's father's favorite overstuffed chair, then moved toward her. "Maria, you could even move into my house with me. I've been waiting for the

240

likes of you for years. I know that what lies beneath that ugly attire is the body of a woman. The woman I could even take as my wife. When your father first described you to me those many months ago, I knew that you had to be what I had been waiting for. Now that I have seen you, I know this to be true." His bony fingers reached upward and touched Maria on the cheek.

She recoiled, as though touched by a snake. But her thoughts were confused, not believing what Nathan Hawkins had just said to her. His wife . . . ? Her Papa had told him about her . . . ? When . . . ? Why . . . ? Her head was spinning from all that was happening. "I don't understand any of this," she finally murmured. "You probably don't even know the meaning of the word 'truth'. My Papa wouldn't tell you anything about me. And you surely can't think I could lower . . . myself . . . to marry such a despicable person as yourself. Do you think you honor me with such a proposal?" She laughed raucously. "Your proposal makes me laugh. In no way could I . . . would I . . . ever let you touch my body. Take your words elsewhere. I don't need the likes of you. Ever."

His eyebrows moved together in their briar-thicket thickness as his face darkened in shadows of yellow-grays. "No one speaks to Nathan Hawkins in such a way," he snarled, taking her by the arm, jerking her to stand next to him. He reached up, grabbing her by the hair, and pulled her face down to meet his, lips searching hers out in a slick wetness, making Maria feel suddenly ill to her stomach. She began to strike out at him, then kicked him in the shins, laughing when he jerked away from her, cursing wildly beneath his breath.

But then his cursing turned to an ugly sort of laughter. "Yes. I do like women to have fire in them," he said, wiping his mouth with the back of his hand. "And, yes, you will be mine. You have no choice."

Maria's eyes widened into two dark pools. "What do you mean?" she snapped. "No one can force me to do anything. And why aren't you after those women who wear beautiful dresses in the town of Creal Springs? Why can't you just leave me and my family alone? Don't you know that all we Italians hate you? You've made us prisoners in this country of America. Papa has told me that he can't even leave to go to another town for fear of what you might do to him. What kind of power do you hold over us all? I don't understand."

Nathan went to a window and placed his back to Maria, letting her only now see the baldness of his head and the small curve to his narrow shoulders. He clasped his hands together behind him and said, "I have explained to you before. I have been generous enough to pay for all your passages to America. This is why you all owe me so much." He swung around and faced Maria. "This is why you owe me. When your father asked for special favors those many months ago, describing you, his daughter, to me, asking that you have special privileges, to let you and your brother believe it was your father's money that was paying your way instead of mine, and because of your beauty and innocence, I agreed, only because I knew that you would be the one I would choose to wed. I am sick of all American women. They bore me. Your description was

242

all that it took to make me realize that you would be the one for me, at long last."

Maria's face had paled. "You say . . . that you . . . planned this? From the beginning?" she whispered. "But . . . Papa . . . ?"

"He had no idea of my true intentions," Nathan said, working with his moustache, curling its ends with the caress of a finger. "He just thought I was being generous."

"But . . . Papa . . . ?"

"Like I said in trying to explain. Your father asked that I let you think it was he who paid for your passage. To let you think that he was no beggar. That he alone was making the kind of money to pay for such things. But that is not the way it is, Maria. I am responsible for your being in America . . . as well as Alberto . . . and your father. You must always remember this."

Maria turned her back to Nathan, hanging her head. She felt humiliated. Degraded. Tears tried to surface. She wiped at her eyes, then turned back to face Nathan. "So . . . you *did* plan all along to . . . seek . . . me out . . . ?" she mumbled.

"All the while," he said flatly.

"Why then . . . did you . . . wait . . . ?"

"Why did I wait until now?" he said. "Because I wanted you to get your fill of living in such conditions as you are living in. Then I knew that you would rush into my arms . . . be my wife . . . to be able to live as any woman dreams of doing. In luxury. With the best of food . . . *and* clothes. Am I right?" His gaze moved around him once again. "Are you tired of living in such a way? Are you ready to live a different way of life? As

243

my wife? In my house? I could see to it that you never want for anything again."

"This is unbelievable," she gasped.

"If you don't agree, I will see to it that you and your family are returned to Italy on the next ship. And while you are on the ship, I will make sure that it will be a voyage of hunger and degradation. I have the power to do so. You know that. The ship you traveled on is mine. Or didn't you know that?"

"This is blackmail," she hissed. "I cannot let you do this to me."

"Call it what you please," he said, laughing amusedly. "But you don't have any choice, my pretty Italian waif."

"You are evil. Just as I have always thought you to be," she said, setting her jaw firmly. She turned once again, and began pacing the floor. She was damned if she did . . . and damned if she didn't. She stopped, facing him directly. "And what about Papa and Alberto? If I do as you request, what about them? Can their lives be made to be more . . . gentle . . . ?"

"No special privileges can be handed them," he said, coughing nervously into a cupped fist. "The only thing I can promise you is that they won't be shipped back to Italy. Other than that, their lives will remain the same. Only you will be the privileged one. But again, you don't have any choice. You will have to forget your brother and father for the time being. For not to do so would be to give all of you a true death sentence, for sure, if you so much as board that ship that heads back to Italy."

"I need . . . time . . . to think," she murmured, so

wanting to lash out at him, to hurt him in some way. But she couldn't. It was he who held her still as a prisoner. It was he who had the power to command. . . .

"You know where I live," he said, placing his hat back atop his head. "I shall be expecting you tomorrow. If you don't arrive, you can expect your father and brother to be without jobs and have tickets in hand for passage back to Italy. I shall do this. Tomorrow."

"I can't believe . . . that. . . ." Maria whispered, paling even more.

"You will believe it when you see it," he said firmly, moving toward the door. He turned to face her, glowering. "Tomorrow?" he said.

"But . . . my Papa . . . and brother," she stammered.

"They are two capable adults. They can do without you," he said bluntly. "And if you will take my advice, do not leave word for them as to where you are until we are together in wedlock. No sense in causing alarm enough for them to come for you when you know the outcome of such a movement on their part."

Maria lowered her eyes, hating this man so much . . . so much . . . she could possibly even kill him. She swallowed hard, remembering the gun that Alberto still had hidden. Could . . . she . . . ? But no. She knew she couldn't. But she would get even with him. Even if it meant having to find a way after actually marrying him.

"I will be there," she said. Her gaze shot upward. "But don't do anything to my brother or Papa. Please. I do this thing . . . only for their welfare. I would gladly go back to Italy. But I know my Papa is too ill to make such a voyage. He wouldn't make it one day aboard that cold, wind-swept deck of the ship. Please just don't do anything to hurt my Papa and brother."

"If you will arrive as soon as you can after the morning whistle's blow from the mine, tomorrow, I will see to it that all will be well with your family. No need to fear. I will keep my word. And you? Will you keep yours? For not to, means only heartache for you. You know that."

"Yes. I understand," she murmured.

"Then I will bid you good day, Maria," he said, bowing slightly, then turned and hurried outside to his carriage.

Maria inched her way to the door and watched, trembling, until the carriage moved from sight. She closed the door behind her, feeling a chill race up and down her spine. Had this been real? Had this truly happened? She leaned against the door, sobbing. She had for so long thought herself to be strong, both physically and mentally. But now? She felt as though she was a child, unable to control her own destiny. She chewed her lower lip while tears crept from her eyes. She knew that she had no choice but to do as Nathan Hawkins ordered. No matter what she would do . . . or no matter whom she would tell of her dilemma . . . she knew the end result. She would possibly be the cause of the loss of three lives. Her own, her brother's, and . . . her . . . Papa's. . . .

The shrill shriek from the mine's whistle drew her mind to the present. She looked down at herself, seeing the ugliness of her garb, then rushed to her bedroom. She had to dress the part of the sister . . . daughter . . .

246

this one more evening. Knives seemed to be piercing her heart, as she thought that this was possibly her last night with her family. "Oh, God," she prayed. "Make it to not be true. Make it to be a nightmare that I will wake up from, and soon. . . ."

She took one last look at her violin, touching it gingerly, feeling the slickness of its varnished exterior, then shut it inside its case and placed it beneath her bed. Then as quickly as she could, she exchanged her chimney sweep costume for her thin cotton dress. She fingered the dress, feeling a creeping eagerness that set her face to flaming because of shame, knowing that deep inside herself she was envisioning herself in other dresses, maybe even fancy hats, like those she had seen on the many women this afternoon in Creal Springs.

She gritted her teeth, wondering how she could let herself think for one moment that what she would be forced to do would be anything pleasant. It would be a life of ugliness . . . so degrading to have been forced into a life with such a man. . . .

But her thoughts suddenly turned to revenge. "Won't I have some control over the lives of the Italians, if I am the wife of Nathan Hawkins?" she said aloud, smiling coyly. "Has he forgotten that to give me his name . . . will be the same as also giving me . . . the power that goes along with . . . that name . . . ?" A feeling swept over her, a feeling of growing confidence in what she was being made to do. "I will make sure my family is well cared for. Nathan Hawkins won't even know I am doing so. He will be too entranced by the way I will use my body with him to even wonder where I will spend my days when he is away. I will go to my family and give them things they have never had before."

She laughed hoarsely. "Yes, Nathan Hawkins. I will repay you for what you have done. I will use your name . . . your wealth . . . your power . . . for the Italians. All Italians. . . ."

Chapter Eleven

Maria lay half asleep, then awakened, startled, when she heard a noise in her room. Pulling the blanket up to hide her thin cotton chemise, she peered through the darkness, seeing a figure moving toward the bed.

"Who's there?" she whispered, growing afraid. Had Nathan Hawkins sent one of his representatives to pluck her away in the middle of the night? She moved to an upright position, inching her way from the bed.

"Maria?" Alberto whispered, reaching for her.

Maria exhaled heavily, relieved. "Alberto?" she whispered. "What are you doing? Why are you sneaking about in my bedroom?" She was remembering him watching her . . . following her to the privy. Had he truly become deranged . . . ?

Alberto moved onto the bed, placing his arm around her waist, pulling her to him. "Maria. Shh. Let's not awaken Papa," Alberto said softly.

Maria began to squirm, feeling embarrassed to have her brother so close to her in this bedroom. It was not Italy. Their Gran-mama was not sleeping in the same room, only a few feet away. Things had changed. There was a respect to uphold when having a bedroom to one's self. "Alberto," she cried softly. "Let me go. Why are you behaving in such a foolish way?"

With his eyes, Alberto sought out her figure in the darkness and could see her outline, making his heart pound fiercely. He moved his elbow up to let it touch a breast. Even though she was his sister, he couldn't help but ache for her in an abnormal way. "I've come to talk, Maria," he said thickly, clearing his throat nervously.

"About what . . . ?" she said, moving away from him.

He ran his fingers through his whiskers, knowing that his movements had been foolish. He didn't dare lose his sister's respect. She was . . . his . . . life. "About someone I just saw at Ruby's," he quickly blurted.

"So you have been there again, Alberto?" she said angrily. "Must you? Every night?" She pulled the blanket upward, shivering from the chill of the early evening. Then she said, "You can't have been gone long. Why did you return so soon? What was this about someone you saw at Ruby's? Did this person cause you to leave so soon? Or did you run out of gambling money?"

"Maria, will you just listen," Alberto grumbled, looking toward the bedroom door, hoping their Papa wouldn't hear the conversation being exchanged between brother and sister in this bedroom of darkness.

"Okay," she said impatiently. "Tell me. What's this all about? Who did you see?"

"Michael Hopper," Alberto said quickly, wishing to see his sister's expression, but without any lights, he just listened to her quick intake of breath. He smiled to himself, anxious to tell her the rest.

Maria's heartbeats skipped as her hands went to her throat. "Did you . . . say . . . Michael . . . ?" she gasped.

250

"At Ruby's? Surely . . . you . . . are . . . wrong. . . ."

Alberto laughed hoarsely. "No mistake, Maria," he said.

"But . . . Michael. . . ."

"Michael was there. I saw him. No way could I be mistaken," Alberto said.

"With . . . one of Ruby's . . . ?"

Alberto laughed once again. "No. He had just arrived and was headed up the stairs, alone, to the gambling room, I am sure," he said. "When I saw him, I ducked out the back door."

Maria's blood surged in a wild thrill, knowing that Michael was so close. She had to find a way to go to him. She had to be held in his arms once again. She knew that he would comfort her as no one else could do. But then she had to remember Nathan Hawkins's warnings. She was to tell no one of their plans. To do so would be possible death for her Papa and brother. Pains circling her heart caused her to gulp back a large lump in her throat, feeling desperation rising inside herself. She had to see Michael, yet she knew she couldn't. "So he was there . . . to only play cards . . . not be with . . . a woman . . . ?" she said softly, trembling.

"He looked as though he didn't have the money for which to pay for one of Ruby's whore's services," Alberto said, laughing. "He looked like a bum. Nothing at all like he dressed while aboard the *Dolphin*. Seems your lover has fallen on hard times."

Maria's eyes widened, remembering how smartly dressed Michael had been, and how he had served her only the best of wines and foods. "I can't . . . believe . . . that he would be poor," she said, sulking. "He is a man

251

of riches. I know this to be true."

"I guess he played one card game too many," Alberto said. "You know the cards can be one's enemy. They have turned on me as of late. You know that. Maybe this is what happened to Michael."

"And you say that Michael didn't see you, Alberto?"

"Hell no. Do you think I'd let him see me? That would only lead him to you."

Maria lowered her eyes. "Then why did you even have to tell me you saw Michael?" she said softly. "Wouldn't I have been better off to not know? Just the same as Michael?"

"I had to tell you that he has lost his luck. I wanted you to know that he is no longer one of the rich kind, that he is as poor as you and I. I hoped that would make you forget him and the damn dreams you must have been having of some day meeting up with him to share his riches. If he has none, you can dream about someone else."

"It is not the riches that attracted me to Michael," Maria said, glowering. "It was Michael. I fell in love with him the first time I saw him. It had nothing to do with money. Nothing at all."

"You...did...love him...Maria?" Alberto gasped.

"Did . . . do . . . and always . . . will," she sighed, feeling tears surfacing. "But it is all lost. For me . . . it is all lost."

"Because of what I just told you about him?"

Maria swallowed hard. "No, Alberto," she said softly. "It's nothing to do . . . with what you have told me."

"Then what?"

Maria's eyes wavered. She reached up and pulled her

hair back from her face and let it settle in deep waves down her back. "Nothing. It is something I cannot talk about, Alberto," she said, knowing that to mention Nathan Hawkins in the same breath would be to reveal too many truths to Alberto. Maria knew of Alberto's temper. She just couldn't let him know that this very next day she would be leaving for Nathan Hawkins's house . . . to become his wife.

"Alberto, will you please leave so I can get some sleep," she said sullenly. "I am so bone-weary and tired."

"Have I upset you, Maria?"

"A bit," she said, stretching out beneath her covers. "But I will be all right. We will all be all right. You shall see."

"What is that supposed to mean?"

"Nothing," she said. "Now, Alberto, please go on to bed. Promise to not leave the house again tonight? I feel much safer when you are beneath the same roof as I. You know that Papa is ailing. You are the strong one of the family now. We depend on you."

"You . . . do . . . ?" he stammered.

"Yes. You know that both Papa and I do."

"I'm glad, Maria," he said, leaning down to kiss her softly on the cheek. "I'm glad. You mean so much to me. I would die if anything would ever happen to you. I would just die."

"I'll be all right, Alberto," she said. "Now, please? I need to be alone."

"To think about that Michael Hopper?" he growled, standing, doubling his fists at his sides.

"Him . . . and much much more," she confessed.

Alberto swung around and stomped from the room,

leaving Maria to stare after him, but glad to now be alone with her thoughts. "Oh, Michael," she whispered, looking toward the window, seeing the blackness of night, wondering how she might arrange to possibly even get a glimpse of him.

"I could go to Ruby's. . . ." she said, sitting upright, biting a lower lip. "Yes, I can go to Ruby's, tell Ruby of my feelings for this man who is in her upstairs room gambling. See if she can arrange for me to take just one small peek at him. Surely it wouldn't hurt."

Her heart thumped wildly against her chest, feeling the excitement building inside her. She knew that this was a dangerous scheme. She knew that a woman did not move through the darkness of the streets at night without taking a chance of being accosted by a drunken man.

"The chimney sweep costume will have to be my disguise once again," she moaned, hating to think of slipping into it another time. But it was the only answer. If she hid herself beneath its looseness and her hair beneath the hat, she could race down the streets without drawing even that first glance from either man or woman. Then even when she entered Ruby's, no heads would turn to stare after her. She would just be another one of the guys . . . in search of a playmate.

She giggled, thinking about it, even wondering if the whores would come to her, thinking she was a "he." "If only one would touch me beneath my jacket," she giggled further. "Wouldn't I surprise her? What a shock would register on that whore's face!"

Trembling from the anticipation of seeing Michael once again, after all these months, Maria finally pulled the last of her clothes on, then her hated shoes that laced up the front. She had no idea how she looked, but she could feel the way each piece hung from her and knew that not even one of Ruby's whores would probably want to draw near her after all. "A man of a six-foot height and lankiness elsewhere surely would be the last thing they would want to take to bed with them," Maria said, giggling still. "And my clothes. Surely they would know I would have no money with which to pay for bedding up with them."

Rechecking to see if her hair was beneath her hat, Maria knew that she was ready to sneak from the house. She only hoped that Alberto had been honest with her and had gone to his room to sleep. If he had gone on to Ruby's, then Maria would most surely be headed for trouble. But she had to take that chance. To see Michael would be worth any trouble her brother could create for her. And wouldn't this be her last night of true freedom? Didn't she have to show up at Nathan Hawkins's house the very next morning? A sick feeling rippled at the pit of her stomach just imagining herself having to be in the same room as that terrible man, much less alone with him . . . on a bed . . . sharing . . . so much more than words with him.

"I mustn't let myself think about that now," she whispered, tiptoeing to the back door, watching cautiously around her, checking and rechecking for shadows in the room, knowing if she did see any, it would be Alberto, possibly up to his old tricks of sneaking, watching her. But when all stayed silent around her and the only shadows were her own, she opened the back door and crept on outside, carefully reclosing the door behind her.

She let her shoulders slump lazily forward, breathing with relief. "Well, I got this far without being discovered," she said, closing her eyes, wiping her brow with the back of a hand. "Now to proceed further."

With brisk steps, she moved across the back yard, around to the front, then on down the middle of the street, dreading having to move across the iron bridge, into unfamiliar territory. She dreaded most of all having to push her way through the darkness of the trees that stretched out between her and Ruby's fenced-in yard, where the dogs browsed constantly, sniffing out any strangers who might come snooping about.

The dogs! The thought of their sharp teeth made pinpricks of fear stab her flesh. She would just have to hope that the dogs would be securely tied . . . that she would be able to reach the front door without being bitten. But surely Ruby had to secure the dogs for the night's business of men arriving. How else could they get to the house . . . to pay for the many types of services that Ruby's house offered?

The moon seemed to be playing games this night. First it would be shining brightly, lighting the area all around Maria, then it would suddenly become hidden by gray, fluffy clouds that appeared to be trimmed in white lace as the moon's rays shone at its edges.

Maria shivered in the chill of the night, pulling her jacket more securely around her neck. She watched on all sides of her as she ran toward the tall Indian grasses in the distance. As was the house she had just left, all the houses lining this street were dark. Maria had argued with her Papa about having to go to bed so early. "Eight o'clock, Papa?" she had grumbled. "I am no longer a child who needs to be pacified by enormous amounts of sleep."

Blowing out the kerosene lamps, her Papa had just ignored her and had crept on into his own bedroom, himself needing all the rest that he could get.

"Boredom is the reason," Maria whispered to herself, stepping high to avoid a pile of horse-dung lying in the middle of the street. "Sheer boredom. What can my people do but work and sleep?"

She had to wonder how her life would change after moving into Nathan Hawkins's mansion. She peered into the distance and could see a bright collection of lights and knew that these were being emitted from Nathan Hawkins's windows. Did he have so many electric lights? She had seen her first at Ruby's. "Such a marvelous invention," she sighed, stopping to listen when she heard the noises that she was fast leaving behind her. The loud guffaws and the tinkling from the pianos at the saloons in Hawkinsville drowned out all other noises.

She was glad to be moving in another direction . . . one that would take her away from the town of Hawkinsville. The town itself, and its deviltry of saloons and loose women, made the Italian people seem to fear even to wander the streets when night fell in its total blackness.

"But maybe I can change all these things for my people," she thought to herself, moving on toward the iron bridge. "Marrying Nathan Hawkins gives me a bitter taste in my mouth, but I have to remember what I might be able to accomplish by being Mrs. Nathan Hawkins."

Pulling her hat lower on her head, Maria moved onto the iron bridge, now hearing a faintness of bull frogs croaking and crickets serenading their mates. It was as though she was entering another world when she stepped from the bridge onto the mossy ground, then on into the thigh-high Indian grass. It was so thick, not even a path had been made by all those who Maria knew had to move through it to go to Ruby's house. The only other way would be to travel across too much of Nathan Hawkins's private estate grounds.

The only thing that Maria couldn't understand was how the men traveled by horseback? Or did they leave the horses at Hawkinsville and travel by foot as she was doing? But then she remembered Ruby's fancy horse and carriage. There had to be a road that Maria hadn't noticed. Had Michael taken that road? Was he now living somewhere besides this place she remembered having been called Saint Louis? Her heart raced, thinking to see him soon. Oh, how she would ache to run to him . . . to fall into his arms . . . to let him carry her away to a wonderland of love. But she had to remember the dangers . . . her Papa . . . her Alberto. . . .

The sounds of dogs barking grew near as Maria made her way into the thickness of brush beneath the towering oak trees. The trees' limbs were whipping around her as the wind seemed to increase in strength, making Maria even more aware of the chill of the night.

She trembled, continuing to move beneath the limbs that hung low, scraping her face, almost knocking her hat from her head. She held onto her hat, lifting her legs high, then tensed when an owl above her let out a loud screech. Her heart pounded and her knees weakened, and she felt so isolated from the world . . . the only world she had ever known . . . a world guided by brother and father. . . .

"Finally," she said, sighing. She reached upward and touched the fence, then recoiled when one of Ruby's dogs raced toward her. Its eyes were two sparkling stars as the moon reflected into them, and its teeth bared in long white points as it continued to have a fit of barking.

"Please," Maria whispered, stepping away from the fence. Now what was she to do? If Ruby let the dogs run loose, how could Maria move on to the front door of the house? And once there, would Ruby recognize her in such a garb? Would she even recognize her at all? They had only met . . . that . . . once.

A sound of footsteps approaching made Maria stiffen. She covered her mouth with her hands, barely breathing. She watched in the direction of the continuing sound, then gulped back words that wouldn't surface when she saw a large, burly Negro moving toward her, carrying a rifle.

He stopped and bent down over the dog, taking it by the collar, talking in soft, soothing tones. Then when he had succeeded at calming the dog, he looked Maria's way, frowning. "Wha' cha' doin' 'round Ruby's place?" he said in a throaty voice. His plaid shirt and dark pants revealed muscles trying to protrude from each. Maria hadn't ever seen such a large person in all her life. But the gentleness of his facial features calmed her insides. His dark eyes were focused on her, waiting.

"I'd . . . like . . . to see . . . Ruby. . . ." she stammered, moving toward the fence.

"What's a whitefolk woman want with Ruby?" he asked, moving toward the fence, now resting the rifle on his left shoulder.

"How did you . . . know I'm a woman . . . ?" she

gasped, eyes wide.

The Negro laughed throatily. "Ain't nevah seen hair as long on a white man befoh," he said, pointing. "An' yore voice ain't that of a white man neither."

Maria reached upward, discovering her hat was missing. "Oh," she said, blushing. Her eyes traveled around her, seeing the hat on the ground at her feet. She stooped to pick it up, hearing the dog growling once again. She hurried to stand in an upright position again.

"Ya knows Ruby?" the man said. "How's ya know mah Ruby?"

"We met one day while I was taking a walk," Maria said, placing the hat back atop her head, working her hair beneath it.

"Not many white womenfolk venture onto this heah property," he said, leaning closer, studying Maria's facial features as the moon came from beneath a cloud. "Wha' cha' wan' with mah Ruby? Huh?"

"Your . . . Ruby . . . ?" Maria gasped, remembering the role Ruby played in this house of girls.

"Mah wife," he said, throwing his shoulders back into a proud square. "Ruby's mah wife from ways back. Now ah asks you again. Wha' cha' wan' with mah Ruby?"

Maria cast her eyes downward, not able to disclose the truth to this stranger. He wouldn't understand. No man would understand. "She told me to visit anytime," she suddenly blurted, watching him again. Her pulsebeat raced. She knew that was a lean explanation. His laughter made her smile awkwardly.

"So's you come visitin' in the daid of night dressed as a man?" he said, chuckling. He motioned with his gun.

"Come on. Ah'll meet you at the front gate. Ah'll then takes yah in the back door. Goin' in the front door would cause some commotion. We don' need no troubles at mah Ruby's house."

When he began to walk along the inside of the fence, shooing the dog away from him, Maria began to follow alongside him. She breathed more easily now, seeing how gentle and kind this man was. And she was relieved to know that she wouldn't be going into the parlor of this grand house after all. The back door was much better. Now she only hoped that Ruby would remember her. What if she . . . didn't . . . ?

Maria swallowed hard when she drew close to the house. She looked upward at the lights flickering through the upper-story windows. Which room . . . was . . . Michael in? Alberto said that the gambling room and the playing of cards was in one of those upstairs rooms. Her stomach fluttered as though it had many butterflies inside it.

"Michael, oh, Michael," she said softly to herself. "If you knew I was so close, would you be as excited? Would you be as eager to get just a glimpse of me?" Then she had to wonder if even a glimpse would be enough for *her*. Once she saw him, could she hold back? Wouldn't she lose her mind and rush to him?

"Here's the gate," the Negro said, opening it for Maria. "Now you jus' follow behin' ol' Clarence. Ah'll takes you to mah Ruby." A chuckle rumbled through him. "Now she jist might laugh a mite when she takes a look at the likes o' you. But she's a woman of good heart. She won' mean you no harm by laughin'. She'll jus' be as me. Ain' used tah seein' no womanfolk in breeches."

Feeling her body being consumed by heartbeats, Maria followed beside him, still eyeing the upper-story windows. She could hear laughter and music surfacing from inside the house and then felt her first moment of apprehension. She had forgotten, in her anxiety to see Michael, just what sort of house she was entering. In the daylight, it had appeared to be a normal house . . . possibly filled with normal people. But now? In the darkness? It appeared a bit foreboding. But she knew that was because she was aware that sharing of lust occurred in the house during the night hours.

She had to divert her attention . . . her thoughts. "Did you say your name is . . . Clarence . . . ?" she asked softly.

"Sho is," he said, stepping aside when he reached the back steps that led upward onto a small square of a back porch.

Looking toward the back door, Maria felt more doubts creeping into her mind. Now could she really . . . ?

"Jus' you go on up to the porch and wait until ah can go and speak tah Ruby," Clarence said, moving on past Maria, two steps at a time.

"Okay," Maria said, swallowing hard. She watched him as he moved on into the house, leaving her to stand alone. She clasped her hands behind her, afraid to move. The sounds surfacing from the house kept her alert and the two dogs now lying at her feet made a tightness, like a band being pulled, form around her forehead. She had never been so bold before.

"Oh, please let Ruby come and see who it is asking for her," she prayed silently to herself. She continued to look around her, seeing only the total blackness of the night crowding in around her. Doubts truly assailed her now. "I'll leave. Now," she whispered. "What I'm doing is wrong. I shouldn't be at such a place. Especially after dark. What would Papa think if he ever found out?" She began to inch her way toward the steps but stopped, startled, when the back door swung widely open.

"Who's there?" Ruby said, stepping out next to Maria. "Clarence said a white femalefolk in man's breeches was here to see me. He didn't think to ask your name. That Clarence of mine. He doesn't use his brains at all."

Maria sighed with relief when she saw the familiar face of Ruby as lights flickered through the back window, then onto her face. She was just as statuesque and beautiful in the semidarkness as she had been in the brightness of day. "Maria. It's me. Maria Lazzaro," Maria said, reaching up to pull her hat from her head. She shook her hair to hang freely down her back. "I had to see you, Ruby," she added quickly, moving toward Ruby, touching her gently on the arm. She eyed Ruby's dress. It was red satin with a plunging neckline, revealing her magnificent bosom.

Ruby laughed softly, tossing her head back. Then she eyed Maria more closely, reaching up to run her fingers through Maria's hair. "Land's sake. It *is* you. I had thought you had forgotten about Ruby's invitation," Ruby purred. "But why now? Dressed in such a way? And in the darkness of night? God, girl. Don't you know the dangers?"

"Yes. I know the dangers," Maria said softly. "That is why I chose to dress as a man. To disguise myself from men's stares."

263

"But you haven't revealed to me why you have chosen to come," Ruby persisted, looking impatiently toward the door, as though she wanted to return inside, where the action was.

"My brother Alberto told me . . . that . . . someone is here that I . . . uh . . . know," Maria stammered, feeling a blush rising from the neck upward.

"Your brother was here? Who did he see?"

"A man I met while aboard ship on our way to America from Italy."

Ruby laughed throatily. "Oh, I see," she said. "So your brother saw this man. What is this man's name? Maybe I will know him from all the others who are here this night."

Maria thrust her hands inside her front breeches pocket and lowered her eyes. "His name is . . . uh . . . Michael Hopper," she murmured.

Ruby emitted a loud gasp. "Michael . . . ?" she said. "You are speaking of Michael Hopper? The Michael Hopper that I also know?"

Maria's heart began to throb wildly. It was true. Michael was at this place. He was only footsteps, heartbeats, away. "Then . . . you do . . . know of this . . . man?" she asked anxiously, looking toward the window, only able to make out fleeting shadows through the lacy, sheer curtains.

"Know of him? Yes. He's been quite a frequent customer," Ruby said. "But I have to ask. Why is it you are so anxious to see him? Did you share more . . . than . . . uh . . . conversation . . . on that ship?"

Maria turned her head from Ruby's imploring eyes. "I cannot say," she whispered. "But I do want to see him. Only see him. Can you help me?"

Ruby moved toward Maria, lifting the tail of Maria's jacket up between her fingers. "You want to see this man dressed in this . . . this . . . outfit?" she said, laughing amusedly.

Maria moved away from her, embarrassment etched across her face. "You don't understand, Ruby," she mumbled. "I want to see *him*. I don't want him to see *me*. Can you help me? Can you arrange this? I only want to take a look at him. I have a need to see him. Just one more time. Before. . . ."

"Before? Before what?" Ruby persisted, placing her hands on her hips.

"Nothing. It is of no importance. The thing that is of importance is that I want to see Michael."

"But why would you want to see him, and him not you? I do not understand, Maria."

"It's hard to explain, Ruby. But that's how it must be."

"You are in love with this man, aren't you?" Ruby said softly, once again lifting Maria's hair from her shoulders. "No need to hide this from Ruby. It is only one person you will have to share this secret with. I talk to no one of gossip. Tell me. You love this Michael Hopper, don't you? You'd like to do more than see him, wouldn't you? You'd like to be with him. As man and woman. Tell me it's true. I sense it is a truth."

Maria's eyes brimmed with tears wanting to surface. "Yes, Ruby. I love him. But it's no use. I can't confess such a love to him. There are too many things standing in the way of such a happiness between Michael and myself. Please. Please. I want to take just one look at him. If you can't help me, then I shall leave."

"No. Don't leave, Maria," Ruby urged. "You want

to be with this man. Right?"

"More than anything on this earth," Maria admitted. "But . . . like I said . . . it is impossible. . . ."

"Nothing is impossible," Ruby said, laughing throatily. "When one is at Ruby's house? Nothing is impossible."

Maria's eyes widened. "I don't understand. What are you saying?"

Ruby leaned down into Maria's face. "Honey, I have an idea. Want to hear it? Ruby's mind works in many directions. At all times. Ruby can sometimes play the part of Cupid. Are you willing to participate in a scheme I have just thought up?"

"I don't . . . know," Maria said, fluttering her thick lashes nervously. "What do you have . . . in mind . . . ?"

"You don't want Michael to know you are here?"

"He can't. . . ."

"Then he won't," Ruby said firmly.

"What are you thinking of doing, Ruby?"

"You will be with Michael. Tonight you will be with Michael Hopper if you are willing to play a role. Are you?"

Maria's pulsebeat quickened. She swallowed hard. "I don't understand . . . ," she mumbled.

"You do want to be with Michael sexually, don't you?" Ruby said, smiling almost wickedly.

"Well . . . I . . ."

"Yes. You do. This truth shows in your eyes. In the way your heartbeat races in the hollow of your throat. So you will be with Michael in this way. Within the hour."

"But . . . how . . . ?"

"Michael usually wants a woman before he leaves

my house," Ruby said. "Once he tires of gambling, he fulfills his desires of the more pleasurable side of life by choosing one of my best girls."

Maria's eyes widened as she let out a loud gasp. She put her hands to her throat, listening further. . . .

"I was the one who personally gave him his pleasures at first," Ruby continued. "But I don't make it a practice to stick with one man too long. It's bad for business. But tonight? I will lead him to a room where there is a new girl. One that will set his heart to racing. One who will make his mind leave him. Are you ready to be . . . this . . . girl . . . ?"

Maria flushed fully. The thought of Michael having been with so many different women made her heart ache. But she had to know that a man had needs . . . needs that possibly needed to be fulfilled each and every night. She had had such needs . . . but had had to leave them to lie dormant, tormenting her insides to shreds it seemed, since having last left Michael's bed on the ship. And now? To have the opportunity to be fulfilled . . . and at the same time to be with the man she loved . . . the man she would always love? She couldn't say no.

"What must I do?" she asked quietly, wishing the trembling would cease inside her.

"Just follow me," Ruby said. "But first. The hat? Place it back on your head. You must look the part of a man for just a short time longer . . . a man I am taking to my room to entertain privately."

Maria's heart lightened. She giggled as she placed her hair beneath the confines of the hat once again. "I don't know about this," she said. "Are you sure . . . ? How will Michael not realize who it is? Won't he

267

see . . . ? Won't he recognize my voice?"

"You'll soon see, honey," Ruby said, circling her arm through Maria's. "Now just act the part of a man. Walk into the house with me very casually, then walk beside me up the steps. My room is upstairs. Next to the gambling room. But keep your head lowered. Damn. One look at that face and those eyelashes and the fellas would think I was going to have fun myself with a female tonight. Don't want to get that reputation. Men are my cup of tea. Not women."

Maria giggled once again, suddenly feeling light-headed. She had never suspected for one minute that anything like this could happen. She had never thought Ruby could be so much fun . . . so full of wonderful schemes. . . . "I don't see . . . I still don't see how you are going to pull this off," she whispered, as they moved into the parlor. It was hard for Maria to not look around her. She heard so many things being spoken between men and women. And the music was soft. Music played for lovers. The warmth of the house wrapped her in its embrace, making her almost sigh, and then she was led up the steepness of the stairs and whisked into a bedroom before Maria could even stop to see the door that led into the room of gamblers.

"We must hasten," Ruby said, already helping Maria with the removal of her clothes. "Michael has been here for some time now. I have to be sure to catch him before he heads down the steps, looking for someone to take to bed. Here. You just hurry with disrobing, splash some of that oil from those bottles over there on my dressing table over your body, then wait for further instructions when I return."

"Where are you going?"

"To go and tell Michael that I have this beautiful new thing that needs to be broken in by the right man."

"But . . . what will I wear . . . ?" Maria said, looking desperately around her, standing cross-armed, partially nude, in the middle of the room.

"Honey, for what I have planned, you don't need a stitch on," Ruby laughed, then rushed from the room, slamming the door behind her.

Maria turned and stared at the room and its plush furnishings. When she looked toward the huge bed and its sheets of red satin, she closed her eyes, trying to not envision Michael on that bed with Ruby. She wanted to think of him as only her own. How marvelous it would be to say that he was hers . . . only . . . to love and cherish forever. But she knew this could not be true. This was a man who had had many women. Would he even think her skilled enough this night to quell his hungers? He at one time had . . . but possibly because she had been the only one available at the time. Had he truly loved her as he had professed to? Or had he only loved . . . her . . . body?

The polished mahogany bedstead and tables shone back at her in dark wines, and the carpet beneath her feet was soft beige, inviting her toes to curl into it. She glanced down at the underthings she still wore and wondered if she could indeed disrobe to only bare skin once again for a man's fingers to explore her body. She shivered, thinking of the thrill of such touches from Michael. Somehow it didn't seem quite fair to not be able to reveal her identity to him. And how was Ruby going to succeed at even doing this?

Maria went and slouched down onto a thickly upholstered chair, biting her lower lip. None of this was real. It just had to be a dream. Surely she would soon awaken and find herself in the bed in her own bedroom, surrounded by the most drab of settings. Her gaze moved around her once again, seeing the red rosebud design of the wallpaper that graced the walls and the brocade draperies that hung in pale beiges at the window. Then the breath caught in her throat when the door opened once again.

"Oh, it's only you, Ruby," Maria sighed, rising.

"It's all taken care of," Ruby said, moving to the bed, smoothing the pillows.

"What did you do?" Maria asked, going to Ruby, to cling to her arm. "What am I supposed to do?"

Ruby swung around, all smiles. She took Maria's hands and squeezed them. "I went to Michael and told him that I have me this new girl who has never been with a man in such a house as mine before," she said. "I told him that to break the girl in, the girl has only agreed to take this man to bed with her if the man would agree to walking into a room of total darkness. I even told him that this girl would be too afraid to speak. He immediately became interested."

Maria paled. "Do you . . . mean . . . he would actually . . . ?"

"Honey, don't you know? Any man would. All men like challenges. What better challenge than this . . . ?"

"But, my brother Alberto said that Michael looked . . . uh . . . down on his luck," Maria murmured. "If he is down on his luck, how can he afford to gamble so much and have women? This all takes money."

"Honey, I know all about this Michael Hopper," Ruby purred. "Only I know his true purpose for being in this area. One day? Maybe you will even find out, whenever you can reveal yourself to the man you love. But until then, just take my word for it. You are just about to be bedded with one of the richest gents in Saint Louis."

"Then he is still rich? Truly? And he still lives in Saint Louis?"

"Correct."

"Then . . . why . . . is he here in this small community? Surely he has better places to visit in Saint Louis?"

"These are things you are not to worry your head about, honey," Ruby said, going around the room, turning the lights out.

"How will he find his way to the . . . bed . . . if the lights are out?" Maria said weakly, looking slowly around her.

"I've told you. He's been in my room before."

Maria lowered her eyes. "Yes. I remember. You did say that."

"Now, honey. Don't let knowing that worry you too much. All men have to have these needs fulfilled. If Ruby didn't do it, someone else would."

"Yes . . . I . . . know. . . ."

"So you just remove the rest of your things and climb onto that bed. Michael should be coming any moment now."

"I just don't see how this will work," Maria said, turning her back to Ruby as she stepped out of the rest of her undergarments. She was glad to see that Ruby had turned the last light out and couldn't make out Maria's nude shape in the dark.

"Just lie on the bed and keep your mouth shut. In the

271

darkness of the room, Michael won't be able to tell if you are Negro or white," Ruby purred. "And because of your olive tones, you'll just blend into the darkness. You'll see."

Maria went to the bed and climbed atop it, feeling the coolness of the sheets next to her skin. She trembled, hugging herself. "I'm a bit afraid," she whispered, teeth chattering.

"Good. Michael knows he's going to enter a room that has a scared girl waiting for him. It's best you play the part to the hilt."

"How can I thank you, Ruby?" Maria said, trying to see Ruby, but not able to even see her outline against the wall.

"Honey, just keep this Michael Hopper happy," she said, laughing throatily. "As long as we have the likes of that man and the riches he possesses frequenting this house, Ruby is kept all smiles."

"Okay," Maria said, stretching out on the bed. "I only hope he doesn't realize who I am. It could cause many complications."

"When a man gets his passions aroused, he isn't aware of much else. Just enjoy it. He's quite a skilled lover. Let him take you away to heights of ecstasy. Don't worry about anything else."

Maria began to speak once again, but was halted when a knock on the door broke through the ensuing silence. "Michael," she blurted, covering her mouth with a hand. "God. Oh, Michael."

Ruby opened the door and moved out into the hall. Maria could hear muffled voices, then felt the thundering of her heart when the door opened and closed once again, giving her only a brief glimpse of Michael's face when the light fell across it when he opened the door. *Oh, God. How can I do this?* Maria worried to herself. When she listened and could hear the rustling of clothes being removed, tears wet her cheeks. Here she was . . . with Michael . . . and not able to even breathe his name . . . or tell him that she loved . . . missed . . . him. . . .

When she felt the weight of his body slide on the bed next to hers, she immediately smelled the familiar aromas of him. It was as before . . . expensive male cologne and cigars. Oh, how could she have been expected to forget such things about him? Their togetherness had been a time of sensuality. She would always be able to remember even the smallest details about him . . . the man she adored . . . the man she loved. She tensed, waiting for that very first touch.

"I know that you're new at this," he said, taking her hand, kissing each fingertip. "I shall be gentle," he added. "I shall make you never be afraid again."

Maria was filled with many emotions. Too many to separate inside herself. His lips . . . his fingers . . . had become his eyes . . . seeking her out in the darkness. His lips were soft against her flesh, yet tearing out small pieces of her heart as he continued to explore her body. Once he let his lips move from her fingertips, he let them move to the hollow of her throat, then downward until he found a breast, the nipple taut, ready.

A warmth seized Maria, remembering the skillfulness of those lips. Yes. It was so easy to recall. As though they had never ever been separated. She groaned from deep inside herself, as his lips moved lower, across the trembling flesh of her stomach, then lower, tracing that part of her body that lay spread

273

between her thighs.

Squirming, Maria chewed on her lower lip, having the need to cry out from passion. But she instead reached downward, until she found his arms, and then encouraged him to move upward, so wanting his lips to crush against her own. Then when he did as she wished, Maria began melting inside, a slow, gentle melting that went from her head to her toes. She moved her body next to his, feeling the hardness of his manhood as it lay against her leg, wanting to reach out . . . touch it . . . but she feared being that bold would cause him to wonder about this girl who wished to remain anonymous . . . the girl who was supposed to be inexperienced.

"You are quite skillful in the way you kiss," he finally murmured, running his fingers upward, through her hair. "And, ah, such luscious, soft hair. Nothing like any I've felt before in this house of girls. Your hair is soft, almost like silk. Not coarse like the other girls of this house."

Maria's heartbeats faltered. Was he guessing that she was indeed not a Negress? Were there ways to tell? Then she forgot her worries . . . her fears . . . when his lips moved to her throat and kissed her there once again . . . so soft . . . so sweet . . . while his fingers made contact on both her breasts, kneading, pinching.

"And now I'd like to warn you before I enter you," Michael said, moving a hand down between her thighs, caressing her there. "Ruby said this was the first for you while in this house. She didn't say if it was the first time for having sex, though. But I will be gentle, just in case it is."

Maria closed her eyes, as the intensity inside her

grew. She was full of wondrous desirous feelings. She felt no guilt . . . no shame. What she was doing seemed natural . . . even expected of her . . . since she was with the man she loved. If she could only whisper of her love to him, touch him where he now throbbed . . . urge him inward. She didn't wish for him to be gentle any longer. She wanted him to take her quickly . . . recklessly even. Being in Michael's arms once again was causing her head to reel with delight. She wanted to tell him this. But instead, she had to continue to lie mute . . . writhing . . . waiting. . . .

With a moan of ecstasy, he entered her. First slowly, then with quick, eager thrusts. His fingers pressed into her flesh, lifting her hips to meet him. His mouth crushed down upon hers, trembling with passion and desire.

"Maria," he then whispered as his body quivered . . . clutching her to him as though she was in a vise. . . .

Maria's eyes flew open, momentarily stunned, having heard her name. Had he truly spoken it? Did he know? How? But soon even these thoughts were taken from her mind when she felt the pleasurable sensations begin as waves in her head, then splashing through her in one marvelous climax after another.

"Ah, Maria," he whispered, caressing her breasts, then withdrew suddenly. "I'm sorry, miss . . . uh . . . I'm very sorry to have spoken another's name. It seems it's a habit of mine. I guess I can't get someone free from my mind. I'm sorry. Believe me. . . ."

Tears moved down Maria's cheeks. She reached for Michael and urged him to lie next to her once again. She wrapped her arms around him, fitting her body into his, clinging. *Oh, Michael. Oh, Michael,* she thought to herself. *You do love me. You do miss me. Oh, Michael. How can I marry Nathan Hawkins knowing this? Oh, God. What shall I do?*

Michael's fingers went to her cheeks, wiping the tears away. "I'm sorry if I hurt you," he whispered, kissing her gently on the lips. "I tried to be gentle."

Maria sobbed harder. She clung to him harder. When he circled his arms around her and climbed atop her once again, she urged him to enter her, knowing that in only that way would he know that he hadn't hurt her. She wanted him. Over and over again this night. For after this night, it would never be possible again. She had to marry Nathan Hawkins. She didn't have any choice in the matter.

"Do you want me to do it again?" Michael asked, smoothing her hair from her face. "Is that truly what you want? Can't you say something? Surely you aren't afraid any longer. Please say something to me. We have shared something beautiful together. Only one other time in my life have I ever shared anything as beautiful."

Maria still kept her lips sealed. Instead, she moved her body so that he could penetrate inside her to the deepest inner part of herself. She moaned in silent ecstasy as she could feel the pleasures sweeping through her once again. And when his lips sought out a breast, she pushed it upward further into his mouth and cried out as his teeth bore into it.

"I think Ruby has herself a little wench here," Michael panted, now working in earnest as his body moved in and out. "God. Your body is so responsive to mine." He pulled her closer to him, attacking her with both lips and manhood now, until Maria began to ache. But it was a beautiful, delicious ache. One that she would store in her memory storage house for the rest of her life. The hollowness inside her was being filled. Then the painful passion was being spent into flashes of multicolors as her body was wracked with spasms in unison with his own.

Maria wanted to cry out his name. But she kept her silence, waiting to listen to his own words once again. Would . . . he . . . ? But this time he didn't speak her name. He just whispered words of love over and over again, until he lay silent atop her, panting.

"Enough for now," he finally said, moving from the bed. "I don't think Ruby has anything to worry about where you are concerned. In fact, I'm going to ask for you every night from here on out. Maybe tomorrow night you might even let me see you beneath the lights. I would like to see the face on the wench who displays such knowledge of lovemaking."

Maria closed her eyes, chewing her lower lip. Again she wanted to cry out to him. Confess to him that this had just been a game devised by Ruby. But she couldn't. She knew that Nathan Hawkins's threats were indeed a cruel reality.

"You'll find a reward for your time given to me on the dressing table," Michael said, then vanished from the room just as quickly as he had appeared, leaving Maria staring blankly toward the closed door, dying a slow death inside. He had paid for her body . . . as though she *was* . . . a whore. . . .

Tossing over to lie on her stomach, she began to beat her fists against the mattress, sobbing noisily. She had found Michael . . . only to lose him once again. And he had said that he would seek her out even the next night. She knew that this next night, she would probably be lying in another man's arms.

"Oh, how I hate you, Nathan Hawkins," she hissed between sobs. "How I despise even the thought of your nearness. But you will pay. Yes . . . you will pay. . . ."

Chapter Twelve

Tears wet Maria's cheeks as she moved around the house she had grown to hate. This was the last time she would see it for a while. Her hate for it was still just as great, but it was the Lazzaro home, a home that she had to bid farewell to, along with her Papa and Alberto. She was torn inside, not knowing how to reveal to them the truth of her parting. If they found her gone, she knew that it might even cause her Papa's health to worsen. But if she left word of where she might be found, she couldn't help but believe that Alberto would come gunning for Nathan Hawkins.

She shook her head, grief dimming her eyes. She knew that she would just have to wait until later, after the marriage to Nathan Hawkins was definitely con-summated. Then Alberto would have no choice but to accept that his sister was indeed married, and no matter if it was to the evil Nathan Hawkins.

She lifted the skirt of her dress, admiring it. She was finally able to wear the dress her Aunt Helena had given her. She knew that she had to be almost beautiful in such a dress of bows and ribbons. She then ran her fingers over the swell of her bosom, knowing that the pleats of the bodice emphasized her greatness there even more. But the neck was staid and tall and the sleeves long and puffed, covering most of her flesh, which she was grateful for. She didn't wish for this evil man to be able to gloat over his prize too soon. She would keep her distance, until she would be forced to do otherwise.

"My violin," she sighed disheartenedly to herself, remembering the long gape down its front. "I guess I shall have to leave it here. It is now broken. I can no longer have it to fill my lonely hours. I shall so miss its whispers as my bow moved across its strings. But one day . . . I shall have all the money required to get it repaired. Then I will play it both day and night."

Taking one last, lingering look, she could envision her Papa sitting slouched in his favorite chair. As of late, his eyes had become so empty . . . sad. . . .

She rushed out the front door, stifling a sob, looking off into the distance, seeing the house she was headed toward. She could understand why Nathan Hawkins hadn't sent for her. His having come in person once to her house had been enough for him. She knew that he had his own reasons for using his representatives to do his dirty business for him. She was just relieved that he hadn't sent a representative this day. That would have added humiliation upon humiliation, to have boarded a carriage with one of those characterless men.

The sun streamed down onto Maria, making her lift her chin upward, loving the warmth on her face. She ran her fingers through her hair, lifting it from her shoulders, letting the wind whistle through and around it. Her freedom was now to be only short-lived. To be married to Nathan Hawkins would be even worse than the prison life of Hawkinsville, except that now, she still had to believe that she could use the Hawkins name and wealth. Wouldn't that be a way of breaking the bonds for most of the Italians? Her pulse raced, thinking about all the possibilities.

Hurrying along, waving to first one Italian, then another, Maria knew that this would be the last time she would be addressing them as Maria Lazzaro. She would soon be Mrs. Nathan Hawkins. She repeated the name over and over again in her mind, trying to find something about it that sounded right. Maria Hawkins. Soon she would be Maria Hawkins.

Then her thoughts traveled to another name. Maria . . . Hopper. . . .

She closed her eyes and clenched her teeth. Oh, God, how she wished to be heading for Michael's house, to soon become *his* bride. She swallowed back the urge to cry, remembering being in his arms only the previous night. When he had spoken her name while making love, she had then known that he loved her still, just as she loved him. But now? Now she knew the possibilities of never seeing him again.

The wind continued to whip her hair upward from her shoulders. To her, it seemed that Illinois wasn't only a state filled with great seas of grasses, but also of great winds. But she loved the wind. If she closed her eyes, she could envision it to be Michael's fingers rippling through her hair, lifting it, as he so often had done. Her passion for him soared at this moment. She would now always think of him when the winds blew. A passion in the wind. . . .

She stepped up onto the iron bridge, stopping to take one last look at the Italian community she was leaving behind. She could see smoke spiraling upward from most of the chimneys, and she knew that most of the women were heating wash water on their stoves, ready to begin their hard day of labor, with no hope for the future of having anything any different.

Some children were playing in the streets, kicking at the coal dust, making it fly upward to settle in gray-blacks on their tattered, worn clothes. Something clutched at Maria's heart, as she wished for so much more for her people. Then she turned and moved into the thigh-high Indian grass, pushing her way through it, smelling its freshness as it continued to blow in the wind. As before, it was like an ocean, dipping and swaying gently, its wine-colored tips edging the sky of blue, resembling an oil painting of magnificence.

Maria's eyes traveled around her, seeing once again the grove of trees that hid Ruby's house so well behind it. A cloud of starlings rose upward from the trees and moved in quivering blacks into the distant sky, and then Maria caught sight of a lone elk cruising in the depths of the brush that surrounded the towering oaks.

Lifting the skirt of her dress, Maria moved onward, seeing Nathan Hawkins's house getting closer. Its magnificence was almost overpowering. It stood two stories high, its many windows resembling eyes, watching Maria's approach. She swallowed hard, then stumbled as she came upon a sudden clearing revealing a freshly graveled road that separated this field of grass in two.

Stepping onto the road, Maria stopped and stared down its full width, first one way, then another. She had just discovered the road that led not only to Nathan Hawkins's house, but almost to Ruby's.

Now Maria knew why she hadn't seen any traces of a road next to Ruby's house. The road stopped abruptly where Ruby's fence began. But on one far side, the side Maria had not been on, a traveled path of muddy ruts sank deeply into the ground.

"So this is how Michael and all those who visit Ruby's arrive? Not over the iron bridge, but on a road that passes right in front of Nathan Hawkins's house," Maria said aloud, holding the skirt of her dress down as the wind continued to lift and pull at it. She set her jaw firmly. "I guess Nathan can't own the roads as he does everything else around here," she said further, turning, making her way down the road, again heading for her new way of life . . . a marriage she already despised. "Knowing this makes me have a bit of hope," she said further. "If he can't own the roads, surely there must be a way to keep him from owning my people."

A thundering of hoofbeats made Maria turn with a start. She stepped from the road just as Ruby's husband Clarence pulled a black, sleek horse to a halt next to Maria. Clarence looked even as burly and dark in the daylight as he had the previous night when he had revealed to Maria that he was Ruby's husband.

This truth still confused Maria. How could a husband agree to a wife's so openly bedding up with other men? It was as though it was only a business arrangement, with Ruby being the main breadwinner of the family.

"Land's sake," Clarence said in a slow drawl, letting the horse's reins grow slack in his hands, leaning, studying Maria. "Don' ya'all have a way of gettin' 'round?" His dark eyes moved quickly over her. "But I mus' say, ya'all sho' look bettah in a dress. Breeches wuz meant foh men. Didn't yore mammie evah tell ya'all that?"

Maria felt a flush rising from her neck upward. She struggled even more to keep the skirt of her dress from revealing her legs to this colored man. She glanced over him quickly, seeing that he was dressed as he had been the night before, in a red plaid, long-sleeved shirt and loose-fitted dark breeches.

"It's nice seeing you again, Clarence," she said, smiling.

"So ya'all does remembah mah name?" he said, straightening his back. His eyes showed the gratitude for her remembering him as they twinkled in dark browns back at her.

Maria shook her head in an effort to remove the wind-blown hair from her face. "Yes," she said. "I remember you *and* your kindness."

"So mah Ruby took care of ya'all's needs last night?" Clarence said, leaning again in her direction.

Maria cast her eyes downward, embarrassed. Surely Clarence knew exactly what those needs had been. She didn't answer. Suddenly her words seemed caught in her throat. She still had such need for Michael. She hadn't liked being reminded. She was much too close to Nathan Hawkins's house now to let her mind fill up with further thoughts of Michael.

"Wheah ya'all headed?" Clarence said, patting his horse gently.

Maria's eyes shot upward, then on past Clarence, to settle on Nathan Hawkins's house.

Clarence's gaze followed hers, then moved back to Maria. "Ya'all be a headin' foh Mastah Hawkins's place?" he said, in an almost whisper. "Is that be wheah ya'all is a headin'?"

Maria bit a lower lip, then answered. "Yes. Exactly,"

she said, clearing her throat nervously.

Clarence seemed to age right before Maria's eyes as his face became all dark wrinkles. "Wha foh ya'all goin' thea foh?" he mumbled.

"For a wedding," Maria said, fighting back a fresh urge to cry.

Clarence's brows tilted. "Whose weddin'? I nevah got word of no weddin' takin' place, and Clarence heahs all 'bout Mastah Hawkins."

"The wedding is to be mine and Nathan Hawkins's." Maria said, then flipped the skirt of her dress around and hurried away from Clarence. She closed her eyes, knowing how she had almost choked on those words. When she heard the horse's hoofbeats following behind her, she tensed, then moved aside when Clarence stopped the horse beside her once again.

"Don' marry up with him," he said. "He's the devil. His house is full of deviltry. Go to Ruby. She can he'p ya'all with whatevah trouble ya'all be in."

Tears brimmed in Maria's eyes as she stared upward into this dark face of compassion. "No. No one can help me," she said. "I have to wed Nathan Hawkins. I must." She lifted the skirt of her dress and rushed away from him once again, glad to hear the hoofbeats move away, instead of toward her.

Wiping her eyes, she moved onward, now seeing through her blur of tears the tiny flowers along the roadside. Somehow, seeing their innocence lightened the burden of her heart. She stooped and picked a bouquet of purple-blossomed blazing stars, sweet coneflowers, yellow with brown centers like daisies, and some pale pink gentians. She tried not to think of Clarence's words, about the house filled with deviltry.

But even a handful of beautiful flowers couldn't erase the words from her mind.

Rising, straightening her back, she stared at Nathan Hawkins's house once again. It looked innocent enough with its stately outer walls of red brick and the tall pillars on the wide front porch. Then her gaze captured what the tall Indian grasses had kept hidden from her eyes till now. It was row after row of grapevines, filled with fresh green leaves. Seeing this made Maria's heart ache, now realizing just how homesick she was for Italy.

She hurried onward, watching the vineyard grow larger and larger as she approached it. It stretched out behind Nathan Hawkins's house on all sides and as far into the distance as Maria's eyes could follow. Though Nathan Hawkins was not of Italian descent, he had not only captured the Italian people and brought them to his town called Hawkinsville, but he had also somehow brought with them their one big love . . . the growing of grapes.

"Why?" Maria wondered aloud. "Does he wish to inflict hurt even more by reminding us all of what we have left behind?" Yes. Seeing this huge vineyard was a reminder to Maria of the freedom she *and* her family had left behind in Italy. Whether or not Nathan Hawkins had planted the grapes purposely as a reminder to the Italians, she knew that would be the way she would always feel about it.

She doubled her one free fist at her side, grumbling. "Oh, how I hate you, Nathan Hawkins. Oh, how I hate and despise you."

Now clutching her small bouquet to her bosom,

Maria moved on in front of Nathan Hawkins's house. The yard was surrounded by thick borders of zinnias and marigolds. Bees buzzed around them and monarch butterflies flitted lazily from flower to flower, as hummingbirds darted in and out among gold and red petals.

Maria moved up a narrow walk of white gravel, stopping to read a plaque that had been placed on a wall constructed of blocks of coal mortared together. On this plaque, she read: August 6, 1890, the first carload of coal was carried from Hawkinsville Coal Mine. Nathan Hawkins, Proprietor.

A sick feeling rippled at the pit of Maria's stomach. Had he been using the Italians as slaves since 1890 . . . ? She glared toward the house and its magnificent stature. Had it been the Italians who had helped make Nathan Hawkins so rich?

The front door opened suddenly, drawing Maria's attention to a short, stocky Negress whose hair circled in masses of gray atop her head. She was attired in a thickly gathered cotton dress of small blue-flowered design and a ruffled apron gave her hands something to do as she wiped her fingers on it, all the while moving from the porch toward Maria. Her face was a mass of wrinkles, almost swallowing her dark eyes into the folds. Only her full lips and nose were prominent, those features alone having been left untouched by age.

"You must be Maria," the Negress said in a squeaky, shrill voice, reminding Maria of Nathan Hawkins's voice. "Ah'm Mama Pearl," the Negress added, moving quickly to Maria, hugging her as she might do a long lost child.

287

Maria squirmed, succeeding at setting herself free, looking at her crushed flowers that now hung limply between her fingers. She let them drop to the walk in front of her, trembling. She had dreaded this day. No hugs from a jolly, fat woman were going to make her feel any better about things.

Mama Pearl grabbed Maria by the hand. "Come on inside, Sweet Baby," she said. "Mastah Hawkins is a waitin' foh ya'all. He's been a pacin' the floah like a true bridegroom for sho. He's proud as punch he is to be gettin' the likes of ya'all as a bride. Now you isn't the first bride on his list, but maybe the last, bless yore heart."

Maria's heart faltered. "Nathan Hawkins has been married before?" she gasped.

"Moh times than ah wants to count on mah fingahs," Mama Pearl said, laughing shrilly, still tugging on Maria's arm.

"But where are these women now?" Maria whispered, her face paling.

"When Nathan Hawkins tires of his womenfolk, he just sends them on thea way," Mama Pearl giggled.

"Do you mean some could still claim to be married to him?" Maria said, paling even more.

"No one would dare ahgue this point with Mastah Hawkins," Mama Pearl said, glowering. "When he says the marriage is ovah . . . it's ovah."

"But . . . the . . . law . . . ?"

"In this county, Mastah Hawkins *is* the law."

Fear and apprehension gripped Maria's insides. It seemed that Nathan Hawkins was even more powerful than she had ever imagined. Would she truly be able to help her people now, knowing the extent of his strength in this state of Illinois? Was he truly the law?

She moved up the steepness of the front steps, onto the widespread porch, then breathed unevenly as Mama Pearl opened the heavy oak door that led inside.

"Come on, Sweet Baby," Mama Pearl said, gesturing with her hand for Maria to move on into the house.

Maria lowered her eyes and lifted the skirt of her dress up into her arms. "Yes, ma'am," she finally murmured, brushing on by Mama Pearl until she found herself standing on a thick oriental carpet that circled beneath heavy oak tables and plushly upholstered chairs and settees clustered about a large, even overpowering room.

Maria lifted her eyes and let her gaze travel across the room to where Nathan Hawkins stood against a large, muraled wall. He was as she remembered. Ugly, short, yet menacing, as his pale gray eyes smoldered beneath his briar-thicket eyebrows. His bushy gray moustache moved as he licked his lips; and all the while he studied her in return.

His black coat fit him perfectly, emphasizing the smallness of his shoulders, and his breeches were tight, showing the bow of his legs.

But it was his bald head that took Maria's full attention. As before, it shone like glass beneath the bright array of electric lightbulbs that decorated a fancy crystal chandelier that hung from the ceiling over his head.

"So you have come as I requested," Nathan said, moving toward her in a slow stride. He clasped his hands tightly behind him, moving around her.

Maria recoiled, moving away from him. "And did I have any choice but to do so, sir?" she hissed, hating it when his bony fingers touched the flesh of her hand.

"Is the thought of becoming my wife so repulsive?" he said. His voice held no emotion. It was apparent that he always got what he wished for. Even if it was a young lady thirty years younger than himself.

"You are unbearable, Nathan Hawkins," Maria said, swallowing hard. She seemed to be weakening under his steady gaze. It seemed that his eyes, though gray and empty as they were, had a way of hypnotizing a person. Maria swung around and placed her back to him. She would show him that, yes, soon he would own her body, but never, no never, her mind.

"Mama Pearl, is my luggage placed aboard the carriage?" Nathan asked, pulling gloves from his coat pocket, working them carefully onto each finger.

"Yes, suh, Mastah Hawkins," Mama Pearl said.

"Then Maria and I will be leaving for the train depot," Nathan said, going to Maria, jerking her around to face him. He looked up into her face, smiling crookedly. "We'll be wed in Saint Louis," he said.

"Yes suh, Mastah Hawkins," Pearl said, grinning from ear to ear, then left the room.

"Saint Louis?" Maria gasped, placing her fingers to her throat.

"Yes. Saint Louis," he snapped. "But upon our arrival there, we will have to see to it that you will have proper attire fitted you. I cannot let a wife of mine be seen in such . . . ah . . . a dress as you have chosen to wear."

Maria's face colored. She looked down at her dress,

having been so proud of it. She had waited forever, it seemed, to find the proper time to wear it. And now that she had . . . he . . . this Nathan Hawkins . . . ridiculed it? But then she remembered the way the fancy ladies had been dressed in New York. Their dresses *and* their hats had been so lovely. So stylish. Yes, she could understand why Nathan Hawkins would be ashamed to be seen in the company of a lady attired in a cheap dress that had been purchased in Italy for only a few lire.

Nathan placed his tall silk hat atop his head. "Let's be on our way then," he said, taking Maria by the elbow, guiding her back outside, where a grand black carriage now sat waiting. A coachman attired in a tall, black silk hat and black coat and breeches jumped from the front outside carriage seat and opened the door, bowing, motioning for Maria to climb inside.

"Thank you," she whispered, then found herself seated on plump cushions of gold velvet. Nathan moved in next to her, closing the door, leaving them to sit alone in an awkward silence. When the carriage began to be jostled along the graveled country road, Maria craned her neck to look from the window, clinging to the seat so hard, the knuckles of her hands grew ghostly white.

"You must learn many things as my wife," Nathan uttered coldly. "The first is to relax while in my presence."

Maria fluttered her lashes nervously, frowning. She glanced sideways at him. "I doubt if I will ever be as you wish," she hissed. "You must remember. It is not of my choosing to become your wife. It is something you have forced upon me. Therefore, I shall act . . . as I shall act." She tilted her chin up into the air, blushing a bit, then gazed out the window again, seeing only barely in the distance the tipple of the coal mine, reminding her of her Papa and Alberto and their fright upon the discovery of her absence. She clasped her hands tightly on her lap, casting her eyes downward, saying, "Sir, I do need something from you," she whispered.

Nathan scooted closer to her, smiling. He reached for her with his gloved hands, covering her hands with his. "And what might that be, Maria?" he said.

She tensed, but left his hand be. She knew that she would have to get used to his touch sooner or later. Why not now, when the layer of glove divided them? She glanced over at him, forcing a smile. "My family will be so worried when they find I am gone," she said. "Can't we send word? Especially now that we're to be wed in another city? What can it truly matter to you?"

Nathan's moustache worked as his tongue wet his lips. "I think something can be arranged," he finally said. "I'll have a messenger boy deliver the message. I'll locate and instruct one before boarding the train for Saint Louis."

An ache circled Maria's heart with another mention of Saint Louis. It reminded her of Michael. Had Ruby been stating a truth when she had said that Michael was still rich? Did that mean that he still most definitely made his residence in Saint Louis?

Maria's hands went to her throat. What if Michael should see her there with Nathan Hawkins? What if he even heard of the marriage? She would just die if he was to hear of this marriage of mockery. How could she even tell him the whys of it? But she knew that her thoughts were on the foolish side. He would never see her . . . nor she him.

Maria grabbed at the seat when the carriage came to a sudden halt. She was tossed a bit sideways against Nathan, making her pull quickly away. "Excuse me, sir," she murmured, reaching up to push some loose strands of her hair back from her eyes.

Nathan's right arm reached around her waist and pulled her back next to him. "You must quit calling me 'sir,'" he said. "You are soon to become my wife. You must act the role." His lips puckered and sought hers out, making her cringe when the stiffness of his moustache scratched her face. "Do you understand, Maria?" he added, letting a hand wander, to touch the outline of a breast.

With her face flaming, Maria said, "Yes. I understand. But for now? Can't you just leave me be?"

"It's all too much too fast for my sweet innocent one from Italy," he said, patting her gently on the cheek. "I understand. Yes, I will wait. We have many years of marriage ahead of us."

Maria's brows tilted, so wanting to ask him the whereabouts . . . or fate . . . of the wives before her. How was she to know how quickly he would tire of her? What would he then do with her? Would she even be free then to return to her family . . . or maybe even to search for Michael?

"But for now, we must move in haste. The train doesn't even wait for Nathan Hawkins," Nathan said, reaching in front of Maria to open the carriage door. "I'm sure George, my coachman, has already seen to

293

my luggage and has it in the rented private car of the train."

Maria stepped from the carriage, all eyes. The black engine of the train sat puffing and wheezing black balls of smoke upward, while a fresh batch of immigrants was being directed from one of the cars of the train. Sympathy made Maria's heart plunge, knowing the kind of life that was awaiting them. She had to wonder just how many more immigrants would be needed by Nathan Hawkins for his slave labor at the mines. The town of Hawkinsville was already too thickly populated for health standards to remain at a safe level. The smell from the privies was already too strong, so strong even, one could hardly stand to enter one's own backyard where the flies buzzed and hatched more flies.

Nathan took Maria by the arm and guided her quickly around the milling crowds. "Do you see that fancier car next to the caboose, Maria?" he said, pointing.

Maria followed his gaze and saw the identical car she had seen once before on the very day of her own arrival to America. She had even seen a partially nude woman when she had stared through its window. "Yes, I see," she murmured.

"You go ahead and go to that car," Nathan said, pushing her away from him. "I will go to the depot to direct a messenger boy to inform your family as you have requested."

"Oh, thank you, sir," she said, then caught herself. She blushed. "I mean, thank you, Nathan."

"You hurry and board. I'll be there soon."

"All right, Nathan," she said, looking around her once again, guilt then causing her to move on toward the train, knowing that from this moment on, her life would be better than the lives of those Italians who stood as though lost, waiting for one of Nathan's representatives to arrive, to take them to their bleak drudgeries of Hawkinsville.

Lifting the skirt of her dress, Maria climbed aboard the private car of the train and stood looking at the luxuriousness of all that surrounded her, leaving her with mouth agape. She moved on into the car, eyes wide. Green fringe-trimmed curtains hung at the few, small windows, and a huge green-velveteen-covered bed filled the space on one far end wall.

A liquor cabinet reflected back at her in different-colored bottles of whiskies and wines, and many plush chairs and two desks filled the rest of the empty spaces around her.

Maria went to a window and pulled a curtain aside, watching the immigrants being loaded onto several wagons. Gulping back tears, she turned her head away and went to slouch down onto a chair. When Nathan rushed into the car, panting for breath, Maria tensed, now realizing how alone they were, and in a car where a bed seemed to have top priority. She eyed the bed, then Nathan, barely breathing.

"The trip will take several hours," he said, pulling his gloves from his fingers, and then the hat from atop his head. "We must make ourselves comfortable and enjoy ourselves." He removed his coat, revealing an abundance of ruffles on his shirt. Then when he moved toward the liquor cabinet, Maria saw a pearl-handled pistol thrust inside the back of his breeches. Her fear of him heightened.

"Why . . . do . . . you wear a . . . gun . . . ?" she stammered, watching his expression, but seeing that her question didn't appear to affect him in one way or another.

He licked his lips and cleared his throat. "Would you care to share some spirits with me, Maria?" he asked, already pouring some red bubbly liquid into a thin-stemmed glass.

Maria fidgeted with the gathers of her skirt, then with a bow at her neck. "I don't think. . . ." she began, but was stopped short when a glass was forced into her free hand.

"Like I said earlier," Nathan said. "You've many things to learn. Share a few drinks with me and you'll find it much easier when I ask you to share that nice bed with me." His gaze flashed from Maria, to the bed, then back to Maria once again, a smile lifting his whiskers from his lips.

Maria's fingers began to tremble. She took a quick swallow of wine, then said weakly, "But you . . . said . . . that you would leave me be. We are not even married. Surely you . . . wouldn't. . . ."

His face was expressionless as he settled down onto a chair opposite her. He crossed his legs, revealing his highly polished boots to Maria. "Did I say that?" he said, sipping on the wine. "I must be more careful with the words I choose to speak. Especially in the company of one so beautifully tempting as you."

Maria's eyes lowered. "But, I do wish. . . ." she began, but was interrupted.

"Your beauty is a unique one, don't you know that, Maria?" he asked, changing the subject.

"Please . . . Nathan. . . ."

"There is only one flaw that I see," he said, clearing his throat. "But maybe with some facial makeup we can hide that ugly birthmark from view."

Maria's fingers reached up and touched the spot on her face of which he was speaking. Her face flushed; she had never felt that her birthmark was so ugly to have to be covered by cheap makeup. "You are wrong, *sir,*" she stated flatly. "I shall not cover my birthmark. You cannot have everything to your liking. My becoming your wife does not mean I have to bow down to you. You will learn that quite quickly."

Nathan rose and put his glass down inside the liquor cabinet. He began unbuttoning his shirt, glowering. "We shall see about that," he said. "I now wish to take you to bed. Undress. Now."

The jolting of the train on its tracks caused Maria to swallow hard, knowing that the train was now traveling away from Hawkinsville and the security she had always felt when in Alberto's and her Papa's presence.

Now? She was left completely to fend for herself. When she saw Nathan reach behind him and lift the pistol from his breeches, she thought this to be cause for conversation to possibly postpone her trip to the bed. She swallowed hard, then said, "You didn't say why you are wearing the gun, Nathan."

"For protection. Why else?"

"Whose . . . protection . . . ?"

"Mine," he said, glowering toward her.

"Protection . . . from . . . whom . . . ?"

He moved the pistol from one hand to the other, as

though weighing it. "There have been threats on my life," he said darkly. "I only recently began to feel the need to carry my pistol."

Maria sipped her wine slowly, then added. "But why would anyone . . . want . . . to kill you?" She knew the answer to that, but needed to lead Nathan further into conversation. Oh, how she hated the thought of sharing the bed with him.

Nathan went to a chair and sat back down onto it, still eyeing the pistol he held in his hand. He pulled a handkerchief from his back pocket and began shining the pistol's barrel.

"It is this damn organization called the United Mine Workers of America that is causing me the trouble," he grumbled. "They are trying to tell me how to run *my* coal mine. But it is *mine*. No one will come to my coal mine and tell me what to do. No one."

"I have never heard of this organization," Maria prodded, relieved to see him settle back against the chair, sulking. She now knew that she had succeeded in getting his mind to wander from things other than what her body could do for him.

"It is called the 'union' for short," he grumbled further.

"Who runs this . . . as you call . . . it . . . Union?"

"At first several union members sought me out. To try to convince me that my mine wasn't safe. And that I wasn't treating my workers fairly. But when I ran them off my property, I heard tell that they then had this one person come to Hawkinsville to do secret investigating to prove my negligence with my mine and people." He laughed sardonically. "I guess they think this one

298

bastard can make Nathan Hawkins change his way of life. Well, they have something to learn about this Nathan Hawkins."

"How is this one man doing this . . . uh . . . investigating?"

"So far my men haven't discovered who it is. We've only heard mention of a name. A man named Hopper. From Saint Louis. I hear tell that he comes to Hawkinsville very well disguised. But one day we will catch up with him. And when we do . . . we will be sure that he will get a bullet through his skull."

Maria almost dropped the glass as her fingers began to tremble violently. Hopper. Did Nathan truly speak of . . . Michael . . . Hopper? She knew that she had paled and took another quick drink of wine in an effort to put more color into her cheeks.

"This . . . Hopper," she said in a near whisper. "How did you hear about him?"

"My representatives. They have ways of hearing things."

"But . . . there are probably many men whose name is . . . Hopper," she said, swallowing hard.

"That's the problem," he grumbled, placing his pistol on the table next to him. "No one has yet found out this bastard's first name. When we do . . . he will no longer be."

"You . . . would actually . . . be guilty of such a violence as . . . murder . . . ?" Maria gasped, clutching the stem of the glass, envisioning Michael, so handsome, so sweet, possibly now in total danger.

"No one would know the deed was done," he laughed. "My coal mine has ways of hiding bodies. No one would ever even know what happened to this man named Hopper."

Maria's eyes lowered. If this was Michael Nathan was speaking of, then she had to find a way to warn him. Her mind was swirling, trying to remember what Ruby had said about Michael. She *had* said that Michael had a "true purpose" for being in the Hawkinsville area. And hadn't Alberto said that Michael had been dressed as one down on his luck? Her heart thumped wildly. Yes. Alberto had said that Michael was dressed as one who was poor. God! This was Michael's way of disguising himself. He *was* the man Nathan was speaking of. After arriving in Saint Louis, she *had* to find him. Warn him.

"And now, Maria," Nathan spoke from in front of her, unbuttoning his breeches. "We have delayed long enough. Like I said before, undress. You are now going to become my wife. We will secure the necessary papers upon arrival to Saint Louis."

"Please. . . ." Maria whimpered.

Nathan knocked the glass from her hand then yanked her roughly up from the chair. "Now you do as you are told," he snarled. "Get undressed and get on that bed. No one defies Nathan Hawkins. Especially not a woman soon to become my wife."

Sobbing, Maria unbuttoned her dress and stepped out of it, then her underthings and shoes, all the while watching Nathan as he undressed fully in front of her. When he moved toward her, she felt a sickness rolling inside her. He was nothing like she remembered Michael being. This man was small, shriveled up, most undesirable to look at, much less be touched by. She

300

recoiled when he touched her on a breast, then shoved her roughly onto the bed.

She closed her eyes, whimpering as he stretched out atop her and lunged his manhood deeply inside her and began to move his body in and out, grunting like a wild animal. She lay there, unresponsive, chewing her lower lip, feeling used, degraded. When his body began to tremble, she tensed, feeling his hands grab at her buttocks to lift her closer to him, then clasped her hands into two fists as he drew his complete pleasure from her body until he was finished and lay panting next to her.

He laughed a bit. "I thought I was marrying an innocent one?" he said, reaching over to pinch a breast. "But I found out that you've been used."

Maria's eyes widened. "What do you mean?" she gasped.

"Don't you know that a man has a way of knowing?"

"I still don't. . . ."

Nathan's hands traveled over her body. "I don't really mind," he said. "It even makes you more exciting to me. To know that you aren't so innocent? It means I can have even more fun with you."

"What . . . do . . . you . . . mean . . . ?"

"Time will tell. Time will tell," he chuckled, then rolled away from her and left the bed. He went and poured himself another glass of wine, then sat down on a chair, still completely nude. "Yes. Our life together will be quite interesting," he added, smiling crookedly.

Maria reached down and pulled the spread over her body, feeling hate grow to even greater intensity inside her for this man who would soon be her husband.

But in name only, she thought darkly to herself. *You will never see me get pleasure from your body. Never. Never.*

She let her thoughts wander to Michael . . . and how she might find him when she arrived in Saint Louis. She must warn him . . . she must. . . .

Chapter Thirteen

Two full days and nights had passed since the necessary words had been spoken between Maria and Nathan to make them man and wife. Since that time, Nathan had kept Maria caught up in a whirlwind of shopping for a wardrobe befitting his new wife, making her now appear a picture of fashion, even more statuesquely beautiful than the models who had pranced across the raised platform at one of Saint Louis's finest department stores, Nugent's.

Nathan had done the choosing. It hadn't taken long for Maria to see his ways of taking over. Though small in voice and stature, when he spoke, everyone seemed to move quickly to do as he bid. So Maria could now boast of having the fanciest hats in the great city of Saint Louis and the necessary attire needed for all occasions.

Hating her newly fitted tight corset, Maria squirmed a bit as she and Nathan moved through the large entranceway at the Planter's House Hotel. Attired in her Eton suit of blue broadcloth, trimmed with folds of matching velvet, and her evening hat in flowered silk and plaited chiffon, Maria could feel many gentlemen's gazes moving along with her.

Tilting her chin up into the air and checking to see if

303

her hair was still upswept neatly beneath her hat, she moved on toward the staircase. She wasn't yet accustomed to such attention. She only hungered for attention from one man. Michael. And she hadn't yet succeeded in finding out where his residence might be. Nathan hadn't let her move from his sight, not for even one moment.

As they moved next to one another up the staircase, Maria glanced at Nathan. He had spoken earlier of being tired and of needing added rest this night before taking the train back to Hawkinsville the very next morning. She smiled to herself, knowing that she didn't require the added rest and would sneak from the room as soon as Nathan's snores became long and lazy.

She had already decided to ask assistance from the desk clerk to show her how to use the telephone that she had seen in the lobby of the hotel. She knew that Michael surely had to own this new invention, if he was indeed as rich as he was said to be.

Nathan reached for Maria's hand. "I'm bone-weary, Maria," he murmured, coughing a bit. "I guess my age is catching up with me." He looked over at her, licking his lips, making the tip of his moustache glisten from the wetness. "I guess your young body is a bit much for my old heart. Tonight I think I'll just leave you be. Now that should make you happy. Eh?"

Maria's eyes lowered. She could feel her cheeks grow hot under his steady gaze. She knew that he had felt her tension each time he had mounted her, panting heavily until his passion had been fulfilled. She was glad that it didn't require much time before he was spent. At least she would know this to be true now whenever he ordered her to stretch out atop the bed, unclothed,

304

open-legged to his demands. But it couldn't erase the thoughts from her mind each time he did mount her, that she was being used, degraded, all over again.

"I must rest also, Nathan," she said, fluttering her lashes nervously, knowing that she had just spoken a nontruth. But it was necessary. All the lies she would ever have to tell Nathan would be necessary. "I'm also tired," she added. "I'm not used to such a fast pace of life as we have had since our arrival in Saint Louis."

"But you do approve of the wardrobe I have chosen for you, don't you?" he asked, sounding even kind. Maria was relieved to see this slight change in his personality. She wondered how long it would last. In Hawkinsville, he had appeared to be the devil himself. In Saint Louis, she had been able to breathe more easily, seeing how much more relaxed his eyes and his mouth had become.

"Yes. It's all very. . . ." she began, then as she looked upward, seeing the man she was going to pass on the stairs, her words seemed to freeze in her throat. She felt a racing of her heartbeat and a giddiness in her head when he moved down several more steps closer to her. Pulling her hand free from Nathan, she covered her mouth, whispering Michael's name. . . .

Nathan stopped and reached for her, placing his arm around her waist. "Maria? What is it? Are you faint?"

Maria looked anxiously about her, knowing that if Michael saw her, he would speak her name as she would his. This couldn't happen. If introductions became necessary, and Nathan heard the name Hopper, and then . . . his name . . . his *first* name . . . Michael, then Nathan would have found the Hopper who he planned to do away with.

Maria touched her forehead lightly, feigning further dizziness. "Yes," she murmured, moving to lean downward against Nathan, hiding her face against his shoulder. "I am a bit lightheaded. Please hold me."

Wrapping his arms around her, Nathan stepped aside so the tall blonde-haired fellow could move on past them. "Maria, I'll get you on to the room," he said, much too loudly, as his shrill voice was so wont to be at times.

Maria tensed, knowing that Michael's footsteps had hesitated. He had heard her name being spoken. . . .

"Maria? Is that you. . . . ?"

When Maria heard his voice, her heart urged her to turn to face him. He was standing two steps below her, looking upward, from Maria, then to Nathan, his face screwed up with amazed puzzlement. "Maria, what the . . . ?" Michael uttered softly, running his fingers through his hair, seeing her attire, so expensive and so stylish. . . . and in Saint Louis? With the likes of Nathan Hawkins? None of it made any sense.

Maria's face flushed crimson. She fidgeted with her hat, speechless. Then she quickly blurted, "Michael *Hampton,* this is Nathan Hawkins." She smiled coyly from one to the other.

Michael's face drained of color. His brows furrowed as he studied Maria's expression. There were traces of fear in her eyes as they gently wavered. Surely there was a reason for her little name game. He quickly extended a hand toward Nathan Hawkins, saying, "Nice to meet you, sir."

Nathan shook Michael's hand cautiously. "And how do you know my wife, sir?" Nathan asked, licking his lips nervously.

Michael's handshake went limp, as well as his knees. His heartbeat faltered. "Did you say . . . wife . . . ?" he blurted, eyeing Maria confusedly.

"Correct. Wife," Nathan said. "Now, how do you know her?"

Michael's hand went to his hair once again, then to a suit pocket to remove a cigar from it. "Briefly, upon passing at the train depot in New York," he quickly answered, lighting his cigar, still studying Maria with a raised brow. He could see the red rimming her eyes and knew that tears were near, so he knew that there was something sinister about this marriage. He knew Maria too well. He knew her sweetness, her kindness. He knew that she wouldn't marry such a man willingly.

Nathan laughed sardonically. "Yes. I can imagine a brief encounter such as that. No man could ever forget Maria," he said, taking her hand. "Come, Maria. We must go to our room. I do need that rest I spoke of earlier."

"Nice to make your acquaintance, sir," Michael said, then more softly, "and nice to see you again . . . Maria. . . ."

Nathan ignored Michael and began guiding Maria on up the stairs. "Yes, nice," Maria said, glancing back at Michael, feeling her heart thundering inside herself, hating being led from the man she truly loved, would always love. When he turned his back to her and moved on down the staircase, she felt bits and pieces of her heart breaking, wanting so badly to run after him. She not only wanted to fall into his arms to profess her love for him, but she had to warn him against Nathan's representatives. Now it was even more risky for Michael to return to Hawkinsville. Nathan had seen him. No amount of disguise would keep the truth from Nathan Hawkins now. He was smart enough to·put two and two together, if given even the smallest of clues.

"Damn strange-acting man," Nathan grumbled, readying his key as he and Maria moved toward one of the many doors that lined this long, narrow hallway of the second floor of the Planter's House Hotel. "If I didn't know better, I would think there was more than just a casual meeting in New York between you and that man." Nathan eyed Maria with his gray eyes that were no longer empty, but accusing. Then he turned and thrust the key into the lock and opened the door with one quick turn of the knob.

Maria moved past him, glad that they had left a dim light burning on the nightstand. She still dreaded dark rooms . . . and Nathan Hawkins. This was a combination she would never get used to. In the dark, he became all hands.

Reaching up, she pulled the hatpin from the plaited chiffon folds of her hat, then lifted the lid of a hatbox and gently placed the hat inside it. She eyed the stacks of hatboxes next to her. At least she was proud to think that at least one of her dreams had come true. She could so vividly remember the many different styles of hats that she had seen worn by the women in New York. Now Maria felt she could look just as beautiful.

Swinging around, she saw that Nathan was already unclothed to just his underthings and stockings, and moving toward the huge canopied bed. Maria didn't know what to do now. If she undressed, it would be more difficult to escape from the room when he was asleep. If she didn't undress, he would suspect something. So she went to the bed and stretched across it, sighing heavily. "Nathan, I am too tired to undress just yet," she said. "After I get my breath, I shall then climb from the bed and unclothe."

She eyed him with fluttering eyelashes. Smiling enticingly, she said further. "And I shall be sure not to make any noise to disturb you. I promise."

Nathan leaned down over her, touching her brow. "Are you ill? You are so pale. Has the trip been too much for you?" he asked, surprising Maria by actually acting concerned about her welfare.

"I am a bit exhausted," she said, putting a hand to her own brow, closing her eyes.

"Then you just lie still and don't worry about a thing," Nathan said, climbing on the bed beside her. "Whenever you are rested enough, just you get up and undress and then turn the lights out. Tomorrow we will return home and I will show you the duties of a wife all over again."

Maria turned her eyes from him, knowing just exactly what he was speaking of. She so hated being his wife. She so hated his touch. *Oh, Michael,* she thought to herself, hungering so for him now. Being near him for only that brief moment had rekindled her passion for him. She set her jaw firmly. She would succeed at being with him this night. She had to. Not to do so meant further unfulfilled desires for her and possible death for Michael. No matter what, she had to succeed in finding out where he made his residence.

Lying quite still, Maria listened for Nathan to slip into a deep sleep. His breathing had become more shallow and his hands had become limp as they lay by his side. Then when he began his long overtures of snoring, she knew that he indeed was fast asleep. From her only brief acquaintance with him, she knew that nothing would awaken him now. Only a clap of thunder shaking the bed could do it. So barely breathing, she crept from the bed, going to the wardrobe to whisk a black velveteen cape from it and throw it around her shoulders, lifting the hood upward to hide her hair and most of her face.

She glanced quickly around the room, seeing it as she had the first time she had entered. It was a warm, inviting room, with brightly designed wallpaper gracing the walls, and curtains hanging in deep pleats at the windows, the furniture consisting of the grandest of beds, with a nightstand by its side, and two matching gold velveteen chairs positioned against the far wall. The room smelled of roses from a large bouquet of opening petals that sat on the nightstand, next to a basin that was always filled with fresh water. It was Maria's first visit to a hotel, and hopefully not her last. The only thing among these comforts that was missing was being with the man she loved.

Tiptoeing, Maria moved toward the door, watching behind her for any movement on the bed. With one hand, she lifted the skirt of her dress and tail of her cape up into her arms, and with the other she turned the knob on the door, making sure that the bolt lock was slipped back so that a key wouldn't be needed to return to the room.

Then, breathing more easily, she moved on out into the hallway. She stopped, shutting the door as quietly as possible, then looked around her, making sure no one saw which room she moved from. She had to be discreet. She had to be sure no one would later tell Nathan that his wife had sneaked from his room while he had been sleeping.

She feared him as a violent man . . . even with women. She still didn't know the fate of his previous wives. Had he done away with them? Possibly in the depths of his coal mine, as he had mentioned possibly doing to Michael, if Michael's identity was ever revealed to him. Thinking such devious thoughts made her shiver and move even more anxiously away from the door.

When she reached the staircase, she moved swiftly down the steps, then stopped, breathless, looking around her. A movement next to her drew her quick attention, and turning, she found Michael moving toward her. She was consumed by her heartbeats when he reached a hand toward her, then pulled her into his arms as he moved next to her.

"Maria. Maria, what does this all mean?" he whispered, hugging her, whispering into her ear.

"Michael, oh, Michael," Maria sighed, clinging.

Michael's hand reached up and traced her facial features as he stepped back away from her. "I can't believe it is really you. You are shatteringly pretty in your new attire. So damn beautiful."

"And you even recognized me hidden beneath the hood of this cape?" she said, pulling the cape more around her face, looking quickly around her. She couldn't be recognized by anyone else. She just couldn't. It was too dangerous for both her . . .

and Michael. . . .

"I would know you anywhere. Don't you know that?"

Maria continued to search around her. "Michael, we mustn't stand here talking," she whispered, tensing when two men moved past her, staring at her, then at Michael. "It is too dangerous. Where can we talk?"

"You are so afraid. What has Nathan Hawkins done to you?" Michael snarled, doubling his fists at his side. "And how in the hell did he get you to accept his hand in marriage when you refused my offer? I don't understand any of this. You are in Saint Louis? How? Why . . . ?"

Maria took one of his hands in hers, pulling him to a dark corner. "Michael, please. We must find a private place. We have to talk. I am so afraid for you," she whispered, reaching up, touching his lips, so wanting those lips to cover hers . . . to send her into another world that only existed when she was in his arms.

"My house is many blocks away. I sense you should not stray too far from this building. Am I right?"

"Yes. If Nathan should awaken. . . ."

"Then I shall get a room here. Just you wait here. I will be only a moment."

"You will . . . get . . . a room . . . ?" Maria's heartbeat quickened. "Does that mean you don't already have a room? Why were . . . you . . . here . . . ?"

Michael's face paled. "That's not of importance, Maria," he said. "What is . . . is that I get you safely to a room where Nathan can't find you."

"All right, Michael," she whispered. Would she and Michael truly get to be alone . . . in such a room . . .

with such a bed . . . as she knew each room of this hotel had to have?

"I shall be only a moment. Trust me," he said thickly, turning to walk quickly away from her.

Maria's eyes continued to dart around her, watching for anyone to stare openly at her, to possibly recognize her as Nathan Hawkins's new bride. And when Michael moved back in her direction, she accepted his arm as he swooped her next to him to guide her back up the steep staircase.

"We will have a room on the third floor," he said, pulling her closer to him. He had dreamed of this moment. He could feel the heat in his loins already. God! She had such an effect on him. But now? She was another man's wife. How? Why? He eyed her with wavering eyes. Oh, God, how he loved her. She would always have his heart. No other woman would ever take her place. Never. But how had Nathan Hawkins succeeded, where he . . . hadn't . . . ?

"Another flight of stairs, Michael?" Maria said, breathing hard.

"We could have taken the elevator," he said, guiding her around the corner that led upward to more steps. "But too many people take the elevator. If you must be discreet, the stairs are the safest. I hope you understand."

"What is an elevator, Michael?" Maria said, eyes wide, lifting the skirt of her dress and the tail of her cape as she proceeded to move upward.

"Nathan Hawkins . . . your . . . uh . . . husband hasn't taken you on the elevator of this building yet?"

"No. He has not. What is an elevator . . . ?"

Michael laughed amusedly. "It is a box that is run by pulleys and takes people from one floor to another in such fabulous buildings as this. I plan to have one installed in my new building that is now in the process of being erected."

"You will own such a building . . . as this one?" Maria gasped, putting a hand to her throat.

"It will be even more marvelous," Michael beamed. "And one day I hope to take you to my penthouse. You will have to sneak away from Nathan Hawkins to see the magnificence of my penthouse when the building is completed."

"And what is a . . . uh . . . penthouse, Michael?"

"I plan to have one of the first in Saint Louis," Michael boasted. "It will be my dwelling unit on the roof of my high building. The name 'penthouse' comes from the Latin words *pendere,* meaning 'to hang,' and *ad,* meaning 'to.' It will be a residence much whispered about in the social gatherings of Saint Louis."

"It sounds very exciting, Michael," Maria said, relieved to step onto the landing that led down another narrow hallway with doors on each side.

"Over here," Michael urged, releasing his hold on her. "This room is ours for the few moments we will have with one another."

Tremulously, Maria waited until Michael had fitted the key into the lock and had opened the door. She waited until he had turned a light on that lighted the room in dim shadows. She then moved on inside, seeing the familiarity of it. It was the same as walking into the room that she had just left behind, except for the lack of the roses that she had found awaiting her

314

arrival when she and Nathan had walked into the room.

"Roses for my new bride," Nathan had said, then had rushed her right to the bed and had taken her sexually even before she had been able to fully unclothe herself.

She trembled now, thinking about it. But she soon put it from her mind when she heard Michael close the door behind them and then had her in his arms, crushing his lips against hers, making her insides begin a slow melting.

"Maria, I must have you," Michael said thickly, moving the hood from around her face, then the full cape from her shoulders, letting it drop to the floor. His lips covered her face in feathery kisses.

"But, Michael. I don't have . . . time. . . ." she murmured. "What . . . if . . . Nathan . . . ?"

Michael quickly withdrew from her and moved across the room, standing with his back to her, staring out the window. "Yes. Nathan," he mumbled, clasping his hands behind him. He turned on a heel, staring at Maria with his eyes changing colors to deeper blues. "How is it that you have become his wife? How could you marry such a man as Nathan Hawkins? You refused me. Why not him?"

Maria stooped to rescue her cape, then carried it with her and placed it on her lap as she moved onto the softness of a green velveteen chair. "There is much that needs to be said, Michael," she said, clearing her throat nervously.

Michael pulled a cigar from his inside suit pocket and lit it, moving to sit across from Maria. "Yes. I do believe so," he said, leaning forward, one foot placed ahead of the other. He so ached for her, but he knew that she was, yes, indeed married. She belonged to another man. Only she could make the choice as to whether or not to move into a bed with a man other than her husband.

Maria's fingers worked with some loose strands of hair, trying to fit them back beneath her comb at the side of her head. "I do not like being married to Nathan Hawkins," she confessed, blushing. "It is only because of my Papa and Alberto that I have done this ugly deed. Please try to understand, Michael."

"I don't understand, Maria. . . ."

"Nathan Hawkins singled me out even before I arrived in America," she said. Her gaze lowered. "It was sort of an agreement between Papa and Nathan Hawkins."

Michael paled. "Good Lord. Your father made an agreement with Nathan Hawkins for you to wed him when you arrived?"

Maria's eyes shot upward. She gasped softly. "No. Nothing like that," she said. "The agreement? It was such an innocent gesture on my Papa's part. He had been told by Nathan Hawkins that Alberto and I would get special treatment aboard the ship, after Papa had begged Nathan Hawkins that Alberto and myself not be told that it wasn't Papa who was paying our passage to America. He didn't want us to know that Nathan Hawkins was doing the paying. You see, Papa had his pride to protect."

Michael rose, his face showing shock. "Then you are . . . of Nathan Hawkins's Italian community,

316

Maria?" he stammered. "You are a part of Hawkinsville . . . ?"

"Yes, Michael. . . ."

He ran his fingers through his hair, murmuring,
"God. God." He slumped down onto the chair once
again, leaning heavily against its back. "And the ship?
Special privileges? God. I didn't see you get any special
privileges aboard that death ship," Michael grumbled,
chewing angrily on the tip of his cigar.

"No. We did not. The only special privileges was the
fact that Nathan *did* agree to let it look as though Papa
was the one who had paid the passage. That was the
only privilege he granted. And this was only agreed to
because Papa had described in such fine detail to
Nathan Hawkins my . . . what . . . he called . . . innocent beauty. . . . And Nathan Hawkins decided to
have my hand in marriage once I arrived. Don't you
see? Nathan had it planned from the very first mention
of my name to him from Papa's lips."

Michael placed his fingertips together in front of
him, glowering. "And you have been in Hawkinsville
all this time? Up to this time of your . . . uh . . . marriage . . . ?"

"Yes, Michael."

"I didn't know. . . ."

"I wish that I had told you while we were on the
ship."

"I should have insisted," he said. "But all of this that
has happened. All of this between Nathan Hawkins
and your father? It didn't mean that once you did arrive
that you did have to go through with such a mockery of
marriage. Why *did* you go ahead and marry such a

317

man? He's not worth the spit from my mouth. And you know that."

Maria felt the need to cry. She turned her gaze from Michael, swallowing hard. "Nathan Hawkins said that he would force Papa, Alberto and myself to board the next ship back to Italy if I refused him," she said sullenly. She wiped a tear away, sobbing softly. "You see? I had no choice. The ship's condition? Don't you remember? My Papa wouldn't live through such a voyage. I know it."

Michael rose and stamped his cigar out in an ashtray. He went to Maria and pulled her up into his arms. "God, Maria. I should have known. I could see the fear in your eyes when I saw you with Nathan on the stairs. And when you chose to address me by a different last name, I suspected even more. That is why I waited in the lobby. I knew you would seek me out. I would have waited all night, if need be."

Maria rested her head against Michael's chest, smelling the familiarity of him, his expensive male cologne, the aroma of cigars, and she could feel the haste with which his heart was beating against his chest. "And, Michael," she murmured, clinging to him. "That is not all. There is so much more you need to know."

He reached and tilted her chin up with a forefinger, their gazes meeting and holding. "What more is there to tell? What is it, Maria?" he said thickly, being suddenly possessed once again by her beauty . . . her nearness. . . .

"Your life is in danger, Michael," she quickly blurted, eyes wide, watching his expression changing to

318

that of disbelief.

"What . . . ?" he gasped, pulling away from her.

"Nathan. He knows there is a man snooping in his community with the name of Hopper. He talked to me of this. I knew immediately that it was you, Michael."

"He knows of my investigations? God. How could he?"

"His representatives. They are quite good at what they do. They have discovered that it is a man named Hopper dressed in disguise who is snooping for this thing called . . . the . . . union. What does it mean, Michael?"

Michael began to knead his brow. "Damn it all to hell," he grumbled. "I belong to the union. We exist because of the need to better the conditions of the workers here in Saint Louis and all over the country. Damn. So Nathan Hawkins does know we have infiltrated his area, huh?" Then Michael swung around, studying Maria closely. "And it sounds as though you know more than what Nathan Hawkins revealed to you. How would you?"

Maria moved across the room, wringing her hands. Should she tell him? What would he think of her? She swung around, smiling coyly. "How did I know that it had to be you when the name Hopper was spoken to me? How would I know this man disguised would be Michael Hopper?"

"Yes. How . . . ?"

"Ruby so much as told me so," she quickly blurted, turning her back to him, not wanting to see his reaction to such a confession on her part.

"Ruby . . . ?" he gasped. So much was becoming

319

clearer in his mind. That night. The darkness of the room. The way that wench had made love with him? When he had returned the next night, requesting the girl who preferred remaining faceless and voiceless, Ruby had acted quite strangely when she had been unable to make this same girl materialize a second time.

Had it been because it had been . . . Maria . . . ? Hadn't she already left for Saint Louis to wed Nathan Hawkins . . . ?

Maria's gaze lowered. "Yes. Ruby," she said softly. When Michael touched her and pulled her to face him, she smiled even more sheepishly, lowering her lashes to protect the truth that was so evident in the depths of her dark eyes.

"You. It *was* you, Maria," he said thickly. "You were the one with me at Ruby's that night. Damn. I should have known." He paused, eyeing her closely. "But how? Why . . . ?"

"Alberto saw you there. He came home gloating to me about how poor you looked. How down on your luck you had become since you were dressed so shabbily, like a bum. When he told me you had been at Ruby's, I just had to seek you out."

"But . . . to . . . ?"

"To be in that room? Waiting?"

"Yes."

"It was Ruby's idea. She said that it would work. I was willing to do anything to get to be with you. But since I had already been made to agree to my marriage to Nathan for fear of what would happen to Papa and Alberto, I couldn't reveal myself to you. Don't

320

you see?"

Michael's fingers worked through his hair. "But, how did you even . . . know . . . Ruby . . . ?"

"We met. One day when I was taking a walk. The first day I was in Hawkinsville, when I just had to get away from that terrible house near the mine."

"God, Maria," Michael said, wrapping his arms around her, pressing his nose into her hair. "My sweet Maria. God."

"But, Michael, what I said about you being in danger? Nathan Hawkins even said that . . . he . . . was planning to kill you . . . if he discovered your true identity."

"He said that?" Michael said, pulling away from her, his expression troubled.

"He even said there were ways . . . of . . . of . . . hiding bodies in his coal mine," she stammered, finding the words hard to speak, envisioning Michael being dragged into the bowels of the earth . . . and . . . left. . . .

"Well, we'll see about that," Michael stormed, beginning to pace the room. "I see now that we at the union have to move ahead with our plans. We don't have time to fool around any longer. But I have to have me an ally. I need someone who is a part of the mines to help me. I need someone to help spread the word of the retaliation I have been planning."

"Michael," Maria said, rushing to him, clasping onto a hand. "Please. It all sounds so dangerous. Can't you just quit whatever it is you are doing? Don't you see? Nathan Hawkins means business. It is his coal mine. He says that no one can tell him how to run it. Isn't he right? How can anyone tell him how to run his own coal mine?"

Michael took both of Maria's hands in his and squeezed them. "Maria, you know the way you and the rest of your Italian friends are forced to live. And you don't even know the half of it. You don't know the conditions of the coal mines. They are death traps. Even much worse than that ship that carried you from Italy. Men are in danger each and every day. And only because Nathan Hawkins refuses to run his coal mine with the proper safety equipment and standards. The members of the union are going to see to it that the Italians get better wages and better working conditions. It is the American way. Most businesses are moving toward the ways of the union. Nathan Hawkins has no choice but to do so also, or it will be he who will suffer in the long run. Trust me, Maria. We know what we are doing."

"But you are in such danger. I know it."

"You must remember. Your father and brother are in even more danger. Each and every day of their lives. When they are lowered into that mine, they never know if they will be raised to the top again. It is as dangerous as that."

Fear grabbed at Maria's heart. She had suspected as much, but just hadn't let the reality linger in her mind. She had known that her Papa and Alberto had no other choice but to work in the mines . . . or be sent back to Italy. "He is the devil," she murmured, biting her lower lip. "The man I married is the devil. Oh, how I hate him."

"So you see what I have to do is quite necessary," Michael said, pulling her into his arms once again.

322

Fresh tears wet her cheeks. She now didn't only have Alberto and her Papa to worry about, but also her dearly beloved Michael. "Yes. I do," she sobbed, wiping her tears with the back of a hand.

"Maria, I even plan to find a way of releasing Nathan Hawkins's hold on you. I cannot bear to think of that man's hands on your body. How it sickens me."

"He is most unpleasant . . . in . . . bed," she murmured, looking up into Michael's eyes, then breathed deeply as his lips lowered to hers, making her mind turn into colorful swirls. "Michael, I love you. Oh, how I love you," she whispered, pulling his lips even closer, tangling her fingers into his hair. When he lifted her up into his arms, she rested her cheek against his chest, sighing leisurely. She knew what was to soon follow. Her thoughts of Nathan were no longer. He didn't even exist. There was only Michael.

"If Nathan awakens and finds you gone . . . ?" Michael said, placing her atop the bed, already working with the buttons of her dress.

"I shall say that I was restless. That I needed a breath of fresh air," she murmured, reaching up, stroking his cheek with the back of a hand. "I had admired the river earlier. I will say I had a carriage take me to the levee so I could look down upon its peacefulness."

She closed her eyes, tremoring as he succeeded at revealing her breasts to his eyes. When his mouth lowered to her and began to suckle on a nipple, as a baby might do, Maria could feel it swelling with warmth. She reached upward, squeezing, kneading her breast, urging it further into his mouth, realizing that a throbbing was beginning deep inside her womb, awakening, desiring, yearning for his manhood to enter her. With her free hand, she unfastened the buttons of his breeches and slid them downward.

"Darling," Michael whispered. "We must undress. Fully. I must caress every curve of your silken body. If not now, I might just explode."

"Yes, Michael. Yes," Maria sighed, moving from the bed. Unable to keep her eyes from him, she removed her clothes in haste. And when he bared his full flesh to her, her heartbeat became erratic, as she saw once again the broadness of his chest that was decorated so with curly, blonde hair. His hips narrowed and now revealed his fully distended manhood, and he knew that his passion for her had fully crested.

"Maria," Michael murmured, moving to her. His hands traced her body gently. "My Maria." He lifted her onto the bed, then stretched out atop her, nudging her legs apart with a knee. He didn't enter her, though. He didn't want to end this moment together that quickly. He wanted to move slowly. He wanted to enjoy caressing her body. He knew that this might possibly be their last time together. He knew that Nathan Hawkins stood between them now, even dangerously so.

Maria squirmed, moaning with lustful pleasure. His hands held a strange magic in them. Each finger was a wand, and as they touched her, sensual sparks were ignited to travel across her skin, upward, settling around her heart, making it to race even more.

His lips sought hers out in a soft warmth, making exquisite pleasure surge through her body. She moved a leg around him, urging him closer. Then she let a

324

hand move downward to wrap around his manhood and guided him inside her.

"Now, Michael. Please," she cried. Her body ached for him. The tension and desire were mounting, making a slow, sweet pain begin deeply inside her. As he began to thrust, over and over again, she arched her back, meeting him. Then their bodies ignited, sending waves of rapture through them both.

Maria sighed languidly, now feeling so content and rapturous. She sought out his lips and pressed hers against them as his hands framed her face and let his manhood move inside her once again. "I love you, Michael," she whispered, tracing his back with her hands, feeling the tautness of his muscles.

He continued to labor over her, kissing her still, first on the lashes, then nose, and down to the hollow of her throat. "There will never be anyone else for me, my darling," he murmured, then kissed and nibbled a breast, making her moan anew.

"I could spend a night, a full night sharing this with you, Michael," she panted, feeling the passionate desire racing through her once again. She wrapped both legs around him and closed her eyes to the spiral of colors that were flashing off and on inside her brain. He continued to press down inside her . . . deeper and deeper. . . .

"This can't, this *won't* be our last time together," he said. He wanted to free her hair from its bondage, to pull his fingers through its softness, but he knew that to do so would cause her added stress when the time came to say goodbye, since she would have to work at it to return it as it was when Nathan had last seen her. This wasn't the time to set Nathan Hawkins's mind to wondering about his new wife's possibly being in another man's bed. . . .

Thinking of Nathan Hawkins and Maria together made Michael thrust almost angrily inside Maria, causing her to let out a small cry, then together they climbed to the highest plateau of feeling until they both lay spent, panting, still clinging to one another.

"It's always so beautiful with you, Michael," Maria purred, tracing his lips with a forefinger.

Michael's brows furrowed. "You should be set free from Nathan Hawkins's bonds. . . ." he said, then stopped when Maria covered her mouth with a hand and gasped.

"Nathan," she murmured, scampering from the bed. "I must return to Nathan." Her face had paled. She began dressing, all the while wondering what Nathan *would* do if he discovered the truth about Michael and herself.

Michael rose from the bed and reached down to pull his breeches on. "If he so much as ever lays a hand on you, I'll kill the bastard," he said icily. "Maybe I should anyway. Then all our problems would be solved. Just that quickly."

Maria moved to him and placed her fingertips to his lips, sealing them. "Shh, Michael. Please don't talk of such violence. Things will work out. You'll see."

Pulling her next to him, he studied her facial features, memorizing them. He knew that his dreams would be filled with only her. "You are so damn beautiful," he whispered. He reached up and traced her birthmark, smiling amusedly. "Even your birthmark. It

326

makes you even more unique, you know."

Maria lowered her eyes. "You've never mentioned it before. I thought because you thought that thing of red was ugly."

Michael's lips touched the birthmark ever so gently, then he ran his tongue over it. "Hmm. It not only looks like a strawberry. It even tastes like one. So sweet. So very, very sweet."

Maria giggled, reaching up to push his lips away. "That tickles," she murmured. Then she grew serious. "You truly don't think it's ugly? Nathan said that it should be covered with a heavy makeup."

Michael laughed hoarsely. "And what does he know? His scraggly face could use some of that makeup he speaks so freely of." His face darkened with thoughts as he turned to walk away from Maria. He went to a window and pulled a drape aside, looking downward onto the nightlife of his great city of Saint Louis. Only recently the gaslights had begun to be replaced by electric, which lit the streets in a more cheerful fashion, encouraging shoppers to be less afraid of the city streets after night had come. And now, both women and men were strolling along, staring into the pane glass windows of the most elaborate shops.

Turning on his heel, Michael suddenly blurted. "How *can* you stand to let that man's lips . . . touch . . . you, Maria? How can you . . . ?"

Maria fastened the last button of her dress, then pulled her cape around her shoulders. "I have no choice, do I, Michael?" she whispered, then rushed to his arms and fell into them, sobbing weakly. "As I have

327

no choice but to take my leave of you now, darling," she whispered. She raised her lips to his and moaned as his crushed downward.

Then when he pulled away, he held her at arm's length. "When are you returning to Hawkinsville, Maria?" he asked, furrowing his brows.

"Early tomorrow morning."

"I plan to be in Hawkinsville day after tomorrow," he said. "Isn't there some place we can meet?"

Maria's eyes faltered. She was not yet familiar with Nathan's house, or his schedule of coming and going. She suddenly thought of Ruby. Could . . . they . . . ? But no. Too many eyes were there. She couldn't take that chance. "I don't know, Michael," she finally said. "Maybe it's too . . . soon. . . ."

He held her shoulders more tightly. "No. It isn't," he demanded. "By God, I will see you. Day after tomorrow. More than likely, Nathan will have business to attend to after being away, so you should be free to come and go as you please."

"But . . . how . . . ? Where . . . ?"

"You're familiar with the iron bridge that leads from Hawkinsville to Nathan's estate and Ruby's house?"

Blushing, Maria's eyes lowered, remembering her night with Michael at Ruby's house. "Yes, I know."

"We can meet near the grove of trees and hide in that deep Indian grass. Around noon. When everyone will be too busy to catch two lovers in the grass."

Maria's pulsebeat raced. She gazed upward into his blue eyes and clung to him one more time, then pulled the hood of her cape over her head. "I will try to be there, Michael," she said. "You know I will try."

Michael walked with her to the door and opened it

328

and kissed her briefly. "Be careful, darling," he whispered, reaching a hand for her as she hurried on away from him. He watched until she disappeared down the staircase, then closed the door and leaned heavily against it. He hung his head, kneading his brow. "Damn that bastard Nathan Hawkins. Damn him all to hell. . . ."

Chapter Fourteen

Having just returned from Saint Louis, Maria was exhausted and glad when the carriage moved in front of Nathan's house. Her corset felt as though it had been laced too tightly and she was ready to shed her dress of London Smoke Cloth with its embroidered silk braid. She was anxious to change into one of her new skirts and shirtwaists. When she had tried them on at Nugent's, she had noticed that they felt quite a bit more comfortable than the fancier dresses chosen by Nathan.

She knew that she was a picture of style, in her hat with its egret plume and satin-faced brim. But all these changes had been thrust on her much too quickly. She only wished to be simple again, to be the Maria her Papa and Alberto would know.

"Maria, I have many things to attend to in Creal Springs," Nathan said, tipping his hat to her. "I may be gone for some time. Maybe even overnight. I have another house in Creal Springs where I can stay. If my meetings go too much into the late hours of the night, I shall stay there. Mama Pearl will see to your comforts."

Maria's eyes widened. She placed a gloved hand to her throat. "You have another house? Besides this one?" she gasped. Was Nathan even wealthier than she had at first thought? This could cause Michael to have an even harder time succeeding with his plans for his union organization.

"Yes. Someday I shall take you there. But now I must take leave of you. You appear to need a bit of rest anyway. You are a bit pale." He reached in front of Maria and opened the door for her. "And your things should have arrived ahead of us. I saw to it that they were whisked from the train and taken to our house so you would be able to change into something more comfortable upon our arrival."

"Thank you, Nathan," Maria said, lifting her bead-covered clutch purse, scooting toward the opened door. She felt a bit in awe at hearing his house now being also referred to as hers. But it was indeed a truth. She was now Mrs. Nathan Hawkins. Oh, how that name caused a bitterness to rise in her throat.

Nathan lifted her free hand and kissed it almost gallantly. "You will be all right, Maria?" he asked.

"Yes. Quite," she answered, pulling her hand free from his. Stepping from the carriage into the fading rays of the late afternoon sun, she moved toward the house, not stopping to look back at Nathan. It was such a relief to be away from him. How could she bear a lifetime with such a man?

A sense of remorse tremored through her, then she tensed when the shrill whistle from the coal mine reverberated through the air. It was a reminder of her Papa and Alberto. What would they think when they saw her so changed? Shame caused her face to burn. But surely they would understand. She had done it for them. For the whole Italian community. She would seek her revenge. Hadn't she already begun?

She looked in the direction of the coal mine, seeing the tipple looming ominously into the sky. She knew that below that earth her Papa and Alberto were coming to the end of their hard day's labor. Then she suddenly remembered Michael's words about the dangers of the mine—how each time the men were carried beneath the earth the chances were quite great that they possibly would not return . . . alive.

"What shall I do?" she whispered, now rushing on toward the house. "What can Michael even truly do? Nathan is so powerful. Nathan is so devious."

The front door swung open, revealing the bulkiness of Mama Pearl standing there, smiling warmly as she wiped her hands on her apron. Her gray hair made a nice contrast with her brown face. And her attire was the same as before—a fully gathered cotton dress that caused her hips to appear even wider than they were.

Maria stepped onto the porch, looking around her at the white wicker furniture, knowing that she would have time to explore this mansion that was now in part hers. She hadn't been able to do so before. Nathan had been too anxious to sweep her away to Saint Louis, where he could transform her from an Italian waif into a grand lady of style.

Mama Pearl moved in a rush for Maria, pulling her into her embrace, hugging her tightly. "Sweet Baby," she purred. "Ya'all looks so pale. Was the first nights of marriage so hard?" Her heavy, thick hands caressed Maria's back.

Maria looked in confusion around her, not understanding this heavyset woman's open affection for someone she had just become acquainted with. But Maria had to think that this Mama Pearl would probably feel a closeness to anyone she had just met. She had the jolly personality of someone who never met a stranger. Maria sighed deeply when Mama Pearl finally released her hold and guided her into the house.

"Your trunks arrived a while ago," Mama Pearl said in her squeaky voice. "I had them taken to your private room. You would probably like a soaking in the tub before doing anything else. I drew your bath and filled the water with some bubblies for you to settle yourself beneath."

Maria's mouth dropped open. "A bath? Bubblies? Does this house . . . have . . . a toilet?"

"Three," Mama Pearl giggled. "One for my quarters, one for yours, and one for Mastah Hawkins's own private bedroom."

"Do you mean that I will have a room . . . all to . . . myself . . . ?" Maria asked hopefully. If she and Nathan weren't in the same bed each evening, maybe she wouldn't have to play the wife so often. Shivers raced up and down her spine, remembering how quickly he had always mounted her and left her lying feeling so used. Never once had he asked if she had enjoyed it. He had just thought of his needs. Only his needs. But, in fact, she had been grateful for that. In no way would he ever be able to arouse any sexual feelings in her.

"Mastah Hawkins's business hours often move into the awkward hours of the night," Mama Pearl said, moving from chair to chair, fluffing cushions. "A private bedroom was his suggestion, so he wouldn't disturb you in the sometimes wee hours of the morning."

"Oh, I see," Maria said, still oh so relieved. Her gaze traveled around the room, seeing more of it this second time. A fireplace that covered the narrower, longer wall grabbed her quick attention. She knew that the chimney would have to be cleaned yearly. Were there chimney sweeps in the area? Would there possibly even be one she would have to hire? It made a strange sensation surge through her realizing that she was now in the position to do the hiring, instead of being the one being hired. But many things had changed since a few days ago. Many, many things.

She looked further around her, marveling at the lightbulbs shining so clearly from the crystal chandelier and the many wall sconces. What a marvelous invention to not have to strike a match to a wick to bring forth enough light to light a room. The lights of Saint Louis had been an incredible sight, as was everything about that marvelous city. She could understand why such a man as Michael would live there. Was he not a great man?

She moved to a back window, staring outward at the row after row of grapevines. She turned to Mama Pearl, eyes heavy with wonder. "Mama Pearl, why does Nathan have such a vineyard? Does he have such an interest in the growing of grapes with his thoughts being so full of his coal mine?"

Mama Pearl moved to her side and pulled a drape aside, also looking outward. "He hopes one day to have a wine named aftah him. How bettah than to start with growin' his own grapes for wine?"

334

"A wine named after him?" Maria said, wanting to laugh out loud. It so sounded like something Nathan would want. He was so egotistical . . . so arrogant.

"If ah knows mah Mastah Hawkins very well, he'll succeed," Mama Pearl giggled. "He usually gets every-thin' he hungahs foh."

Maria moved away from the window, working her gloves from her fingers, one at a time. "You do like Nathan, don't you?" she asked softly.

Mama Pearl straightened the drapes, smoothing their lines with her deft fingers. "He's been good to me," she said. "Can't ask foh more than that." She moved to Maria's side. "Now are you ready to be shown your room, Sweet Baby?" She reached up and touched the softness of Maria's hat. Envy showed at the depth of Mama Pearl's eyes. Maria understood such envy. Up until only a few days before, she had felt such envy, almost a hunger inside when she had seen beautifully attired ladies.

Smiling, Maria reached up and removed two hatpins from her hat and lifted the hat from her head. "Do you like the hat, Mama Pearl?" she asked softly, handing it to Mama Pearl.

"One of the prettiest ah've evah seen," Mama Pearl sighed, running her fingers along the satin-faced brim.

"It's yours," Maria said, taking one of Mama Pearl's hands, easing her hat into it.

"Mine . . . ?" Mama Pearl gasped, eyes wide. "But ah'm sho Mastah Hawkins wouldn't want you to. . . ."

Maria straightened her back and set her jaws firmly. "I don't care what Nathan Hawkins thinks," she said. "If I want to give a gift to you, it is my right to do so.

335

Please accept this hat as a gift from me to you as a souvenir from the great city of Saint Louis."

"But . . . it's yours. . . ."

Maria sighed heavily, loosening her hair from its combs and pins. "Mama Pearl, didn't you see the many hatboxes delivered to this house? Nathan must have purchased one of each style for me. I won't miss just one. Please believe me."

Maria placed her combs and pins on a table, then went to Mama Pearl. "Here. Let me place it atop your head," she said softly. She took the hat and arranged it over the tight, gray bun, seeing a softness in Mama Pearl's eyes as she did so. Mama Pearl reached up and touched it gingerly, making Maria proud. Maria stepped back, eyes wide, smiling. "Like it, Mama Pearl?" she asked, clasping her hands together in front of her.

Mama Pearl's fingers moved over it, then she broke into a fit of giggles. "Land's sake, Sweet Baby," she said. "Nevah, no nevah have ah had such a thing of style on this head of mine."

Maria giggled also, then tensed when a loud banging on the front door forced an awkward silence between her and Mama Pearl. When the knocking persisted, Mama Pearl rushed to the door and opened it, exclaiming loudly, "You again? Why do you continue to pestah me so?"

Maria's heartbeat skipped when she heard the loud voice of Alberto traveling across the threshold into the room.

"I'm here to see Maria Lazzaro," he boomed. "Just like I have been for the past several days. Has she arrived back here yet? If so, I must see her. I'll put it even more strongly than that. I *insist* on seeing her."

With weakened knees, Maria hurried to the door and stepped in front of Mama Pearl. "Alberto? Oh, Alberto," she cried, rushing into his arms.

"Maria, what is this all about?" he demanded, pushing her away from him, holding her at arm's length, studying her. His eyes raked over her, over and over again, seeing the fanciness of her attire. He had never seen his sister look so beautiful. But in Nathan Hawkins's house? Explanations were due!

"Did you and Papa receive word by messenger, Alberto?" Maria asked, wiping a tear from her eye. She now realized that a part of her had just been put in place again. She and Alberto had never been separated before. Seeing him now made her ache, knowing that she had put him from her mind so easily.

"Yes. We received word all right," Alberto growled. "Word that you had ventured off with Nathan Hawkins to Saint Louis."

"Didn't the message state that I was to become . . . Nathan Hawkins's wife?" Maria gasped, paling. Had Nathan felt it safer not to include that tidbit of information? Maybe he had guessed the anger of Alberto. . . .

Alberto dropped his hands to his sides, eyes wide. "Did you . . . say . . . wife . . . ?" he gasped, also paling.

Maria's gaze lowered. She fluttered her lashes nervously. "Yes. I am now . . . his wife . . . Alberto," she confessed.

Alberto grabbed her by the shoulders and began shaking her violently. "No," he screamed. "No. No. It just can't be. You . . . wouldn't. . . ."

Mama Pearl pushed Alberto away from Maria and stood with hands on hips between brother and sister. "I don't think ah'd lay anothah hand on Mastah Hawkins's bride, suh," she said firmly.

Maria moved to Mama Pearl's side and took a hand in hers. "Mama Pearl, this is my brother Alberto," she said softly. "Please don't fret over me. My brother has reasons for such anger."

"This is ya'all's brothah?" Mama Pearl said quietly. She frowned toward Alberto. "And why didn't ya'll tell me earlier? All the othah times ya'll came knockin' on this heah door?"

Alberto's hands went to his whiskers and began to caress them. "I didn't think it . . . uh . . . wise," he stammered.

Maria spoke again. "You see, Alberto and my Papa work in Nathan's coal mine. Alberto feared . . . Nathan. . . ."

"Feahed . . . Mastah Hawkins . . . ?" Mama Pearl whispered. "How can anyone feah Mastah Hawkins? He has always been so kind to me."

"To hell with you," Alberto exclaimed, glaring. "It is Maria whom I am so concerned about. Maria? Tell me. How could you do this? Have you lost all love and respect for Italians? You know how badly Nathan Hawkins treats all of us."

Maria felt tears surfacing. Alberto looked so tired. His dark eyes were heavy with sadness, and his face was lined with coal dust. His clothes were even dirtier than when he had worn his chimney sweep costume. Maria's heart ached so, knowing even more now that Alberto hadn't bettered himself by traveling to America. "Alberto, there's so much to tell you," she said, reaching for him.

Mama Pearl stepped away from them both, watching silently as brother and sister stood arguing with one another. Mama Pearl didn't understand any of this. Hadn't Maria willingly married Mastah Hawkins? Had he forced her . . . ? She knew that he had done this many other times before. Lawdy, she had learned to keep her mouth shut about things. She had no other choice but to. . . .

"Tell me then," Alberto shouted. "Maria, tell me. Now!"

Maria looked at Mama Pearl who still stood glowering, ready to pounce on Alberto if he made another approach toward Maria. Maria didn't feel free to talk while in Mama Pearl's presence. She knew that anything they said would more than likely be repeated to Nathan. Mama Pearl appeared to have great loyalty to her . . . master.

Turning with wavering eyes, Maria whispered, "Alberto, I cannot tell you now. Please. . . ."

Alberto's rage increased. His eyes bulged as he yanked Maria into his arms and kissed her strong and hard on the mouth, feeling an inner excitement at such softness against his lips. He knew that he was swelling beneath his breeches, and felt shame, utter shame and contempt for himself, not having been able to control his feelings for Maria any longer. But love had almost become the same as hate, as he now realized what she had done. She had betrayed him. She had given herself to a man who was no better than a snake in the grass.

He clung to her for a moment, feeling his heart

pound wildly inside him, then released her, watching her expression turn to one of mortification. He then rushed from the porch to the wagon and shouted loudly to the horse, anxious to get away from what he had just revealed to his sister. He now even knew the cause of his being incapable of making love to another woman. All along, it had been because of his secret passion for his lovely Maria. Tears burst forth from his eyes as he slapped the horse with the reins, yelling loudly into the wind. He knew of only one place to go. He couldn't face his Papa. Not after what he had just done.

Maria lifted a finger to her lips, stunned. She raced to the edge of the porch and watched as Alberto grew dim in the distance. Why had Alberto done such a thing? Had his hurt caused him to become suddenly deranged in the head? Then she remembered. The blow to his head on the ship. Was it still causing him trouble? She vividly recalled how worried she had been about him for so long after he had supposedly recovered. And now? To kiss her? As a man kissed a woman . . . ?

Lowering her eyes, she rubbed her lips furiously. Her brother. Her own flesh and blood. *Now* what was she to do?

"Sweet Baby," Mama Pearl said, moving to Maria's side. "Your brother. He has taken leave of his senses."

Maria swung around, tears streaming down her cheeks. "I must go to him," she said. "I have to talk with him. There's so much that needs saying. But my clothes. I can't go dressed so expensively. You did say that my clothes had arrived . . . ?" She paused, then added quickly, "I need to change into something less

340

fancy to go to my Papa's house."

Mama Pearl moved toward the staircase, motioning for Maria to follow after her. "Yes, ma'am. Ah've already placed a few things across the bed for ya'all. Ah'll take ya'all to the room that's to be yours."

Breathless, Maria lifted the skirt of her dress and climbed the staircase. She couldn't help but let her eyes wander around her, seeing the greatness of all that she continued to find in this house. The staircase led upward to a hallway of many rooms, and as she passed each, she peered into the rooms, seeing many styles of decorated walls and draperies. The furniture was all large, comfortable pieces, and the floors shone back at her as though never walked upon.

"In heah. This is your room," Mama Pearl said, stepping aside. "Do you want me to assist you change ya'all's clothes? Or do ya'all want to be left alone?"

Maria stood wringing her hands. "Please leave me be, Mama Pearl," she murmured. "Please go on about your duties."

"Now you just quit frettin' ovah things. Don't ya'all know things will work out? Mastah Hawkins will see to it. He's a kind man. Sho nuff is."

In anger, Maria closed her lips tightly together. Then she said, "Please, Mama Pearl." She moved toward the bed. "Please. I'd rather not speak of Nathan at this time."

"If ya'all needs me, ah'll just be down the hall."

"I will be leaving as soon as I change," Maria said, already unbuttoning her dress. "And please don't tell Nathan. He wouldn't approve. I am sure of it."

"If that is what ya'all wants," Mama Pearl said,

shrugging, then left Maria standing alone in a room totally unfamiliar to her, though she knew that it now by legal standards was hers.

As she stepped out of her dress and began to unlace her corset, her gaze traveled around her. A great mahogany bedstead sat against a far outside wall beneath a window. The drapes hanging at the one window of the room and the bedspread covering the bed were of pale orchid velveteen. The bureau and night table were of a matching mahogany, as were the carvings of the legs of two velveteen-covered chairs.

Seeing herself in a pier glass that was set into the wardrobe's door, Maria quickly shook her hair to settle around her shoulders and down her back. Then she slipped into a full-length, black serge skirt and white shirtwaist, feeling now more ready for her first appearance in Hawkinsville since she had been forced to wed the man whose name the town bore.

She threw a simple knitted shawl (one of her personal choosing in Saint Louis) around her shoulders, then she raced down the staircase, on through the spaciousness of the brightly lighted parlor, to the outdoors, and began to run down the gravel road. Oh, if by fleeing now she could only escape the memories of Nathan's hands and lips. They would always be revolting to her. But now she was remembering another's mouth against hers. It was as though her lips were burning even now. "Why, oh, why, Alberto?" she whispered to herself.

Lifting her skirt, she stepped from the road, into the Indian grass, slowed by its thickness. But she continued to push her way through it, feeling the breeze lifting her hair from her shoulders, making it whip around her face. She wiped it back from her eyes, hurrying onward until she reached the iron bridge.

Panting, she ran across it and began to move in front of all the bleak houses that made up this town of Hawkinsville. Aromas from the privies rippled through the air, and the breeze carried coal dust upward to settle on her lips and face. She sneezed, then rushed on up the steps that led inside her Papa's house.

A fresher aroma met her as she moved into the front room. She recognized it as the distinct aroma of turnip greens with only a faint fragrance of vinegar intermingling. As she drew nearer to the kitchen, she could hear movement from within. She hurried her pace and stopped when she entered, seeing her Papa even more slumped, and much, much too thin, making her heart ache.

"Papa?" she whispered. When he turned, she saw the familiar distortion to his face, knowing this to be the usual wad of chewing tobacco he kept formed into a cheek.

"Maria?" he said, paling. "My . . . Maria . . . ?"

Maria went to him and hugged him to her, seeing through his thin wisps of hair the signs of coal dust on his scalp and in the lines of his face as he searched hers.

"Are you truly all right, Maria?" he said, tears causing his eyes to redden. "I was so worried. I had no idea why you would have gone with that . . . that . . . Nathan Hawkins."

"This is why I have come home, Papa," she said, sniffling. "To tell you the reasons. But, first. I have to see Alberto. Has he come home? I have a desperate need to speak with him first."

"No. Alberto isn't here. Why? What has happened?" He pulled away from her, going to pull the pot of turnip greens from the stove. Then he slouched down onto a kitchen chair, wheezing hard.

Maria saw the laboring of his breath. She went to him and touched his brow. "Papa. You aren't breathing naturally. Has your . . . health . . . worsened?"

He hung his head, inhaling and exhaling even more laboriously. "No. I'm all right," he mumbled. With his hand, he covered the area over his heart, sighing deeply. "No. Now I am all right." His gaze met Maria's and held. "Now. What is this about Alberto?"

Maria swung her skirt around and went to stand at the back window, wringing her hands nervously. "It is something between Alberto and myself, Papa," she murmured. "Please understand. I cannot tell you."

"He's done something foolish. Tell me what it is. He's acted strangely since coming to America."

Maria went to the table and pulled a chair from beneath it and sat down onto it. "Like I said, Papa," she said, her eyes wavering. "It's between me and Alberto. Where is he? Please tell me."

"He took the wagon just as soon as we arrived home from the mine," Giacomo said. "I have no idea where he went."

Maria knew. She cast her eyes downward, thinking her Papa might be able to see some truth in the depths of her eyes. "Well, then I will have to seek him out later," she murmured. Again she met her Papa's gaze. "Now I must explain why I went away with Nathan Hawkins." She swallowed hard, then held her left hand

344

toward her Papa, letting him see the largeness of the diamond that had been given her after the words had been spoken between her and Nathan, the words that had sealed . . . their . . . union. She chewed on her lower lip, watching her Papa's expression change to disbelief . . . then anger. He pushed himself up from the chair, breathing hard once again.

"You can't tell me that you have wed that . . . that evil man," he said, amost choking. He leaned his full weight on the edge of the table, teetering. "Maria, why? Why?"

Maria rose and rushed to him, trying to embrace him, only to be brushed angrily aside. "Papa, if you will let me explain, then you will fully understand," she cried. "You will see that what I have done was . . . quite . . . necessary."

"Nothing would be explanation enough, Maria," he said, moving from the room.

Maria felt an iciness fill her veins. Had she been wrong? Should she have refused Nathan Hawkins? Had he only been bluffing? Maybe he wouldn't even have done what he had threatened. She hung her head in her hands, sobbing. She cried for a few moments, then followed her Papa into the front room where he sat, staring out the window into space.

Maria fell to her knees in front of him. "Papa?" she whispered, taking his hands in hers. "Now you listen. You just listen to what I have to say. Then you will know that I only did this to make all of our lives better. . . ."

His dark eyes sought hers out, heavy and brooding. "You mean *your* life, don't you, Maria?" he said, accusingly.

"No. No, Papa," she cried. "Please listen."

"All right, tell me," he said thickly. "Tell your Papa why you have disgraced the Lazzaro family's name . . . and all the Italians in this community. Tell me how you can let that craggly faced devil . . . touch . . . the flesh . . . of your beautiful . . . body. . . ."

Chapter Fifteen

Alberto drew the horse to a halt next to Ruby's fence, staring at the house. He knew that he was a bit too early and that he wasn't cleaned up as usual after his day of working, but he had nowhere else to go. Ruby's had become his second home. She seemed to know him so well now. She had even consoled him when he had failed to have sexual success with any of her girls. He wiped at the tears in his eyes, feeling so weak, so unmanly. He needed to prove himself a man even more this early evening than at any time before. Maybe Ruby herself could take him to a room and bring out the man inside him. He had the desires . . . the needs of a man. Surely someone as skilled as Ruby could ease his inner torment. Up to this time, her consoling had only taken the form of words.

He jumped from the wagon and tied the reins to a hitching post, then entered through the gate, eyeing the dogs cautiously. They came to him, sniffing, then went on their way. He was glad that they had finally grown used to him. He had always feared dogs and the sharpness of their teeth, especially these two that Ruby depended on for safety.

Trembling, Alberto went to the front door and tapped lightly. Thrusting his hands in his rear breeches

347

pockets, he stood with bowed head. He could still feel the softness of Maria's lips and what they had caused to stir inside him. Shame once again flooded his thoughts. How . . . could he . . . have . . . ? What must Maria be thinking . . . ?

When the door opened, Ruby's brown eyes traveled over Alberto, seeing the state he was in. "Alberto? What's the matter?" she said in her slow drawl. "You've never come to Ruby's house so early. And you look so distraught. What has happened? Have you finally succeeded in finding Maria? Are you upset . . . about . . . your findings?"

Alberto looked quickly from side to side, swallowing hard, then eyed Ruby with pleading. "Can I come in, Ruby? I need to talk with you. I have nowhere else . . . to . . . go," he stammered.

"Yes. Come on in," she said, smiling awkwardly. "But what do you mean . . . you don't have anywhere else to go? You have your home in Hawkinsville. What's happened, Alberto?"

Once inside, Alberto lowered his eyes, feeling so awkward in the position he had put himself in. "Like I said," he mumbled. "I'd like to talk with you. In private."

"Do you mean . . . in . . . my room . . . ?" she said softly.

Alberto's eyes wavered as his face flushed crimson. "Yes. If you only would," he blurted. His eyes raked over her and her skimpy attire. Seeing the fullness of her breasts and the way they came to such sharp points beneath the chemise made a throbbing begin in his manhood. He had never seen her dressed so skimpily.

348

He had most surely caught her as she had emerged from her bath, or possibly as she had begun to prepare for her evening's activities. His gaze traveled lower and saw the darkness of the vee between her legs. The brown flesh of her thighs looked like velvet, making Alberto lick his lips hungrily. Maybe Ruby could help him. She was already affecting him in a strange way. He even felt a bit giddy being so close to her as she began to guide him up the narrow staircase, then on into her private room. Once inside, all he could see was the greatness of the bed and the red satin sheets and pillow coverings. But instead of guiding Alberto to the bed, Ruby directed him toward a chair.

"Now, Alberto, please tell me what has happened?" Ruby said, stretching out on her stomach on the bed, resting her head in her hands.

"I don't know where to start," he stammered, stretching his long, lean legs out before him, flushing once again when he realized just how dirty he was. Coal dust. The damn coal dust that he seemed never to be able to wash off. It was worse than the dust from inside chimneys. Oh, how he hated it all. His existence had become almost unbearable.

"The beginning," Ruby said, moving to an upright position, reaching for a cigar, lighting it. She began to blow circles from between her thick lips, waiting.

"Maria has returned from Saint Louis," he began, speaking so softly he wasn't even sure if Ruby could hear. But he had hated to say the words aloud. He hated to say that Maria was now . . . Mrs. Nathan . . . Hawkins. It still didn't seem possible. His Maria. His sweet, innocent Maria. . . .

"She has? When did you see her? Have you talked with her?"

"I went to Nathan Hawkins's house. Only a short while ago. Maria was there," he said, then lowered his head into his hands, cursing softly to himself.

"You knew that Maria was with Nathan Hawkins," Ruby said, drawing once again on her cigar. "What has upset you about that? I thought you had had enough time to get used to it. What has renewed your anger so?"

Alberto rose and began pacing the floor. "She not only was with Nathan while in Saint Louis," he said, now angrily, "but she came back to this area with Nathan Hawkins . . . bearing . . . his name."

Ruby jumped from the bed and took Alberto by the arm, stopping him. "What did you say?" she said. "What do you mean . . . bearing his name . . . ?" Had Clarence been telling the truth then that day he had come racing back on horseback? When he had told her that Maria was marrying Nathan, Ruby had laughed in her husband's face. Should she have taken him seriously? She hadn't . . . for . . . so . . . long. . . .

"What the hell do you think I mean?" Alberto stormed.

"That she is now . . . Mrs. Nathan Hawkins?"

"Yes. She is now Nathan Hawkins's wife," Alberto said, suddenly weeping, holding his face in his hands, as his body shook in violent trembles.

Ruby mashed her cigar out in an ashtray, then went to Alberto and pulled him into her embrace. "My God, Alberto," she murmured, running her long, lean fingers through his hair. "Oh, my God. Maria? I hadn't under-

350

stood for one minute why she had gone to Saint Louis with Nathan. That was a puzzler. But now? To find that she's married him? Maria? Why? Why would she do such a dumbass thing as marrying that bastard? She doesn't love him. She loves. . . ."

Alberto tensed and withdrew from Ruby. "She loves? What do you mean? What did you start to say?"

Ruby covered her mouth and swung around, placing her back to him. She had almost mentioned Michael Hopper's name. She went to her liquor cabinet and poured a glass of whiskey and swallowed it in two fast gulps. She turned to face Alberto once again. "I meant to say that no one could love Nathan Hawkins," she said. "There has to be more to this than what you've told me."

"That's all one has to know, isn't it?" he said. "She's married to the man who imprisons all us Italians. She is no better than him now. Marrying him meant that she must approve of his evil practices." He stomped back and forth across the room, glaring. "No. I cannot think it was for any other reason than that she had grown tired of the kind of life that has been forced on us in America. She took the first chance she was offered to free herself of such blight. Maria is no longer a Lazzaro." He gulped back more tears. "She is no longer . . . my . . . sister. . . ."

Ruby went to him and tried to console him once again by whispering soft murmurings into his ear. When Alberto reached and touched a breast through the thin chemise, she leaned into his touch and moaned softly. "Alberto, what has taken you so long to desire me?" she whispered, beginning to unbutton his shirt.

351

Her fingers were quick and sure as she reached downward and unbuttoned his breeches and helped to lower them to the floor.

"Ruby, there's something I need to tell. . . ." Alberto began, but was hushed by her fingers sealing his lips.

"Hush. I'll help to erase all sadness from your mind," she said, urging him to step from his shoes, then guiding him onto the bed.

"But, Ruby. . . ." he said, almost choking on his words, fearing the worst . . . that he once again wouldn't be able to be a man . . . not even with Ruby. What then? Oh, God. What then . . . ?

"First some soft oils to perfume your body with," she whispered, pouring some sweetly fragranted liquid into the palm of each of her hands. "After being in the depths of the earth all day, this will take the stench from your body. You will smell like a spring flower when I get finished with you. Then I shall slide my body up and down yours until you will beg to be finished with."

When her fingers made contact with his flesh, Alberto closed his eyes, groaning softly. He moved his body with her as she rubbed and kneaded him, first his taut stomach muscles, then lower, to ease the liquid onto his manhood.

"Ruby," he moaned. "You are making my mind leave me."

Ruby laughed wickedly, then quickly removed her chemise and climbed atop him. She reached into her navel and removed the ruby and placed it on the table next to the bed, not wanting to scratch Alberto with it when she would scoot her body along his. Then with all the skills that she had learned, she began to slide her body back and forth over him, feeling the stiffness of his manhood, feeling desire mounting inside her, as no man had caused for some time now . . . not since Michael Hopper.

She had grown so fond of Michael's skills at love-making that it had frightened her. She had worried that Clarence would grow suspicious of her going with only one man. Clarence. Her husband—who had been so savagely castrated by some furious whites so many years ago, after it had been discovered that Clarence . . . had raped . . . a young white girl. Ruby had wanted to kill Clarence herself after finding out the ugly truth, until she had found what the men had done to him. It was Ruby who had then nursed him back to health, loving him even more as each day passed. But Clarence, not being able to quench her desires for a man any longer, had agreed to let her start this house of girls . . . enabling Ruby to hide her own lusts behind the skirts of so many other girls.

Ruby's lips crushed down onto Alberto's, making Alberto's mind begin a slow swirling. He reached upward and squeezed first one breast then another, arching his body upward until his manhood was swallowed deeply inside Ruby. She moved her hips up and down, moaning softly, but when Alberto began to tense, realizing that it was happening again, that he was becoming smaller instead of larger, Ruby's eyes opened wide, searching his face, seeing pain, torture, grief. . . .

She reached upward and caressed his brow, whispering, "Alberto, relax." She continued to move her body up and down, but she felt his manhood come from inside her to lie limply beneath her.

"Ruby, please," he said, clenching his teeth. He was once again humiliated. And this time with Ruby. God, how he hated her knowing. "I just . . . can't, Ruby. . . ."

Ruby reached downward and began to caress him, but saw that it was of no use. "Honey, why?" she said, moving from on top of him, handing him a towel.

Alberto climbed from the bed and began to wipe himself down with it. He knew that his face was crimson from the embarrassment. He had just proven to himself that he still was not a true man. In any sense of the word. "I don't know what causes me to react so," he said, reaching for his breeches. He stepped into them, anxious to hide his manhood from her probing eyes.

"Is there someone else, Alberto?" Ruby asked, moving from the bed, toweling herself off. "Is that the reason you still cannot enjoy me or any of my women? If so, who is it?"

Alberto looked quickly away from her as he pulled his shirt on. "I do need to talk to someone about it," he said thickly.

Ruby repositioned her red stone inside her navel, then pulled a robe on and tied it in front of her. "You can always talk to me," she said, trying to hide the disappointment in her voice. She had so hungered for his body. And damn. He was the first man who had actually been unable to have sex successfully with her. Whoever this female was who had captured Alberto's heart had to be truly something extra special.

"I don't know how to say it," Alberto said, kneading his brow. He slumped down onto a chair. "It's such an unnatural thing. I don't know what to do."

"What is it, Alberto?" She sat down on the floor in front of him, staring upward into his dark pits of eyes.

"I actually kissed Maria a while ago," he stammered.

"All brothers kiss their sisters, Alberto. What's so unnatural about that?"

"What's unnatural?" he stormed. "I enjoyed it as a man enjoys kissing a woman. It gave me strange stirrings. I desired her. This is why it was unnatural. I've desired her for years now. I am tortured. Day and night. What shall I do?"

"I see," Ruby exclaimed, rising, pacing the floor. "Yes, I see," she said once again, lighting another cigar.

"And when I kissed her, I know she realized that it wasn't the kiss of a brother," Alberto continued. "She must think I'm a freak. I don't know what to do."

"Well, you said she was no . . . longer . . . your sister," Ruby said. "So why even worry yourself about anything she will think?"

"But don't you see? That doesn't help me with my state of mind. I can't enjoy a woman the way I should. I should have been able to enjoy you. God, Ruby. You're beautiful. You had my mind and body going for a while. I don't know what happened. Just suddenly, it just quit feeling good. I couldn't feel anything. So see? What am I to do?"

"What are you to do? Wait until the right woman comes along. Just as most men do. You'll see, that will happen. This thing for your sister. It is just a passing thing. One day soon a beautiful, innocent thing will just happen along and your heart will be gone from you. Also thoughts of your sister."

Alberto's eyes wavered as he looked upward at

Ruby. "Do you really think so?" he murmured.

"I'm sure of it," Ruby said, going to her wardrobe to search through her many dresses, choosing one for the night's activities.

"But until then? What shall I do? And what about Maria and that damned Nathan Hawkins?"

"About Maria? I am sure you will find there is more to her marriage than what you have permitted her to tell you. And as for the other problem? Why not go to the gambling room and have some fun? Gambling is sort of a way to seduction. You have learned that. We should have a wild game going soon. Go on and have some fun."

She went to her liquor cabinet and pulled a bottle of port from inside it. She handed it and a long-stemmed wine glass to Alberto. "And in the meantime, get drunk." She laughed hoarsely, guiding him toward the door. "You just make yourself at home. There might already be some action in the gambling room. Maybe some have come as we've been . . . uh . . . talking."

Alberto turned to Ruby and lowered his eyes, then looked at her sternly for a moment. "I do appreciate your friendship, Ruby," he said. "Without it, I don't know what I would do."

She slapped him on the back, laughing throatily. "And I also enjoy you. One day, I plan to enjoy you to the fullest, if you know what I mean."

"Yes. Let's hope," Alberto said, then hurried from the room, and having both hands full, kicked at the door that led into the gambling room. When the door swung open and Alberto found himself face to face with Michael Hopper, he felt an inner excitement that he had momentarily forgotten. He smiled crookedly, and said, "Well, look who we have here. My ex-sister's ex-boyfriend."

He moved on past Michael, feeling Michael's eyes following him, then sat down at the gambling table and poured himself a drink. His eyes traveled around the room, seeing only one other man in the room besides Michael. He then focused his eyes back on Michael, grinning absently. "And are you ready to lose your balls at poker, Michael?" he laughed hoarsely. "I've not lost at poker for some time now." Now that Maria was married, Alberto no longer had to stay hidden from Michael. Michael was no longer a threat. Hawkins had taken care of that.

Michael wouldn't have recognized Alberto behind the whiskers, but since he now knew of Maria's presence in the area, he was quickly aware of the identity of this man who appeared to be so full of cynicism and bitterness. He lumbered across the room and sat down at the gambling table, working with a deck of cards, flipping them onto the table, one at a time. "I know you're some kind of a fool, Alberto," he grumbled. "And if I remember correctly, crazy as hell and don't know half of what comes from that mouth of yours. But I would like to know what you meant by those damn remarks about Maria."

Alberto felt a tearing at his heart at having to speak further of her, but he forced an ugly laugh and said, "My sweet innocent Maria? Seems she's not so sweet and innocent any longer." He poured himself another glass of port and swallowed it in fast gulps, then added, "When a woman marries Nathan Hawkins, she's no longer sweet and innocent, wouldn't you say?"

Michael glowered. He reached inside his suit jacket pocket and pulled out a cigar. He thrust it between his teeth and lighted it, tilting a brow as he continued to watch Alberto. "You appear to be a bit jealous, Alberto," he snarled, laughing hoarsely. "Why is that?"

Alberto lunged from the chair, anger making his eyes bulge. "You just shut your damn filthy mouth, Michael," he said. "And what the hell brings you here bumming in these parts?" He laughed loudly, taking another fast gulp of port. "Your luck run out? Huh?" His eyes raked over Michael's attire of flannel shirt and faded breeches. "Play one too many games of poker? Lose your life's savings?" He laughed once again, settling back down onto a chair opposite Michael. "Do you even have enough money to play me a few hands tonight? I feel my luck is a-rolling." He lowered his eyes, then murmured, "With . . . uh . . . cards, that is."

"Sure. I'd like to play you a few hands, Alberto," Michael said, picking up the cards from the table, shuffling them. The door opened and two more men entered and settled down around the gambling table, now making a total of five men ready to be dealt a hand to.

Michael continued to shuffle the cards, puffing eagerly on his cigar. "So you say Maria married up with a Nathan Hawkins, eh?" he mumbled, furrowing his brow. He had to act as though he didn't know. He couldn't take the chance of arousing Alberto's curiosity. Alberto had only just suspected that Maria and himself had been intimate anyway, he thought to himself. He must never know that only last night he had held her in

358

his arms, made love to her. Oh, how he ached for her now!

"You don't seem a bit upset about Maria," Alberto growled, slamming the glass on the table, scooting the wine bottle away from him. "Is that because you had only thought to use her on the ship? Just like I thought? Once we had arrived in America, you knew that she wasn't good enough for you? Huh?"

Michael's face paled. He looked anxiously around him, seeing eyes on him. He knew what the men had to be thinking. What ship? They had to be wondering what *he* would have been doing on a ship that had carried this immigrant called Alberto and his sister Maria to America. They had to know by his appearance that he was American, not Italian, and would have no cause to be aboard such a ship.

Damn. Would Alberto cause his cover to be exposed? Could one of these men even be a representative for Nathan Hawkins? Hadn't Maria warned him that Nathan Hawkins was suspicious . . . ?

"Let's just play cards, Alberto," he grumbled. "I don't wish to talk about Maria, nor anything else this night. I've come to earn a few dollars. Not toss words idly around. Most of the time words come from between your lips that don't even make sense. And these men at the table will soon know that is because you are only a half-wit, with only a portion of a mind."

Michael stopped shuffling for a brief moment and glowered toward Alberto. "You see, I don't know what ship you are talking about. I've never been aboard any ship. I've never even had enough money to travel much further than the city of Creal Springs. Only recently

359

have I had enough money to purchase me a fine cigar and be able to come to these card games. No, Alberto. I only know you and your sister from the streets of Hawkinsville."

Alberto's brows raised in confusion. What the hell kind of a game was Michael trying to play? Alberto knew that he should be raging because of Michael's words about his being a half-wit. But hearing all this other garble confused him to the point of speechlessness. He pushed his chair back and tipped it to rest on two legs, still studying Michael. There had to be a reason behind Michael's drab clothes. There had to be a reason behind this story he had just made up. Damn. Alberto had to know. After the poker game, he would follow Michael from the house and confront him. Maybe then he might even knock the hell out of Michael for talking so casually of Maria, as though he had never even known her, and for speaking so loosely of Alberto's mind not being right.

But now Alberto was ready to play poker. His insides were glowing, thinking to have those cards in his hands once again. He could even forget his brief moment with Ruby, and how he had failed once again at becoming a full man. He pulled his chair back to the table, feeling his heart thumping wildly against his ribs.

"And what's your pleasure, gents?" Michael said, straightening the cards, ready to deal them.

A dark-skinned man, attired in a brown woolen suit with an initial of "B" sewn on his suit pocket leaned forward and said, "The usual." A diamond stickpin twinkled in blues and golds from his silk cravat and his dark hair was slicked down with pomade and parted in the middle. His dark eyes moved from man to man as his fingers worked with his neatly trimmed moustache. "Five card stud. Jacks or better to open," he added. He placed two one-dollar bills in the center of the table. "And an ante of two dollars should suffice," he grumbled further.

Michael watched this man's eyes. Was he one to be trusted? Could he be one of Nathan Hawkins's men? Then his eyes moved to the next man. He was being much too quiet. This man's blue eyes traveled from man to man, almost suspiciously, then he placed his ante in the middle of the table, saying, "Suits me fine."

Alberto laughed gruffly, placing his own ante atop the other bills. "Just beans," he said. "When this night is over, you'll see just who is the greatest at playing this game of poker." He looked at Michael, sneering. What luck to have run into him this night. Alberto's other problems had quickly dissolved from his mind. He had been anxious to play Michael a game of poker. He had been anxious to beat him all to hell. If not by fists, then in the next best way—with the skillfulness with which Alberto now knew how to play this game with cards. So far, luck had been with him.

Alberto knew that Maria hadn't been the only one to play games with the Lazzaro family. Since Alberto's first night at Ruby's, he had been winning at poker and had been hiding his money away from the rest of the family. At times, he had felt guilt for this, but mostly he had felt hope for the future. His future. He had plans. He was going to be able to move from Hawkinsville. He was going to have his own place of business in Creal Springs. Then he could take his Papa away from this hell hole of a town. But he could only do this by saving his winnings. If his winnings were used for household expenses, he would go the way of all the other immigrants. The household expenses would be paid . . . but nothing else. No. He couldn't let himself feel guilty for what he was doing. Maria had hidden her own jar of money. Why couldn't he?

The other ante was placed atop Alberto's money, then Michael began to deal the cards until all were holding five cards apiece in their hands. Low grumbles surfaced from all around the table, and even Alberto joined in. Damn. He hadn't gotten openers. He glanced over at Michael. Had he?

Michael clenched a fist on his lap, studying his cards. Damn. No openers. He glanced over at Alberto. Had he any?

"Well?" Michael finally said, looking all around him. He placed his cards on the table, face down, and lit a fresh cigar. The man next to him lit a cigarette, scowling. "Check," the man said, slapping his cards face down onto the table, looking at the next man.

Many grumbles of "check" floated around the table, then all threw their cards onto a pile in the middle of the table and anted again. The cards were dealt a second, then a third time, then Alberto smiled broadly. He had drawn better than openers. He had drawn four of a kind. He looked the cards over once again, then glanced around the table, his gaze stopping at Michael. He tensed. Didn't he see something in Michael's eyes? A glimmer of sorts? Had Michael also drawn something as great as Alberto? Damn. Alberto so wanted to beat the hell out of Michael. He had waited so long for such an opportunity. He would never forget the way Michael had kissed Maria on the ship. . . .

Michael's pulsebeat quickened. He glanced first at the outspread cards in his hand, then with a furrowed brow, looked quickly at Alberto. He chewed on his cigar, studying Alberto's expression. In his dark eyes, Michael could see something similar to triumph. Damn. What the hell had Alberto drawn? Michael wanted to beat the hell out of this bastard who had caused him nothing but trouble since the first time he had laid eyes on him on that death ship.

Michael glanced back down at his cards, seeing that he would be drawing into a straight flush. If only he could be dealt an eight of Clubs. Then he would have it made!

The dealer looked toward Michael. "What's your bet?"

"One dollar," he mumbled. He would try to bluff his way through this. He didn't want anyone to suspect such a great hand.

The bet moved around to Alberto. "Okay. I'll call you," he grumbled, feeling a twitching of his cheek, knowing that bluffing was the best way. Yeah. That's what he'd do. Bluff. He glanced toward Michael and saw Michael's eyebrows tilt in surprise. Alberto wanted to laugh, but instead glanced on around the table to the next man who was the next to bet, then the next, until it was time to discard.

The dealer took a deep drag from the cigarette that was hanging from the corner of his mouth, blew the smoke out, then asked, "How many cards, Lazzaro?"

Alberto straightened his back and said, "One."

All faces quickly turned toward him, making Alberto smile smugly. He knew that his bluff was fast coming to an end. But it was time. . . .

"How many cards, uh, what did you say your last name was?" the dealer asked, looking toward Michael. He moved his cigarette around with the tip of his tongue, then puffed on it once again.

Michael ran a hand through his hair, then mumbled, "I didn't say." He eyed the man suspiciously, then added, "But you can call me Michael. And how many cards do I want?" He laughed a bit throatily, glancing toward Alberto. "One. I need one."

Alberto's face drained of color. Damn. Could Michael . . . ? He placed his cards face down on the table in front of him after throwing in his discard. When the dealer dealt him his one requested card, Alberto shuffled it into his other four and picked them up, continuing to shuffle them in his hands, almost afraid to look at them. If Michael had only needed one card, Alberto knew that his own chances weren't so great. He continued to shuffle the cards, watching Michael's expression as he lifted his dealt card before his eyes. Alberto's heartbeat faltered when he saw Michael's light up in various colors of blues, and his face flush a rose color. Then when the bet was passed on around to Alberto, he tossed in ten one-dollar bills, knowing he would have even bet more if ten hadn't been the limit set down on the first bet passed around the table.

Then when all the men dropped out and Michael was the only one left to call Alberto's hand, Alberto grumbled, "I'll raise you ten more dollars." He threw out ten more one-dollar bills.

All grew silent in the room. It seemed that even the three men who were now only observers had ceased to breathe. The continuation of spiraling smoke in the air was the only indication that there were more in the room besides Alberto and Michael.

"Okay. I'll call you," Michael said, slapping his money on the table. He glanced down at his cards, seeing his three, four, five, six and seven of Clubs. He had hoped for an eight, but having been lucky enough to be given the three, he knew that had been just as good. His heart pounded wildly. He chewed and puffed on the cigar, waiting for Alberto to reveal his hand.

Alberto glanced downward at his cards, trembling inside. It was at times like this that he was reminded of the weak side of himself. He felt as though he might retch from the excitement. His four twos and Jack of Spades normally would be a winner for sure. But he had to remember that Michael had also drawn only one more card.

"Well? Alberto?" Michael prodded, growing impatient. He placed his cigar on an ashtray, spreading his cards out face down, close to the middle of the table, letting Alberto and the rest of the men see them.

"Ah hell," Alberto grumbled, then spread his cards out onto the table, face up. He felt the sickness at the pit of his stomach increase in intensity when he heard a low, throaty laughter emerge from deep inside Michael. I'm beaten, Alberto thought to himself. Or why the laugh . . . ? He watched as Michael flipped the cards over, face side up, one by one, until all five were revealed to the staring eyes of all the men, who had grown even more stone silent.

"Well, I'll be damned," Alberto said, hitting his fist against the table top. "I'll be damned. A damned straight flush."

"Got cha beat, Alberto ol' boy. Four of a kind just isn't good enough," Michael laughed, scooping the money over in front of him. "Ready for another hand?"

"You bet," Alberto said, already counting money, placing it in the middle of the table. "You'd better know I am. I'm going to beat your pants off, if I have to play you all night."

Michael laughed, scooting his cards to the gentleman next to him. "Deal," he said, fitting his fingertips together in front of him, still watching Alberto.

The card game went on for hours. Michael would win one hand, then Alberto, with an occasional win from one of the other men at the table. When midnight was drawing nigh, Michael and Alberto had won an even number of hands. And when they were the only two left at the gambling table, Michael slapped the cards down on the table and scooted the chair back and said, "Well, I guess that's all for now." He watched Alberto amusedly, seeing that he appeared to be upset by this night's cards.

Alberto slammed his cards on the table, then placed his winnings inside his front breeches pocket. "None of this turned out the way I wanted it to," he grumbled.

"Well, I have to admit, I would have preferred to have done a much better job at beating your ass off," Michael laughed.

"And now that your card playing is over, you're going to have one of Ruby's girls, huh?" Alberto said, eyes wavering.

"I don't think so," Michael said. "Guess I'd best be running back to my hotel. I'm kind of beat. I've got a few things to do tomorrow that will have to be done with a clear head."

Alberto laughed hoarsely as he pushed his chair back and rose from it. "Well, I now know your plans can't have anything to do with Maria," he said. "It seems Nathan Hawkins beat you inside her breeches."

Michael pushed his chair back and went to Alberto and grabbed him by the throat, threatening him with a doubled-up fist. "Alberto, if you know what's good for you, you'll keep your damn mouth shut about Maria," he said. "If you don't, you may not have any teeth left in that warped head of yours. Do you hear?"

"Hey. Ease up, Hopper," Alberto gulped, straining, feeling the color fast draining from his face. He didn't care to fight Michael. He knew who would be the winner. He had dreamed of one day getting even with Michael, but now that he felt the strength in Michael's hands, he knew that another way would have to be found.

Michael dropped both arms, then straightened his coat, shrugging his shoulders. "Okay. As long as you understand," he mumbled, then left the room.

Alberto swallowed hard, lifting a hand to his throat. He could feel the pulsebeat growing stronger. God. Would he ever become a man in every sense of the word? First not to be able to bed up with a female in the proper way, then not be able to defend himself . . . ?

He rushed from the room and down the stairs, moving on through the parlor to the kitchen, and out the back door. He didn't want to run into Ruby again tonight. He didn't want to run into anyone. He wanted to rush home, climb beneath his covers and try to go to sleep to forget all that had happened both that day and that night.

As he rushed down the back steps, he stopped, hearing some scuffling in the dark. He tensed, then eased on around the house, wondering who might be fighting. He stumbled over something in the dark and gasped when he glanced downward and found both of Ruby's dogs lying still in the grass. He bent and checked them over carefully. Were they dead? What had happened to them? Then muffled cursings drew him to stand next to the house, in the shadows, growing frightened. When the three wrestling figures moved out into the open, beneath the direct rays of the moon, Alberto gasped even further, seeing that one of the men was Michael Hopper. The other two were two of the men who had been playing cards with them all evening.

Alberto recoiled even more, but when he saw the flash of a knife, and saw that it was moving toward Michael's stomach, something made him jump for the man who was holding the knife. He grabbed the man by the neck, panting, and wrestled him to the ground, relieved when the knife fell to the ground beside them.

With one blow, he clipped this man on the chin, then another blow, and another, then rose, panting even more when the man lay quiet, breathing shallowly. He wiped his brow when he saw Michael lumbering toward him, blood streaming from both his mouth and nose.

"Thanks, Alberto," Michael said, placing his arm

around Alberto's shoulder. "If you hadn't happened along, I'd have been a goner for sure. Clarence seems to have disappeared tonight. I sure could've used some of his muscles." Michael wiped at his mouth with the back of a hand, then studied Alberto. "And are you all right? I saw the knife just as you jumped that bastard. Did he have a chance to get you before you knocked him to the ground?"

Alberto grew weak in the knees, realizing just how close he had come to being dead. He slumped to the ground, nearing the stage of retching. He hung his head in his hands, moaning. Michael dropped down beside him. "Alberto? Are you all right?" Michael's hands went over Alberto, searching him for wounds. "Damn it, Alberto. Speak to me. Tell me you're all right. I don't hate you enough to want you dead."

Alberto's head flew up, his dark eyes weary. "You sure about that?" he said, forcing a laugh.

"Then you're all right?" Michael prodded, once again wiping at his mouth and nose, staining his shirt sleeve to make it even redder than it was.

"I'm fine. And you?" Alberto finally said. "What the hell was that all about?"

Michael slumped down on the ground beside Alberto, breathing hard. His eyes moved from one lifeless figure to the next, then to Ruby's dogs. "Damned if I know," he mumbled. "Maybe for money, maybe for . . . something . . . else. . . ."

"What else could it be, besides the money?" Alberto asked, wiping his brow with the back of his hand. His eyes traveled over the lifeless bodies, hoping they weren't dead. But he knew the man he had dealt the

369

blow to wouldn't be dead. Alberto didn't have the strength to hit anyone so hard as to cause death. But the other? Alberto could see a pool of blood at the base of his head.

"Alberto, I'd like to tell you about it, but I think we'd best get the hell out of here. Don't you?"

"Do you mean . . . just leave them here . . . ? Not tell anybody?"

"Ruby isn't going to like it one hell of a bit," Michael said, rising, offering Alberto a hand. "Her dogs? Those bastards had already taken care of the dogs before jumping me. I don't know if they are alive or dead." He placed his arm around Alberto's shoulder once they were standing side by side. "And, Alberto? I owe you a lot for stepping in and doing what you did. If you hadn't, it would be me lying beside those dogs. But I would have been filled with many knife wounds. Not only knocked in the head."

"I've never liked you very much, Michael," Alberto said, clearing his throat nervously. "But, hell. I couldn't stand by and watch you get murdered. Glad to have been of assistance."

"Well, then, since we have our thank yous cleared up, let's get the hell out of here. I think I may have just found the person I've been searching for."

"Huh?" Alberto said, moving along beside Michael, on out onto the gravel road.

"Yeah. I think you and I can work together, Alberto," Michael said, smiling broadly. "How's about it?"

"Hell, I don't have the least bit of an idea what you're talking about," Alberto grumbled.

"Come. We'll go to my hotel and I'll tell you all about it."

"Where's your hotel?"

"In Creal Springs. But you'll have to climb onto the horse behind me. That's the best I can do."

"I've got my own horse and wagon hitched over there," Alberto said, motioning with his head.

"Well, then, follow me," Michael said, laughing throatily. "Yeah, Alberto. I think between the two of us, we can take care of that damn Nathan Hawkins."

Alberto began to walk toward his wagon but stopped when he caught sight of a body lying partially in the brush. He felt his heart lurch, then shouted, "Michael! Come quick!"

Michael rushed to his side, then stooped when he saw the cause of Alberto's alarm. "My God, it's Clarence," he gasped.

Alberto took a few steps backward. "Is he . . . is . . . he dead . . . ?"

Michael checked Clarence over carefully, then rose, frowning. "No. Just has a blow to the head," he grumbled. "We've got to get him to the porch. We'll just leave him there for Ruby to find."

"Are you sure he's not . . . dead . . . ?" Alberto stammered, afraid to lift Clarence. He knew the weak side of himself was surfacing once again, but he just couldn't seem to help it.

"Damn it, Alberto," Michael said. "Grab hold of his legs. I'll take his arms. Let's get him to the porch and *then* get the hell out of here."

"Okay," Alberto mumbled. "If you say so."

They struggled with the heaviness of Clarence's body

371

until they had arranged him beside the door for a quick discovery by anyone making the next exit from Ruby's house.

Michael brushed his hair back from his eyes, panting hard. "Now, Alberto, let's head out," he said, moving down the steps.

"I'd sure like to know what you've got up your sleeve, Michael," Alberto said, moving alongside him.

"You'll soon know, Alberto. Soon. . . ."

Chapter Sixteen

The night sounds in this state of Illinois were peaceful and serene. Wrapped in her velveteen cape, Maria paced the front porch of her new home. She shivered in the chill, clasping her arms around her, hugging herself, looking into the distance, listening. A whippoorwill was echoing across the stretches of land that lay on all sides of her and crickets hummed along, it seemed in unison. But it wasn't these sounds that had brought Maria to the porch in the wee hours of the morning. She had heard the sound of a wagon's wheels and horse's hooves, sounding almost like those of the wagon that she had called her own, but was now only her Papa's and Alberto's.

Thinking it to be Alberto returning to apologize for his nasty behavior, Maria had rushed to her wardrobe and had pulled the cape from inside it and wrapped it around her chemise, hoping to meet Alberto just as he stepped from the wagon, headed for her front door.

But nothing. When she arrived at the front door and looked toward the road, all she had seen had been just a bit of dust in the air, swirling upward from the road, the only signs left of any wagon having just passed by.

Maria continued to pace, sighing heavily. She knew that she could return to bed, but she hadn't been able to sleep. Closing her eyes in the new surroundings, beautiful though they were, had become an absolute impossibility. She had lain there, listening for the familiar steps of Nathan, fearing his return would carry him right to her room, to demand more from her body. Did she have a lifetime of dread ahead of her? Wasn't there any way out of this complication she had gotten herself into?

She feared not, for it seemed that Nathan was even more powerful than she had at first suspected. How many wives had there been before her? How could Mama Pearl not have grown suspicious before now? But maybe Mama Pearl was being held against her own will, and being forced to pretend such joviality.

Maria knew that she would have to agree to anything Nathan would demand of her now. The thought of possibly being taken and left deep inside the bowels of the earth frightened her so. Would he truly add her body to those that she suspected he had already taken to the coal mines and left to die?

She shook her head, trying to make her mind quit traveling in such vicious circles. She was letting her imagination run wild. This wasn't the time. She needed her rest. Hadn't Michael said that he would meet her this very next day? She needed to be fresh, to make him love her even more.

Sighing, she turned and went back inside, walking quietly up the steepness of the stairs, on to her room. She tossed her cape aside and stretched out on her bed, resting her head on her hands as her elbows pushed against the mattress. She gazed out the window, suddenly feeling as though she was in Italy. Didn't the setting outside the window resemble Italy? Beneath the soft velvet rays of the moon, row after row of grapevines sat in clusters, as though they were people, stooped, with rounded backs. Only by daylight did they show their true forms, which then resembled fingers, as their tendrils reached out to the next cluster of vines.

A deep sadness crept through Maria's heart. She missed Italy. She missed her Gran-mama and her Aunt Helena. And she now missed Alberto and her Papa, and they were only a stone's throw away. "One doesn't have to be across the ocean to be separated," she whispered, settling down onto a pillow, feeling her eyelids grow heavy. She reached up and lifted her hair from beneath her head, letting it drape across the pillow behind and beside her, then let herself drift off into a restless sleep. She dreamed of Michael, his lips, his hands, his voice, and then she was awakened abruptly when she heard a noise outside her door in the hallway. She tensed, thinking it was Nathan, seeking her out in the dark. She rose, pulling a night robe around her shoulders, then crept to the door, opening it slowly.

"Maria . . . ?" a voice spoke from somewhere beside her.

Maria put her hands to her throat, turning on her heel, peering through the darkness. "Alberto . . . ? God. Alberto, is that you? How . . . ?"

Alberto moved to her side and took her hand in his. "Maria, I've got to talk to you. Now. Tonight," he said thickly. He glanced quickly around him. "Where's Hawkins?"

Maria was in a state of semi-shock. "Alberto, how did you get in here? Why . . . ?"

375

"The front door was unlocked. I just walked in. I had to see you."

"But what if Nathan had been here? What if he had heard you? Wouldn't you be afraid of him shooting you like a thief in the night?"

"I had to take that chance," Alberto grumbled, taking her by an elbow, guiding her back into her room. Once inside, he shut the door behind them. "Now. You must tell me. Where *is* Hawkins?"

"How did you know he wasn't even here in this room where I slept . . . ?"

Alberto laughed hoarsely. "Maria, if Hawkins had been in that room with you, I know you would've steered me away from it long before now." His eyes moved around him, seeing what was possible beneath the dim rays of the moonlight streaming in through the one window.

"I still cannot believe you would enter this house as you have done," Maria whispered.

"I can feel my way around any house. Especially if it's to find you, Maria."

Maria went to her nightstand and turned on a light, flooding the room in shallow yellows. Alberto went quickly to the light, looking beneath its shade. "Electric," he said. "So Hawkins *has* brought you to a house of riches, huh?" He began to walk around the room, touching the softness of the upholstered chairs, and then the bed. He bounced onto it, laughing shakily. "God. What a bed. Now I can understand why you would agree to live here."

Maria went to him and sat down beside him, taking a hand in hers. "Alberto, *that* is *not* the reason at all," she said sternly. "Now that you're here, you're going to hear all the true reasons. You shall not leave this house until you listen."

Alberto ran his free hand through the thickness of his beard. His face became serious. "Maria, I already do know," he said thickly.

Maria's face paled. She rose, moving around the room, hugging herself. "How do you know, Alberto?" she said. She swung around, facing him. "Only two people know besides myself. Papa . . . and. . . ."

Alberto rose and moved toward her. "And Michael?" he grumbled, tilting her chin with a forefinger. "And Michael Hopper? Is that what you were ready to say? That you had also told Michael Hopper?"

Maria swallowed hard, seeing much in the depths of Alberto's dark eyes. It wasn't a mockery. It was an understanding. "How did you . . . know . . . ?" she whispered.

He walked away from her and slouched down into a chair, stretching his long, lean legs out before him. "It's the damnedest thing," he said, laughing amusedly.

Maria sat down opposite him, leaning forward, eyes wide. "What are you talking about, Alberto?" she prodded, feeling the rapid beat of her heart. How would he know of Michael, without . . . having . . . talked with . . . him?

"Michael," he grumbled. "He's not so bad after all. I guess I've been wrong about him all along."

Maria flipped her hair back from her eyes. "What has happened to change your mind . . . ?" she uttered softly.

"Michael. He's what has happened," Alberto said. "He and I. Well . . . uh . . . we met once again tonight. We met at Ruby's."

Maria's fingers went to her throat. "At Ruby's?" she gasped. "You and Michael . . . ?"

"We joined in on one of the damnest poker games," he laughed more amusedly. "Cutthroat as hell. But neither of us won over the other. We split even."

"Then you got along all right? You didn't have bitter words between you?"

"More than that," Alberto chuckled.

"What do you mean, more than that . . . ?"

"Well, Michael left before I did, and when I got outside Ruby's, I found him being attacked by two fellows. I decided I didn't dislike Michael enough to let him get knifed so I jumped into the fight with him. Between us . . . we gave the two bastards the licking of their lives."

"Then you and Michael . . . are . . . all right . . . ?"

Alberto thrust out his chest, hitting it with doubled-up fists. "Don't I look all right?" he laughed.

"And Michael . . . ?"

"Fit as a fiddle."

"Why would these men attack . . . ?" Maria began to say, then paled, remembering what Michael had said about being so involved in this thing called the "union." Had Nathan . . . found out . . . ?

"Afterwards, I went with Michael to his hotel room in Creal Springs," Alberto said, rising, pacing the floor. "He told why he's in Creal Springs. He's asked me to help him."

"What do you mean, Alberto? Help him . . . ?"

"This 'union' he speaks of? Well, Michael wants me to be his and the 'union's' ally. To speak the truth to all the coal miners. To set them against this Nathan Hawkins. To cause them to demand better wages and different, safer working conditions. I'm to mingle with the men, whisper these truths. When all agree that Nathan Hawkins has to be dealt with, then we will make our move and we will no longer be prisoners in this town called Hawkinsville."

Tears burned at the corners of Maria's eyes. Now not only did she have to fear for Michael's safety, but also for Alberto's. "Alberto, it is too dangerous," she cried. "You don't want to get involved. Surely Michael has his own men that he can send in to talk to the coal miners. Why . . . you . . . ?"

"Nathan Hawkins's representatives are everywhere. They can sniff out a union man. Don't you see? I'm sure that's why Michael was getting attacked tonight. That's the reason he needs someone who is already of the Italian community to infiltrate and set our people's minds to wondering about these things that the union promises for our people."

Maria rose and began pacing the floor, chewing on her lower lip. "I just don't know," she whispered. "I just don't know."

Alberto went to her and took her by the shoulders, glowering. "Maria, I have to do this. Don't you see? I need this to make me feel as . . . a . . . uh . . . man. Doing this could make me feel so important. Up to now, I have groveled in pity for myself. And don't you even remember what I did . . . uh . . . earlier . . . to you? How I . . . uh . . . kissed you?"

Maria's gaze lowered. She swallowed hard. "Yes. I remember," she whispered. Her eyes shot upward. "And why *did* you do such a thing, Alberto? You made me feel . . . so dirty afterwards. I was never so confused."

Alberto moved away from her, with head bent. "I do not understand myself at times, Maria," he murmured. He began to knead his brow, trembling. "I guess I was so angry at you for having married such a beast as Nathan Hawkins. I didn't understand how you could do this to me . . . Papa . . . and all of our people. You knew that it was he who had caused us to live like dogs . . . animals. . . ."

Maria went to him and took his hands in hers. She looked into his eyes, nearing tears. "But I *had* to, Alberto," she said. "I had no choice. He forced me. Don't you see? I wouldn't have otherwise. Don't you know my hate for that man? If you knew how I hated . . . for him . . . to touch me. . . ."

Alberto closed his eyes and shook his head violently. "Don't even say it, Maria," he shouted. "I don't want to hear the words. Just the thought of him being near you repulses me. I don't want to think of him doing anything further to you. . . ."

"I know," she murmured, caressing his cheek with her hand. "I'm sorry, Alberto. I'm sorry."

His gaze met hers and held. "Anyway, Michael explained it all to me," he mumbled.

Maria felt a blush rising. "He . . . did . . . ?" she gasped, pulling away from Alberto. She wondered just how much Michael had confessed to her brother.

"I understand. Fully," he said, moving to plop down into a chair, head bowed.

She went and sat down on the floor in front of him, looking upward into his face. "Do you? Honestly? Do you know that if I hadn't, that man I have been forced to call my husband would have sent us all back to Italy? Do you realize that would have been the end for Papa?

380

He isn't well enough. . . ."

Alberto framed her face between his hands. "Hush. Maria, don't speak anymore of it," he whispered. "Like I said, Michael told me all. He told me of your encounter with him while you were there with Nathan in Saint Louis. I even now approve of Michael and you getting together. Honestly, I do. He's one hell of a man. I don't know why I didn't see it sooner. He's someone I'd like to be more like. And maybe one day I will."

"I'll always love Michael, Alberto," Maria confessed, flushing once again.

"I know," he said, lowering his eyes. "And he loves you. He plans to have you. One way or another. He confessed this much to me tonight."

Maria's heartbeat increased. "You did say you were with him tonight?" she said. "Michael had said that he would be in town tomorrow. But he hadn't said anything about tonight. Where is he now, Alberto?"

"In the Saline Hotel in Creal Springs," he said, blinking his eyes nervously, suspicious of what her next words might be. . . .

"Take me to him, Alberto," she quickly blurted, rising, moving across the room to pull her cape around her shoulders. She tied the bow in front at her neck, watching Alberto with pleading in her eyes. "Please? I must see him. Tonight. I fear for him. I don't want to wait another moment. Please take me to him?"

Alberto pushed himself up from the chair and moved toward her. "But what about Nathan Hawkins?" he said, opening the bedroom door, looking outward.

"He's supposedly in Creal Springs," she said. "He said that his meeting might last into the night, and if it did, he would be staying at his other house for the night."

Alberto's eyes grew wide. "The damn bastard has two houses . . . ?"

Maria giggled. She had had the same reaction. "Yes. He has another house in Creal Springs."

"But what if he does decide to come to this house later on tonight?"

"If he does, I am sure he will move on to his room. He won't be aware of my absence. This is why we have two separate rooms. For his late arrivals. He doesn't want to disturb me, so I will be, shall we say, 'fresh,' for whatever he desires of me the next night."

Alberto groaned, reaching for Maria's hand. His eyes raked over her, remembering her night robe beneath the cape. He knew what she had in mind when she would meet with Michael. He tried to keep the thought from his mind, but he couldn't help it. Even now he could feel desire rising for Maria . . . his own sister. He closed his eyes and stepped back away from her, almost reeling. He reached for the edge of the door and steadied himself.

"Will you take me to Michael, Alberto?" Maria asked once again. She cast her eyes downward. "I know what you truly think of my asking this, but I do have a need to talk with him. Please understand."

"If you must, you must," he said. "But what if Nathan Hawkins finds out? What then?"

Shivers raced up and down Maria's spine. She pulled the hood of her cape upward, to cover her hair and most of her face. "He won't," she answered. "I shall see to it that he won't."

"Okay, then. Come with me," he said, motioning with his hand. "If I found my way to your room, I can

382

surely find my way back to my wagon."

"We must do it in darkness," Maria whispered. "I wouldn't want Mama Pearl to see me. I'm not sure if I can trust her."

Alberto leaned into Maria's face. "Who the hell is Mama Pearl?"

Maria covered his lips with her hands. "Shh," she replied, then hooked her arm through his and followed alongside him down the steep stairs, then breathed more easily when they rushed through the parlor and on outside, to the wagon. Once again Maria cautioned Alberto. "The wagon. It creaks so," she said, settling down beside Alberto on the seat, seeing the restlessness of the horse as it stamped a hoof into the ground. "Please move slowly from the house. The house seems to have eyes. Please be as quiet as possible, Alberto."

"What you're doing is foolish, Maria," Alberto grumbled, snapping the reins. "Your sense of adventure—won't it ever leave you? Do you realize the hour of the night? What will Michael say when you go knocking on his door?"

Maria scooted next to Alberto and cuddled, seeking warmth. The chill of the night was settling all around her in a wet dampness, causing her teeth to chatter. "When he sees me, I only hope he will be happy," she finally answered.

"And am I to wait? Will your conversation be brief . . . ?"

Maria's face flushed. "As brief as possible, Alberto," she said. "But surely you can find something to do to pass the time while you wait. Maybe a beautiful . . . lady . . . ?" Maria giggled, then placed her hand over her lips when she saw the cloudiness suddenly appearing in his eyes. "Or something. . . ." she stammered, tensing inside.

"It's quite late. I shall just snooze in the wagon until you return," Alberto grumbled.

Maria blinked her thick lashes nervously, watching all around her as Alberto urged the horse onward. The tall Indian grasses were rippling in the breeze, making shadows appear to be jumping about on all sides of them. She grabbed Alberto's hand and held on to it when a dog raced up to the wagon barking and showing its teeth. Then when houses began doubling at the sides of the road, Maria pulled the hood of her cape closer to her face, wondering if one could even be the one that Nathan owned. Would he see this horse and wagon wandering on the quiet streets of the night? Would he wonder about its passengers?

"How much farther, Alberto?" she whispered, trembling suddenly.

"The hotel is the one in the square of the town," he said.

"He's in such a nice one?"

"Well, you might say that," he laughed, then guided the horse to a halt in front of a building that stood four stories into the sky. "He's in the basement rooms," he said, laughing softly. "You know he has to appear like a bum. Well, he couldn't take a room that's usually only inhabited by the richest gents visiting this fair town of Creal Springs."

"Which room, Alberto?" Maria asked, inching her way from the seat.

"When you go down those stairs over there, it's the first room to the right when you step into the hallway," he answered. "And watch out for the rats. They're

384

almost as big as dogs."

Maria shuddered. "What?" she gasped. "Rats . . . ?"

Alberto laughed hoarsely once again, tying the reins to the seat, moving to stretch out onto the wagon's floor. "Sorry to have frightened you, Maria," he said, placing his arms behind his head, resting on them. "No rats. Go on. Just tap lightly. I was supposed to tell you earlier that Michael had asked to see you. Just thought I'd play a little game with you by not telling."

Maria's eyes flashed and her hands formed two tight fists. "How could you, Alberto," she hissed, then flew from the seat and headed for the building, watching close around her, seeing no other travelers on the roads or sidewalks at this time of night. The large clock on the building that sat in the center of this square of the town began to strike and ended after striking twice. "Two in the morning," Maria said, feeling a wickedness sweep over her.

Never in her life had she been so daring. But she was going to see Michael again. Another rendezvous of rapture. And Alberto had even okayed it this time. She felt that she had accomplished something this night. She and Alberto had become an alliance once again. She relished the thought. She idolized her brother. It was nice to have him on her side once again.

Glancing fleetingly from side to side, seeing nobody approaching, Maria rushed down the four narrow steps, then pushed open a door that led into a dark, smelly passageway. Swallowing back her fear, she inched her way to the door that Alberto had directed her to. With a doubled fist, she knocked, then stood, trembling, listening. When the door yanked open, flooding her face with light, enabling her to see the

385

figure standing before her, she waited no longer, but fell into Michael's arms.

"Michael, my love," she murmured, reaching up, caressing his face, his lips, then lifted her lips to his and let his swallow hers in total warmth, softness. She felt the hardness of his body and the urgency in which he was pressing her to him, realizing that this night heid more than mere talk for her. She was going to let him guide her into another world that included only their united passions. The desire flooding her became almost painful when his hands reached beneath her cape and found the skimpiness of her attire.

"I'm so glad you came, darling," he said, now kissing the hollow of her throat after having released the ties of her cape, letting the cape cascade to the floor, to settle around her feet. His free hand reached and closed and bolt-locked the door, then with both arms, lifted her up and carried her to a small bed that sat against a far wall.

"I need you, Michael," Maria purred, reaching up to run her fingers through his hair, then seeking his lips once again.

"And I you," he whispered, placing her on the bed.

Maria lifted her night robe, then her chemise over her head, all the while watching him unbuttoning his breeches, feeling anxiety making her head begin to reel. Oh, if only he were her husband. What nights they would share! Every night they would explore one another's body, make their minds soar from within them.

"You don't mind the nastiness of the room?" Michael asked, lowering himself down beside her, stretching his legs next to hers, rubbing his toes up and down the inside of her thighs.

Maria looked swiftly around her and giggled. "It's not much worse than most houses I've lived in," she said, seeing the stained, yellowed walls, and the upholstered chair that was losing its stuffing in wadded brown masses. One lone window looked back at her with tattered gray curtains. But all that mattered was that she was with Michael, and that Michael needed her as badly as she needed him. Talk would come later. Now she only wanted him to make love to her. Over and over again.

He took her face between his hands and searched it with his blue eyes. "You are all right, aren't you, darling?" he asked softly. "Nathan Hawkins hasn't hurt you in any way?"

She puckered her lips, inviting a kiss. "Hush. Please. No mention of that madman," she whispered. "Later. Let's enjoy our moments of bliss first. Please, Michael?" She took his hand and guided it between her thighs, parting her legs, letting his fingers enter her. With her other hand, she guided his to a breast, squirming when he began to knead and caress. "I'm so hungry for you, my love," she whispered.

"I don't wish to disappoint," he laughed hoarsely, then moved atop her and replaced his fingers with the hardness of his manhood. He began to work in and out slowly, enjoying each and every moment. His lips trailed kisses over her face, then lower, to suckle on a nipple, making slow moans rise upward into Maria's throat. "Oh, how I love you, my love," she sighed, trembling. "Oh, how I love you. . . ."

Michael's fingers moved behind her and lifted her

hips to meet his more eager thrusts, groaning with each thrust of his own hips.

She clung to him, pressing her breasts to his own, pleasure sweeping through her like electrical currents, causing her body to move in quick jerks when he reached passion's peak. When his spasms had been quenched, she felt her own come to a halt, then clung even more tightly to him, not wanting this moment of bliss to end. It was always as before. He would make her mind leave her for a brief moment, to be replaced by different colors, melting, blending together. His mouth crushed down onto hers and left her lips as he moved from atop her, leaving her to lie panting, tracing his face with her fingertips.

"You must think me a whore to come in your room and give myself so quickly and easily to you," she murmured, drawing her lips downward into a pout.

"Only *my* whore," he laughed, running his hands over her silky curves. "As long as you don't act as wanton with anyone else, who am I to complain?"

Her expression grew serious as she set her jaw firmly. "Alberto told me what you have asked of him, Michael," she said, moving to an upright position, trembling when his hand reached for her and touched her between the thighs, making a want for him sweep through her once again. But she had come for more reasons than making love. She had to find out about this thing she knew to be dangerous for both Alberto and Michael. Would it in the end be worth it? Could Michael guarantee these things he spoke of for all the Italians? Or was it just because Michael wanted things for his "union"?

Reaching down, she grabbed her chemise and pulled it over her head, then her night robe. She was glad to see that Michael also pulled his breeches back on, this alone helping her to forget her further passions for him.

Michael went to an ashtray and pulled a half-smoked cigar from it and lighted it. He drew deeply from it, inhaled slowly, then began to pace the floor. "Maria, I've been unsuccessful at being able to reach the mine workers," he grumbled. "It seems most are still too afraid of Hawkins to open their mouths about any grievances they might have. And when I *do* find someone who is willing to listen, they listen, then saunter off, blank-faced. Now what Alberto can do for me is talk to the men while working. He can get them off alone, one at a time and explain the dangers they are working in at that damned coal mine of Hawkins's."

Maria pulled her legs up to her chest, hugging them. "Is it truly as dangerous as you profess, Michael?" she asked. "And what can you and your union do about it if it is? Nathan owns the mines. No one can take it from him. Why, to do so isn't even American."

Michael's thick brows furrowed as he continued to chew on his cigar. "Maria, we only wish to speak in behalf of the coal miners," he grumbled. "We only wish to organize them so they can speak openly of their desires for better wages and safer working conditions. You speak of being American. In no way are any of your people living as true Americans. Can't you see that? That damn coal mine has a bad reputation for 'bad top'. We need to get investigators in there and demand that Hawkins take care of such shortcomings in his mine."

"What is 'bad top,' Michael?"

"Much of the rock over the men's heads is faulted and threatens to fall when the coal which supports it is cut out from under. But that is only one small danger. I know there is danger of explosion. Constantly. Now that I've talked with Alberto, I know that black powder is being stored in the mine in violation of the law and that ventilation is far below adequate safety levels. Damn it, Maria, I predict an explosion soon if something isn't done about all of these things."

Maria rose and went to Michael to cling to his arm. "But, Michael, what *can* you and Alberto succeed at doing? You even say that you've been unsuccessful up to now. What can Alberto do to make our people listen?"

"After he's had a chance to talk with them all individually, I will give him some secret ballots to pass around for the men to sign stating that they want to join the United Mine Workers of America. And, damn it, if Nathan Hawkins doesn't pay any attention to that, I may have to organize something else, but most unpleasant for that bastard husband of yours."

"What, Michael?" Maria asked, feeling fear rippling through her. She feared violence . . . a violence that could possibly cause the death of many. She feared for her Papa, for Alberto, and oh, God, for Michael.

"We'll just have to wait and see," he grumbled, mashing his cigar out in the ashtray. He turned to her and pulled her into his arms. "But for now, I think you'd best get back to that mansion you now live in. One thing we *don't* need is for that bastard Nathan Hawkins to come looking for you."

"He's gone from the house. For the night as far as I know," she said, lowering her eyes.

Michael tipped her chin up with a forefinger.

"Yeah. I know," he whispered. "But his representatives? They're everywhere."

"How do you know that Nathan isn't home tonight?" she asked, eyes wide.

"Darling, I make it my practice to know where he is at all times," he said, laughing sardonically. "This is why I have been chosen to be the union's spokesman in this area. I'm good at what I do. I could even join Pinkerton's men I've got such a good reputation with my men for being so good at investigating."

"Then where . . . is . . . Nathan . . . ?" Maria whispered, looking toward the window.

"He's been in a meeting with his men this whole damn night," Michael said, sneering. "You see, I also have a couple of my own representatives keeping an eye on things for me."

"Do you know . . . what sort of a meeting?"

"Not truly. But I'm sure we'll all be finding out soon," Michael said, moving away from her. He began to run his fingers through the thickness of his blonde hair, pacing the floor once again. "He's got something up his sleeve. I know it. And I will find out. But it sure scares me *not* knowing."

"Do you expect him to cause more trouble . . . for you . . . soon . . . ?" Maria whispered, going to him, clinging once again.

"Oh? Alberto told you about the incident at Ruby's?"

"Yes, my love," Maria purred, laying her head on his

shoulder. "I am so frightened for you. Don't you know that? Why can't you let someone else do the dirty work for your union? Why must it be you?"

"Like I said. I'm best at what I do."

A light tapping on the door drew Maria's breath from inside her. She recoiled, putting her hands to her mouth.

Michael inched his way to the door, then jerked it open quickly. "Alberto, you scared the shit out of me," he said, now laughing.

"One of your men alerted me, Michael. They've seen some of Nathan Hawkins's men leaving the building where they've been meeting all night," Alberto said, entering the room. "Maria, you've got to leave now." His eyes raked over her, seeing the disarray of her hair and her night robe. He stooped and picked up her cape and thrust it toward her, furrowing his brow. "Now. You must leave with me *now*," he quickly added. "It's getting a bit uneasy out there in the streets right now."

"So they've broken up for the night, eh?" Michael said, going to the window, pulling the curtain back a bit, peering outward.

"Seems that way," Alberto said, helping Maria with the cape. "Your man told me to tell you that Nathan Hawkins hasn't left yet. But he might at any minute. I wouldn't want to be the one caught with Maria in my wagon if he should happen along the road beside me."

Michael swung around on a heel and hurried to Maria. He pulled her into his embrace and kissed her gently on the lips, brushing her hair back from her face. "You be careful, darling," he whispered. "That damn fool could even be using you for his evil purposes.

392

Maybe he has found out some way that you and I . . . well . . . knew one another. Maybe he knows who I am and is only playing games. One never knows about such a man. So you just watch yourself. Especially in the darkness of night."

Maria began to tremble. "Michael, you scare me so," she whispered.

"Damn it, Maria, I mean to," he grumbled, kissing her once again. "You have to be on your guard. At all times. Watch that bastard. And if he discloses any information to you, you know to tell either me or Alberto. Maybe between us all, we can manage to settle this thing once and for all."

Alberto pulled at Maria's arm. "Come on, Maria," he grumbled. "We must leave."

Maria reached upward and traced Michael's face, as though it might be their last moment together, forever. "Tomorrow, Michael? In the depths of the tall Indian grasses?" she whispered.

"Tomorrow. . . ." he answered.

She rushed on out to the wagon with Alberto, feeling her heart aching, as though it was tearing from inside her. She glanced back toward the building, then huddled next to Alberto, shivering still, watching all around them as Alberto slapped the reins, urging the horse to move quickly away.

"I am so frightened, Alberto," she said, sniffling.

"With both Michael and myself to protect you, nothing is going to happen to you," Alberto said stiffly.

"But when I am alone with . . . Nathan . . . ?"

Alberto reached inside his jacket pocket and handed something toward Maria. "Here. You will need this

393

more than I ever will," he said thickly.

"What . . . ?" Maria asked, letting Alberto place a heavy object in her hand. Then she gasped aloud when she looked downward and saw that it was the gun that Alberto had found aboard the ship. Her gaze turned sharply toward Alberto. "The gun? What are you doing . . . with . . . the gun . . . ?"

"I usually carry it with me," he said, looking her way, his eyes wavering. "Tonight I almost had to use it when I began fighting alongside Michael. But my fists were weapon enough this night."

"But . . . what . . . do you think I can do with such . . . a violent thing . . . ?"

"Keep it with you. Mainly at night when Hawkins can enter your room and demand from you what you don't . . . want to . . . give him," Alberto said sullenly. "And when trouble between the coal miners and Hawkins begins wholeheartedly, I want to be sure you are protected in some way. A gun is the best. All you need is to pull the trigger if you are in a position to have to protect your life from either Hawkins or his men." He looked toward Maria, his eyes having become two dark coals. "Do you understand, Maria? Do you?"

Maria shifted the gun from one hand to the other, not liking the feel of the heavy, cold steel. "I don't know, Alberto," she whispered.

"You had just better heed my warning, Maria," he grumbled, slapping the reins angrily.

"But you? If I have the gun, what will . . . you . . . have for protection . . . ?"

"Papa has a very adequate shotgun. I shall get it out from storage and shine and clean it. It can do for myself."

Maria hung her head, feeling the tears wetting her cheeks. "Alberto, I hadn't thought that being in America would mean . . . violence. . . ." she murmured.

"Being in America means many things, Maria," Alberto grumbled. *"Many . . .* things. . . ."

Chapter Seventeen

Having just poured the used washwater down the back steps of her Papa's house, Maria wiped her hands on her apron, making sure to not soil her new dress. Its silken folds rustled about her as she moved to the back window, peering into the distance. She had heard a constant hammering since having kissed her Papa goodbye this morning. It seemed to her that the hammering had begun as soon as the whistle from the coal mine had reverberated through the air. What could it mean? It was surfacing from the coal mine's direction. Neither her Papa nor Alberto had mentioned anything new being added to the community nor to the coal mine area.

Maria shrugged, pulling her apron from around her waist. She only hoped that by laboring so hard she hadn't destroyed the sweet smells of the perfumed bath she had taken earlier in the morning. But she had so wanted to return home to help her Papa and Alberto in any way she still could. Doing their laundry and removing the dust from their meager possessions was all that she could do at this point. She hadn't yet made any progress in securing any of Nathan's money. Only then could she purchase a wooden ice box for her Papa's kitchen. She would even purchase a fancier stove for him, with embossed nickel trimmings. But now? All she could do was make them as comfortable as possible.

Going to the bedroom, she looked slowly around her. Maybe she could at least purchase a new bedspread and curtains the next time she was in Creal Springs. She could tell Nathan she needed the money for a new . . . hat. . . .

"Even a mirror is needed in this house," she fussed aloud, reaching upward to touch her hair, wondering if it was in its upswept mass of curls, remembering taking so much extra time with it early this morning, knowing that Michael would see her in whatever way she would happen to arrive at their appointed meeting time.

Her eyes traveled downward. She loved the trimming of this dress with its open-work embroidery of soft colors and the low-cut bodice emphasizing the firm grace of her breasts. The dress, of a rose color, seemed appropriate enough for this fine day of spring. The fullness of its skirt would make it even more accessible for Michael's wandering hands.

Maria's heartbeat increased as she headed toward the door. The time was right. Michael would be waiting. The only thing that was causing uneasiness inside her were the threats of the night before from both Michael and Alberto. Would Nathan have ways of knowing about her and Michael? He did have many . . . representatives. . . .

As Maria moved from the house and down its front steps, she tensed, listening. The hammering thuds had increased in intensity. She moved out onto the street, peering in the distance, toward the coal mine tipple, and what she saw made her heart skip beats. "Why would they be building a . . . fence . . . around the coal mine . . . ?" she whispered to herself. She looked around and saw others on their porches, watching . . . silently watching. . . .

Something grabbed at Maria's heart. There was something threatening in what she was seeing. A fence . . . meant . . . even a worse kind of prison for the coal miners. It didn't make any sense.

She lifted the skirt of her dress into her arms and began to run, gasping for air, until she reached the iron bridge, then stopped once again, looking behind her. The fence was quickly taking shape, surrounding the whole coal mine. . . .

Turning, she rushed toward the tallest of the Indian grasses, looking anxiously around her, hoping to see Michael's familiar stance, but she saw nothing. All that surrounded her was the slowly weaving grasses and an occasional bee buzzing around her head. All else was as it had always been before. Silent. No movement. Nothing.

Maria's hands went to her throat. "Michael," she whispered. "Where are you?" She stumbled through the grass, desperately seeking around her, hoping to find him lying, waiting. But still nothing. She went to stand, waiting, hearing only the thuds of the hammers and the sound of the wind as it whipped around her, lifting her skirt upward, and pulling her hair free from its pins.

When another sound surfaced from beside her, she swung around and grew limp as Michael moved into her direction and soon had her in his arms, hugging her tightly to him. "I almost didn't make it," he said thickly.

"I'm so glad you did," Maria sighed, lifting her lips to his, searching. She moved her body into his, feeling the same rapturous quivering of excitement flowing through her as his hands reached down and secured a breast.

"Maria, my Maria," Michael said, moving her to the ground, settling next to her, lifting her dress, caressing her. "Things are quickly changing, my darling," he said, withdrawing his hands, looking away from her.

Maria followed his gaze. He was also hearing the hammering. He had also seen the fence. "Michael, what's happening?" she asked, reaching up to trace his facial features with a finger. "Why...the...fence...?"

Michael's blue eyes softened as they turned to search her face. "As we had expected," he said gruffly. "Nathan knows too much about the plans of our union. He's preparing for the worst."

"The worst . . . ?" she gasped.

"The meeting last night?"

"Yes . . . ?"

"I guess his men told him about me . . . and . . . *my* men," Michael said, plucking a weed, thrusting it between his teeth.

Maria's insides turned cold. "No, Michael," she whispered. "He just can't know."

"He's readying himself for the union. I guess he is going to fight us all the way."

"Hold me, Michael," Maria said, lifting her arms to him. "Please hold me. I'm so frightened."

Michael leaned down over her, covering her body with his, a fortress. "We shouldn't be here, Maria," he said. "What if I was followed? What if you were followed?"

"Please don't think about that now," she said, running her hands over his back, loving the feel of the tightness of his muscles, then her fingers lowered and touched the bulge beneath his breeches buttons. "The tall grasses. It would take someone a long time to search us out here. The wind is our protector. It will continue to blow the grasses around and over us. As it weaves and dips, it will be as though nothing is disturbing its flow. Please kiss me. Please hold me."

"I only have a moment, Maria," he said thickly, flicking his tongue over her lips. "My men are awaiting my decision on our next move." His lips lowered and covered the throbbing flesh of her bosom. He reached upward and pulled a breast free and devoured it with his lips, inching his hands downward until he was touching her in the softness between her legs.

"Take me now, Michael," she whispered, trembling. "No preliminaries this time. I only hunger for you to be inside me. I need you to fill me completely. Please take me. Now." She lifted her hips, making it easy for him to pull her underthings down. Maria became dizzy with passion. She felt her desire for him increase in momentum as his hands released his manhood from its confines and leaned it down into her. A groan of ecstasy flowed from between her lips as he began to thrust inside her. Her body began to move with him, her hair falling free, settling around her face like a crown. She had become as part of the wind, thrashing against his body as she lifted it to meet him. She no longer cared about the dangers of being discovered. She was as the tall grasses around them, weaving, dancing, as Michael continued to move inside her.

"Michael, oh Michael," she sighed, tossing her head

sideways, clamping her teeth together, desire for him a never-ending thing. His tongue, his lips, were as pollen to her, so sweet, so very, very sweet. She was the bee, taking from him, enjoying, always enjoying. . . .

"Now, Maria," Michael whispered, feeling the ache inside him turning to a hungry pain that needed to be quelled. He felt the perspiration rising on his brow and even felt it on her body as she moved so quickly against him. His hunger for her was so great, would he ever be completely fulfilled? As now, the explosion inside himself was almost ready to begin. . . .

He groaned, then let the spasms engulf him in wondrous splashes, smiling to himself when he felt her own similar spasms of delight, pleasure, joining in with his own. Then he pulled from her, panting. He began to laugh hoarsely, reaching to touch the softness between her thighs once again.

"What's so funny, Michael?" Maria whispered, leaning into his fingers, feeling almost wicked, knowing how easily she continued to give of herself to this man. Did he think her shameful? Was he even now laughing at her and her weaknesses for him?

"Us," he said. "Here we are in broad daylight, with dangers all around us, and we still are able to make love. I find us both a bit amazing, don't you?"

"Yes. Quite," she purred. Then she tensed when she was aware once again of the hammerings in the distance. She frowned. She rose to a sitting position and looked toward the sounds of the racket.

"And what shall we do when it is impossible for us to meet one another?" Michael said, buttoning his breeches, also rising to a sitting position. He reached and smoothed Maria's hair back from her face. "And you? Won't everyone know you've just been with a man? Oh, Maria, I've missed you so."

Maria's face drained of color. She hadn't thought to worry about that. She looked down at the disarray of her dress and reached up and felt her hair. She had even lost its pins in the depths of the grass. "I didn't think. . . ." she murmured. Then she smiled coyly. "But, my love, it was worth it," she said, smoothing her dress down after pulling her underthings back up. "I would even die to get to be with you. Don't you know that?"

Michael helped her up from the ground, and they stood arm-in-arm looking toward the coal mine tipple and the fence that was being erected. He hugged her to him. "We shall make this thing right," he grumbled. "I must leave now. I must meet with my men. See what our strategy will be. That damn Nathan Hawkins. What does he think he's doing surrounding his coal mine with a fence? Doesn't he know a fence won't keep men from talking? Doesn't he know that a fence won't keep his men from being unhappy with the conditions of the coal mine once Alberto discloses the dangers to them?"

"Alberto. He and Papa . . . how will they react once they see the fence?"

"Mad . . . scared. . . ." Michael grumbled. "Damn. Who knows?"

Michael framed Maria's face between his hands. "But, Maria, I must truly leave. I don't know what this day will bring for us all. Please understand my haste in saying goodbye."

"You don't know when we can meet again?" she whispered, leaning into his hands, loving the warmth they evoked.

"I think we'd best let some time pass before our next rendezvous. Nathan Hawkins will, well, he isn't a dumb man. In time, he would find out."

"I see," she murmured, tears burning at the corners of her eyes. "Then, my love, kiss me once more. Long and lingering."

She wrapped her arms around his neck and felt the usual giddiness of her head when his lips covered hers; then he was gone from her almost as quickly as he had appeared, waving, leaving her there alone with the wind and the grass, still wiping a few tears from her eyes. She waved over and over again, then lowered her eyes when he disappeared from her sight.

With an emptiness inside her, she moved through the thigh-high grass until she reached the road that led to her home, a home that she could not feel comfortable in. She knew that it had been home to many women before her, and that it would always be Nathan's, even when she was just another passing thought in his mind.

Reaching up, she tried to straighten her hair. But without pins, she could not make it presentable. Then she looked downward. Her dress. It was so wrinkled. How could she explain it away if she was asked? She had to hope that Nathan was still away at his meetings. He hadn't arrived home yet when she had left near sunrise. Maybe she would continue to be as lucky.

Hurrying her pace, she moved up the steps of her house, then on inside, past the noise surfacing from the kitchen, up the stairs until she entered the privacy of her own room. When she closed the door, she turned with a start when she heard a noise from behind her.

Her eyes widened and her pulsebeat raced when she found Nathan moving toward her. His eyes had never appeared so narrow and bottomless. They were all grays, washing over her appearance. His briar-thicket brows bounced as his eyes moved back up to search her face.

"And where have you been, my sweet?" he said in his usual high-pitched voice. His fingers reached up and began to caress his thick moustache as his lips continued to be wetted by his flicking tongue.

"I've been out. Enjoying the beautiful day," she said, trembling. She laughed nervously, reaching up to push her hair back from her shoulders. "It seems the March winds continue to play havoc with my hair," she uttered softly.

"And your dress?" he accused. "Is the weather so rough that your dress gets so wrinkled by the harshness of the wind's breath?"

Maria's gaze lowered. She began to fidget with the gathers of her dress, waiting for his further accusations. She knew that her words were frozen deeply inside her. No way could she talk her way out of this discovery.

"Come here, Maria," Nathan said strongly.

Maria's gaze moved toward him, seeing him unbuttoning his breeches. "What . . . ?" she gasped, swallowing hard.

"I said to come here," he ordered, his voice seeming to have dropped an octave. He reached inside his breeches and pulled from it his drooping manhood.

"Why . . . ?" Maria whispered, putting her hands to her throat, feeling suddenly ill. She didn't want to think that she would have just left Michael and his caresses to have to be plunged into such an ugly sexual confrontation with Nathan, even if Nathan was her husband, and Michael not. She stood her ground, shaking her head back and forth.

"I'm going to show you just who is boss around here," Nathan said, moving toward her. He reached up and wrapped his hands around her neck and forced her down.

"What . . . are . . . you doing . . . ?" she gasped, feeling ice water filling her veins, having to have her face so close to. . . .

"Just shut up," Nathan growled, forcing her face into his crotch.

"Please. . . ." she gasped, struggling. But he soon had her mouth quieted by something of revulsion to her. She gagged and kicked as he began to thrust inside her mouth, over and over again, until tears fell from her eyes, not even then helping with her utter disgrace of the moment. When he finally became all tremors, she felt pain down the back of her throat and gagged even more, then wiped at her mouth when he pulled away from her, laughing hoarsely.

She closed her eyes and fell forward, crying hard, hitting her doubled-up fists against the floor. She would never be so humiliated again. Why had he done this to her? Why had he chosen to take her in such an abnormal way? She hadn't even known such ways existed. Oh, how her throat ached. Would she even be able to face another human being after such an ugly violation to her . . . mouth . . . ?

"Get up, you bitch," Nathan growled, reaching down to grab her roughly by the arm. "Don't you think I know what you've been up to?" He laughed shrilly. "But I'm going to let you continue to play your games with that union fellow. Maybe you can even get me some information to help me with my plans." He placed his fingers through her hair and yanked her head back. "Do you hear, slut? I should've known better than to marry a luscious wench like you. From what I've found, you're all whores. Damn, dirty whores."

"Please let me go, Nathan," Maria whimpered. "I'll never do anything else to make you angry at me. Honest. Please don't hurt me, though." Her thoughts went to her gun. She had placed it deep inside her closet, beneath her hat boxes. If she could only act innocent, play the role of someone who meant to apologize, then she could possibly get the gun and use it on him.

"Beg," he hissed, jerking even more strongly on her hair.

"I *am* begging," she cried. "Please don't hurt me any longer."

His hands dropped to his side, letting Maria crumple to the floor in a heap. She continued to cry, hoping he would leave the room. But he continued to stand there and wait for her to reach composure of some degree. She sobbed another time, then pushed herself up from the floor, looking upward at the ugliness of his face and the emptiness of his eyes once again.

Oh, how she hated him. Oh, how she loathed him. He was even more vile than she had ever imagined another human could be. She inched her way toward the closet, but once there, she knew she couldn't use the gun. She just couldn't shoot another human . . . being . . . even if this one was the lowest of all forms.

Nathan walked to the window and stared outward,

laughing shrilly. "No. I won't hurt you," he said. "But I can't say as much for those who try to disturb my coal mine employees." He swung around, glaring. "You see, Maria, after the fence is completed, I plan to have machine guns mounted atop blockhouses constructed of oak logs. Then if anyone should try to intervene in my business, I shall shoot to kill." He laughed once again, moving toward her. "So you see, my pet, my plans to keep my coal mine running with my Italian . . . uh . . . friends will continue as in the past."

"But . . . machine . . . guns . . . ?" she gasped, inching her way from him as he continued to move toward her.

"Machine guns. Bang . . . bang. . . ." he said, pointing a finger at her. "Shoot to kill. That's going to be my motto."

"You're sick," Maria hissed, forgetting her fears of him. She now could only think of Michael and the danger he was in. How could she tell him? Or would he have already found out? Surely his men had found out the gruesome details of Nathan Hawkins's plans. There would never be a way to win. Never.

"Not sick," he said, kicking at the skirt of her dress. "Rich. Filthy rich. And I intend to remain so." He rushed from the room, leaving Maria to stare blankly after him.

Rising, she walked as though in a daze toward the window, seeing the peacefulness of the vineyard stretched out for miles and miles. The green leaves were swaying gently in the breeze and the sun's rays rippled in velvets onto the vines, so peaceful, so calm and peaceful. But that was the only thing that was peaceful in this area of southern Illinois.

Maria lifted the window, listening. The pounding and hammerings at the coal mine had ceased. Had they completed the fence? Were they now constructing the blockhouses, readying them for their machine guns? Slamming the window shut, Maria began to pace back and forth. What could she do? She felt in a worse prison now that Nathan knew of her involvement with Michael. Then hope sprang forth. He hadn't mentioned Michael's name. Maybe he truly didn't know. Maybe he was just playing another game with her?

Going to the bedroom door, opening it, Maria listened. She heard voices, then crept to the top of the staircase and listened even further. She tensed when she heard Nathan giving orders to his representatives.

". . . And I want it posted all over the town of Hawkinsville that all persons in the possession of firearms, equipment and munitions of war are required to surrender the same to you and that all assemblages in the streets, either by day or night, are prohibited."

Someone besides Nathan spoke up. "Okay. But what are we to do if anyone gives us trouble?"

"Damn it. Shoot to kill," Nathan responded angrily. "And tonight, I want you to make sure all of Hawkinsville's businesses are closed. Especially the saloons. I will have no one loitering the streets where it is possible for anyone to speak of this thing called the 'union' to the coal miners. Then if anyone ventures out onto the streets after dark, give them a fair warning to return home, and if they don't, shoot. Don't hesitate. Shoot. I can always bring another shipful of dumb bastards over from Italy. If killing just one of them is needed to show our power over them, if this is needed to encourage them to listen to me, then damn it, do it."

"And Ruby and her half-wit husband? You know that he succeeded in surviving our attack the other night. You know that information can be exchanged at Ruby's by the men while they're gamblin' and whorin'."

"You go to Ruby. Order the house shut for the time being," Nathan said. Then he chuckled, saying further, "And you tell Ruby to remember what happened to Clarence that one other time when he didn't succeed at coming through the attack as well as the other night. Remind her that if I can order my men to castrate a man, I can also order them to do worse to a woman."

"Okay. As well as done. Then what about your wife?"

"I have ways of taking care of her," Nathan said. "And you be sure nothing happens to her brother and father. They are of use to us. Remember that. When the time comes, we'll just take care of them all at one time. Do you understand?"

"Yeah. Sure."

Maria's hands went to her throat. She began to tremble violently, then crept back on to her bedroom, closing the door gently behind her. Was it all truly happening? How could anything such as this happen in America? She and her family had been transported to a place of war. She threw herself across the bed, sobbing. How would it all end? Oh, what could she do . . . ?

A sudden determination seized her. She rose from the bed with a set jaw. She knew that she couldn't solve anything by weeping like a baby. She had to warn Michael. Only by doing so could any of them have any hope for the future. She hurried to her closet and searched beneath the hat boxes, then cringed when her fingers made contact with the cold steel of the gun. She wrapped her fingers around it and pulled it out, holding it away from her, looking at its pearl handle and the glint of the steel of its butt. It was a threatening piece of equipment to her. But she knew that she needed it. After hearing Nathan speaking with his representatives, she knew that everyone needed to be armed. Wasn't he ready to shoot them all as though they were dogs?

Hiding the gun inside her beaded purse, Maria crept to her door and opened it, listening once again. There were no voices surfacing from the parlor. Maybe they had gone. She would just have to take that chance. Ruby's house was her destination. Ruby needed to know, as well as Michael. Maybe Ruby and Clarence could even manage to get to Michael and warn him. Maria knew that she couldn't travel to Creal Springs. She knew that it would be too risky. Nathan Hawkins's representatives were everywhere . . . like hornets . . . ready to attack.

Tiptoeing, Maria began her descent on the staircase. She clutched at her purse, feeling its extra heaviness, wishing she had no need for a gun. But it was her only protection now. Michael's arms were no longer around her . . . her Papa and Alberto were deep inside the bowels of the earth. When they came to the surface, what would be awaiting them? Would the fence frighten them too much? Would her Papa's health weaken even more seeing that he was a prisoner for sure in this land of . . . freedom . . . ?

"I've got to quit worrying and hurry onward," she whispered to herself. "I must move through the Indian grass just like the Indians must have all those years ago.

I mustn't let Nathan's representatives see me. I have to get to Ruby's before they do. Maybe Clarence can figure out what to do."

But Maria felt coldness circling her heart when she remembered Nathan's words about Clarence and what Nathan had ordered done to Clarence all those years ago, and now what Nathan threatened to do to Ruby. . . .

Inching her way down the hallway that would lead her past the kitchen, Maria's breath came in short gasps. She still wasn't sure about Mama Pearl. Could Mama Pearl be trusted?

Maria stopped and listened, then swung around when she heard footsteps approaching. When she saw Mama Pearl moving toward her, Maria stood as though frozen, now not knowing which way to turn. Mama Pearl would know that she was planning to leave, because Maria held her purse tightly in her hand. And Maria hadn't been known to leave through the back door. Mama Pearl would have many questions.

"And where ya'all headin', Sweet Baby?" Mama Pearl asked, wiping her hands on an apron, eyeing Maria questioningly.

"Out," Maria whispered. "I need . . . some . . . uh . . . fresh air."

"But ya'all were ahready out this mohnin'," Mama Pearl said, lifting a heavy brow. "Why on earth do ya'all needs to go out again? Ain' ya'all a feisty thing?" Mama Pearl cackled and moved on past Maria, into the kitchen.

"Mama Pearl," Maria said softly, looking from side to side.

411

"Yes'm?" Mama Pearl said, lifting a rolling pin, placing it onto a wad of pie dough in the center of the kitchen table.

"Please don't tell Nathan I'm out, should he ask," Maria blurted, flushing.

"Lawdy be. Why's not?"

Maria cast her eyes downward, fidgeting with the beads of her purse. "Well, Mama Pearl, you know how busy Nathan is," she said softly. "Why worry him about my . . . uh . . . restlessness."

"Sho' nuff has been keepin' his nose to the grindstone lately," Mama Pearl said, puffing as she pushed the rolling pin back and forth. "Just did see him leave with those workin' men o' his a minute ago. Guess the poh soul will be workin' till nightfall. Yes'm, Sweet Baby, I guess yo' be right. I won't speak of any restlessness to him. Mighty sweet of ya'all to care so much."

Maria felt the heat of her anger inside herself, hating to pretend a liking for the man who had so recently humiliated her in such a degrading way. She forced a smile. "Yes. I do worry about him being so involved," she said, then moved toward the door.

"Goin' the back way, Sweet Baby?"

"I like to walk through the vineyard," she replied weakly. "Reminds me of Italy."

"Yes'm. I understand," Mama Pearl said, giggling softly.

Maria rushed on out the back door, stopping to breathe a deep sigh of relief. She had gotten past Mama Pearl without any difficulty. Now she had to be sure to evade the watchful eyes of all of Nathan's representa-

412

tives. She moved toward the thickness of the vineyard, then stooped, hiding as she moved quickly from one row to the other, glad to finally reach the tall Indian grasses that would lead her to Ruby's house.

The sun beat down on her head and back, making perspiration bead her brow and her heartbeat become erratic, making her become almost lightheaded, but she continued to push her way through the thickness of the grass until she finally reached the fence. She moved slowly around it, watching all around her for any signs of movement, and when the dogs came barking and howling at her, she began to chew her lower lip, knowing that alone was reason for discovery.

Rushing, she reached the gate and ignored the leaping dogs as she moved toward the front door, then fell inside, gasping for air. When Ruby appeared before her, Maria rose and clung to her arm, panting.

"Ruby. Ruby, you just don't know what's happening," she cried.

"I think I might," Ruby drawled, turning, beckoning with a nod of the head toward the door that led to the back rooms of the house. When Michael and several more men made an appearance, tears sprang forth from Maria's eyes. She rushed to Michael and fell into his arms. "Michael, oh, Michael. You're safe. Oh, thank God. You're safe," she blurted clinging to him.

"I failed to tell you that my meeting place was so close by a while ago," he said, holding her to him. "I guess I should have. Maria, you are panting so. What's happened?"

She brushed tears from her face with the back of a hand and looked upward into his eyes. To her, blue

413

most normally meant a restfulness, a peacefulness. But in Michael's eyes, there was no trace of such feelings. She could see so much more. And this made her even more frightened for his safety. She now knew him to be a man of daring.

"Michael, I've just overheard much being said at my . . . uh . . . at Nathan's house," she said. "It all frightens me so. You need to know. I fear that we all might be dead in the end."

"What did you hear, darling?" he said, glancing an already knowing look toward the men, glowering.

"Not only is there going to be a fence around the coal mine, but machine guns mounted, as well," she blurted. "And then no one is to be allowed to be on the streets of Hawkinsville after dark. Anyone who disobeys will be killed. And all firearms are to be surrendered to Nathan's representatives."

Michael's arms went limp. He moved from Maria, running his fingers through the thickness of his hair. "God. It's even worse than I ever imagined," he grumbled. "Machine guns? He is a madman. What will be next?"

"No one is safe, Michael," Maria cried, going to cling to him once again.

"Maria, you know you shouldn't have put yourself in any more danger by coming here," he said, suddenly clutching onto her shoulders, shaking her a bit. "What if Hawkins or his men had seen you coming here?"

"I have a gun . . . in . . . my purse," she stammered, lifting the purse, showing him.

Michael's face paled. "A gun? Where did you get a gun, Maria?"

414

"Alberto. He gave it to me last night. He said I needed it for protection."

"But sometimes a gun is more harm. If you should pull it to shoot it and became too afraid to do so, it could be taken from you and used on you," he stormed. He released Maria and began to pace the floor angrily. "This is becoming way out of hand. I never intended you to get so involved."

"If Nathan. . . ."

"Yes, if Nathan hadn't forced your hand in marriage, you would be free," Michael further stormed, throwing his hands up into the air in despair. "But he did. You are. Now what?"

"What can I do, Michael?" Maria asked softly, lowering her eyes.

"You must return to Hawkins's house. Stay low. Don't interfere. And above all, don't antagonize him. Lord knows what he might pull with you. Force you to do."

Maria's face turned crimson. God. If Michael knew what Nathan *had* already done. But she couldn't tell. She could never tell anyone what she had been forced to do. "Then I should return to his house?" she blurted, eyes wavering as she sought out Michael as he continued to pace the room in long, angry strides.

"Yes. I have much to figure out, Maria," he said. "And if you just keep a low profile, surely Nathan will leave you out of this mess." He went to her and grabbed her by the shoulders. "You must listen to me. You have to go back to him. To stay with me *or* your brother and father is much too dangerous at this point. If Nathan wants a war, he will have a war."

415

"What . . . do you mean . . . Michael?"

"Like I said, I have that to figure out. But he's gone a bit too far this time. Machine guns? Ha. They won't even keep me from my duties."

Maria's gaze went to Ruby. Maria paled, now remembering Nathan's threats against Ruby. "Ruby, there is something you need to know," she whispered. "Nathan has made threats against you. He has told his men to make sure you close this house down until this all is over, or he . . . he . . . will see to it . . . that you . . . are injured in a terrible . . . way. . . ."

Ruby's hands went to her hips. "Just let him try to force me into anything," she shouted. "My Clarence was outdone by Hawkins and his men once. They even tried a second time. But by God, no more. Clarence is bitter enough to shoot all the damn bastards who try to step on our property. And I have enough guns to pass around to my girls to complete the job. Just let him try."

Maria smiled awkwardly. "I just felt . . . I should warn you. . . ." she murmured.

"And now that you have, darling," Michael said thickly, "please go back to Hawkins's house. If you need to, just stay in your room. Feign illness. That way he won't even touch you."

Maria's eyes lowered. "Okay, Michael. Whatever you say," she whispered. Then her eyes shot quickly upward. "But how will I know what's happening? I don't think Nathan would even approve of my returning to see my Papa."

"I will get word to you. One way or the other," Michael said, guiding her to the door. He pulled her into his arms and gave her a long, lingering kiss, then

416

opened the door and said, "Now. Go on. Everything will be all right. You'll see. Good will prevail. It always does."

"I truly hope so, Michael," Maria said, then moved on down the steps, and through the tall Indian grasses, feeling a heaviness of her heart that she felt might never lift. . . .

Chapter Eighteen

For one week now a giant searchlight and its unearthly beam had scanned the wooded area surrounding Nathan Hawkins's coal mine, turning night and day. Maria stood at her bedroom window, glad that daybreak had finally come, wondering when the strained silence between Michael and Nathan and his union men would be broken.

Maria hadn't seen Michael nor her Papa and Alberto for these many nights and days, since Nathan had ordered the electric light wires be strung to his coal mine. He had decided to go all out where the protection of his mine was concerned, having then placed the searchlight halfway up the mine's tipple.

The beams from the searchlight hadn't only penetrated the tall Indian grasses in the distance, but also the hearts of all the coal miners, having planted the seed of fear too deeply for the words of Alberto or Michael to permeate. The beams had shown the true force with which Nathan had chosen to act.

Everyone now knew that Nathan Hawkins meant business, that in no way would he permit the United Mine Workers of America to have any say in the operation of the mine that he had opened with his own hard-earned money those many years ago. The mine

418

was Nathan Hawkins's. The workers . . . were . . . also his. They had been bought and paid for. None had a choice to leave or stay. No one even spoke of such things anymore.

Sighing resolutely, Maria went to her bed and threw herself atop it. She had done as Michael had suggested. She had feigned illness. Even Mama Pearl had believed her. Maria's stomach seemed to splash continuously with chicken soup and beef broth. She burrowed her head into a pillow, wondering just how much longer she could stand it. There seemed to be so many ways of being a prisoner in America, and she had found . . . them . . . all. . . .

Even Ruby's words had been in vain. Even she had bowed down to Nathan's representatives, having no choice but to do so when they had surrounded her house with guns shining threateningly from the holsters hanging from around their hips.

Who could fight the machine guns at the coal mines and the hordes of gun-slinging men hired by Nathan Hawkins? It seemed that all was lost. Michael? Maria worried about Michael all hours of the day and night.

The sound of a loud explosion erupting from somewhere in the distance rocked the bed beneath Maria, making her jump with a start. She rose from the bed and rushed to her window, seeing a darkness rising into the sky. Her heartbeat faltered. What had that noise been? Why was the sky . . . darkening . . . ? Then she gasped, putting her hands to her throat. "The coal mine," she mumbled. "Oh, no. It can't be. . . ."

She turned when Mama Pearl rushed into the room, gasping for breath. "Come quick, Maria," she said. "It seems something terrible has happened at the coal

419

mine. I'm sure there . . . has . . . been an explosion."

Maria's insides became a mass of trembles. She rushed to her closet and chose a black serge skirt and white shirtwaist, slipped into her shoes and then rushed down the staircase, not stopping to wait for Mama Pearl. All Maria could think about was the welfare of Alberto and her Papa. *Oh God,* she prayed silently, *Please don't let anything have happened to them.*

Moving on outside, she peered into the distance and felt a bitterness rising into her throat. She could see the rolling clouds of black billowing upward from the area of the mine. She covered her ears when the mine's whistle began to blow in sharp, short whistles. "It *was* the mine," she screamed, moving down the front steps, running down the road, then on through the Indian grass. "Michael warned that there would be an explosion. God, he was right," she murmured, breathing hard.

Fearing the worst, Maria ran until her legs ached and her head throbbed. And when she got to the fence that surrounded the mine, she stopped and clung to it, chewing nervously her lower lip. All the area around the entrance to the mine was a mass of confusion. The mine continued to belch black smoke, and bodies were being carried from the dark pit of the earth.

Maria continued to look anxiously around her, trying to see the familiar faces of Alberto and Papa. Then when the crowd of women and children from Hawkinsville arrived to stand beside her at the locked fence, loud wailings and cries from the women tore at Maria's heart. She went to the main gate and joined the others in tugging and pulling at the chain that looped through and around the holes of the fence, where a lock secured its ends together.

"It's no use," Maria cried. "Our men are locked in as we are locked out." Then her cries became muffled by her hand covering her mouth as she watched Alberto move from the crowd of men who had been busying themselves with carrying the wounded and dead from the mine. He was a mass of black. She could hardly even see his eyes through the black of his face. But the closer he came to her the more clearly she could see the streaks of wetness on his face where his tears were making a path through the black on his cheeks. When he caught sight of Maria, his shoulders sagged heavily and he began to shake his head slowly back and forth.

Maria thrust a doubled fist between her teeth and clamped down. She knew what Alberto was saying without words. "Oh, no," she moaned, looking on past him at the bodies, wondering . . . which . . . one was that . . . of her . . . Papa.

When Alberto reached the fence, he reached his fingers through it, covering Maria's. He squeezed and fell into heavy sobs along with her.

"Tell me it isn't so," Maria whimpered, feeling an emptiness at the pit of her stomach, feeling such a loss without having even seen her Papa yet. She knew that he was gone. She knew that this coal mine had snuffed the breath from his lungs. She knew that she would never be able to hug him to her again.

"Papa . . . is one . . . of the fifty. . . ." Alberto said, hanging his head, sobbing still.

"Fifty . . . ?" Maria gasped.

"After the explosion and after the dust cleared a bit,

421

there seemed to be bodies all around me," Alberto said, almost choking on his words.

"Papa . . . ?"

"He was right beside me, Maria," Alberto said, crying loudly, his body wracked with grief. "Why couldn't it have been me? Why did that earthen wall have to take our Papa from us?"

"An earthen . . . wall . . . ?"

"It fell right on top of him. . . ." Alberto groaned. "When I scraped it free from him, he . . . was . . . no longer . . . breathing. . . ."

Maria turned her head away and closed her eyes. Her hate for Nathan Hawkins was so great, she knew that she could take her gun and shoot him now. He had just the same as killed her Papa. He had been warned about the mine's being unsafe for workers to be lowered into it. But he hadn't listened. Instead, he had taken the money which could have been used to meet the safety standards and erected a fence . . . an ungodly searchlight that had frightened the Italian people into utter silence . . . and then machine guns, which were the final threat. She would never forgive him. Never.

Loud shouts brought Maria's head around. She saw the surviving coal miners moving toward the fence with shovels in their hands and hate in their eyes. When Alberto pulled free from Maria and began to move toward the men with cleanched fists, Maria yelled after him. "Alberto. No," she screamed. "Please. No violence now. Remember poor Papa. . . ."

But it was of no use. Alberto picked up a pickaxe and joined the men at bashing in the fence until it was lying in a mangled heap at everyone's feet. "We should've done that long ago," Alberto shouted, raising a doubled fist into the air. "Death to the prisoner ways of life. Birth to the United Mine Workers of America. If we had joined earlier, none of this would have happened. . . ."

The loud rat-a-tat of the machine guns filled the air, causing everyone to run in panic.

"Alberto," Maria screamed, covering her mouth with her hands. She began to run toward the crowd, seeing Alberto falling to the ground. When she reached him, she found him breathing anxiously with his arms covering his face.

"Are you all right?" she shouted, looking frantically around her, seeing that the crowd had quickly dispersed and had disappeared from sight except for the women and children who had moved to sit beside the dead and mourn for their loved ones.

"Yes, I'm all right," Alberto grumbled. "The bastards weren't aiming at us. They were aiming in the other direction. But they accomplished what they set out to do. They scared the hell out of us all."

"Maybe next time they *will* mean business, Alberto," Maria said, reaching for him, urging him upward. "Please don't be so foolish. Please. Right now we must think of Papa. We must think of his . . . burial. . . ."

"I know," Alberto grumbled, rising, brushing at his clothes. His eyes grew heavy as he looked toward the stretched-out bodies. "Come on, Maria. I'll take you to Papa. . . ."

The fifty pine caskets were lined up in a row at a clearing that was shadowed by the huge image of the coal mine's tipple. The wind whipped Maria's black skirt around her, and her black veil that hung in gathers across her face wasn't enough to hide her deep mourning for her Papa who was one among the fifty who were being buried this day.

Sniffing into a white, lacy handkerchief, she looked around her, hoping to see Michael standing somewhere away from the crowd. She hadn't seen him since this tragedy. But she knew that Nathan Hawkins had even succeeded at putting a fear into Michael. Nathan had added more men to his armed menagerie. The streets of Hawkinsville were silent except for the low chatter of the gun-toting men who stood at each street corner, watching for any suspicious moves around them.

Since the coal mine's explosion, Maria had refused to return to Nathan's house. She had sat beside her Papa's casket, day and night, so full of mourning that nothing could have pulled her away. And this day, once her Papa was lowered into the earth for his final rest, Maria still didn't plan to return to her husband's house. Her Papa was dead. He was the main reason for Maria's having agreed to such a marriage.

Alberto? Maria now knew that Alberto could take care of himself. Alberto was capable of much Maria had never thought possible. Though weak in many ways, he had found much courage in himself ready to emerge, to blossom, to make him into the man he had always wished to be.

Maria reached over and took Alberto's hand in hers. She could feel the trembling of his fingers. She could hear the low, throaty sobs emerging from her brother. She knew that he was mourning deeply, maybe even more deeply than she. She knew that Alberto had had many plans for the Lazzaro family. He had wanted to be the one to say that he had bettered their lives, had taken their Papa away from a life of drudgery. Alberto had confided in her the past two days, since the accident, that he had been saving money with which to invest in his own business . . . one that would be away from Hawkinsville. His gambling had been profitable. But not enough . . . not soon enough. . . .

But now? Only the Lord had taken their Papa. Only the Lord could give their Papa the peace he had sought all his life. . . .

A low whispering from behind Maria made her turn her head slightly. She listened closely. Her eyes widened when she was able to make out what was being said.

"Tomorrow night. We will make our move tomorrow night," one man grumbled to another. "Pass the word along."

Alberto was nudged in the side. Maria looked quickly toward him as he leaned his ear down to listen. Maria tensed when she heard the same words. . . . "Tomorrow night. We will make our move tomorrow night," the man said. "Alberto, pass the word along. It is time. Now . . . or never."

Alberto wiped a tear from his eye, looked carefully from side to side, then leaned forward, speaking into another's ear. Maria recognized the same exact words. Her hands went to her throat, finally realizing what was being planned. Nathan had made sure no groups had gathered, knowing that hatred of him was now at its highest, also knowing that gatherings could be plots being planned against his welfare. But Nathan hadn't considered the gatherings of a funeral being a place for planning. Funerals were a place of mourning . . . a place of silence. . . .

Maria watched the word being passed on from one man to another. She reached for Alberto's hand once again and squeezed it, both fear *and* hope making her insides ripple like the Indian grasses in the wind. She glanced upward and saw a trace of a smile beneath Alberto's thick whiskers. His tears had ceased to fall. Yes. Alberto felt confident that soon revenge would be fulfilled. Not only for himself, but for his Papa, his Maria, and all the poor immigrants in the community.

A priest dressed in full black moved in front of the gathering. He held tightly to a Bible and said, "Let us pray for our fallen brothers." He bowed his head and spoke briefly of his Italian friends, with whom he had crossed the waters from Italy, having received a calling to come to this community, where God had warned him that the devil reigned.

Then when the brief eulogy was spoken, the priest stepped back, sweat glistening on his haggard face, and motioned for a young woman to step forward.

Maria's eyes widened as she suddenly recognized the woman. As the woman began to place single red paper roses atop each casket, Maria remembered vividly their encounter and how they had competed for the street corner in Creal Springs. When she heard a loud sigh next to her, Maria looked into Alberto's eyes and saw something she had never seen before. She could see that he had just, for the first time ever to Maria's knowledge, been taken aback by the loveliness of a

426

woman who was not his own sister.

Alberto leaned down next to Maria. "Who is that . . . ?" he whispered. "She's so lovely." His face turned crimson, and he thought, *Even lovelier than you, my sweet Maria. Even lovelier than you. . . .*

"She is one of us," Maria whispered back. "But I do not know her name."

"I must find out," Alberto said, then felt shame for having such feelings while standing at his Papa's funeral. How could such things enter his mind, when his Papa was lying lifeless, ready to be lowered into the depths of the ground?

But he couldn't help himself. He had never . . . no . . . never . . . seen anyone to stir him so. . . .

Young, long-haired pallbearers, dressed in ill-fitting black suits, moved to stand beside the caskets, and after the paper roses had been put in place and another prayer spoken, the pallbearers lifted the caskets and lowered them into the ground.

The women of the gathering, tightly grouped, began to weep loudly and cried words incoherently into their handkerchiefs as the dirt began to be shoveled atop the caskets. Maria chewed on her lower lip, also wanting to cry out, but she felt a greater need to mourn silently. She lowered her eyes and began to move away from the graves. She didn't wish to see the final shovel of dirt placed above her father's grave. She didn't wish to think of him in the ground at all, where he would soon be wet, and then bothered by the crawling life that burrowed through the ground and all that was lowered into it.

Hurrying, she circled around the coal mine, then

onto the street that led her to her Papa's house. The house would be stone quiet, like a grave itself. It would be almost unbearable for her. But she had to go there. She would not be a part of Nathan's life. Ever again, even if he chose to send her and Alberto back to Italy. She knew that to do so, he would have more than a fight on his hands. There would be Michael *and* Alberto to contend with. She only had to hope, though, that what the gathering of coal miners had planned would soon become a reality, to end the whole nightmare of Nathan Hawkins. . . .

Turning momentarily, Maria wondered about Alberto, why he wasn't following alongside her. Then she saw the reason. He was standing talking with the young woman who he had been so enraptured with at the gravesides.

Maria gazed toward the woman and could see something in her eyes. It was a look of liking. Instant liking. She also . . . found . . . Alberto . . . interesting.

Maria smiled to herself, then rushed into her Papa's house, stopping to look slowly around her, seeing the chair where her Papa had spent so many lonely hours. Then she glanced toward the spot where the casket had rested the last two days . . . where she had sat . . . looking down upon him . . . keeping him company during his last hours on earth. . . .

Choking back a sob, she rushed to the bedroom that had been hers and now was again. She leaned down and reached beneath the bed, feeling the violin case that she had left there. With tears rushing down her cheeks, she pulled the case from beneath the bed, placed it on the bed, opened it and peered down onto the violin and its broken body.

She lifted the violin to her bosom and cradled it to her, rocking it back and forth, feeling so much at this moment. When she heard a knocking on the front door, she hesitated, then thought it might possibly be Michael and rushed to the door and opened it. She almost dropped her violin when she saw Nathan standing there, looking even more craggy than she remembered. His narrow, gray eyes were pools of emptiness, and as he removed his hat, revealing his head of shining wax to her, Maria stepped back away from him. He wasn't anything but a threat to her and Alberto. She swallowed hard and said, "What do you want, Nathan?" She turned her back to him, lowering her eyes. "You have caused this family nothing but grief. You are evil. You will always . . . be . . . evil. . . ."

"You are to return home with me. Now," he demanded. "Your place is by my side. You are my wife. You have no place in this . . . this rat trap . . . of a . . . house. . . ."

Maria swung around, her lips trembling almost uncontrollably. "I'll never return to your house with you," she screamed. "Get out. Do you hear? Get out. My Papa was just buried because of you. Do you understand? You are the cause of my dear Papa's death. I hate you. I'll always hate you. You'll never get the chance to touch me *or* my life again."

"Hah!" Nathan exclaimed. "You say I am the cause of your father's death? Well, I have news for you. This Michael Hopper and his union men are responsible."

Maria's face drained of color. "What did . . . you say . . . ?" she gasped, feeling her knees weakening.

"Don't you know that violence travels side by side with those union men? It's become a well-known fact that once the United Mine Workers of America intervene, there is violence. No. I am not the cause. There was no trouble until Michael Hopper began spreading lies about me and my coal mine. He is the cause. No one else."

"Lies! It is a lie," Maria shouted. "You are the cause. You alone."

"I don't lie," Nathan said, licking his lips nervously. "You have chosen to be loyal to the wrong man, Maria."

"Get out, Nathan Hawkins," Maria shouted, moving toward the door. "Get out with your filthy lies. And leave me alone. Do you hear . . . ?"

"No. I won't leave you alone," he warned. "You will return to my house. I will see to it. In time, you will wish you had never come back here. You are meant to be my wife. Nothing else."

Maria stomped a foot as he moved from the door and toward his carriage. With a pounding heart, she slammed the door, then went to her bedroom and placed her violin back inside its case, now full of wonder. Could Michael and his men be made to feel responsible for this disaster? Had Michael somehow even caused the blast . . . possibly to scare the coal miners into joining the union? Had Alberto even had a hand in such a thing . . . ?

She clenched her fists to her side. No. It was all wrong. Neither Alberto nor Michael could cause such a thing. They are good. Nathan is the evil one.

"Maria . . . ?"

Maria swung around and found Alberto standing there with the woman from the funeral . . . the woman from the streets of Creal Springs who made and sold flowers.

"Yes? What is it, Alberto?" Maria said softly, wiping tears from her eyes with the back of a hand. Her eyes traveled over this woman, again seeing her beauty. She had delicate features, with a small nose, tilted, not at all like most Italians noses, but her olive skin tones and her long, flowing hair and dark eyes showed the Italian in her. She smiled sheepishly back at Maria, then moved toward her. "We've met, haven't we?" she asked, reaching a hand of friendship toward Maria.

Maria laughed softly. "Yes, I believe we have," she murmured, accepting the hand, also in friendship. "You make beautiful flowers."

"And you make beautiful music, Maria," the woman said.

"This is Angelina Monteleone," Alberto said, moving next to Angelina. His eyes showed it all. He had found the woman of his dreams. "And this is my sister, Maria. But, of course, you already know this," he added, laughing lightly.

Angelina smiled warmly. "Yes. Like I said, Alberto, Maria and I have already met."

Alberto's brow furrowed. "Did you say something about Maria and her music?" he asked, looking toward the bed, seeing the violin in its case. "How would you know . . . ?"

"We met one day in Creal Springs," Maria said, swinging around, securing the locks on her violin case. She bent to slide it beneath her bed once again. Seeing

431

it reminded her too much of her losses. The music she could no longer pull from the violin . . . and her Papa . . . and possibly even Michael. But surely Nathan had been wrong about Michael. . . .

"And . . . ?" Alberto said impatiently, clasping his hands tightly behind him.

Angelina cast her eyes downward. "I was selling my flowers for pennies, and Maria . . . was . . . uh playing her violin, also for coins to be tossed at her feet."

Alberto's face first shadowed, then he burst into a fit of laughter.

Maria's jaws tightened. "What's so funny, Alberto?" she said, eyeing him questioningly.

"You must have drawn such crowds," he said, softening his mood, wiping his eyes. "Two such beauties? Wish I had been there."

Maria began to pace the floor. "That's where Nathan Hawkins first saw me," she blurted. "I only wish I had stayed where I belonged. In this house. Where no one like him could have discovered me."

"Let's not talk about Nathan Hawkins, Maria," Alberto said, going to her, grabbing her by the arm. "By tomorrow night, there won't even be a Nathan Hawkins to talk about. So . . . let's . . . pretend . . . this is tomorrow night."

Maria's eyes wavered as she reached for Alberto's hand. "Alberto, I must talk about Nathan," she whispered. "He was here. Only moments ago."

Alberto's face reddened with rage. "He was here? That bastard was here? Immediately after our Papa was lowered into the ground?" He hung his head, kneading his brow. "He never gives up, does he?"

"He said many things, Alberto," Maria said.

Angelina spoke up. "Let's move to the kitchen. I shall make some tea. Maybe that will make everyone feel better about things." She went to Alberto and touched him gently on the cheek. "The kitchen. Please direct me to it?"

"Yes. I guess a bit of tea is what we all need," he grumbled. "Hell. I need something stronger. But that can wait."

Maria followed along behind them and helped Angelina until they were sitting around the table, sipping on the warm liquid.

"Nathan said that Michael was the cause of the explosion," she suddenly blurted, swallowing hard, seeing the lines deepening around Alberto's eyes.

"He'd say anything to persuade you to hate Michael. Maria, Nathan Hawkins is completely responsible. Don't doubt that for a moment."

"But he said that violence follows alongside the union men. Could it be true? It was quiet at the mine until the union began spreading its tales around."

"Tales?" Alberto shouted. "Tales? You speak of tales when our Papa is lying dead? It's because of these tales of truth that Nathan Hawkins resorted to fencing in the coal mine and placing machine guns everywhere, and that searchlight on the mine's tipple. If our men would've listened sooner to these 'tales,' as you choose to call them, then we would've seen investigators coming to this coal mine and would've seen improvements in everything about our life around here. No. Nathan Hawkins is a liar. Don't ever doubt that for a moment."

"What are the whisperings about? The ones I heard at the funeral?"

"We are going to get Nathan Hawkins. Tomorrow night. When all his men are asleep. In the middle of the night. We are going to get Nathan Hawkins."

"Do you . . . really . . . mean . . . ?"

Alberto laughed hoarsely. "Yes. Exactly."

Chapter Nineteen

"It's all such a nightmare," Maria said, pulling the satin drapery aside, looking down upon the hustle and bustle of the crowds along the streets and walks of Saint Louis.

"What is, darling?" Michael asked, turning her, sweeping her into his arms. He traced her birthmark with the tip of a finger, then kissed it gently.

"That last terrible night in Hawkinsville," she murmured.

"The night you became a . . . uh . . . widow?"

Maria lowered her eyes. "Yes. Yes, that night," she gulped, remembering it so vividly, she felt as though she was experiencing it all over again. If she closed her eyes, she could see again the way the sky had lit up in bright red. Against the blackness of the night, it had been so evident what had happened. The mob had set fire to Nathan's house. And when she had heard the one gunshot being fired, echoing over and over again in her ears, she had known who had been the recipient of that lone bullet. The coal miners had gone to rid the earth of Nathan and they had succeeded. One act of violence had sparked many more, to end up with the death of Nathan. The men had acted while Nathan's men slept, and once Nathan's men had been awakened

435

to the sure sounds of violence, they had fled, leaving Hawkinsville to its Italian inhabitants.

"Can't you just forget it?" Michael asked, holding her closely, putting his nose into the depths of her hair.

"But how could the Italian people perform an act of murder so easily? Don't they have . . . any . . . conscience?"

"Darling, please. . . ." Michael whispered.

"To all be involved in the way they were," she continued. "It was a conspiracy. I still can't believe it, even though Alberto warned me before it even happened. I didn't believe they would go through with it. And Alberto? He was among those who circled Nathan's house. How do I know that it wasn't even Alberto himself who pulled the trigger of the murder weapon?"

Michael pushed her away from him, to hold her at arm's length, scowling. "But, darling, don't you see? That's why all are protected," he said. "Each man who chose to go that night held a gun. Each had pointed that gun toward the house, waiting for Nathan's exit. The men were clever enough to have emptied the chamber of one bullet of each gun, all but one gun, held by the man who would shoot Nathan, so that all the guns would have the same amount of bullets left in their chambers once the fatal shot was fired. Only the coal miners know who it was who fired that fatal shot. No one else. And no one is talking. No court in America would send fifty men to jail for that one crime without having proof or a witness to swear to the one who had fired that one shot. So will you please quit worrying your mind so over it? In the eyes of the law, all have been cleared of the crime. So must you. You hated the man. Now he is gone. He's no longer around to make lives miserable. The world is rid of vermin. Think of it that way."

"I know," she sighed. "But I guess my mind will be full of the terror of that night for much longer than I have control over."

"Darling, I. . . ." Michael began, but was stopped by Maria's further words.

"I am so glad you weren't involved. Oh, so glad," she murmured. "If you had been, I would always wonder if it had been you who had pulled the gun's trigger. I don't think I could bear such a life of doubt about you."

Michael's face reddened. He had come close to confessing his role in the shooting . . . that it was he who had sneaked the guns to the men . . . that it was he who had devised the whole thing. He had thought she would be proud, but instead. . . . She could never know the complete truth. No. Never!

"Just be glad that Mama Pearl's life was saved," he said. "At least she escaped unharmed."

"But what if she hadn't?"

"But she *did* and she is now with us. She will remain on as our maid. We couldn't have gotten better."

"Yes, you are right, my love," Maria said.

Her eyes raked over Michael and she thought how handsome he was on this fine day that was to be the opening of the Saint Louis World's Fair. He looked quite dignified in his navy blue, pin-striped suit, worn with a pale blue pure silk shirt with a detachable collar. His diamond stickpin shone back at her from his navy blue cravat in colors of the rainbow and his eyes were twinkling in many different shades of blue.

She reached up and ran her fingers across the smoothness of his golden hair, then over the gentleness of his jaw. When a smile lifted the corners of his lips, she felt as though she was melting inside. Would he always have the same effect on her? She leaned into his embrace, sighing heavily. If anyone could make her forget the torment she had only recently gone through, Michael could. Footsteps entering the room made Maria turn with a start. Then she smiled. . . .

"I think I've got the weddin' gown ready for ya'all, Sweet Thing," Mama Pearl said, moving toward Maria with an armful of what appeared to be only white lace. She then held this gathering of lace up before her and watched Maria's face light up.

"It is simply gorgeous, Mama Pearl," Maria gasped, going to run her fingers over the lines of the gown. It was of organza and Alencon lace, studded with seed pearls. It would be worn with a lace face veil in front, and a fingertip veil in back. Also, a chapel-length train would be added on the day of the wedding, also covered with lace appliqués.

"So mah Sweet Baby likes it?" Mama Pearl said, squinting her dark eyes that were already mostly hidden by the wrinkled flesh of her face.

"It's breathtaking," Maria sighed, lifting the skirt of the gown, letting it ripple slowly back in deep gathers in Mama Pearl's arms. "I can hardly wait," she added.

"It won't be long now." Mama Pearl giggled. "And do ya'all think Alberto's Angelina will have such a gown? A double weddin' sho will be somethin' special. A weddin' of twins marryin' up with their loved ones. Both brides should be extraordinarily beautiful."

"Yes. I've spoken with Angelina by phone," Maria said. "Angelina and I don't want exact gowns, you know. So she has ordered a gown that will have tripled layers of ivory silk organza, with a chapel-length train and embroidered bodice. It will also have a pouf-sleeved jacket with a peplum and a high ruffled neckline. Her veil will be in Alencon lace and organza."

Michael laughed heartily as he took Maria's hands in his. "How'd you memorize all of that?"

Maria blushed a bit. "Whenever it is a wedding gown being spoken of, a woman remembers each and every detail."

"I'm so glad that Alberto and Angelina will arrive on time for the ceremony."

"Alberto seems to have everything in order at Hawkinsville now. Once the state investigators okayed the return of the men to the coal mine, it took a load off Alberto's shoulders."

"If anyone should know that, I should," Michael said, kissing Maria's right hand, then releasing both, to move to the liquor cabinet. He poured himself a glass of port. "Want a glass, darling?" he asked, tilting a brow in her direction.

"No. Not really," she murmured.

"And you, Mama Pearl?" he asked, extending a full glass in her direction.

Mama Pearl giggled a bit. "No, Mastah Hoppah. I've got chores waitin'. Just ya'all and my Sweet Baby enjoy." She swung around, heavy-hipped in her cotton attire, and lumbered from the room.

Maria went and eased onto a deeply upholstered velveteen chair. She looked around her, seeing the expensive furnishings of this hotel suite, which she and Michael had been sharing with Mama Pearl until Michael's penthouse apartment would be finished. This hotel suite was quite comfortable, with its richness of furnishings and draperies. Its pale green carpet-ings stretched out from wall to wall and from room to room. The wallpaperings were of peaceful designs in pale gold, and the electric lights added a pleasurable glow to the room.

Michael settled down across from her and lighted a cigar. Then with a cigar between his fingers of one hand, and his glass of port in the other, he sighed leisurely. "Yep. Sure glad to have Mama Pearl around," he said. "Then when we start having our children in twos, you can just sit back and relax and enjoy watching them grow."

"In twos . . . ?"

"You and Alberto? You're twins. Maybe we'll add another set of twins to the family."

Maria laughed lightly. "I'm not so sure. . . ." she said.

He laughed amusedly, then said, "Do you like the idea of having a double wedding, darling?"

"Yes. It will complete the bond between Alberto and myself. Then we can make our much needed separa-tion—when he walks from the church with his wife . . . and I walk from the church with my husband. I think it's quite appropriate. And thank you for doing this for us all. You know that Alberto wouldn't be able to have such an expensive wedding otherwise. And the gown you have purchased for Angelina! Michael, you con-tinue to amaze me with your kindness."

"Well, I like happy endings," he laughed gruffly.

"And this will be just that," Maria said. "This will be."

"You look quite beautiful today, darling," Michael said thickly. "Do you know how beautiful?"

440

Maria glanced downward at her suit, fingering its velvet trim. She loved this Eton suit in blue broadcloth trimmed with folds of matching velvet. And then she reached up and touched the hat that she already had perched atop her head, ready for their escape into the afternoon sun. It was of a toque style with a velvet brim and a silk crown and bow. She knew that she was a picture of style, but she still hated the tightly laced corset that kept her panting for breath at times.

"I do feel fit as a fiddle in these clothes," she finally answered. "Again, Michael, you are too kind."

"You must get used to my whims," he laughed throatily. "Each day I might pop in with a new hat for you. Who knows?"

Maria's face darkened, remembering the large array of hats that had burned in Nathan's house. He had been as generous in his own devious ways. He had almost bought out the stores their one time in Saint Louis. She turned her eyes away from Michael, trying to hide the shadows that had crept across her face. She wanted so badly to forget. She had to forget. It was all behind her now. The Italian community was safe now. Their living conditions were being improved as each day passed. Alberto had taken charge. With the money loaned to him and the families of Hawkinsville by the United Mine Workers of America, running water had been installed in each household, electricity had been wired, and a siding of sorts had been nailed outside each house, enabling the people to stay warmer in the upcoming storms of winter.

"Darling," Michael said. "You are lost in thought once again."

Maria turned her eyes to him, fluttering her lashes

441

nervously. "Yes. I do that. I'm sorry," she murmured.

"You know the mine is safe now," he said. "Alberto is safe working the mines now as are all the other coal miners. Isn't that what we were striving for? Didn't the union make coal mining safer and more secure economically for your people? You shouldn't fret any longer."

"But my mind has been drawn back to . . . what was found when the investigators searched deep inside the coal mine," she uttered, covering her mouth with her hands, feeling sick inside all over again. If not for Michael and the persistence of his men, would she in the end have also been found there—decapitated . . . dead . . . ?

Michael took a quick swallow of port, then puffed angrily on his cigar. "Yes. I know what you are thinking of," he said hoarsely. "You are remembering the . . . uh . . . women's bodies found when the investigators worked their way to the back of the mine. The earlier wives of Nathan Hawkins."

"Yes," she murmured. "I'm remembering that. What if . . . ?" She couldn't help but shudder.

"But, he didn't get the chance, did he?" Michael reassured her. "Now we know *all* the reasons for his protecting his mine from the snooping of investigators. He had used the mine for a grave. A dark, deep grave." He looked heavy-lidded toward Maria. "You are safe. Thank God you are safe. Nathan Hawkins didn't get the chance to do . . . uh the . . . same with you. . . ."

"Only because I was with him for such a short time," she stammered. "What if . . . ?"

"Enough of such talk," Michael said, rising, taking his empty glass to the liquor cabinet. "Let's concentrate on pleasanter things. Let's head on to the fair. What do you say?" He mashed his cigar out in an ash-tray, then offered her his arm.

"Yes, let's," Maria said, pushing herself up from the chair. She accepted Michael's arm and walked with him from their suite, on out into the hallway, and watched as he pressed the button for the elevator.

"Ready to ride the moving box once again?" Michael teased, laughing.

Maria's heartbeat began to hasten. She didn't like to disclose her fears of this box to Michael. She didn't want him to think her a child, with childish notions. But the elevator always set her worst fears in action. What if the box fell? What if the box doors didn't open and they were trapped . . . ?

"Well? Darling?" Michael persisted, guiding her on inside the elevator as its doors rattled open.

Trying to hide the trembling in her fingers, Maria watched the door as it was shoved shut. Then she barely breathed as the box moved downward in awkward jerks. And when the door opened once again, revealing the hotel lobby to her and all its merry chatter of people coming and going, only then could she force a smile and move on next to Michael out into the busy streets.

"Angelina, you might appear to be tiny-boned," Alberto said, breathing heavily, feeling an aching in his arms. "But you are quite heavy."

Angelina giggled as she clung to his neck. They weren't married yet, and this was only a fun way to practice. She began to kick her feet slowly as Alberto stepped on across the threshold that would lead them into what would soon be their honeymoon suite at the grand Planter's Hotel. "But, Alberto, I'm heavier on this, the day before our wedding," she murmured.

"Why is that?" he scowled, kicking the door shut, then heading toward the bedroom.

"Because I'm so filled with love, darling," she whispered, brushing her lips against his. "My love for you must weigh hundreds and hundreds of pounds. But you know that."

Alberto's eyes raked over her, feeling the quivering of his insides, so wanting her, yet afraid. Just looking into her eyes . . . so dark . . . so imploring . . . could set his heart to racing and the blood to boiling inside his manhood. But he had failed so often while trying to make love to a woman.

With Angelina, he had up to this point managed to put off the inevitable, telling her that he wouldn't seduce her before the wedding, saying that he had wanted her to remain pure at heart, as most women should, if they weren't wanton whores, giving their bodies to every man who asked. But now he had decided that he had to try this night, so that if he couldn't succeed, he would set her free to let her marry someone more worthy.

"You look so beautiful, Angelina," he said, placing her tenderly atop the bed. He moved away from her, thrusting his hands deeply inside his front breeches pockets. He went to the window, placing his back to her. "But your dress," he murmured. "Before . . . uh . . . going any further with our caresses, maybe you'd best remove it and hang it carefully in the closet. I don't want to . . . uh . . . muss it."

He turned and fled from the room, his heart pound-

444

ing so hard he felt he couldn't breathe. He was afraid she would sense his weakness. Up to this point in their relationship, she had seen only the stronger side of his personality. She had been proud to know that he had led the mob of coal miners who had killed the dreaded man Nathan Hawkins. She had been proud to believe that he had been the one to pull the trigger of the gun that had fired the one fatal bullet that night. . . .

Going to the liquor cabinet, Alberto poured himself five fingers of whiskey and gulped them down, trying to let the whiskey burn the memory of that night from his mind. He lowered his head and stroked his clean-shaven face. He couldn't help but think back once again. . . .

It had been so dark that night. A starless night. The sky had been almost as dark as the insides of a coal mine. But the dark cover of night had made it easier for the coal miners to move unnoticed toward Nathan Hawkins's house. There had been no sounds, except for the anxious breathing of all men who had guns drawn and ready. Then when they had reached Nathan Hawkins's house, the scratching of a match had begun it all. Torches had been passed around and the house had quickly become consumed in flames.

All poised and ready, everyone's eyes were focused, unblinking even, on the front door of the house. When Mama Pearl had rushed, screaming, from the house, she had seen the circle of men and had fled down the road toward Ruby's.

Then when Nathan Hawkins had come gasping from the house, Alberto had tried to pull the trigger, but had frozen to the spot. When the gun was grabbed from his hand and the shot fired, Alberto had been surprised to find that it was Michael who had once again proven himself to be more of a man than Alberto, causing Alberto's hatred for Michael to begin anew. . . .

"Alberto? Are you all right?" Angelina asked, moving to his side.

Alberto swung around and felt the thumping of his heart go wild when he saw her standing there in a white, lace-trimmed chemise, oh, so seductive as her dark hair lay in deep waves across her shoulders. He reached and lifted one end of her hair, feeling its softness, then kissed her on the curve of the shoulder. "No. There's nothing wrong," he said, tasting the sweetness of her.

"Then why are you in here, and not in the bedroom?" she asked, touching him gently on the lips. "We've waited so long. I think I shall just burst if I have to wait another minute."

Whirling around, Alberto poured himself another drink. He was thinking about Maria. Could Angelina erase all the boyhood thoughts of Maria from his mind? Oh, how he had hungered for her, and how dirty it had always made him feel afterwards.

He put the glass to his lips and emptied it, gasping as the whiskey burned another path down his throat.

"Soon, Angelina," he said thickly. "Soon." He slammed the glass down onto the cabinet's surface and framed his head with his hands, groaning. It was back. The dull pounding in his head. Only recently it had begun again, similar to the pounding in his head after Sam had dealt him that blow.

"What is it, Alberto?" Angelina asked, clutching at his arm.

"My head. It throbs so," he groaned.

Angelina urged him to a chair. "Darling, just sit here

446

and relax," she said. "Maybe there's been too much excitement for you, with our wedding day so close."

"Yes, maybe so," he said, loosening the top button of his shirt. He stretched his legs out before him, resting his head against the back of the tall wing chair. He closed his eyes, sighing deeply. "I want so much for us, Angelina," he said quietly. "So very, very much."

Angelina settled on the floor at his feet and rested her chin on his right knee. She looked upward at him adoringly, her brown eyes wide. "We already have much," she said softly. "We have each other."

Alberto's eyes opened as he reached to smooth a forefinger down the slight tilt of her nose. "Yes, we have each other," he said. "But I'm going to see to it that we have much more."

"Like what, Alberto?"

The pounding in his head had lessened, letting him breathe easier. "My dreams have changed," he said. "I wanted to own a place of business in Creal Springs. A small place to just call my own. But now? I plan for something bigger and better."

Angelina frowned. "Alberto, I wish you wouldn't talk in circles."

"I plan to own Hawkinsville," he quickly blurted. His dark eyes gleamed at the thought.

Angelina pushed herself up from the floor, paling. "You what?" she gasped.

"Though I let Michael pay for your wedding gown and this hotel suite, it wasn't because I couldn't do so myself."

"Then . . . why . . . ?"

"I didn't want Michael to be aware of the wealth I've accumulated gambling. I want to spring it all on him at once."

"Alberto, you're not being yourself. . . ."

Alberto rose from the chair, glowering. He began to pace the floor in wide, even strides. "Yes, I shall rebuild the house where Hawkins lived, I shall take over the vineyard, and you will be mistress to the finest mansion in all of southern Illinois."

"You truly can . . . do this . . . ?" Angelina asked, going to Alberto, clutching on to his arm. "We can truly live in such a way?"

"We will. You'll see," he said, grabbing her by the shoulders, squeezing. "No more coal mining for me. We will reign over Hawkinsville. You . . . and . . . I. . . ."

Angelina began to laugh, throwing her head back. Then she grew serious. "You really can do it, Alberto? Truly?"

"Yes. I can. I shall."

Angelina moved away from Alberto, twirling in slow circles, giggling. "I will never have to make another paper flower again," she shouted. "I will have my own gardens filled with real flowers."

Alberto grabbed her and pulled her into his arms. "You are my flower," he said with a sudden yearning for her. He could feel the desire for her mounting, sending waves of sensual longings splashing through him. "You are my rose. My sweet, sweet rose. Come to the bedroom and let me caress your velvet petals."

"Oh, Alberto," Angelina sighed, all trembles.

Alberto moved into the room next to her and lifted her chemise over her head. With trembling fingers, he reached for her breasts, almost melting on the spot when he felt the softness of her skin.

"Kiss them," Angelina begged, leaning toward him

with eyes closed. "Let me feel your lips . . . your tongue . . . on my breasts," she purred.

"Angelina, my Angelina," Alberto sighed, and buried his nose between her breasts, then moved his lips to suck on a nipple, until it was hard and erect. His heart was beating with a rapid pounding as his hands began to trace her body, then his lips searched out her lips and bore down upon them in a demanding, fiery kiss.

When he felt her fingers working on his clothes, trying to remove them, Alberto tensed. What . . . if . . . ?

"Please, Alberto," she begged. "Let's go to bed. Please undress. I want you. Now."

"Yes, yes," he said. He watched her stretch across the bed, so seductively, and he couldn't undress fast enough. The pounding in his head had ceased, but the pounding in his manhood was fast taking over. He *had* to succeed this time. He *had* to. If not, he knew that he never would. . . .

Fully unclothed, he crept to the bed, and almost shyly even, moved to her side.

"Are you still feeling pain, Alberto?" she asked, touching his brow.

"Yes, darling," he said. "But of a much sweeter kind."

He moved atop her and opened her legs with a quick movement of his knee. Still trembling, he sought her soft spot out with his manhood, and once found, quickly moved inside her. If he worked quickly, surely he would succeed. He loved her. He *had* to be able to make love to her.

"Oh, Alberto," Angelina sighed, now moving her hips with his. "Why did we wait? My love, why did

449

we wait?"

He crushed her to him, over and over again, his heartbeat consuming him, feeling the pressures inside himself building. He closed his eyes and gritted his teeth, feeling something he had never experienced before . . . it was a warmth . . . rising . . . rising . . . making his mind leave him . . . becoming multicolors crashing . . . crashing . . . then his body seemed to explode in the most marvelous of sensations.

He groaned as his body spasmed, over and over again, realizing that he had done it. He had become a man! Then his breathing ceased momentarily as he experienced Angelina's quiverings.

"Darling?" he whispered, kissing her softly on the cheek.

She clung to him, breathless. "It was so good," she finally whispered.

Alberto beamed. "Yes. It was. Wasn't it?" He pulled from her and scooted to lie on his back, his head resting in his raised arms. "Damned good," he shouted.

Angelina began to trace his body with a forefinger, then began giggling.

"What's so damn funny?" Alberto said, tensing. Had he done something wrong? Had he been . . . too . . . clumsy . . . ?

"You have a birthmark in the strangest place," Angelina said, giggling again.

Alberto's face reddened. "Yes, I know," he said. "Maria . . ." he began, then stopped, knowing his hangups for his sister had finally been put behind him. He laughed merrily. "Yes, Maria also has such a birthmark."

450

"She does?" Angelina gasped. "In the same place? I've seen the one on her face. She doesn't have two, does she?"

Alberto roared with laughter, suddenly feeling so lighthearted. "No, my love. Only I have one in such a private spot. Now, wouldn't Maria look funny with one in the *exact* spot as mine?"

Angelina giggled as she placed her fingers around his manhood, then traced the birthmark. "It looks like a strawberry. It's shaped like one, and it's as red," she murmured. She eyed Alberto wickedly. "And does it even taste as sweet?"

Alberto's heart thumped wildly. He eyed her questioningly. "There's one way to find out, Angelina," he said thickly.

"I know," she whispered . . .

Maria clung to Michael's arm with one hand and her hat with the other, moving with him toward a stately black carriage. The city of Saint Louis buzzed with excitement. The Saint Louis World's Fair had brought dignitaries from all over the world. They had all come to celebrate the Centennial of the Louisiana Purchase, an event in American history having an importance second only to the Declaration of Independence.

Michael had explained to Maria that the territory acquired from France by the purchase embraced all the land lying between the Mississippi River and the crest of the Rocky Mountains and that its ownership by the United States made possible the extension of the nation's boundaries to the Pacific Ocean.

"I'm so anxious to see the array of flags your

451

company made, Michael," Maria said as he aided her inside the carriage. "There must be so many if every state and territory of the United States plus scores of foreign countries are represented!"

Michael moved in next to Maria as the coachman closed the door behind them. He reached inside his pocket for a fresh cigar, then lit it, settling back against the plump cushions of gold velvet. He crossed his legs and arms in unison, puffing leisurely on the cigar. "Yep. There will be many flags to see today," he boasted. "And in all different colors and designs. I'm quite proud of what my company has produced. It has been nice to move into another area besides making shoes."

"And now that the flags are completed, what will your sewing machines be used for?"

"High fashion, darling," Michael said, flicking an ash from the cigar out the carriage window. "You think you've seen beautiful dresses on the Saint Louis women? Just you wait until I'm finished with the ones I will have designed. Models from all over the country will flock to Saint Louis just to have the opportunity of wearing Michael Hopper's fashions. Yep, that's what is in my future."

Maria scowled, envisioning Michael's coming face to face with many beautiful women each day. Jealousy stung her insides. And Michael thought she would sit home having babies? He would see just how wrong he was! She set her jaw firmly, thumping her fingers nervously on her lap. She had plans of her own. She would enter into politics and see to it that all women had the same rights as men. She had seen enough of

452

rights being kept from people. Hawkinsville had shown her enough of this kind of life. She would never feel as though she was in bondage again. Not in marriage . . . and not in life.

She would study the laws of the land, and then she would show everyone that women could speak out about women's rights and slavery of all kinds. Maria had just recently heard about a Susan B. Anthony and her leadership of a women's suffrage movement. Maria wanted to be more like her. Maria wanted to be a part of fighting for these rights being spoken of all over the country.

She sighed leisurely, knowing that would come. Yes, that would come. But for now, she would just enjoy the day at hand. She gazed out the carriage window, seeing people entering and exiting the famous French pastry shops of the city, and then she was all eyes when the carriage carried her and Michael on past the grand Union Station where trains stood lined up beneath a large roof both day and night. This building that reached up into the sky was an architectural marvel, as were the buildings that Michael had told her about that she would soon see when they arrived at the World's Fair grounds.

"You've suddenly turned quiet, darling," Michael said, leaning next to her, taking her hand in his.

"This city," she sighed. "It is so beautiful. There is nothing like it in Italy. I just know it." ·

Michael laughed hoarsely. "Yes, there is," he said. "It's only because you never got any further than that town of Pordenone. Ah, Rome. One day we will go there. I will take you back to your country and show you what you were unable to see as a child."

453

Maria frowned. "Not by ship," she said stubbornly. "I shall never forget that ship that brought me from Italy."

"Darling, when we travel to Italy, it will be on a luxury liner," he said, patting her hand fondly. "It will be the same as in a luxurious hotel. You won't even know you are on the water."

"I can't believe there could be such a ship," she sighed, eyes wide.

"You've much to see and learn," Michael chuckled, flipping his cigar from the window. "And we will begin now. I believe the carriage has arrived at the fair."

When Michael reached around and opened the door for Maria, she let out a loud gasp, seeing so much already. The crowds were thick and everyone was attired fancily in their best hats, suits, and dresses. Aided by the coachman, Maria stepped from the carriage onto a red carpet that had been spread from the curbing to the entranceway of the fair, where all fancier carriages moved to a halt, discharging the most elite of passengers.

Maria's eyes moved upward. She let out a loud gasp, covering her mouth with her hands. "My word," she said. "What is . . . that . . . Michael?"

Michael's gaze followed Maria's, hiding his eyes from the rays of the sun with the back of a hand. "My God," he exclaimed. "They've succeeded at getting that damn thing up into the sky. That's some of my union associates. They bought that contraption for this occasion." He laughed hoarsely. "See what's written on the balloon's side?"

Maria read "United Mine Workers of America."

"But it's so fascinating," she said. "How does such a balloon . . . as you called it . . . get up into the air? And aren't the men afraid they might fall out of that flimsy-looking basket, or that the balloon might just suddenly drop from the sky?"

"Darling, that's a hydrogen balloon. The balloon is able to rise because the gas inside the bag is much lighter than the air around it," he said, guiding her onward. "If you will notice, my friends were not brave enough to let the balloon fly itself. You do see the rope securing the balloon to the ground."

"I would hope so," she sighed, looking on ahead. "What shall we see first, Michael?" she added, feeling excitement rippling through her.

"We can't see it all in one day," he said. "But we shall start at the Sunken Gardens."

Michael guided Maria down steps that led to a richly planted parterre. A graceful slope of fine turf that was a combination of color and charming design spread out before the eye. The scene was kaleidoscopic, the colored bits of flowers seeming to change patterns constantly. The aroma was like a mixture of different perfumes combined.

Maria's eyes couldn't move fast enough to take it all in. "I believe I've walked into heaven, Michael," she sighed. She leaned down and sniffed at one flower then the next, and then Michael guided her on to the next unique display. This was the area of the fairgrounds that was called "The Pike." It was a long, wide street of large amusement concessions.

Maria and Michael clung to one another, laughing, as they passed the "Temple of Mirth," went into the

"Jungle of Mirrors," where they saw many of themselves staring back at them, then on to "Hagenbeck's Wild Animal Show," where every kind of animal could be found walking stealthily back and forth behind fenced-in areas.

"I don't think I've ever had so much fun in my entire life, Michael," Maria purred as Michael purchased a swirl of pink candy floss from a vendor and handed it to her. She set her teeth into it, laughing as it seemed to melt onto her tongue, then swallowed the sweetness.

"I don't think you'd get too fat eating that," Michael laughed, buying himself an ice cream sandwich from another vendor.

They moved on past two more exhibitions, where the announcement sign stated that a young Irish tenor, John McCormack, was singing in one, and a comedian named Will Rogers performing in the other.

Michael nodded with his head toward a tent with a red-and-white-striped covering. "And under that tent, they boast of some new invention called the hot dog, and a cool drink called iced tea," Michael said, licking his lips as he swallowed the last of his ice cream sandwich. He reached inside his pocket and pulled a cigar out. He placed it in his mouth and lit it.

"Hot dog?" Maria giggled. "Such a strange name. Surely it isn't . . . a thing . . . made from a dog . . . ?"

Michael doubled over with laugher. "No, my dear," he said. "It is something quite good made of a mixture of pork and beef. Before we leave this day, we will try it. Maybe have it for our lunch."

Maria's gaze moved upward. Her heart pounded against her ribs. "And what is that thing . . . called . . . ?"

she whispered.

Michael looked upward. "That is the 'Observation Wheel,'" he said. "One can climb aboard those seats and make a circle into the sky and see for miles and miles. Want to board it? Experience it?"

Maria swallowed hard. She could vividly remember her feelings about the moving box at the hotel. She knew that this ride that moved in a circle into the sky could be even more dangerous. "No, Michael, I think not," she said. "Please. Let's move onward. There's so much to see. The buildings. Each one is so very beautiful."

Michael chuckled and led her away from the squealing passengers. Their day was then spent moving from one building to the next, seeing exhibits, checking out the flags that waved atop each of these buildings, seeing that Michael's seamstresses had done quite well for the Hopper Shoe Company, that was soon also to be known as Hopper's High Fashions.

And when the sun began to dip toward the horizon in brazen oranges, Michael guided Maria back to the carriage, to head back to the hotel. He smiled when he found her head resting on his shoulder. The day had exhausted her. But he knew that his surprise waiting for her would quickly awaken her. He only hoped that Maestro Von Heifschmitz hadn't let him down. . . .

The carriage came to a halt and the coachman opened the door. "Maria?" Michael whispered, touching her softly on the face. "Darling? Wake up. We've arrived back at the hotel."

Maria's eyes fluttered open and looked around her. She smiled warmly when she found Michael's face so

457

close to hers. "Michael? Are we back at the hotel already?" she murmured.

Michael laughed softly. "Yes. You've been asleep. But now it's time to step down from the carriage."

Maria sighed heavily, then reached a hand to the coachman and let him assist her down. She swirled the skirt of her dress around, waiting for Michael, then locked her arm through his as they went inside the hotel and once again traveled inside the moving box to the fourth floor of the popular Planter's Hotel. When they were finally inside the hotel suite, Michael swept Maria into his arms and kissed her long and lingering, then stepped back, smiling sheepishly.

Maria giggled, lifting her hands to her hat. She removed first the pins, then the hat. "What's wrong with you, Michael?" she said. "You look as though you might be the cat who swallowed the canary." She walked to the couch and dropped onto it, so very, very tired. She placed her hat beside her and threw her head against the back of the couch, breathing heavily.

"I've got a surprise for you, darling," Michael said, removing his suit jacket, placing it on the back of a chair. He moved toward the bedroom. "I'll only be a moment," he said from across his shoulder.

Maria leaned forward, watching. A surprise? What could he be talking about? She had been with him almost every hour of the day and night since having arrived in Saint Louis. How could he have . . . ?

When he reentered the room, carrying a black case, Maria's heartbeat quickened. She rose quickly and rushed to Michael, all eyes. "It looks like . . . it . . . *is* . . . my violin case," she gasped, taking it from him.

She stood still for a moment, hugging it to her. "Michael, how . . . ? What . . . ?"

"You've talked of having missed your violin? Well, Alberto brought it to Mama Pearl one day while we were out. Then I contacted a Maestro Von Heifschmitz, the director of the Saint Louis Symphony Orchestra. He said that he would arrange to have it repaired."

Gasping, Maria rushed to the couch and placed her violin case on it. With trembling fingers, she released each lock, then raised the lid, feeling tears surfacing as she lifted her instrument into her arms. She hugged it to her, feeling as though a part of her had been returned . . . and all in one piece. She held it away from her once again, letting a finger trace its highly varnished body. The crack was no longer there. By some miracle, it had been removed. She plucked at the strings, filling the room with a soft, sweet sound, then placed the violin back inside the case and flew to Michael and into his arms.

"Oh, Michael, this is the best surprise you could have handed me," she cried, clinging. "I just didn't think anything could ever be done for my cracked violin." She looked upward into his eyes. "How can I ever thank you? Darling, how can I?"

Michael laughed hoarsely, his fingers already working with the buttons of her dress. "There's always a way, darling," he said quickly. "And you know what that is, don't you?"

Maria reached back and continued to release her buttons, watching as Michael began to release the buttons of his shirt. "But we must move to the bedroom, my love," she purred. "Mama Pearl. We must remember we're not the only ones occupying the small space of this hotel suite."

"Mama Pearl?" he laughed. "She's just down the hall for this entire night. She's staying in another hotel suite that I've purposely arranged for her so we could have this place all to ourselves. Shall we take advantage of it?"

Maria's gaze lowered. "Before we're even married, Mr. Michael Hopper?" she teased.

Michael stepped from his shoes, then his breeches, laughing. "Even before we're married, wench," he said. His underthings were quickly discarded, then he moved to Maria and aided her with her corset, laughing when he heard a loud breath of relief when it fell to the floor in a heap. He lifted her into his arms, smothering her lips with kisses as he carried her to the bedroom.

When they reached the bed, Maria clung to his neck, savoring the soft warmth of his lips. His hands began caressing her, causing the pleasure waves to splash around inside her, a storm of passion rising and falling with each of her erratic heartbeats.

As he placed her on the bed, he leaned over her with his blue eyes burning with desire, then with a fierceness, he was beside her, holding her, his mouth bearing down upon hers in hot demand.

Moaning with sensuous pleasure, Maria's fingers moved over his body, feeling the familiarity of it . . . the wide expanse of shoulders tightened now as he held her in rapturous imprisonment against him . . . the soft, velvety skin of the curve of his buttocks . . . then the fuzz of hair that led her fingers around to where his manhood lay throbbing against her thigh.

The wondrous desire for him was now causing her to writhe, trying to position herself, when he suddenly released his lips from hers and lowered them to a breast, as his manhood slowly entered her.

"My darling," he whispered. "I thought I had lost you for sure."

"I was always yours," she murmured. "From that very first instant that I looked into the blue of your eyes."

He laughed amusedly. "Do you mean that day on the ship when I discovered that you were indeed a female?"

"Yes. That day, my love," she purred. Her heart was beating with a reckless passion now, recalling all their times together since that day . . . all of their rapturous rendezvous . . . from the first bed she was stretched out upon on the ship, to the time they had made love in the depths of the Indian grasses.

"How could I have ever for one moment not known you were female," he said, kissing her sweetly on the hollow of the throat.

"Remember the day you made love to me while the tipple of the coal mine seemed to be watching, as though it was a person?" she whispered, tracing his lips with a forefinger.

"Yes, my darling. . . ."

"Then Michael, let's pretend. . . ."

"Pretend?" he said, tilting a brow.

"Yes, my love. Pretend."

"How . . . ?"

"Lay me down, my love, amidst the tall Indian grasses, and watch me become as the wind, ah, so passion-filled. . . ."

Michael then took her in one swift movement. With a moan of ecstasy, she gave to him all he desired, while at the same time, she smiled, content.

She was free . . . at last free . . . yet always a prisoner . . . when in his . . . arms. . . .

More by Bestselling Author
Hannah Howell

__Highland Angel	978-1-4201-0864-4	$6.99US/$8.99CAN
__If He's Sinful	978-1-4201-0461-5	$6.99US/$8.99CAN
__Wild Conquest	978-1-4201-0464-6	$6.99US/$8.99CAN
__If He's Wicked	978-1-4201-0460-8	$6.99US/$8.49CAN
__My Lady Captor	978-0-8217-7430-4	$6.99US/$8.49CAN
__Highland Sinner	978-0-8217-8001-5	$6.99US/$8.49CAN
__Highland Captive	978-0-8217-8003-9	$6.99US/$8.49CAN
__Nature of the Beast	978-1-4201-0435-6	$6.99US/$8.49CAN
__Highland Fire	978-0-8217-7429-8	$6.99US/$8.49CAN
__Silver Flame	978-1-4201-0107-2	$6.99US/$8.49CAN
__Highland Wolf	978-0-8217-8000-8	$6.99US/$9.99CAN
__Highland Wedding	978-0-8217-8002-2	$4.99US/$6.99CAN
__Highland Destiny	978-1-4201-0259-8	$4.99US/$6.99CAN
__Only for You	978-0-8217-8151-7	$6.99US/$8.99CAN
__Highland Promise	978-1-4201-0261-1	$4.99US/$6.99CAN
__Highland Vow	978-1-4201-0260-4	$4.99US/$6.99CAN
__Highland Savage	978-0-8217-7999-6	$6.99US/$9.99CAN
__Beauty and the Beast	978-0-8217-8004-6	$4.99US/$6.99CAN
__Unconquered	978-0-8217-8088-6	$4.99US/$6.99CAN
__Highland Barbarian	978-0-8217-7998-9	$6.99US/$9.99CAN
__Highland Conqueror	978-0-8217-8148-7	$6.99US/$9.99CAN
__Conqueror's Kiss	978-0-8217-8005-3	$4.99US/$6.99CAN
__A Stockingful of Joy	978-1-4201-0018-1	$4.99US/$6.99CAN
__Highland Bride	978-0-8217-7995-8	$4.99US/$6.99CAN
__Highland Lover	978-0-8217-7759-6	$6.99US/$9.99CAN

Available Wherever Books Are Sold!

Check out our website at
http://www.kensingtonbooks.com